Blessed the Devoured

Frances B Corvo

FBC

BLESSED THE DEVOURED
by
Frances B Corvo

This is a work of fiction. Names, characters, places, and incidents either are products of the author's imagination or are used fictitiously. Any resemblance to actual events or locales or persons, living or dead, is entirely coincidental.

Copyright © 2026 Frances B Corvo

Cover illustration by Nathan J. Anderson

Print Paperback ISBN: 978-1-966133-04-9

Print Hardback ISBN: 978-1-966133-05-6

E-Book ISBN: 978-1-966133-03-2

CONTENTS

Introduction

A general pitch I've used to explain this book is that it is "loosely based on the myth of Cronus," but you won't find a Zeus and Rhea analog here. Instead, it's more the sentiment that has survived, twisted by the framing of a dark medieval-ish fantasy story. I realize for some, this is essentially a blind-box purchase, and you don't have any reason to trust me as an author. All I can say is, as much as I love dour men in fantasy, a man with a big sword tearing everything up for rule-of-cool's sake does not a story make. You might hate it anyway, but I hope that manages expectations.

While I hesitate to label this story as a grimdark fantasy for fear of disappointing genre fans, given this has a lesser dedication to grit and nihilism most definitions tend to expect, the premise and subjects presented may be outside your comfort zone. I prefer to avoid shock-factor moments such as graphic depictions of sexual violence or graphic depictions of self-harm, but my limits and lines are not everyone's. At the end of the day, the point is for this to be a piece of entertainment that lets you know what to expect when you read the label and allows others who may not be interested to turn it away.

Any concerns or desire for additional warnings are welcome: crowfashionable@gmail.com

For those of you who prefer more explicit content warnings, you can find them on the next page.

Content Warnings

- violence, gore, mutilation, cannibalism

- elements of verbal, and physical abuse

- someone is restrained, drowning, choking

- torture, non-consensual intimacy, references to rape off-page

To all the birds in the nest.

And to the gentleman I met on the Amtrak bus that terrible winter of 2015.

The Deathless

In my prime, war was a clean occupation. A man swore fealty to his liege
lord and prayed to his gods. He honored his oaths. He killed barbarians.
He passed his land on to his sons.

My brothers in arms walked the well-trodden path to manhood with me
from babes to squires to knights, reveling in every titled promotion. We
killed for grander names than the ones we came screaming into the world
with.

I sacrificed mine for my legacy. They anointed me with oils and fed me
to the beasts so that I, in my monstrousness, might rid the world of greater
monsters. My old name was cast aside, and when I was not Hellhound or
Warbreaker, I was Savior.

There was a time when war sowed peace, a time when a little blood in
the soil gave way to good harvests and good men. But as the years tolled,
children forgot the meaning of such sacrifices. They languished in the lush
green around them and wondered why the fields beyond the river were
their neighbor's and not theirs. Inch by inch, they salted the earth. Body
by body, they blackened the water. What came after was too thin to be war.

Sniveling lordlings following the doctrine of new, young gods sent me
after old grudges: rivals whose families and serfs would gut one another
over a stray cow in the wrong pasture. I burned manors and carried heads
in a bag. When the lordlings strangled one another with rusting circlets, I
strung up the mercenaries who tore down abandoned kingdoms for gold.
When coin became meaningless and the mercenaries were destitute, I hung

the vagrants who ravaged lone homesteads. When the vagrants were as extinct as the homesteads, I began to hunt the vermin. One in particular.

He had started life as a battlefield vulture with hollow eyes and knobby knees, following war camps the way wolves follow drovers. There was a time when I thought him harmless, pitiable, even. Then I learned how cold his blood ran under lice-bitten skin. It had started the night he cut into his brother's chest to please a Young God that promised him power and immortality, and he has only grown bolder since.

He traded his straw shoes for a lord's leather boots. His gambeson belonged to a superior whose throat he slit. The pouch of signet rings on his hip marked the myriad dead he had murdered, robbed, and betrayed. His hair had grayed, and his nose was scarred, but his patron god had preserved his face's youth. I had seen that face gasping for air, splattered by blood, laughing with toothless glee, but never still and breathless.

After narrowly escaping our last encounter, he had sought out safety in numbers and joined a company of Acolytes of the Unblinking Eye, cousins pledged in service to their own Young God. Watching them travel together was like watching swans adopt a water rat. While the Acolytes glided across the misty hillsides, garbed in light robes that billowed like wraith cloaks, he trudged against the bitter wind with his lambskin coat pulled tight to his chest.

Clannish as the devotees of the Young Gods tend to be, the world was not as rich as it once was. No more cities. No more bustling ports. No more quilted patchworks of laborers bent over wheat and beans. Even the immortals were starving. The children of the Young Gods knew the value of sharing in these scarce times. Lambskin was a Heartless outsider, but he would want a different piece of the game they hunted.

The Acolytes and Lambskin combed the Blue Mountains and the Silk Banks in search of mortal men and women. Fifty years ago, they had only to pick a direction and demand a sacrifice from the first village they came across; the promise to spare the others earned them an easy meal. That had devolved into hunting through miles of brushland for one abandoned hut in the hopes that a secluded huntsman had not yet died of starvation and spoiled before they could cut what pieces they needed from him to please their gods. Months, sometimes years, passed before they found another victim.

It was only when they were as far east as the Splintered Hills that they saw a promising sign of life: smoke, black and thick, billowing up from a lone structure of tar-darkened pine. It was once a temple to Amivia, first of the gods, but her circular symbol had been defaced, and her wooden statue had been splintered into firewood. The Old Gods had been reduced to such indignities in this new world, if they were remembered at all.

The door was barred, the windows were barricaded, but the grain loft teemed with rats, and a fire burned inside. The promise of fresh communion flesh nearby could not go ignored. So Lambskin and his Acolytes began their siege on this pitiful fortress.

I'd seen Acolytes gut a village before. They combed through the limp gardens and fishermen's caves that'd kept hungry men alive in this withering world. They sniffed out trapdoors and hidden alcoves. They took those hooked knives on their hips and carved the eyes out of the sockets of every corpse they created. Brown, black, green. They strung every color through the sclera on delicate chains of gold as if they were fine gemstones.

What easy meal had they fantasized about inside the Black Pine Hall? Did they scratch their tiny nails on the door, thinking of scarecrow-thin mortals with hollow stomachs and bulging eyes? Did they smell the rot on their skin and think of fevered children paralyzed with plague? They chipped away at the barricaded door, knowing whoever was on the other side could hear them.

It took three days for them to breach the Black Pine Hall's front door. The party of five stumbled inside with gleeful vigor that quickly melted into silence. Instead of cowering chickens in their coop, they found a slaughterhouse.

The last unbound, mortal men of the Splintered Hills lay almost as if they were asleep. Their bodies were tangled between the narrow lines of benches. Their skin was dry and untouched by maggots.

That had been my doing.

I manned the fire in that rotting hall, baiting the promise of the defenseless godless trapped inside. I burned incense day and night to keep the flies away and preserve the flesh. Thick smoke spilled out from the hall in noxious tendrils. Lambskin bent over in a coughing fit. The others covered their noses and peered out into the hall, unbothered.

I lay still and quiet as the smoke thinned to a gray haze. They were hesitant at first, but it only took a few unanswered shouts into the hall for them to dismiss any danger and file in. While they took their hooked knives to the sockets of the nearest bodies, Lambskin surveyed the scene with a grimace. He crept up to the hearth fire, hand on his short sword and eyes set over the bundles of wetted wood. Someone had been here, he warned, but the Acolytes insisted an unbound man must have hidden when they heard them at the door. There was little reason for them to feel threatened by a mortal, much less to guess they were being hunted, but Lambskin knew better.

I crept out from my bed of flesh, my longsword sharp, my body light and quiet without plate armor. The closest Acolyte did not hear me at all.

His wrists were thin but calloused, and the faintest tangle of black curls peeked out from beneath his coif as he pinched a corpse's eyelid open. I pulled him back by the mouth, muffling his initial scream. I felt a small scar beneath the pads of my fingers as I cut his throat. Our brief struggle had been subdued, but it was enough to announce my presence to the others. All four turned toward me.

Unarmored, with only a longsword in my hand, they might have thought me an unbound man hiding in the hazy air. My arms were lean, and my face was haggard. One of the Acolytes whistled at the sight of his friend writhing at my feet. "We'll have to take your eyes for that."

Swords and daggers slid from their scabbards with a menacing hiss.

"Ugly old sprout, isn't he? I didn't think mortals lasted so long anymore."

All laughed except for Lambskin, who was clearly struck by a sense of familiarity. For my part, I was deciding how best to kill them. There was a definitive muscle among the Acolytes: a one-eyed man carrying a war hammer that needed no accuracy to be deadly. He strutted with an easy confidence behind his friends.

A sightless Acolyte approached from my left, empty sockets stitched closed. She carried a spear with a dexterity that I couldn't discount. The other two, a half-blind Acolyte and Lambskin, were closest to me but retreating. The strategy was clear: the Hammer with eyes woven into his beard was the tower they hid behind. They only needed to distract me long enough for him to take care of me.

"How old are you, boy? Fifty?" the Hammer called. His voice bounced across the vaulted ceiling. "Lay that stick down, and we'll only take one. You owe our friend the other."

If they'd thought me godless, their pace would be slow, their form lazy. Though one of their brothers lay gurgling his own blood, this was entertainment to them. They were sure they would make a meal of me and restore their friend within seconds. That is, until Lambskin placed me. I saw the moment his pinched expression slackened to one of bewildered fear.

"Deathless!" he shouted, no doubt remembering how he had left me with a knife between my ribs the last time we'd met.

I charged at Lambskin and his Acolyte friend, thrusting my longsword in front of me. Lambskin split off, but the Acolyte met me with a swing of his sword. Having yet to take me seriously, he aimed to overwhelm me with a show of strength. I let my blade be batted down by his and stepped back with his blow. Encouraged, the Acolyte came after me, and I had him alone.

The second time he swung, I countered him. The edge of his blade rang against the flat of my own that I had raised to my shoulder. Before he could pull back, I extended my arms and brought the blade careening down into his collarbone. Ill-kept mail snapped under my sword, and blood spilled onto that all-seeing blue eye on his chest.

Surprise had earned me two quick deaths; I felt this one whisper into me. Ambrosial satisfaction shivered through my chest. But I was not afforded more than a moment to indulge in the feeling. Lambskin returned sooner than I expected, dagger drawn in one hand, short sword in the other.

I dragged my longsword from the Acolyte's neck, but I could not bring it around soon enough to counter Lambskin. His dagger scratched my shirt sleeve.

I took a step to the side. Lambskin took a step forward. His short sword followed through.

I didn't have the freedom to counter yet, so I kept moving to give myself enough distance to control my longsword. Three steps into my retreat, the blind Acolyte appeared at my side. She thrust a spear at my stomach. Though I tried to twist away, her strike pierced through my gambeson into the flesh beneath my rib cage.

I ripped myself away before she could twist the point. Escaping her sent me straight into Lambskin. The swipe of his blade was too wide to have cut me, but it did force me to stagger back into the Acolyte's range. Though both of them put on a show of flashing blades, they were not *pressing* onto me. They nipped at my legs and my arms in the hopes of maneuvering me to the Hammer, who was now charging toward us.

I had to break their pattern. Instead of trying to dart away from both of them, I let Lambskin's short sword cut my thigh and dropped my sword to grab the Acolyte's spear. I wrapped my arm over the pole and locked it in place. When she tried to pull back, I pushed her to the floor with enough force to wrench the spear from her grip. The moment it was free, I swung it around wildly.

Lambskin sprang back to avoid me, and I let him go. I turned to the Acolyte instead and drove the point of her spear into her chest. Chipped iron punched through her padded shirt and into muscle. I laid my weight on the shaft, feeling the hard crack as a rib split.

I heard a name being called, a harsh cry, and turned to face thirty unblinking eyes. The Hammer had arrived. He swung his weapon down with a force so furious that it would crush my ribs and collapse my lung if it made contact. I fell to one knee, my elbows locked, and pulled the spearpoint from the downed Acolyte to extend the butt of the spear into his stomach. Though harmless, the jolt stunned the Hammer for a moment and gave me time to slip out from under him.

I was back on my feet, my body light from the rush of such a quick encounter. The Hammer and Lambskin were both collecting themselves the same way I was. They were armed, however, and I was not. We began to circle, my gaze dipping to the ground in search of my sword. It was then that I slipped and noticed a streak of blood under my feet. When I looked back up, Lambskin was smiling. His black eyes lingered on my torso. There was a heat in my belly, and when I looked down, I saw the blood seeping from my abdomen. A thin flap of flesh spilled from my torn padding.

I thought Lambskin had gone for my thigh, but no. He'd stabbed through my shirt into my stomach. It was a killing blow; I knew the instant the heat flared out in its first nervous tendrils. The wound was too deep for proper pain.

Blood. The banner of life's surrender seeped out of me. From somewhere far off, but just behind me, I heard the groan of fury and felt the rapid excitement of my heart. My eyes caught on a shining piece of metal on the ground. My sword? An Acolyte's? It did not matter. I had it in my hands, and I wielded it without composure or form. All thoughts of careful preservation were gone. I charged forward the way I had across blood-slicked fields for a century on end.

The Hammer might have landed a blow that crushed a leg. Lambskin might have cut me again. I did not know. I hardly felt them. I was an animal, tearing with my teeth, scratching with blunted nails, and striking again and again and again—until I found myself standing over the Hammer with Lambskin's sword in my hand.

In that heavy pause, I noticed I was not holding the short sword by the pommel, but by a twitching hand that looked to have been ripped away at the wrist. I might have been shocked if the Hammer beneath me had not gurgled. But he did, and I struck him with that grotesque amalgamation once more. A whine seeped out from him, and I let the sword fly until the whining stopped. I felt the whisper of death pass from him into me.

Only then did I drop the wrist and short sword.

I stared at the twitching hand of Lambskin. His glove had been ripped off, revealing calloused fingers. His nails were clean and pink, cut short and even, and I stood there for too long wondering who had taught him to maintain them.

Fifty years... I thought. Pain flared in my chest. Hot blood pooled in my stomach and trickled down my legs. It'd be in my lungs soon. I'd hunted that vermin for fifty years, and he was dead. That had been his end, and I hardly recalled it. He was supposed to have been too crafty for such a mundane end, too skilled. Yet there was his hand. Behind me was his body. And here I stood . . . What now?

A sharp whistle arrested my attention. I turned just as the burn of a short blade prickled through me. Lambskin was there, alive. His right wrist was a stub, but his left still held that hooked knife. It vibrated in my neck, biting when I tried to swallow. I tried to breathe, but I could only attempt a half-cough.

"You," he wheezed against my neck, "should be getting tired, old man."

Ashen and shaking with the cold of death, Lambskin's threat was a whimper to my ears. His calloused hand wrapped around my throat and tried to squeeze, but he had the grip of a child, too shaken to do any real damage. I looked down at his mangled wrist.

I wanted to grip him by his collar and pull him close to reply. Tired? Men tired. I could be bludgeoned, broken, or cut open, but I would never tire. He'd made an enemy of a creature less than a man. I was a Deathless. This hunt would go on for as long as it took. I would haunt his shadow across continents, through the decades. Whether five or ten thousand steps behind, I would be on my way to him. But I had no breath for such promises.

Looking into that youth's face, into those coward's eyes, I could see he understood all the same. I would kill him. Not today, no. But the only way this ended was with my knife through his heart.

My knees gave out, and Lambskin collapsed with me, pulled by the knife. He looked down at his right wrist, mangled at the stump, and cried out. The boy ripped the knife from my neck, and it was as if my body had become a stone. My breathing was shallow, my skin cold. Before I fell into the heavy veil between worlds, I caught a flicker of movement, a twitching, writhing thing—a rat gnawing at my finger.

THE BARREN LANDS

In the space between breaths, I glimpsed into the domain of Morthia, King of the Flies. The first time I had seen it, cold terror had seized my chest. Though I knew not where I was, I had understood even then it was not a place made for men. No living thing belonged on those ashen sands. After a thousand visits, the endless black expanse of dunes where great towers cracked and ancient trees withered to bone-white husks did not seem so wrong. No living thing belonged here, and I was no living thing.

To come and go from this god's den was my right as his pledged servant. I lay as a Deathless in that stillness, where the slightest breeze would sweep up the hills of dust like a tidal wave and wash us all away into darkness. It was cold and dark to every horizon, except the one I could not look directly upon. Behind Morthia, draped in a veil as black as midnight, was death, the After, the land from which I was exiled.

Morthia loomed over me as he had hundreds of times before, his face obscured in his cloak. With an exhale, the final sigh of a bedridden man, the crack of an old tree root, he raised his arm. A thin hand gripped the fabric draped over my eyes and drew it away.

A cold front passed over me.

I awoke in the violent, fitful way I'd repeated over the centuries. My body, heavy and aching, was dropped into the shock of sensation. I gasped the early, brittle breaths of my resurrection.

A fit seized my whole body with a force that threatened to crush me from the inside out. Cold fingers braced beneath me. My nose ground against the pungent stench of iron and saccharine rot. And just as soon as I could not take any more, the tension released and my muscles went lax.

I collapsed onto the soft bed of dirt. Sunlight pouring in from the broken rafters warmed my cheek. I was in the Black Pine Hall, its blood still brittle on my collar. And I was not where I had fallen. My body had been moved.

I had been laid out like a casualty of war to be counted among my brothers. It was almost an insult to see the Acolytes of the Unblinking Eye on either side of me, as if we had been anything but dogs tearing at one another's throats before our deaths. Lambskin was not among them, which did not surprise me, but the sight of three bodies instead of four gave me pause. I noticed then that the blurred vision in my left eye had cleared, but the right could not focus.

When Morthia had me wrapped in his domain, Lambskin must have taken a hooked knife to my eye and plucked it from my skull. The fresh flesh would do nothing for him, as he'd pledged himself to Koroe the Flaming Heart, not the Eye. If he fed it to an Acolyte friend, however, one I had gravely wounded but not killed, they might be saved. Sure enough, I saw it was the blind Acolyte whom I'd taken the spear from, the woman I'd stabbed through the ribs, who was missing among the dead.

The Acolyte I'd cut at the collar lay with his chest sliced open, rib cage split. A maggot nursery flourished in the cavity that once held his heart. I pieced together Lambskin's frantic efforts. He'd taken my eye and fed it to an Acolyte he could restore with her communion. Then, with her help, they'd selected a dead comrade whom they could quickly strip of familiar padding and cut into his chest. They'd cut out his heart and fed it to Lambskin, who must now be wandering the countryside with a staunched stump for a right hand but alive.

I took some petty satisfaction in the limitations of the Young Gods. Lambskin, with a heart fresh and oil-slick with viscera sacrificed to his god, would never be fully restored, while Morthia, merciless and demanding as he was, had returned me with my eye intact and only the faintest ache to remind me of the lives that had paid for its restoration. In a day or two, my vision would be as sharp as a hawk's. Lambskin would go without his hand for the rest of his immortal life.

Upon closer inspection, I saw both eyes had been taken from the dead Acolytes. Perhaps with the bounty of five total, the surviving Acolyte knew their patron would be sated for months longer than she could preserve the flesh. Perhaps my eye was one too many and would have been a worthless harvest. Still, I couldn't help but wonder if the Acolyte feared bad luck if she consumed the flesh of a Deathless; the servants of the Young Gods had such superstitions.

Lambskin was an exception. He'd always picked his meals from the scraps of corpses, and immortality made him no more selective about it. He had eaten my heart before, and surely fed my eye to the Acolyte.

Still, he had his own odd limitations. Only one heart had been harvested. I knew Lambskin could go much longer than an Acolyte of the Unblinking Eye without a fresh meal, but that did not mean he'd have no use for a spare. It'd be two years or so before he needed to take communion again to appease Koroe, but he chose to travel with no reserve to save him from a mortal injury.

I couldn't help but imagine chasing Lambskin across the hills only to cut off another piece of him—perhaps his foot or his other hand. He'd turn on his Acolyte friend like a rabid animal and tear into her chest before the severed flesh could hit the ground, and it would be his arrogance, not I, that killed her. When I next saw him, perhaps I'd take only an ear or an eye to teach him some prudence.

I was unsure of how long had passed since our fight and my resurrection, but I did not rush to give chase. I chipped off the flakes of blood that'd crusted over my gambeson's collar and collected the armor I'd hidden beneath Amivia's empty pedestal. The greaves and mail had lasted me decades, but the helmet was new, and my gauntlets had been scavenged from two different men a century apart.

I strapped on the bracers and greaves, but carried the mail folded in a bag on my back and my helmet on my hip. There was no need to walk for miles with all that weight pressing on my chest. I might have been able to forgo the armor altogether if I'd ever thought to scavenge replacements from the bodies I would find on my travels, but I was precious about comfortable pieces; with no smiths or tinkers left in the world, the burden of preservation fell to me.

I set out from the Black Pine Hall, thinking longingly of my days on campaign. I did not miss riding. Horses were fine creatures, but it had been so long since I'd seen one that I could not imagine how their pace compared to my feet. Even in the days when I had been awarded my own destrier, I had been annoyed at how the beast had tired. My company of Deathless men had marched in step as the moon and sun chased each other across the sky, stopping for neither food nor drink until we arrived at our next camp. The steady tempo of the drums and bawdy tunes locked us in a trance as we went.

Now, I walked alone in lands far less heat-stricken with a leisurely gait. Intercepting Lambskin before he reoriented to the exclusive use of his left hand would take the challenge out of our next fight. Best to give him time. I would, of course, find him.

I was a Deathless servant of Morthia; distance and direction mattered less than time. The years, in fact, had cleared this world of the obstacles between my prey and myself. Forests withered in sick soil, the bandits and soldiers left to waylay me had all but died out, and there were no fortified borders or guarded bridges. There was not a cell or castle I could not walk into and claim as my own. The world was wide open, and it was so terribly small.

I often wondered if the priests who'd dragged me from my home, thrown me on my knees, and pledged me to Morthia knew this would be his true price. Did they know that with their sacrifice, a bell had been rung? It tolled, and we did not hear it, not until a time after their grandchildren's grandchildren. If they looked now, they would see the salt in the fields they sent us to protect and the poison in their wells. They could not see, of course, as I was all that remained of their time. And I looked out on this withered world and wondered if Morthia's ashen domain was a place or a premonition.

If any godless men and women remained, they were already well on their way to joining Morthia's legion of the dead. Servants of the Young Gods like Lambskin were the ones who could endure the droughts and rotted harvests. While I had never felt the pang of hunger for want of a sacrifice to Morthia, I knew the Young Gods had limits. Years at most. Months for many.

Their sustenance was flesh, fresh-cut and bloodied. When mortal marks became scarce, they took to hunting one another. Lambskin was not immune to hunger, and he would seek out his own prey soon enough.

Until then, there was the road ahead and a long march with no tune.

THE CANARY

I found him in the summer. The smoke of a wildfire a continent away clotted the air. The grass was tall and yellow, the trees sparse and low. An Acolyte lay in the shade, chest cut open. The drag marks by her feet showed a struggle, perhaps a betrayal in the night. There were no flowers, but he'd braided grass into a wreath and set that on her stomach. His footprints continued west, into the haze, where sunlight warred with smoke.

The hills were burning. Stripes of dry grass crackled and snuffed themselves out. Plumes of thick brown smoke drifted like clouds across the plains.

Within a day, the shadows gave way to solid form. A wall appeared. The ivy coating its stone face was green and supple; its roots were thick and strong. In such parched times, I marveled, half convinced it was a trick even as I plucked a leaf from the vine. Green, healthy, and plentiful.

Lambskin's boot prints walked a well-worn path in the shadow of that wall. I heard no steps ahead of me, saw no firelight, but I knew I was close.

Then I came to a break in the smoke where the wall stretched high and opened for me. I stood in front of a massive, arched tunnel. The ivy that dangled from the walls had been trimmed back over the years, but that was the only proof of maintenance I could see. Thousands of little masons' tool marks had been weathered away, and the stones set in the floor had long since been warped and cracked. I stepped into the tunnel, feeling as if I were walking into the throat of a primal beast. I half expected the ceiling to rumble, reveal its teeth, and snap shut once I was in deep enough.

I heard wind buffering against the other side. I felt the cool touch of fresh mountain air tug on my braided hair. I thought of Varlemont, my home, and the smell of the trees and old stone. This was a close cousin with the same grand expanse promised in its scent. A part of me was sure I had to be mistaken. I had just come from open plains. Yet, when I reached the other side of the tunnel, I stood at the top of a bridge. On either side of me was a drop into a gorge that was too deep to see the bottom of. The wall that had abruptly cut across the plains seemed to be an extension of that sharp, cavernous wall and looked more like the result of nature's carving than a craftsman's.

What was more remarkable was the bridge ahead. Heavy slabs of stone had been laid across piers a quarter mile in width. Each pier was not only cut but decorated with reliefs of blooming, thick-trunked trees and spiraling patterns. Small clouds drifted between those supports and tumbled over the deck.

The walk across took half a day. Twice, I thought of going back, imagining myself having wandered into the realm of something beyond men. The bridge's scale and decoration alone felt as if it would serve the needs of gods and their behemoth beasts. Perhaps this long walk across an endless bridge was Amivia's eternity or Sibdeot's path, a divine landscape divorced from the material world. To think such a structure would have an end seemed naive.

There was an end, however, and someone was waiting for me on the other side.

I heard him before I saw him at the foot of the bridge; a man in a bright yellow liripipe sat under the shadow of a ramshackle guardhouse. His long brown fingers caressed the neck of a mandolin and pinched its strings. Despite its foreign melody, the tune he plucked reminded me of the peasant songs that made their popular rounds in war camps. I had not heard music in a century, nor seen an instrument.

In addition to that, I hadn't seen a domestic bird in twenty years, yet this man had a menagerie. More than fifty were penned in a twine cage beside him.

I stopped there, knowing such displays for what they were. Nothing reeked of such decadent life anymore. Nothing sang for joy or pleasure. No one was so bright and obvious unless they wanted to be seen. This was a fisher of men, hiding his hooks behind his obvious lures.

I surveyed the high windows of the guardhouse and its banisters for a sign of others, but could see no one else. All the same, I did not trust this scene.

It must be an ambush, I thought.

And it was then that the mandolinist noticed me and waved.

"Good tidings, Outlander! Come! Don't make me shout for long, now!"

I remained where I stood. Lambskin would have known this trap for what it was. But I hadn't seen his footsteps wandering away from the wall. Had he gone through this man? I could see no fresh blood on the stones, no signs of a skirmish.

"What a skittish lot you are!" the mandolinist called again. "I'm alone, my friend. Here, come. I have a gift for you on behalf of King Evarund!"

I knew of no King Evarund, nor did I know the stranger's crest or colors. He announced both with such excitement, as if either should elicit a reaction from me.

"Come, man!" the mandolinist called.

Suspicious as it was, I approached. Before I reached the end of the bridge, the mandolinist opened the birdcage and pulled out a blue-capped pheasant by its feet. He unsheathed a knife and set it against the pheasant's neck.

"Which is your pleasure, my friend?" he asked. "The eye? The heart? The toes? King Evarund sees to it that no man steps into his kingdom hungry."

A gift from a king? The last king I met had been butchered for parts by his immortal servants in a barricaded stone hall. Were we still playing at heraldry in the age of extinction?

The mandolinist had no armor and no weapon, save the dagger he held to the bird. His clothes were of good make, and his shoes were delicate wool pieces with lengthy points, the kind made for lounging around inside. I chanced a glance beyond his little post and saw a straight path into empty green hills. For now, it seemed we two were alone in the world.

"I'm searching for a Heartless dressed in a lambskin coat," I told him.

"He speaks!" the mandolinist rejoiced. "But that's no introduction. I know it must have been so long for you, friend, but please, there are customs. I am Geocelin of Pulrodge, a humble guard to these the Hallowed Lands, watchman of the Thousand Hand Wall, and lyricist to a thousand boastful tunes."

"Are you now?" I asked, finding no words to match the pomp of this strange presentation.

"And who are you, stranger?" the man asked, all earnestness and good-will. "Who do you serve?"

"Neither answer has any meaning now."

"Cheerful one, aren't you?" Geocelin slighted. "No matter. You are still welcome. Now, how about it? Eyes? Hands? Heart? Tongue? Skin? If you're a man of Deiviknot, we set aside dogs' teeth here." He flicked open a small box to show me a collection.

He was offering me a communion, a piece of the bird to sate my patron's hunger, assuming I served a Young God. Most men did, of course, but Morthia was not satisfied with scraps. I would snap this bird's neck to feel the whisper of its life fade away, or I would have nothing at all. The whole offer was symbolic, of course. A fowl was not comparable to a man.

I imagined Geocelin day after day approaching Acolytes of the Unblinking Eye or the Cretinous Flayed with jovial cheer. He'd hold out the knife to the parts they wanted and let them pluck them from the bird like fruit ripening off a tree. Lambskin must have smiled and bantered with this jester. He'd have been as tempted as I was to discard the bird and take the man. He *was* the brightest canary of the flock. Yet, for whatever reason, Lambskin had left him alive and unharmed.

"This is quite an offer for a stranger."

"King Evarund provides for all his subjects, and he wishes for any man seeking refuge to know that he is welcome. We serve the highest of the high, after all."

The mandolinist then thumbed a chain from around his neck with his knife hand to show me a silver medallion stamped with an ascending bird and three burning roses. I recognized the crest at once and almost laughed.

There was not a man on the continent who would not know the All-Father's iconography. He was not a king of the material world, but one of legend. Not a god. Not a man. A story. An ideal. Lords of my time poured a cup for him at the start of every feast. They set his token on their war room tables and strove for the piety, honor, and greatness he demonstrated.

He was faceless and nameless, and this man's liege lord.

I had come from a scorched earth where kings were as good as paupers and the field hands strung up their landlords. I expected him to flounder, for his smile to break as he explained his poor joke of serving a sham crown. If he claimed the All-Father to ease my suspicion, he accomplished the opposite. Yet, there were four dozen birds all chirping on beds of hay beside me. Here was a man who looked unmarked by bloodied sacrifice.

There was something strange happening here; I would not deny that.

"How long have you been at this post, boy?" I asked him.

"Boy, is it? I have a good face, friend, but there's no need to flatter. We're all old men here. I have served my king at this post for forty years, but I've been pledged for much longer than that," he said. To his credit, I knew he had to be older than most.

After the wars of earth and water, I saw plenty of mortal children rush to pledge when their backs had yet to broaden and their faces were still soft.

However, it used to be a requirement that men who pledged to the Young Gods already had children and were of high enough status and repute to be trusted with immortality. They would be infertile and relinquish the legal claim of their titles and holdings to their sons once they were bound to a god. Legally, they were dead.

Geocelin had the face and frame of a grown man, but time had not weathered him fiercely. Soft lines marked his brow. Strands of gray lined his temple. If he aged as a mortal, I would think he was forty. He must have pledged before cities crumbled and empires burned, but he would still be younger than me.

"And which is your patron?" I asked.

"Why, the Seven Hands, friend."

A Fingerman. That explained his casual behavior. In the early days, when pacts with the Young Gods were still deemed a duty for the lesser nobility, every house had at least one. Easy to sate, difficult to kill.

In their ceremony, when the priests pledged them to the Seven Hands, it was tradition for them to use the fingers of loved ones or enemies of their masters to forge the bond between man and god. In the years after the wars of earth and water, they were a common sight. Unlike Acolytes of the Unblinking Eye, who were as aggressive as wolves over eyes, Fingermen were vultures, obvious but distant and not troublesome. A single finger cut off a man I killed paid for many months in their long lives. They picked pockets and stole scraps long before they tried to hunt anyone themselves.

Sensing what I must have known, Geocelin spoke.

"Enough with the sour face, my nameless friend. I know the Barrens out there have robbed you of decency, but that will not be the case here. As a guard to the Hallowed Lands, I can't let men with bitter blood pass without demonstrating that he is still a man, yet. This is an invitation to seek out Evarund's hall in the Green Castle, to feel sated and make merry." He dangled the bird and flipped the knife in his hand, holding the hilt out to me. "All we ask is that you accept and reciprocate the good gesture of our invitation when the time comes."

I killed the bird, feeling the smallest rush, like the softest of breezes, against my skin. It did not relieve the *ache*, but it was enough to warm me to the offering, the way a sip of wine does not quench thirst but is a pleasant sensation all the same.

"Isn't that better, my dear Heartless friend?" Geocelin asked.

"There was another like me. You sent him to the castle as well?" I asked. I continued to carve until I could pull the heart from the pheasant's breast and feed his assumption. "We've been separated too long, and I'm eager to be reunited."

"A close friend of yours? A son, perhaps? You two did not have the most striking of resemblances, but that's the truth for any man who leaves their wives on campaign."

I grunted in affirmation a moment before I realized the meat of his words.

"Did you send him along?" I asked again, at the limit of my patience.

"He'll likely be at the foot of the Green Castle as we speak," the mandolinist said. "When you get there, speak my name, show your bird, and you will find friends waiting."

Like that, the guardsman had let a wolf like Lambskin into his home. What a pathetic way to fall to a parasite. If I were lucky, he would not do too much damage before I arrived.

"You should reconsider your test of character, boy," I said, shaking the bird.

"I think it tells me all I need to know about my new friends."

"With your kind of charm, jester, you never feared a man taking a knife to *you* instead of the fowl?"

The mandolinist smiled, then stilled, realizing it was not a joke. The teeth remained, but there was the flash of steel beneath those gaudy yellow feathers.

"If this is your way of expressing that temptation, I can only say that how you enter the king's domain is how it shall receive you. The Hallowed Lands are vast, but they are not those endless wastes behind you. If you wish for a place to live under grace, you'll find there are rules of decorum we all must obey."

I laughed then, a cracked thing warped by disuse. I strung the pheasant and tossed it over my back, leaving the fluttering feathers and the mandolinist behind.

THE AMBUSH

The Hallowed Lands, like the All-Father, were understood to be a fable. It was a storied kingdom that had been, a fertile land where the kings and princes of our past arrived on silver boats from the heavens and tilled the first soil. All men came from these lands and scattered across the continent, but none could place it. None would dare such arrogance.

The All-Father was the first of the first men and the greatest. With unmatched might, he tamed beasts of the heavens and built a city—a country—on the backs of giants. My father used to say that when the ground shook, it was the giants snoring beneath the grass.

Such tales had been absent from my mind for centuries, but swept forward now with boyish clarity.

I could almost believe such a fantasy. Grass grew tall here, swaying like a sea of green. Trees shaded me with bold, supple branches—not brittle, petrified shells of bark. Little blue and yellow flowers I did not know the names of sprouted along my path.

It was unfair how such small, delicate things urged a man to dream.

Whoever this King Evarund was pretending to be, he was still a man. Most likely, he was a boy playing at governance. His guardsman had no sense of judgment, but perhaps that indicated some miraculous haven awaited. Perhaps there were gardens and soil insulated from the world's rot. Perhaps men reached adulthood here and pledged their souls to gods through proper ceremony even now. Perhaps I had listened to a broken man spouting fantasies in a dying world from his crumbling guardhouse.

I more readily believed the latter, especially given how solitary this walk was. A multitude of birds flew overhead, but the canary at the gatehouse had been the only other man I had come across. Now that I'd had a conversation, brief as it had been, these imposter Hallowed Lands felt all the more lacking.

In my youth, I would walk with my brother, Mica, from our villa at the top of a hill down to the central market. Every day, I'd walk with the mule's harness scratching against my palm, hot sweat plastered on my forehead. We'd complain that we had servants to fetch water from the well, but this was our task. In the blistering heat of summer or the crackling cold of winter, we scaled up and down that road like any other peasant in Varlemont.

It was never solitary. We would wave to neighbors on the road, laborers in the field, herders pushing their sheep to a new pasture, or a hunter with a string of rabbits flung over his shoulder. On occasion, my brother would offer me a small mercy and let me ride on the mule's back. Its sweat-damp hair would stick to my legs.

The boy in me longed to walk to the Green Castle and declare myself to its keepers. He would have been enthralled to step into the halls of the fantastical king and clasp arms with the courtly men who had inspired him to follow in his brother's footsteps, to serve as a page to Sir Lasyterie of Howlengaurd, to squire for Lord Forestier at the seat of the Bear's Stronghold, to pledge my life to the King of Bevelon—a man who would never compare to the All-Father.

That boy had not seen his kings grow old, their children grow selfish, and their land grow nothing. The man looked at King Evarund's fortress with morbid curiosity.

I had seen the corpses of cities shine bone-white on the outside and found their splattered red insides. Gutted beasts, rotted to the marrow. The canary promised grandeur, but I could see a bed of fur-lined skeletons in my mind's eye.

When the sun fell and dusk purpled the sky, I stopped on my trail in awe as I saw orange light seep out from the Green Castle, a sign of life not smothered behind boarded windows and doors. Though I stood miles away, voices leaked over the stone wall; the clamor of a *crowd* and the collective shout of songs were carried to me by the wind.

It was their voices, not the light, that arrested me.

There were enough of them living there to sing. I sat and listened, suddenly hesitant to continue. Approaching a fortress of so many in the dark would only set the stage for me to be greeted with suspicion and ire. If Lambskin had already ingratiated himself with them, he would frighten the hens with the threat of a fox at their door. In the morning, I could meet these children in more favorable circumstances. Either they'd fling open the doors with the same naive trust as the canary, or I would have a headcount of the guards and good enough aim with a sling.

I doffed my armor, built a fire, and waited for the sun to rise again.

The licking tongues of orange and red in the flame were usually enough to trance me into a timeless state. I kept my hands busy braiding grass, but this place discouraged the simple absence I'd once maintained. My gaze drifted to the lights spotting the inky black horizon, and I thought of Mica's face alight on the other side of a feast hall. I thought of us as children striking a flint over a bed of dead leaves to roast frog legs with other village boys. I could not recall the last time I'd thought to cook.

All day, I had carried the pheasant with no plans for the meat. Ants now circled its body on the ground. They burrowed into the flesh between feathers.

I was about to nudge over the bird to inspect the swarm beneath when I heard a snap and then silence. The silence was the tell. When prey animals fled through the underbrush, swiftness was more important than sound. Hunters stopped. Hunters hid.

There was only a brief warning as a shaft whistled through the air. Then came the familiar bite of metal after the dull punch of impact. Fletching protruded from my collar in the corner of my vision. I'd been shot with an arrow. I stood in time to avoid the second one and traced the arrow's flight back to its archer.

I rushed and tackled him to the ground. He'd been easy to spot. The weasel wore a bright yellow liripipe. I straddled him, one hand to his throat, the other clenched in a fist.

"Easy, friend!" Geocelin said, dropping the bow and showing his empty hands. He wanted me to talk, to hesitate. I pulled back my fist.

"You don't want to do that," he said, entirely too calm.

I punched him hard in the jaw. The arrow snapped inside my shoulder.

"Well!" He spat, still smiling. "*I* didn't want you to."

I hit him again, harder. Something cracked under my knuckles. I wound back to hit him another time when suddenly there was a hand on my shoulder, and it tugged. I was thrown to the ground. Two sets of hands flattened and pushed down to pin me in place. Two figures loomed over me in the dark.

I recognized the smell of the Flayed on my right—the linseed oil stung my nose. An Acolyte of the Eye likely held down my left side; petrified eyes brushed against my skin.

There was a moment of stillness, an exhale before they started to drag me. They heaved, and I was being pulled along. My heels dug in. My back scraped against the grass until I felt the heat of flames licking at my neck. They'd brought me back to my camp. In the firelight, I could see my assailants. I was right on both counts.

The Flayed was a woman with strong arms patched with raised scars. Concave shadows under her hood suggested a missing nose. The Acolyte was puny, with spindly arms and four lean fingers that held me with a soft touch. His chain of eyes dangled low on his neck.

Just as I had gotten my bearings, the canary leapt onto my chest. Blood dribbled from his nose. I felt some satisfaction knowing I'd done that to him. He was quick to repay me in kind.

"I told you you'd receive what you gave. We could have been friends, you know? This world doesn't do well without them. I've got plenty. What do you have?"

He hit me again. My ear started ringing when he punched the side of my head.

Then, I felt the shift on my left shoulder.

"He smells wrong, Goss," the Acolyte said.

"What's it matter what he smells like?"

With what movement I had, I wrapped my hand around the Acolyte's gold chain. I yanked it down and broke his hold on me. I stole enough movement to snatch the hooked knife from his belt and jam it into the canary's thigh. He sang out in pain, and his weight shifted. I ripped out the knife and struck the Acolyte. As soon as I cut his ankle, his hands flew from my arm to the sting.

With my left side free, I had enough momentum to throw the canary off and pull away from the Flayed.

All this struggle ended with me on the opposite side of the fire, hooked knife in hand and my back to the grass. My lungs strained against the arrow rod embedded in my upper chest, but I knew this pain. A Deathless did not get by without knowing what pain will last him days and what will cost him minutes. I could breathe. I could move. If I were to die, it would be from a direct blow from this band of hyenas, not a festering arrow.

The Acolyte's hands shook as he inspected the blood seeping from his leg and forearm in the firelight. Both were superficial, but he cursed and spat all the same. He gathered the golden chain, biting an eye off the string.

The Flayed had risen and drawn a short sword that seemed ill-suited for the stance she took. I suspected her weapon had been a prize from a recent robbery. Squares of skin hung on her hip from an iron ring. The oils used to keep them must have been in the folds of her sackcloth robe.

And then there was the canary. Bright red blood glistened on his golden hood. A striking line ran down his thigh. He smiled, and a red trail ran between his teeth. This time, I knew why he looked so pleased. I heard the grass snapping behind me.

The fourth member of the canary's band sprang out from his cover. The other three had been a distraction. They attacked first, and if they couldn't kill me, their fourth was waiting in the wings. He used a dagger, which forced him into close quarters. I turned, palmed his weapon at the flat of the blade, and tucked his arm into my side. I tugged, and he fell into my hooked knife.

The two of us were suspended: he in surprise, I in euphoria as I felt his sigh and a rush of stolen life flood through me. It was only when he dropped that I could truly see him. Tongues dangled around his waist like a sash. He'd been a Silver Tongue, a devotee of Malmon.

I grimaced at the canary. "A Silver Tongue, a Flayed, an Acolyte, and a Finger Man. Where's your Heartless? Together, your piecemeal gods may make one."

I was boisterous, overconfident, and uncontrollable in the rush of lightness sweeping through me. The canary raised his hands.

"That can always be you, friend," he said. "You're a strong one, man of Koroe. Direct. Now that you've made a meal of our friend, it'd be a wasted opportunity not to unite. How about it? You carve out his heart, and we'll divide the rest of him among ourselves. Or—we could make this ugly for you."

The Flayed and the Acolyte both adjusted their grips on their swords. The Flayed nodded with a jerky tilt of her chin.

My hand shook. My shoulder throbbed. Pain, my jovial companion, slowly crept through my arm and stuttered my breathing. The *ache* pooled in me.

Never mind meals, I had a banquet. Three different worshippers of three Young Gods stood before me, and I could harvest from each of them. I could stop their hearts, cut out their tongues, pry out their teeth, and snip off their fingers. I could burn each part of them to deny scavengers the satisfaction of my scraps.

The ache urged me to sate my hunger. But I recalled the Acolytes I'd butchered and still lost to. I was in a worse state now than I had been in the Splintered Hills. Taking on all three of them could end with the loss of my eyes, my fingers, or my tongue. If I lost and woke again at the feet of Morthia, the tax asked of me might be more than I could pay. I might lose Lambskin in that time.

But, oh! The lightness of that dead man bewitched my insides. Words I had been forced to speak in my pact panted in my ear. *The hunt begins. Thee or me, Morthia shall feast.* I was only a man, and the shadow of Morthia crept close. If he did not have them, he would have me. I would not let him have me.

I rushed the canary first; I would guarantee his death before the others.

But he did not draw the sword on his hip. He did not reposition to counter my blow. Instead, he turned and sprinted into the tall grass.

All three of them ran.

I stood in bafflement, watching them scatter.

How could they afford to flee now? They'd been injured. They would need pieces of me to recover.

How could they simply—*they could simply*. This was a land of plenty. They could afford to flee because the cache of eyes, fingers, and skin on their person was fresh enough to pay their tax to whatever god they served. The use of such rations would not be catastrophic, only impractical.

Geocelin had his trap set at the gatehouse with his pen of birds. The birds showed them exactly which god I submitted to. They'd taken my measure and ambushed me in the night like any other prey. I was a missed kill. There would be others. They could afford to flee.

I wouldn't allow that. I sprinted after the slowest shadow. It was the Acolyte of the Eye. I returned his knife to him. Lodged it in his neck. And I breathed in the sweet scent of his final gasp.

I turned to face the others only to find myself alone. Where there'd once been disorder, there was now the harmony of the swaying grass. The blades whispered against me, unaware of the beasts they protected. I'd only had time to kill the one vagabond. It annoyed me that it hadn't been the canary. For tonight, though, I could not give chase. They knew these fields. I did not. They could recover with a communion. I needed to see to my wounds before they festered.

When I returned to my campfire, I intended to strip the Silver Tongue's corpse, gather my armor and sword, and abandon the camp. The fire was too conspicuous in this denser country. But my armor, my sword, and my half-empty pack were not waiting for me when I returned. The Silver Tongue had been flipped onto his back. His fingers had been cut, and his nose was gone. I had not been away for long, but it'd been long enough for the thief to take everything of value to them.

Where there were three, there were four.

Where there were four, there was *a fifth*.

A chest piece, a pauldron, greaves, bracers, and gauntlets were not as heavy as full plate but cumbersome to run off with. Perhaps there was a sixth man. I wondered if the thieves had hidden just a few hundred yards away. Were they a part of the canary's pack or rogue scavengers? Either way, I'd been robbed of all but the clothes on my back, and I was beginning to feel it. The arrowhead burned in my shoulder. A sore pinch in my spine promised to worsen by the morning. There was a loose tooth in the back of my mouth that I would have to dig out.

I searched the Silver Tongue's corpse. There was nothing of use except for flint and the dagger. The five tongues he strung on a rope were little more than morbid decorations now. It was laughable to think these were once such weighty sacrifices when men like this treated a length of tongues like a harvest. I was as disgusted as I was envious. Not for the first time, I wished I could consume some part of him and watch my flesh stitch together.

I threw the chain of tongues into the fire. Something about destroying their use made me feel satisfaction, as if that was the vengeance I needed more than his death.

I took the flint and the knife. The rest I bequeathed to the ants.

THE GREEN CASTLE

Though Deathless and pledged to Morthia, I was not rewarded when I gave him a feast. My reward was my soul and my sanity. My body would be remade, and his hunting dog would be repaired when it was truly useless. The lives I took now only acted as proof to him that I would hunt of my own will again and convinced him to resurrect me with my full faculties.

Without any hope of divine healing, I walked with an arrow shaft deep in my collarbone to the Green Castle. Unencumbered by armor, it was not the bitterest of sentences, but one that made me feel small and naked. I was toothless without a sword. The dagger in my palm was little more than a cat's claw—something that could scratch but wouldn't do more than annoy a skilled swordsman.

I walked on unsteady feet. I cursed the canary. I imagined the hundreds of ways I would tear him apart once I had a proper weapon in my hands again. I would hang him from his feet like one of his birds and offer travelers a slice of him as a welcome gift.

It was morning when I reached the foot of the Green Castle's walls. The gate was raised, leaving only a heavy set of doors to seal off the fortress from the world.

"That's far enough!" a voice called from overhead.

I should have felt some wonder that there were men mounted on the wall—*clean* men in *polished* armor and *laundered* surcoats. The canary had been a beggar compared to them.

"Who are you, and what has brought you to the King's door?"

The man crowing down at me glittered in full plate armor lavishly decorated with streaks of gold. The green cloak fastened around his shoulders bore no insignia, but instead a complex woven pattern that marked his allegiances. That was a pattern used by the countrymen of Thyremozt. I knew the colors and shapes would have told me his family name and lands, but I did not have the memory for them.

I'd fought beside those philosophers and poet warriors in the Jillianus Wars. He was groomed like a Thyremoine: a long black braid leaked out of his helm. His beard, visible beneath his visor, was short and styled. The bright blue wrap around the grip of his sword was similar to the green, gold, white, and pink tassels I'd seen his countrymen wear.

From what little I could see under his helmet, he seemed at least as old as the canary. He was remarkably intact for his age, all ten fingers flexed in his gauntlets—though that might not signify. No tongues on his neck. No flayed skin. No obvious mark of self-sacrifice showed on his person

He was flanked by two archers who were markedly more youthful and in padded jackets closer in style to the canary's. I could have mistaken them for boys of twenty. Their hair, curly and dark, was woven with gold rings. Their faces were clean-shaven. The designs on their tabards were more detailed than the symbolic shapes used in my home country of Bevelon. They wore bright emblems: a cornucopia and a single feathered wing.

"Speak up, Piglet!" the Thyremoin shouted down from the ramparts. "Who are you? What business brings you to King Evarund's door?"

"A king, is he?" I scoffed. "Of wet nurses and foals? He has his grandfather answer the door, does he?"

I should have introduced myself with decorum and grace, but pain overruled me, and to pretend ceremony now, at the end of times, felt exceedingly ridiculous. I had not played with toy soldiers since my boys were four, and I would not start again a century and a half later.

"What else is a man to do in retirement?" He smiled with too many teeth. "You've seen plenty of springs yourself. By the looks of that leg, there may not be another on the way. I ask again, who are you? What business brings you to the All-Father's home?"

The All-Father again? He really was pretending to be such a godly being? Curiosity burned in me to see the snot-nosed changeling that sat boosted on his throne. My tongue traced along my teeth as I deliberated joining this child's play. Words that had no reason to cross my mind in over a century came as easily as breathing.

"I am Sir Darl of Rugenmont. Knight in service to Lord Forestier at the seat of the Bear's Stronghold. Protector of the lands of Pyrgne and servant to mine own and the king of kings, the All-Father. I come requesting sanctuary."

"Lord Forestier and all the Forestiers of his time are long dead now, are they not?" the Thyremoin said. He dismissed the Forestiers with surprising confidence. Perhaps he was old enough to know the affairs of my country. Perhaps one of the Jillianus campaigners himself. Perhaps he guessed. "Your knighthood must not have survived, either, for you to come here without a sword or armor!"

"I lost both to the brigands who declared themselves to be our king's servants at the gatehouse."

"Our king?" the Thyremoin repeated. "*My* king is not *your* king, Doll of Rouge-mount. We will not dole out charity to flattery."

My teeth set. "What shameful hospitality is this? The All-Father is king of all kings. King of all men—"

"Yes, men. Not beasts. I can smell your rot, Outlander, from a mile away. Hundreds have come before you. These are trying times, and not ones that have been weathered by guards waving in every vagabond blown in from the Barrens. If you have a qualm with the yellow-capped heathen at the bridge, take it up with him. You'll find this castle has more to attend to than petty skirmishes."

I surveyed the empty green hills around me. "Such as?"

"Tell me, Doll, which god do you pledge to?" he sneered.

"The Flaming Heart," I lied. The Young Gods might all despise each other, but they were as kin as brothers when faced against Morthia. "I'm searching for my son pledged to the same patron."

"Then I wish you the best of luck in finding your Heartless brat, but you won't find him behind these walls. The Green is for men loyal to the King before their gods."

What a noble yet antiquated virtue. My neck had been cut for king and country. Morthia was a lion I chained myself to with the understanding that I would use his hunger for them. The ungrateful cowards of my grandchildren's time had an influx of restless, immortal usurpers. Many made pacts with gods to conquer or to feast. Many men lost faith in the dream that was their country.

Yet, the canary had welcomed me to his king's country while he served the Seven Hands. The boys with crossbows on either side could be unbound youths if I believed any could grow to such an age looking so healthy. The Thyremoine wore old armor and kept the old fashions, evident in his braid and accent. Perhaps he kept to the old, good code of honor.

"Tell me, dear Piglet, when's the last time you drew your blade for the name of your liege lord and not your own hounding sickness to supplicate to your higher power? If you aim to make use of the barbarity that's kept you breathing these last hundred years, I suggest you find your marks *out there*."

He grinned in a way that made me want to scale his wall and knock out two of his teeth.

"My son wears a lambskin coat and is missing his right hand."

"Is that so?" the Thyremoin cooed. I waited for him to call me on my bluff, but he did not. "He took after his mother, I assume. Fortunate for him. He was here two days ago. I sent him away, the same as I am sending you."

There was a lie in there somewhere. I could not tell what, but I saw that glint of deception, the lilt of carefully chosen words. Had Lambskin endeared himself to this encampment? Was he sheltered by the very walls that were guarded to keep a parasite like him out?

"Have pity on an old man," I told the Thyremoin. "I won't ask for communion, only a bed to rest in."

I moved to try the doors. The pups held the crossbows too loosely to be expected to use them. This was all bluster. But, just as I leaned my weight against the first door, I felt something punch into my leg. My knee gave out, and I collapsed with it. When I oriented myself, I was kneeling on the floor, staring at the fletching of an arrow stuck in my calf. One of the pups had shot me. Though meeting his eyes, he looked more startled than I.

"Touch the iron again, and we'll send the next arrow through your neck. Go back to the Barrens and die honorably on the sword. If you came here to escape that, seek out the city of Lorenial in the Elder Wood, and you'll find the Blight will bring a soft end to your miserable existence."

Unprompted, the other crossbowman leaned over the wall to join the taunt. "You can ask the White Knight for your son while you're there!"

"Run along, *Sir Darl*," said the Thyremoin. "Your glory awaits you."

I hated the way the Thyremoin wiped his boots with my name. I hated *him*—this ignoble, pompous man among boys. But what was I to do? Force my way in on the chance Lambskin had earned this cad's sympathies?

I took a breath and stood. My leg spasmed, protesting its use, but I would not show weakness here. The pain would not kill me. I made sure to walk straight down the path, without once looking back. I only collapsed when I was certain I was out of their sight.

I sat there, under the blistering sun, seething with renewed pain. Before I could think of any way to pick up Lambskin's trail or humble the Thyremoin, I had to fix my body.

The pain in my shoulder had dulled—a terrible sign if it started to smell of rot by nightfall. The arrow in my leg was easy to extract, but my bag had been stolen with my armor. Any tinctures or herbs I could use to prevent a sickening of the blood were gone. I might be forced to succumb, but I knew from the ache inside me that I did not have enough to pay my debt to Morthia. Resurrection would return a creature less than a man.

I needed to hunt or to heal.

I was oozing and slow. If any stranger saw me as I was, they would keep their distance and wait for death to take me before looting my body. The tall grass whispered mirthfully. Shadows hid in these vast fields, cutthroat and quick. I'd met and seen no one on the way here, and I saw no one on my horizon now, but I knew they were there.

The Rat King

Feral sheep grazed the valley. Abandoned farmhouses, overgrown with moss and ivy, stood as relics to the shepherdless herd. Perhaps the peasantry had all fled to the Green Castle.

Or perhaps the more faithful sought refuge under a god's roof. There was a temple overlooking the shepherd's village. Its bell tower had crumbled, but its seat of prominence was unmistakable. I had not seen lights coming from its direction the night before, but I hoped to find salves abandoned on high shelves or a cot for me to await an unpleasant death and resurrection in solitude.

I scaled along narrow ridges to dead stops and crumbling footpaths to reach the temple on its raised peak. The ground gave out under me once, and I slid down nearly sixty feet. The terrain might have been less of a nuisance if my leg was not shrieking in protest and my shoulder was not growing stiff. What a comfort it was to feel them, at least. Pain lavished her burning kisses on my body until it was only her heat I felt, not her sting. She wanted me to sit, to rest, and let her touch pulse through me. Her promise was false, but she was ever tempting.

When I summited, I knew at once something was amiss.

I'd seen mass graves before: square ditches where the bodies were laid like bricks and the markers were little more than splinters. Troughs for the crows. Those bodies would have been stripped of boots, rings, and belts during the good days; fingers, tongues, and teeth in these new ones.

This was not so impersonal. A graveyard had been excavated. Where once there had been a dignified row of headstones, there were now empty pits. It was not that the bodies were looted but missing.

I walked along the first row, inspecting every ditch. Beside one grave would be a fresh mound of dirt, rank and wriggling with worms. The next would be packed down by age and growing healthy tufts of grass.

I peered down the slanted curve of the hill. As far as it stretched, the graves were uncovered. Had they been ordered to be moved? Had fresh bodies been scavenged for strips of flesh? It would be too much effort to take a whole corpse if that had been the intention. Even the Flayed only took a small square of skin from the back or chest.

The temple itself was unkempt. Vines coiled up its pillars and slipped in through the broken windows. A dead yew tree had been left bone-white and limbless in the courtyard.

As I rounded the building, the mounds of dirt were notably fresher. The coffins had strips of canvas, the remnants of bedding, and tatters of clothes. The smell of fresh earth was ripe there. The newest line of unburied graves was a short walk down the hillside. In the first pit, I saw no bodies, only a rusted greave and bracer. In the next, there was a sabaton with a corpse's foot still strapped inside. In the third, there was a wraith. No. A man in a tattered moss-green hood. He knelt at the bottom of the grave with an open sackcloth in one hand and a rusty chest plate in the other. Suddenly, he stopped and looked up at me.

Once, I saw a bear and a fox spook each other approaching a creek bed from different directions. This was much the same. We both startled. I hobbled back a half step. The green creature leapt out of the grave like a cat and took off downhill. He raced into the trees and vanished.

I stood and watched, feeling the impulse to chase. Happening upon strangers was still an unusual sensation. I'd gone five years meeting no one else unless I'd sought them out. When I did happen upon strangers, it always ended in blood, as either of us was, inevitably, starving. People here ran as a habit. I'd have to make peace with that.

The creature had abandoned his sackcloth in his flight, and I could see the treasures inside. He'd been collecting the armor and tools of dead men. I did not believe in the malice nor the compassion of gods, but this felt like an especially cruel design to stare down at a sword that I so desperately craved and know that my leg would not let me climb out if I jumped down to take it.

Bitter, irritated, hot—I limped back to the front of the temple.

Its gutted insides lay wide open to the graveyard. As if nature itself had decided to storm this fortress, saplings had wedged themselves between the rotting doors and fixed them ajar.

It was customary for a statue to stand at the entrance of any temple. In my home, ours was dedicated to Amivia, Mother of Morthia, Goddess of All. Her stony visage instilled pious fear in me as a boy as three of her four hands surrounded her bare heart. I had been expected to offer water and bread as payment for my life before I entered. My brother, Mica, used to place my square of bread in her only outstretched palm while I slipped inside behind him.

In this temple, there was no statue asking for alms, but I knew it had once belonged to Amivia. Her symbol, the snake circling its own tail, was carved into the wall, and the pedestal where she would have stood remained, though it bore no display. She reigned here once. And the Young Gods had killed her here too. The inner chambers housed the conquering pantheon.

A wooden statue of Koroe tore open her own chest to release the flaming heart that burned up her shoulders. Malmon the Liar's face was obscured, save for the snakelike tongue that dangled at his chest by a ball and chain. Toothless Deiviknot's fingers pried open his gummy mouth, unhinging his jaw to his navel. The Unblinking Eye stood tall and lithe, armless and featureless, save for a single lidless eye in the center of what should be its head. The Seven Hands cocooned a body hidden inside its nest of arms and fingers. Rivialt the Cretinous Flayed stood on four legs joined at the hip and split again as the torsos of a man and woman sprang away from each other.

The mural painted on the plaster walls must have once been vibrant with rich reds and blues to portray the Young Gods tearing apart their predecessors with their bare hands and devouring them. How the yellows must have shone on their teeth, how the red must have glistened in their hands.

I knew each god pressed beneath their feet: Amivia, Sibdeot, Lotinus, Fuemog, Wroungemout, and Bellium. Each met their end in dirt, and the victors stretched out into the skies. My patron was not among the consumed. Even in their arrogance, no one dared claim dominance over the King of the Flies. I'd long since cooled my temper on such paintings. Lord Forestier's grandchildren took comfort in those murals. They saw gods that defied destiny and buried the natural order, and that blasphemy appealed to them.

In these lean years, no one sought out the mercy of such petty gods. The pews had not been pushed to the walls to make room on the floor for sleeping. Blankets that should have been passed around had rotted in their chests. The hearth fire that would burn in the iron basin in the center of the temple remained only a decorative pile of logs, adorned with dried flowers. The emptied graves outside had been fresh, but it seemed no one had business inside the temple.

No offerings lay at the feet of this mighty coalition. No groundskeeper scraped the elements off their stone skins. The Old Gods had died in blood and battle. The Young had starved themselves in their sickly harvest.

In the back of the altar chamber was a door that would lead to the housing quarters of the temple. The priests and seers would have lived in the dormitories I'd seen attached to the right of the building. Somewhere there would be a kitchen and steps down to a storeroom. I hoped that any useful tinctures had been left undisturbed.

Someone had tried to drag something heavy through the halls. The door to the back room was loose on its hinges, and there were scratches on the doorframe and the floor. Looters? An evacuation? Many scratches had built up over time. Repeat trips with something slightly too cumbersome to navigate elegantly through the narrower halls must have been the cause.

The scratches led me to the kitchen, which was in better shape than I expected. No meat had been left to rot. The fruits and grains had been cleared, and the rats had no stores to nest in. A few tools and sealed jars gathered dust, but none of the labels encouraged me to inspect them further. There was little else of interest except the scratches on the floor that continued under a shelf. From behind, I spied where the wall ended and stone gave way to a dark corridor.

I pushed the shelf aside to expose a narrow hallway, crudely dug but sturdy. Hidden rooms weren't uncommon for a temple. Usually, such passages stored the bodies of the important dead, the silver and gold, and the expensive stores. With my mind set on the latter, I walked through the tunnel.

I took a gnawed candle from the storage shelf and lit it. The tunnel was quiet and dark, but it seemed to go on in only one direction. Sparse alcoves housed a marked tomb for dead priests or stored scrolls and religious texts.

It was not long before I found a room, a small cavity in which a stone floor had been set. A table covered in papers bisected the space, and thick, labeled cabinets lined the far wall. The dried herbs in each box were identified, but the compounds they could be used in were less intuitive. I knew garlic was boiled with bandages, but I did not know the mischief of mugwort. I squinted in the soft candlelight for a label, a book where the healer might have kept his notes. And it was when I finally *looked* at the bench beneath the shelves that I saw the contents of the notes.

Diagrams of arms, shoulders, and elbows lay strewn about me. I'd seen anatomy drawings before where the flesh was peeled back, and the patterns of muscle beneath were documented for study. The subject did not disturb me in principle, but there was an imagination to these images that did. Hands sewn together at the wrists. Fingers fused to the nodules of the spine. Cavities hollowed out in the head to set eyes into newly bored holes.

The notes were written in a language I could not understand, but I could decipher the meaning of the experiments from the illustrations. I looked at the table in the center of this room. Polished scalpels, saws, and forceps sat at its side, still glistening with moisture from when they'd been cleaned. I recognized, too late, the distinct tang of lye in the air.

And something else that had drifted in—something pungent like a crowded market or donkey sweat. Something else was in the tunnel with me.

I grabbed one of the smaller jars on the shelf and made to leave in haste, but when I turned around—*it* was there, waiting at the entryway.

It stood just shy of the candlelight. What little I could see took on the shape of a man, but poorly. Its head was either distorted by the shadow or bulbous—*swollen*. The candle flames caught on tiny pinpoints scattered along its mass. It wasn't until one blinked that I realized each reflection was glimmering off the moisture in an eye watching me.

It could see me. I raised the candle slowly, and the eyes rolled up to follow the light, showing off delicate, attentive whites in each socket.

I blew out the light, and, suddenly, there was a clamor of many slapping feet. I lunged for the medical tools and felt my hand grip around the pommel of *something*. My shoulder twinged as I flexed my dominant grip. My leg shrieked.

Damn pain. Damn weakness.

I felt the brush of fingers against my shoulder and lashed out. The wooden handle of the mysterious weapon vibrated under my palm as it connected with flesh.

Whatever this beast was, it had a voice. Its shriek might have been the agony of a man if it did not come from more than one mouth. Its muscles writhed under the toothed edge of the blade in my hand. The skin I brushed felt tacky and loose.

I felt a hand—two hands—two *left* hands. Their thumbs circled my wrist from the same angle, closing from the same side. I released the weapon and stuck the hot wax of the candle into the closest wrist. The creature yowled and curled back into the shadows, releasing me with such force that I fell flat on the floor.

I could hear it groaning above me. It slapped about on many feet. Pots smashed. Pages fluttered to the floor. The metal tools jostled together. While this mass flailed about in the dark, I had to make my escape or succumb.

I darted in the direction of the hall. By some meeting of luck and memory, I did not run into a wall first. In my best form, I might have been able to bolt back down this secret corridor, up the pantry, out of the kitchen, and into the grass before the altar, heaving, clutching my leg that had been lightened from the exhilaration of a near brush with death. But I was not in my best form, and I was not fast enough.

My damaged leg could not bear my weight, and I felt it collapse under me every fourth step or so. I knew I would not reach the graveyard when I heard the creature tearing down the path just behind me, its wail now a cackle.

When it did grab me, it was not one hand. A spiderlike mass of limbs circled around my waist, my legs, my torso, my neck. Sometimes there were three hands to an arm, each coiling about me like a snake. A dozen arms together flung me up into the ceiling, then smashed me down on the ground. They shook me like a dog trying to snap a rabbit's neck.

I felt pain, briefly, then the euphoric distance of numbness. Then nothing.

THE HUNGER

I was not a man when I awoke.

I'd paid Morthia, and I'd been found wanting.

The thing shoved back in me was not whole. Peel away the layers of a man, and you'll find one thing at its core, beneath the chivalry and valor to which knighthood aspires, beneath the lusts and musings of base men. It lives so deep in us that to pry it out is to husk our souls from our mortal shells.

Its teeth are sharp. Its eyes are keen. It never sleeps. It's always there, digging in at the edges of hunger. It raises its head when another man's face turns red and his hand goes to his sword. Most men mistake it for fury. But it has no rage nor malice. It is only quick and violent.

When it returned to my body, it understood one thing: it was ravenous.

The smell of refuse was sharp against my nose. The scent was bitter on my tongue. The backs of corpses gave under my feet like a bed of moss. I knew I stood among the dead and gave no thought to their purpose. No meal could be made of them. That is all.

So I moved on, seeking a hunt.

It was dark. The air was stale.

I stumbled into a pile of treasures. Steel glittered like starlight in the dark.

I pushed aside a gauntlet-gloved hand and grasped the pommel of a sword. It was snapped and rusted at the edges, but I needed teeth.

The blade came with me.

I walked on, following a familiar, putrid scent. I had a mark. The tumorous mass of a man who'd felled me was here.

I could smell him. Lye and sweat and iron.

A thousand eyes and a thousand hands would be my feast.

Then, I heard something else. A voice called out to me.

Life. A man.

Two arms, two legs, but too far for me to reach.

The iron bars of the cage that separated me from him were clear in my memory.

A thick crosshatched wall embedded in the stone. It was a holding cell where a sliver of light seeped in from a tiny hole in the ceiling.

There was a lock. My prey stood behind it.

There were words. *You're alive*, perhaps? There'd been more.

I broke the lock, and my meal stood up—to greet me? To fight? I didn't know.

I ran him through—the dull blade graceless in my stiff fingers. All the same, I embedded it deep in his chest.

A rasping gurgle bubbled at the back of his throat. I groaned in relief, like a parched man feeling the first taste of cool water against my tongue.

Then, I saw another beside him. I made a meal of that one just as quickly.

I drove him back into the wall he'd seeped from. The shock of stone rattled the steel. I basked in the euphoria of that final sigh and longed for more.

There was a third. I was upon him, but the clash and shake of steel vibrated down my palms.

A bar of broken iron had batted my swing away. I grabbed for his slender neck. He struck me across the jaw with another wild swing. I staggered, and a flash of vibrant blue fluttered past me.

If there was pain, I didn't know it yet. I saw the color, alive with promise.

Morthia's *ache* and the euphoria of the other two deaths urged me on. They sang in my chest, pounding on drums that quaked my body. *Hunt. Hunt. Hunt.*

I gave chase.

I could see the barest flashes of him in the dark. He scurried, but I was gaining. Then he ran through a door.

A new light, soft but persistent, stunned me. Fresh, cool air brushed over my skin. The earthen walls on either side of me had vanished, and I smelled it again.

Sweat and fresh-turned earth. I stood in the hillside graveyard.

A black shadow loomed over the static graves, wriggling with life. The flat moonlight reflected off a thousand little eyes. Its body, rounded to mock the idea of a man, was digging with its thousand hands to pull up dirt one fistful at a time.

It dug like an animal. Bare hands scraped layer after layer of earth away to plunder the coffin beneath. Hands sprouted from the ankles and, like the roots of a yew sapling, held fast to the edge of the grave it was excavating.

Excitement thundered through me. I felt like a wolf that had caught a deer drinking from a pond. This clumsy, swollen thing begged to be popped with tooth and claw.

Sword in hand, I charged forward.

The thousand eyes shone. I tasted the acrid tang of its sweat as it stopped its shoveling. It tried to raise its lumbering arms from the grave. Clumps of dirt rained down from newly opened palms. I cared not for them, but those stout legs.

I lunged for the ankle and slashed at the tender flesh the way a boy swung a hammer. No skill or form ruled my arm, only the *need* to cut, to strike, to sink my teeth into flesh.

My heart sang, and the sweet ache sighed as I felt my blade slide deep into its skin and cut a tendon in its ankle. The beast buckled. Its knee sank, missing the edge of the hole it'd dug.

Its body plummeted into the grave.

Hands stretched out to catch itself before it fell too deep. Arms flexed, overlapping and tangling themselves. I swung the sword down like an ax, severing a hand at the wrist.

Two more punched out and struck my torso, but it was like a man slapping away a rabid dog.

I scurried to my feet and threw myself back at the beast. The sword, little more than a dagger after snapping in the creature's flesh, was sharp and true in my hand. I stabbed one of the thousand eyes. It shrieked, and I brought my knife to the elbow protruding from a thick-muscled calf. I pulled away and stabbed again.

I slashed.

I bit.

I hacked away at what little give I had until I felt bone strain and tendons snap.

I recalled sinking. Arms, legs, feet, and hands all curled for me like the limbs of a dying arachnid. Fingers fisted my hair. Legs looped around my stomach. They squeezed. It might have been painful. I would not know.

All I knew was that with each punch of my sword, I drove both of us a little deeper into the grave. Dirt clumped between my fingers. It sprayed my eyes and coated my lips.

I tasted mud and blood and pus.

Then the rush.

Every hollow of my bone could feel it quicken through me like mercury. A light as clear and pure as the stars could have offered itself to me then, and I would not have known the difference. Morthia offered me no taste of divinity, but in these moments, I felt as if I were eating of Amivia herself. This was satisfaction. This was pleasure. I shuddered with power and collapsed upon the corpse I had wrested such satisfaction from—exhausted.

Alive.

THE BLUE KNIGHT

I tasted the tang of blood on my tongue when I recovered from my frenzy. The crust of it had dried on my skin. Maggots brushed against my palms like wriggling blades of grass.

Slowly, I peeled myself away from the carcass beneath me. In the bare morning light, I saw the malformed creature I'd slain in its entirety. It should have been grotesque—stiff legs and arms curled around me in a sickly embrace.

I had seen the bodies of war: lidless eyes withered in living sockets, skin bubbled by fire and hot sand. The hanged, the flayed, the conquered, the starved. I had felt horror at the sight of men warped by war's hand, but not for this creature. Curiosity, perhaps, and a mild fascination. There were many limbs, dozens of eyes embedded in shoulders and arms, and teeth growing between folds of skin and bubbling lumps. I knew not where a man ended and a creature began, only flesh and more flesh. Skin cured and stretched like leather stitched this beast together.

Should I have been aghast? It was not human, no, but impossible? I had seen the possibilities of cruelty and ingenuity, and this seemed as reasonable as those inflicted mutilations.

I climbed out of the grave, against the protesting ache of my limbs and the snag in my chipped fingernail. Absently, I rubbed at a sore spot in my jaw, trying to recall its cause from my haze.

Bright blue flickered behind my eyelids.

Yes. There'd been someone else besides this creature. There had been voices. I'd been underground at one point. Catacombs. Dimly lit halls and a mass grave where flesh had been picked from steel.

I looked at my own state of dress and, for the first time, noticed my right sleeve had been torn off at the shoulder. My arm felt stiffer, numb in places. The scars I'd carried for six decades, dark and nearly black against my skin, were gone. The smooth, supple flesh of a young man's sat over lean musculature, its coloring a somewhat lighter umber than the rest of my body. I tried to touch my fingertips together on my right hand and did so with slow, uncoordinated success. I'd regrown a new arm entirely in my resurrection.

The bloodstains on my breeches and my bare feet suggested my legs had been crushed, but they hadn't been ripped from my torso. I pulled some grass from the graveyard and tested my fingertips, clumsily braiding the blades together. Morthia's hunger was sated, and the arrow wound in my leg from the Green Castle was a thing of the past. I recalled two piles in the tunnels. There'd been the grave, and there had been the smaller lump of personal effects, clothing, belts, and swords.

I needed a weapon.

Behind me was the entrance. A rusted iron gate lay jammed open at the base of a scarp running along this side of the graveyard. The temple that stood proudly at the top of the hill seemed so far away from this vantage. The grassy overhang tickled the tunnel's edges and would have hidden the sharp drop from above.

I walked to the gate, orienting myself to the new balance in my legs from bones set in death, some long-aching pains remedied, others remaining untouched. When I stepped into the tunnel, I found the interior to be as bright in the morning as it had been at night. They were not illuminated by pale sunlight, as I'd thought, but moonstones—a luminous rock quarried not too far from my home. The Varlemont mountains were known for their rich deposits of ore. When I had served Lord Forestier, finely cut moonstones had been set in the rafters of his assembly hall to look like stars, emitting a faint glow from the sunlight they caught during the day.

I followed the glowing stones back to a holding cell first. Two bodies lay crumpled inside the cage. The first was a man in white robes. His throat had been cut. Though I could not place the moment, his death was, surely, my doing. There were no weapons on his person, nor calluses on his hands. He hadn't been a fighter. The ring on his left hand bore an unfamiliar crest, but in a style I recognized as belonging to the continent far south. I knew him as a servant of Malmon by the punctured tongue looped on his belt.

The other was a man in a quartered tabard of blue and black and a pouch of fingers on his hip. It was not the bright blue I recalled chasing. He seemed to be bigger than the other, with familiar calluses on his palm. He was the swordsman of the two, and the prominent medallion on his chest told me his occupation. A heart burned at the base of an engraved silver tower. He was of the order of the Southern Light Holy Guard, loyalists to Amivia in a time when her worship had faded. They often served as escorts for priests and holy nobility. These men were foreigners like me. They'd come into this land together and died together.

Neither of them was armed, which was of no use to me. I continued deeper into the tunnels until the damp air became thick with rot and the hum of flies clogged my ears. In that chamber, there were three mounds.

One pile seemed to be the discards; slabs of muscle tissue had been piled together like scraps of a butchered chicken. The flies nested in the freshest morsels. The near-skeletal and shrunken bodies mixed among those cuts must have been the ones pulled from the unburied graves.

I assumed I rose from the second pile, a collection of corpses still dressed in their funeral garb and largely intact. The third pile was the one from which I'd plucked my rusty sword.

Most pieces were rusted through from years of exposure to the cold and damp. The surviving clothes were tattered rags. I salvaged half a cloth tunic, a bracer, a set of greaves, and a backplate from that pile.

As I sorted through helmets, I tried to rearrange my braids in hopes that flattening or curling them about my head like a skullcap would help them fit better. Every helmet in decent condition, however, reeked of blood when I closed it. I returned them all to the pile, with no shortage of disappointment.

As for swords, there were fewer to choose from. Among the remnants, I found an arming sword of decent make: an unimpressive slab of steel rusting at the edges and by the pommel. It was the most acceptable of the lot. *A chipped tooth is better than gums.*

I stood there, armored and armed, and suddenly had a sense of uncertainty. Not in myself or my gear but in what I was arming myself for. I'd come to this temple to fix injuries that Morthia had repaired in my death.

Morthia's thread tugged so softly I couldn't feel it now. The ache was gone, the hunger inside me gorging on the soul—or souls—of the chimera rotting outside. Where to now?

Should I storm back to the Green Castle and pull the Thyremoin off the ramparts? It'd amuse me, at least. What about Lambskin? Presuming the gatekeeper had not been lying to me and had not let him through, I had a whole country to search.

In his taunt, the Thyremoin had mentioned a city. Lorenial, was it? Lambskin would be arrogant enough to challenge some foreign champion, eager to humiliate another swordsman through trickery and brigand's tactics. Would there even be a crowd to watch? Was Lorenial a populated city like the Green Castle promised to be? Would I see lights in the forest the way I had seen them in the fields?

Would I see *men* in these strange cities?

Servants of the Young Gods prowled the grasses, but the Thyremoin's archers did not carry communion flesh on their person. Were they men? Normal, human men who would die within sixty years with no despair or depravity limiting their time or their sanity? Could they have children? Did they plow these lush green fields and harvest crops somewhere I could not see? I'd crossed miles of unworked farmland and wild herds of livestock. Were there richer, better reserves somewhere I was not allowed to see? Behind the Green Castle's walls? In this city of Lorenial?

I was not left to my musings for long since once I exited the tunnel, I spotted a stranger.

"Greetings!"

The man was armed with a broadsword, but he had not drawn it. He had not even touched it. Nimble fingers twisted the threads of his light blue tabard. His chain jacket hissed with the movement. He'd set his helmet aside, baring his face to me. The first thing I could think of was how young he looked—so round in the face and unwrinkled. The sunlight warmed his clean-shaven cheeks to a flushed russet. His eyes were striking—common and black at first, but in the sunlight they appeared almost wine-red.

"Greetings, Sir," he said again, lifting his hand in a half-hearted wave.

I said nothing. He was more doe-eyed than the canary. I stepped out from the entrance, checking the hillrise over the tunnel. If there was an ambush waiting, it would spring out now.

"Have the spoils of your victory been satisfactory?" he asked. "I saw Leoric dragging you through the tunnel, and I said to myself, 'There's another poor soul to be butchered.' But it seems you had the upper hand on him, didn't you? Quite a—er . . . direct strategy you have. I've found my training as a knight demands a little more finesse. But in your case, it's effective, I suppose. I thought I saw you dragged into that pit, limp as a corpse. Yet, here you stand."

This was the moment his eyes traced my bare arm, and he waited, as if he expected an announcement. When I gave him nothing, he chewed his tongue. I took in his rounded face, the handsome curve of his nose, and the black hair that fell in thick curls. Not a scar on him. Not a finger, tongue, or eye missing. And as far as I could tell, he was completely alone.

"What do you want?" I asked, hand resting on the arming sword.

The stranger flinched but reached for nothing. "My apologies, we haven't even been properly introduced. I am Theodoulos of Emvinberg." He spoke with his chin up and a toothy smile that felt more polite than gleeful. "And you, Outlander?"

"Darl."

"Do you have a surname, Sir?"

These countrymen were far too fond of formal introductions. "They'd mean nothing to you."

"Due to distance or age?" He was far too excited by his question to wait for an answer. "You're a Deathless, aren't you? You'd be from before the collapse of the Illian Empire."

Illian? He read my confusion as anger and quickly threw up his hands.

"I mean nothing by it, Sir Darl. You may be an outlander, but you know our gods. I think that makes us closer to brothers than some of the foreign heathens that have stormed our lands. Besides, if it were still possible to pledge to Morthia, I'm sure a great many of my brothers would still be honored to accept such a privilege."

A privilege, was it? "And which young feet do you kiss?"

"Deiviknot is my patron," Theodoulos said. *A Toothless*; any bone preserved their lives, but the popular communion was easiest to access. "I earned the right to servitude and laid my back teeth on the altar to contract myself to him."

The years before his pledge could not have possibly amounted to more than twenty. More distasteful than that was the beaming pride in his voice. His first pledge sacrificed his own teeth? A Heartless, by their nature, sacrificed others. Those who chose disposable parts, skin, bone, tongues, fingers, or eyes would be appalled to stoop to self-cannibalism. Even Acolytes, who tended to take their own eyes on ceremony, gave them to another.

"Are the pledged in that castle all as young as you?"

"In the Green? Not as many as before. Some of the faithless fifty-six were younger than I, but they squandered their gifts and were exiled from King

Evarund's halls. Narrow-minded children. The rest of us are grateful and moral, even in these challenging times. Most men of the Green now are from my grandfather's grandfather's time. The priests have plans to grant immortality to young and worthy nobility in another decade."

As a foreign soldier, I was used to catching on to the politics of strangers in their strange lands. To meet a people so covetous of a fate worse than death with no apparent need was surreal. I understood skeletal youths who had picked through rotted crops cutting off their own fingers in the hopes of exchanging their starvation for a different kind of hunger. To hear the nobility, round-cheeked in this lush garden, were honored by their own sacrifice rattled me.

"And you are . . . a soldier of the Green?"

"Yes, sir."

"What are you doing out here?"

"My former brothers in arms abused the status of their position. They were more loyal to their own gods than the king, and King Evarund does not abide by traitors littering his countryside. I was sent to ensure that they face justice and hang from the neck until dead—truly dead."

It still sounded strange to hear him speak of King Evarund. I could only imagine the farcical display of their court. Little knight heads peeking out of breastplates twice their shoulders' widths. Ladies and lords in robes that swallowed them whole, playing at politics in their parents' clothing. What a ridiculous country this was.

"You? Alone?"

Theodoulos' smile strained. "There were others. You sorted through their bones in Leoric's tunnels. The old physician had hidden away here fifty years ago, and King Evarund was willing to leave him to his experiments. We hadn't imagined he'd turned himself into . . . that." He looked into the grave where the many-limbed creature putrefied.

"He was a great healer in the Green Castle. He delivered me and many other members of the nobility. I remember thinking he was the oldest man

I'd ever seen. He left when I was a boy. I remember the relief the day we . . . Even before most healing was a matter of communion, he'd pay the peasantry in silver when they overbred to cure their children. He did great research. He moved here with his books and his apprentices to continue his studies undistracted."

Theodoulos took a steadying breath and surveyed the unburied graves.

"I think this place may have poisoned him. He was never a fanatic; we've done away with such illogical sentiments after Evarlyn, but you've seen the walls and the statues. I can imagine living in the House of the Pantheon, with nothing but those idols and graves, might make a man believe the gods are mightier than they should be. Most of his communication with us after he settled here was ill-mannered and . . . odd.

"Naturally, when my brothers and I set out to hunt the fifty-six, King Evarund also sent us to retrieve Leoric. We thought to shackle him and return him within the week, but as you've seen, he transmuted himself into something . . . less. One of my cellmates was the last of his apprentices. He said the others had been bludgeoned and stitched onto his skin, or they'd fled into the Elder Wood. It seems the White Knight and the Blight were preferable to facing their master."

There was a discomfort in his tale that he was trying to hide, like a man in a shirt stitched a fraction too tight. There was something he was keeping from me.

"Did I kill your friends in that cell?" I asked, in no mood to be caught in a drawn-out plan for revenge.

"The outlanders?" Theodoulos scoffed. "No. Leoric killed the apprentice a month ago. The ones left with me were vagabonds who took refuge here when the Green turned them away. Most foreigners who come to ravage our lands stumble here when the Green smells the wolves beneath their sheepskin—N-not that *you, Sir Darl,* would ever be—"

I interrupted his stammering. "And the soldiers you left with?"

"They're gone. They died as well. I was saved for last."

I didn't believe him, but what did it matter to me? He was alone; that's all the truth I needed. "So, that is your physician. What decrepit god did he seek out to transform himself into that?"

"I'm told he'd been studying communion: how the consumption of flesh restored us. The apprentice said he thought restoration might be in the flesh itself, not a pact with the divine—yet he has all these symbols of divinity in his notes and about these tunnels. He tore off his dying flesh and replaced it. The apprentice thought him godless, but I think he tried to bond himself to any that would have him. His form must have pleased Koroe's bloodlust, or the greed of the Seven Hands, or, perhaps, Rivialt. It's grotesque. What is the point in eternity if you cannot keep your humanity?"

He looked to me as if I'd weigh in with some heavy philosophical remark. Of course, I didn't. We both were already less than human. What was there to say?

"Have any other outlanders passed through this place since you were imprisoned?"

"A few," he said. He hid his disappointment with my dismissal poorly. "Are you asking after someone in particular?"

"A Heartless dressed in a lambskin coat," I said. "He had one hand and would have arrived little more than a week before I did."

"The Green wouldn't take a foreign Heartless. Servants of Koroe were banned, save for the existing knights. If you didn't find his bones here, he likely set off into the country. Perhaps he'll stumble into the lairs of King Evarund's enemies—some coalition of peasantry and exiled knights—or the hedge witches. Who is this Heartless to you?"

"No one of your concern."

"It might be. You intend to find him, don't you?"

I had little patience for leading questions. "You should be running back to your boy-king."

"King Evarund's name is not one to be belittled, Sir Darl. You and I are alive by the charity of men like Evarund. He will not be ridiculed in my presence."

I took a step forward. The little knight scurried back. I'm sure my amusement was plain on my face. "You're here with a mission from your god-king. If you go back now, you'll have failed him. Instead of striking out on your own, you waited this long for me to wake. So let's cut to it. What is it you want from me? And what can you offer in exchange?"

Theodoulos swallowed. Those striking dark eyes flitted to mine. "I believe you and I can benefit from a partnership. They don't make men as . . . durable as you anymore. And I . . . I have the lay of this land . . . I can help you find your Heartless if you help me in turn. We'd be searching in all the same places anyway, and while you rescue your friend, you need only chop a few heads on the way to him. You're a stranger here, and you can be subject to painful surprises like Leoric, or . . . you could avoid them with me. Who knows? If you impress me enough, I might even put in a good word for you to be let into the Green."

I scoffed. "What makes you believe I want to enter the Green Castle?"

"What else is left for any man to want?" Theodoulos said primly.

I'm sure he thought he presented a striking offer, standing tall with his chest puffed in untested armor, eyes bright with unearned confidence. All at once, I realized how frighteningly young this little knight was, and how quickly this world would skin him alive if given the opportunity. I thought of Lambskin creeping in his shadow. What else, really, was there to do?

THE LEADSWINE

It might have been faster to reject Theodoulos' offer. It was obvious that he had exaggerated his expertise and authority. He knew these lands the way someone who left the castle for sparse hunting parties and peasant festivals might.

Yet, he was not born nobility. I could say his mannerisms gave him away—something in how he held the pommel of his sword or how he set his feet. The enunciation of his vowels was too conscious for confidence; the same way the sons of stable hands spoke when one of them was raised to be a page. I preferred the expression that men older than I had used for generations: I could smell it on him.

In the forest, however, he proved not to be a peasant's boy either. He didn't know the local plants and stumbled away from a well-trodden hunting path the locals would have used in favor of cutting through a thicket to keep our direction south.

Despite our slow going, I enjoyed that he talked.

Silence is like noise: you don't notice it until it ends, and then you don't want it to start again. Not that the boy prattled on for hours, but it was enough: a short recount of some brigand thwarted at a crossway, a local legend invented to scare children about some creature dwelling in the cave we hurried by, the odd question for me when he ran out of anecdotes.

He was loud and unobservant. Lambskin would consider him an easy mark when they eventually crossed paths. He would be good bait. After all, if I spent the next year cutting down this boy's enemies for him, he could afford to be a lure for mine.

"Who is this Heartless you're hunting, again?" Theodoulos asked for perhaps the fifth time. We were in a grassy valley with little to speak of under the sweltering sun. He had been babbling questions all afternoon to distract himself from the heat.

I hadn't answered the first four times, but the sun wore me down as well. "His father would have been a rancher before the war came through. The army would have confiscated his stock and taken up residence in the barn or his home. They would have taken liberties, and he, no doubt, would have been driven away for one reason or another after that."

"Which army is this?"

I shrugged. "Mine or another's would have met his homeland the same way."

"You'll have to be more specific, Sir Darl. I was tutored in history, but there are an awful lot of invaded homelands and an awful lot of armies."

"Sur Duomgah was what the land was called when I was a boy. Changed to Serrentez when the Southern Emperor took it over, some gilded pup named Silo or Alfonso. They bred fine horses on those hills and were excellent riders. Boys and girls could ride before they could run. The herdsmen had a whistle that they used to speak to one another across mountains and bring in their livestock. Their voices bounced across the mountains, and if you heard them when the fog rolled in, you would think they were passing spirits. I rode through that valley a century and a half apart. The men changed, the villages were larger, but the whistles stayed the same."

"And your Heartless friend came from one of these occupied villages?"

"He started following our war camp around the time we marched on Tibre . . . no, Auster's campaign against . . . it must have been Wustraghal . . . no. We were fighting someone."

"Someone?" Theodoulos repeated flatly.

In truth, it startled me a little as well that I could not remember the specifics. A century and a half of marching and sieges blended together. The only campaign I remembered in full was my first. I could recall every stopped heart that had brought me one step closer to home. By my tenth, I'd long since left the matters of the home in Varlemont to the gaggle of strangers who vaguely resembled me, and did not fret when I returned to be greeted by another.

"Have you forgotten the specifics of his story? That'd make you a poor—er . . ." Theodoulos' playful insult died between his clamped teeth. I wondered how many superiors had corrected him in his lifetime to make his fear instinctive.

"The story of his land is his story. He was from a region of horse lords who became cattle barons, who became stablemen. Whatever specifics of his life made him different are of no consequence. He lived in a country that was pillaged from both sides by two armies. He survived it, and now his country is gone and so are the armies."

The facts of wartime disturbed young Theodoulos. He walked with an uncomfortable stiffness, as if he'd never considered such a tragedy before.

"Did he have a family?" he asked.

"Yes." There was that mop of curly, dark hair that had followed him around in his youth. The one who had climbed over bodies with bare feet and stolen scraps from the camp cook. The one who had carried a carved wooden horse around his neck. "His little brother died before him."

"My condolences. I know . . . I lost . . ." Theodoulos seemed to be warring with what to say next, but then he turned his head like a hare on lookout. He stood still as stone, listening. Before I could understand, he pulled me down into the grass.

His breath puffed against the dirt, his vibrant eyes fixed on that obscure point in front of us. For a while, there was nothing: the pitch of the wind, the sway of the grass, a line of ants skittering between my fingertips. Then, there were the sudden, heavy footfalls of an animal charging, and the shrill squawk before an abrupt crunch of bones. A boar-like beast not a hundred yards from us threw back its head and snapped its mouth closed, crushing a chicken caught in its maw. Tusks, the width of my forearm, shifted with its lower jaw. Its long, sleek lion's tail whipped across the top of the grass.

Then, as if it had been pelted with a stone, it stopped. Wide nostrils flared out and in. Slowly, it began to turn toward us.

I heard the creak of wood straining. Theodoulos had strung his bow and nocked an arrow behind me. Stiff fletching slipped just past my ear, loosed by the delicate straightening of his fingers. A sharp, trilling whistle like a birdcall whipped past me and flew deep into the brush.

The boar-creature turned and charged after the noise.

Theodoulos guided us back to the trees. We were silent and slow until we were sure we were beyond the boar's senses.

"Leadswine," Theodoulos explained. "It's the giant's magic. He resurrected them, and they bring what they hunt back to him in exchange."

"A giant?"

"Yes, but we only need to concern ourselves with the swine. They're difficult beasts, not quite animals, not quite alive." Theodoulos pointed to a distant rocky mound barely visible on the western hillsides. "They're usually not this far down from High Mound."

Not only did this land have the All-Father incarnate, but *giants and magic.* In Varlemont, we said our mountains were stone giants lying on one another, but that was a tale for children, a saying. *Bepiv, Bevi, Kuri.* While I knew of some foreign servants of Young Gods who had an ability to weave strange magics, I knew nothing of these beasts.

Theodoulos pointed out a line of trees nestled into the rolling hills called the Elder Wood. The land to the northwest of those trees, Theodoulos said, was the leadswine's usual territory.

"The White Knight took the Puldregrot Fort first, but after he left, the leadswine came in," he explained. "The House of Revesaurs is little more than a stone mound since they charged the eastern wall . . ." and so on.

"What was that arrow you shot?" I asked.

My question interrupted his history lesson, and he seemed quite thrown by it. "I-it's my own invention. I hollowed the center to make it sing. It's like a whistle, see?" Theodoulos plucked another from his quiver.

The arrowhead was made from carved wood and blunted with a hole bored at an angle through its hollow frame. I flicked it through the air a few times to hear the soft whistle. I arched my brow, impressed with its design.

"It felt more practical than charging in. I know it's not how things are done, but it seemed going in swinging would only end in my . . . I thought this was a fine solution."

"It's a decoy."

His bright eyes flashed as if I were admonishing him.

"Wise men avoid danger when they can," he muttered. I hadn't said otherwise.

THE SWAMP

I didn't sleep around Theodoulos.

I feigned it the first night and listened to his breathing to count the hours. I tried not to tense when he stood and walked to me. I imagined what I would do if I heard the scrape of his knife slipping from its scabbard or the soft groan of a bowstring pulled taut. Neither happened.

A feather-soft touch on my shoulder roused me for the second watch. As soon as I stirred, his hand retreated. Theodoulos fell asleep in front of me within the hour.

On the second night, when he suggested a formal schedule, I admitted to my eternal wakefulness. Another night staring at the vacant darkness was too tedious, and he already knew my patron. Still, it surprised me that he was not disturbed. In fact, he marveled at the "gifts of the Old Gods" and dropped like a sack.

Ridiculous boy, I thought. I plucked up some blades of grass and braided them until sunrise.

In the mornings, he'd stretch like a child—all ease and unbothered rest. Sometimes, he would fish out a tooth to swallow whole from a pouch on his hip. He didn't try to hide taking his god's communion, but he preferred not to mention it. Theodoulos promised me the Green Castle in the mornings and praised the view from its walls at sunset like a holy man spouting a sermon. I never said anything to the contrary—let him think that promise kindled my spirit.

We were walking the lowlands by then. Moss gave way to skunk cabbage, and the smell of wood rot perfumed the air.

One night, when we had reached the thick of the swamp, we settled down beneath the sloping trunk of an old tree. Dark water lapped at slick mud traps just a few yards away. Theodoulos complained about mosquitoes and the damp late into the night. Though I agreed the swamp was miserable, it was a welcome kind of irritation to hear the constant croak of frogs and the hiss of plentiful cicadas. Life thrived even in this soggy muck.

It wasn't until much later that I remembered that a plentiful landscape was not devoid of dangers. After Theodoulos had fallen asleep, a shadow crept out from the swamp to the edge of our camp. It sat very still. If I had not seen it approach, I might have mistaken it for a lithe stump on the yew's branches. We watched one another in the tattered moonlight. Perhaps it was waiting for me to fall asleep. Whatever its aim, it startled when Theodoulos began to thrash in his sleep. He muttered something into the floor and shouted. Just as he jolted awake, the shadow skittered away, leaves and sticks snapping underfoot.

"What was that?" Theodoulos asked. He was in tears.

"Heron."

Theodoulos was unsettled for the morning, but his spirits lightened when we finally set eyes on our destination.

"The House of Oghir!" Theodoulos announced. "Home to Alanus the Alligator Queen."

I expected some sinister darkness: gnarled roots, dark canopies, carnivorous vines choking out the trees. The swamp was disappointingly common. Thick bald cypress trees flourished in ample sunlight, and purple milkweed bloomed all about us. A congregation of alligators sunbathed on the bank of a dilapidated manor.

The swamp had already reclaimed most of it. The windows were clotted with dust. Its plastered walls were chipped and overgrown with thick clusters of ivy. A fallen tree had partially collapsed the west wing, but survived and sprouted fresh, full branches at a severe angle.

"When the fifty-six fled, many went to seek out Lady Alanus. She was the first of the traitors, after all. She has speakers wandering the countryside to recruit the naive and the desperate. Your Heartless might have been drawn here to her. The Green will be glad to see her head mounted on their wall."

When Theodoulos had said he was on the hunt for traitors to the king, I had expected his targets to be nameless souls. Foreign invaders. Peasants. This one had a title? A manor?

"What has she done?"

"There's *little* she *hasn't*."

The insinuation in his tone was intended to scandalize. My expression made his pleased little smile evaporate.

Soberly, he went on, "When Holy King Evarund's great-grandson, King Evaright—divine save his soul—perished, there was speculation on the nature of the illness that had taken him. See, he had not been well for years, and Lady Alanus had been advisor and consort. Before his death, it was an open secret Lady Alanus was ruling in his stead—"

"He was *human*?" I interrupted.

Theodoulos stopped, his lip twitching. "What do you mean?"

"He died of an illness. He was a *man*. He grew up, grew old, *died*."

Theodoulos chuckled, a nervous, reedy thing. "He had no patron. None of King Evarund's descendants nor their consorts took a patron. They would not give up something as precious as their fertility for physical power."

"Then they die of age? They have children?"

Theodoulos' mouth flattened. "Those who do not serve as knights continue the family bloodline, yes."

"All one family?"

I dismissed the question as soon as I said it. The nobility had bred among themselves even before the wars of earth and water. I didn't see any farmland worked, but enough must be maintained within the walls to sustain their settlement. What mattered was that the Green Castle was ruled by a *human*, one impersonating the All-Father, but a man nonetheless.

"Were they sickly from the start? How old was Evaright when he died?"

"I've never seen you this excited," Theodoulos said wryly. "King Evaright lived to be thirty-two. Upon his death, he had no heir. Lady Alanus had been withholding her wifely duties in the hopes of succeeding him without a direct heir to challenge her.

"King Evarund, however, stepped up to rule his lands again with his sons and grandsons gone. He was generous and offered the lady clemency. He was willing to accept her as his bride, and she would be queen mother as she was promised when she bore children with him. Evaright was not cold in the ground before she rallied a coup and tried to banish our divine king from the Green Castle. We squashed her play at rebellion and cast her out.

"I thought we should hang her," he added hastily, "but our commander at the time thought the barbarians littering our countryside would gain more satisfaction finishing her—not you, of course."

Of course.

"Then she struck a bargain with Cretinous Flayed Rivialt. See, she was beautiful once, and so she sacrificed that, I think, more than flesh to him. A year later, she stormed the Green Castle wearing a silver mask—we thought to hide her identity, though she was obvious in her grandfather's armor. When we pulled the mask off her we, revealed her shame. She'd cut the skin of her face!

"We drove her back into her swamp that night, but she never stays there long. For forty years, she's used this waterlogged hovel as her fortress. With the dismissal of knights in the Green Castle, I would not be surprised if some fell straight into her bosom. The ones who had no principles wouldn't care who ruled the Green so long as they were back in it. I know for a fact there were older knights who knew the House of Oghir when it was alive who would gladly exchange favors with the lady. So, you see,

Alanus' death would destroy a more powerful enemy to the crown than any of the fifty-six."

That was forty years ago, was it? I doubted Lady Alanus' circumstances were as simple as Theodoulos' sensationalized telling claimed, but I didn't care to interrogate his exaggerations. Theodoulos had promised me a hunt. I'd promised him a dead traitor. There was nothing else I needed to know.

THE TUNNEL

Bronze sunlight tinted the alligator spines drifting in front of the House of Oghir.

A path must have once led from the manor's courtyard to a road in drier times. Now, everything short of the front door was flooded. The hissing hymns of its subjects bounced across the water. The pungent perfume of fish and old blood tainted the bank. No one would simply walk in through the main entrance.

Theodoulos took us behind the manor, where the water was shaded and the reptilian court thinned. He pointed out a small cluster of rocks, overgrown with moss and bramble. There was a hidden gap between them, a small crevasse that led to the cellar under the manor.

"They called it a secret entrance, but it's been referenced so often in accounts of trysts and sieges, I doubt it's been secret since my great-grandfather's time. The flooding must have put Lady Alanus off from sealing it—if she knew about it to begin with. I'll go farther up the bank and splash about, get the attention of anyone outside. In the meantime, you slip in through there."

While he played in the water, I'd storm the House of Oghir alone. That was our agreement, of course. I was the hunting dog. However, I'd expected him to have more than a secret entryway to offer as preparation. He didn't know the count of who I'd find inside nor their gods. Alanus pledged to Rivialt the Cretinous Flayed and was an accomplished fighter. The rest would, apparently, be a surprise.

"How deep does it go?"

"I wouldn't know. It shouldn't be higher than your hip most of the way. There's a brief point at the end where it said men crouched for a few steps under a low ceiling, but the rest should be above the water level."

I wondered what circumstances would make Theodoulos study the records of old castles without venturing into one himself. Limp-spined survivors tended to carry a wealth of untested information. In the old days, they were the ones peering down from their books to lecture fieldmen on how they'd gone wrong in the bloody fray. For young Theodoulos, I expected no better. I nodded and began to strip the little plate I had, peeling off Leoric's scraps piece by piece.

"You're going unarmored?" Theodoulos asked, scandalized.

His naivete made me laugh. Some men said they felt naked in anything less than full plate. It'd been decades since I'd had such a suit, and I would give up every scrap of my precious armor now before walking into water. I had never passed by drowning, but I'd seen its consequences. Morthia denied death to men, but he did not remove the body from danger.

In the early days, when Deathless were new, we were reputed to be unkillable, but we were not unstoppable. I remember charging past a shallow moat where bodies in full plate armor would suddenly slap about like writhing fish. Fresh bubbles of air from some wanton kiss of life would escape from the slits of their visors. Either their depleted strength, the disorientation of their awakening, or the weight of their mail prevented them from pushing out of two feet of water. When that one breath passed, they'd fall back under Morthia's cloak for another day or two before the bubbles came again.

It became the job of pages and war boys to fish out the flapping soldiers. One Deathless on the battlefield was worth a division of cavalry to our liege lord. When those Deathless woke, they often maimed their rescuers. The few I spoke to between sieges had a skittishness to them, a shake that never settled.

Normally, we Deathless were an undaunted lot. In war, the tax to Morthia was well paid and scarcely considered. The ache of his dissatisfaction was never present. Some of us jumped from high places, ran ourselves through, or crushed ourselves to reflect on the sensation when we woke anew. We shared such conquests as proudly as brothel stories, but the drowned were men who had succumbed. They woke and died again and again for days, months. None of them ever explained what the water felt like. It was known among the other Deathless to avoid them.

Within a few days, they'd start to antagonize others in the hopes of provoking a duel. They wouldn't go after mortal men where the only risk in crossing swords was waking up again. They would seek out other Deathless. It *had* to be another Deathless or else there would be no *end* for the loser.

What an irony that the only thing that could grant freedom to a slave of Morthia was the hand of another slave.

I would take my chances in a gambeson coat. I'd resharpened the worn arming sword on our journey here, and that would have to be enough.

Theodoulos fumbled with the ties on his belt and offered me a twine-netted rock that gave off a soft glow. A moonstone. "Best have a pocket to hide it in once you're in the manor, but it'll be dark as pitch in the tunnel."

I was pleasantly surprised by the boy's willingness to hand me such a rare resource. Against all sense, he trusted me to return with it. I tied the moonstone to my belt, noting the soft blue light catching on nearby cattails. It was not particularly strong, but it had absorbed the sun all day and would last hours.

"I'll be waiting," Theodoulos said, as if I should be reassured by his presence outside. I would be surprised if he wasn't stripped and hanging from a tree by the time I returned.

He ran off to splash in the water after that, and he drew the attention of the most active bulls. They slithered through the algae in a great hissing pack to investigate. The ones that remained seemed to be the sedentary lot, but I did not take their disinterest for granted. I waded through the water under their watchful gaze, my sword at the ready and my back exposed. I arrived at the entrance without having to wrestle one of the beasts, but I was sure they'd be waiting for me on my way back.

The familiar sweet rot of soaked wood wafted from the tunnel's entrance. The moonstone on my hip cast the stonework in a pale light. If this had once been a servant's entrance, it would have been a poorly formed and maintained one. Tools had widened the natural formation of a narrow cave enough for a single man's shoulder width. Lugging barrels and crates to a cellar from this path would have been cumbersome and impractical. Before it flooded, it would have served better as an escape route or a spy's entrance.

As I progressed, black water rose to my knees, to my thighs, then to my hips. The path became so narrow my scabbard scraped against the stone unless it was pressed flat against my leg. It was not long until I reached a point where a slight drop in the sand would submerge me to my shoulders. The water level made me wary.

I pulled the moonstone from my hip and pushed it under the water, illuminating the rock and walls. The dip went on beyond my vision's capacity. A little school of minnows swam under the rock in a wide circle, suggesting there was a path farther ahead. If I breathed in too deeply, my chest pushed against the opposite wall. If it narrowed just a fraction more on the other side, I could be wedged into place and drowned. But there was only one way forward. I thought of those wild-eyed Deathless and knew not even Lambskin could tempt me to endure such a fate.

I went slowly, establishing my footing and keeping the moonstone ahead of me. If it proved too narrow, I would retreat and tell Theodoulos to find another hound. I took a breath and submerged myself. Cold water rushed up into my ears. Silt stirred beneath. I walked forward with one hand tracing the ceiling above me. The narrow sides of the cave did not close in and squeeze against me. In fact, they opened past the third step. On the fourth step, I felt a slight tilt upward in the ceiling. By the sixth, I broke from the water.

I blinked droplets away and pushed my braids out of my face. I stood in a man-made tunnel with tool-hatched walls and wood beams. The walls were wide enough apart for two men to walk abreast, but it curved slightly to my right, a precaution against a siege. It must have been the cellar, judging by the smell of sour rinds. Outside had been almost unbearably humid, but here, despite the flooding, the air was temperate.

Within yards, the water receded to my knees.

In pure darkness, the moonstone's dull light cut off just beyond my arm's reach. Water slapped loudly against the walls as I waded onward.

And then, two little turbulent waves crashed together in a sudden snap, one coming from me, one from the bend in the tunnel. That was all the warning I had before a shadow swept in my direction. Instinctively, I lunged for my opponent.

Or, I meant to do so. My elbow banged against the right-side wall as I tried to swing the arming sword. A swift shadow bore down on me. Heavy metal collided against my shoulder, and my body crumpled under the momentum of the blow.

I collapsed into the wall. The cramped conditions of the tunnel had worked to my attacker's favor. Disoriented and half-blind, I had only a moment to recognize the figure of a man in front of me before an iron mace came down again.

This time, I let myself fall, dropping into the water on my back to escape the blow. My assailant seemed to count on it, as I suddenly felt a foot on my chest, which quickly rose to press on my neck. *Fuck.*

The boot heel pinning me began to press on my neck. Reaching for the foot was a gamble. I didn't know my attacker's strength or stability, but that was the point. They wanted me confused.

If I'd flailed out, flapped my arms, and scratched at sturdy leather, I would have strangled myself. I forced myself to go still, to wait, to think.

I was on my back, but my attacker had a mace. They had to rely on suffocation or momentum, not the point of a blade. They would drown me from here unless I found a way to shove their weight off of me. My arms could spread and brace along the floor, but I wouldn't be able to push myself up on arm strength alone. My feet had a good purchase on one wall, but the press of the boot seemed too sure to slip out from under. If I tried to kick out and slip away from the hold with force, I might expend all my energy on a gamble. But I had space to *move* my arms. My hip brushed against the sword I'd dropped in the chaos. Slowly, I recovered it, hand over hand, until I felt the point slide against my fingertips.

I didn't swing; I just took a firm grip of the hilt and pushed upwards. When I felt the blade start to press against flesh, slowly but with consistent pressure, the solid weight over me tried to draw away. The hold on my neck loosened from that instinctive retreat, and I kicked out, taking advantage of the moment of weakness. I pushed myself out from under my attacker and slammed into the opposite wall. I burst from the water, gasping in the darkness.

The moonstone illuminated the water a few yards in front of me, but it only served to make me feel more exposed. I held my sword out to defend myself against the shadows. Whoever was down here no doubt could pick me out of the darkness already. I heard the water shift, and I had no idea where it had come from. The arming sword seemed to have doubled in weight. My left arm was injured. Not broken, but my grip was weak and strained. My right side would have to compensate.

"I'll give you one warning now," I bluffed. I could barely make out the shadow of someone standing just at the edge of the moonstone's light. "Step aside, and we can end this here."

There was a long silence. I watched the water. I listened for breathing or for the subtle click of metal against stone. The hammering of my heart and the burn in my left shoulder, however, were difficult to ignore.

"No," a woman answered suddenly—far to the right of where I thought she'd been. "But I am willing to negotiate."

The Devotee

"May I?"

I dipped my sword to gesture at the moonstone. There was a long silence again.

I reached for the stone.

"Stay there."

When she said that, she stepped *into* the light. She stopped *on top* of the moonstone, and revealed herself in its faint glow. Her boots were high, oiled leather, perfect for wading in the water. Her padded vest ended above the knee, skimming just above the water line. The light was too dim to illuminate her face, but her hair was close-cropped, and the mace glinted on her shoulder. She cradled it in a confident two-handed grip.

I expected her to bend down and pluck up the moonstone, smothering us in darkness again. Instead she stood in the light while I was encased in shadow. Why put herself at a disadvantage?

"State your business, stranger," she said. Her voice and posture were both at ease. "What brings you to the House of Oghir?"

She was so confident she could best me that she'd decided to show herself. It was frankly insulting. Was she a guardian of the cellar? Surely not. Posted in the dark? It was a good way to kill one's own sentinel. Yet, she appeared to have taken advantage of her environment.

"The lady of the house herself," I answered.

"How so?"

"King Evarund has closed the—" She turned her head away from me. It was such a sudden movement that I expected to hear a third party rushing in behind her, but there was nothing to hear, and she gave no other reaction. "—the Green Castle to myself and my brothers in arms. I set out in search of new leadership. I . . ."

Her head remained turned, and it was then I realized her body was still tilted toward me, her head turned to *listen*. Acolytes of the Eye who had given up their sight stood like that.

"I . . . May I light a candle? It's pitch-dark here."

"No," she said sternly.

Blind. Blinded Acolytes could not see the way a man could, but they tended to have a sense of space even if they were missing both eyes. Light and dark would be indistinguishable to her unless it touched one of her other senses.

Moonstones were uncommon sources of light outside of fixtures. To produce a light equal to a burning wick would require a cumbersome slab the size of my foot. They made no sound and had no noticeable warmth unless they lay in your bare palm. The waterway entrance I'd come from forced any form of firelight to be put out and she waited as close to the dip as possible. This was her hunting ground, I realized. I wondered if any of the true fifty-six had been caught in this snare.

"You're a soldier of the Green?" she asked.

When I spoke this time, she moved, slowly, only a step, but nearly soundless in the water.

"Not anymore. I've come here to endorse the true queen of The Hallowed Lands–"

She was using the sound of my voice to cover her movements as she stepped almost out of the light of the moonstone, circling to my left.

"Yet another green-back flees the flooding hull by jumping into the swamp. Do you know what waits for you on the other side of this tunnel?"

"I intend to find out."

"Why is that? What has the All-Father done to you inside those gates? I hear tell of the Butcher, a Deathless heathen, harbored in your walls. That's the will of your divine leader."

Theodoulos would have fallen for her provocation. Perhaps any knight of the Green would swing at the shadows that dared to mock their king.

"I know you care not for my loyalties or history. You failed to kill me, my lady. I wish to carry on, but you will not allow me. So, what shall we do to resolve our impasse?"

She moved partly back into the light before I'd finished. She wasn't going anywhere in particular; she didn't want me to know exactly where she was after she spoke. Her hand drifted out and tapped the stone to her right. She noted the distance and adjusted her stance.

"Teeth are my price. Four. Remove them and place them on the ridge of stone two steps to your right." *Teeth*. Not an Acolyte, then. Yet, she *was* blind.

I moved as she instructed and felt along the wall. It took some doing. When I found the ridge, I rubbed against what felt like the head of a nail. My numb fingers brushed something off, and it clattered against the rock. It took me a moment to realize the item was dangling from a string attached to that nail. I followed the string to the small pair of pliers hanging at the bottom.

This must be a fruitful routine for her. Trapped in the dark, a few teeth is an easy toll to pay for escape. I half-considered Theodoulos playing a part in this, but he'd given me the light. What a fruitful coincidence that a moonstone was exactly what I should need. Yet, she *was* asking for teeth.

An amused little part of me wondered if one of us had been betrayed.

"How long have you been a rat in Lady Alanus' cellar?" I asked.

"I will be here long after you've pledged loyalty to another false prophet." The resentment in her voice was not what I'd expected.

"You're speaking of Lady Alanus now?"

No answer.

"What insight does she claim is the will of the gods?"

She remained silent. I could leave it there, but given how easily I saw her, I thought a measure of transparency was warranted.

"I am truly curious. If I may confess, I've lied to you. I am not a soldier from the Green. I've been sent here by a man of questionable motive to kill the lady in her own manor. He claims she's a power-lusting usurper, and I find myself at a disadvantage in this new world."

"Who was this nobleman?"

I hadn't suggested a title. She had someone in mind. "Theodoulos of Emvinberg. Heard of him?"

"No."

Her tone gave nothing away. My fault for being candid with my questions.

"Alanus is a woman who misunderstands her place," she volunteered, remarkably. "A woman must be devoted to her god. A communion sacrifice is an exchange of gratitude for the privilege of the life we are given. Alanus has stripped herself and laid her pelt before the Cretinous Flayed. She has demanded his grace like a child. She sought power, not enlightenment. It is slothful faithlessness like hers that brought the Blight upon us. Faithlessness has been growing in this country since Evarlyn's time. He died combating such pestilence, but still it grows. In our continuous efforts and relation to the divine, we are worthy of this life eternal. It does not come from one expectant gesture. Alanus makes a mockery of her family's patron and house."

To be bound to Morthia was to relinquish one's own life for a greater purpose. To think of him as a guiding hand to a spiritual awakening felt more absurd than Alanus' attitude. Acolytes were often reverential, but a Toothless? I'd never seen an organized temple for Deiviknot alone and, rarely, a shrine. Her resentment of the slothful, at least, worked in my favor.

"Is this your endorsement of my quest to behead her?" I asked the devotee.

"You will not be able to. Her skin is unyielding steel. No war hammer can crush it. No sword can cut it."

"Then her little god answered her, regardless of her understanding," I said.

A long silence followed. I'd insulted the shucking of her humanity, and now the child was feeling petulant.

"Leave your teeth and turn back," she said. "If you wish to live up to your knightly vows, warn the exiled away from dying for King Evarund's lie. No man can provide succor for the gods' designs."

My interest pricked at that.

"What lie does he offer?"

"A price with a steeper cost than a god's, though he'd say otherwise."

"Steeper than teeth?"

She did not reply.

I ran my thumb along the ridges of the pliers. Judging by the throb in my left side, something was dislocated. My assailant was exposed to me here and now. If I chose to attack, I had an advantage over her. Or, I could demonstrate good manners and pull out four teeth for her gluttonous god.

❖

I flexed my jaw and my hand as pain throbbed down my neck and caressed my arm like a lover. My tongue ran against the hollows where four molars used to be. They'd grow back the next time Morthia revived me. Still, I couldn't help but agitate myself by prodding the new gaps.

The effort of the act had taxed my grip strength and my arm more than my faculties. I had not been magnanimous in my choice, however. It had been the easiest way past her, given that there was not enough room to swing a sword, which had been growing progressively heavier to my throbbing arm.

When I had left, I had maneuvered to pass over the moonstone and collect it. She did not move from my path as I neared, confident in the darkness. I stood so close I could smell her—musty clothes, leather oil, and sweat. The toe of my boot settled on the stone and slid it a little closer to her. The light reflected dimly against intact, sightless eyes. They did not so much as squint in my direction. It was odd to be facing the ear of someone so close.

"Were you blind before you pledged to Deiviknot?" I asked impulsively.

Her lip twitched into a frown.

"Why not pay The Unblinking Eye?" I went on. "Yours were of no use to begin with. From what I understand, the eyeless Acolytes can *see beyond* for their sacrifice." A vague term, but I had watched them move with a certainty that had suggested they'd had an impression of the area around them, if not a full picture.

Her grip adjusted on her mace, ready to swing. "It's not a sacrifice to offer what you do not have. They have no interest in something I have not used since birth. Besides, Deiviknot looks after his devotees in ways the others do not."

Her pride in her choice irritated me more than the notion of her deep relationship with her god. I'd long since accepted that servants of the Young Gods made their bargains with little regard for how their lust for power spat on the sacrifices men before their time had made for them. They did not have the character to resent their positions. But to be proud of one above all others? Deiviknot was said to heal more grievous injuries faster than others. Koroe's longevity appealed to Heartless. The Flayed felt less pain. The Acolytes had their paradoxical sight. What did the differences matter when a pact with any came at the cost of their humanity?

She spoke as if her choice had been the *best* one. I left the moonstone there, exposing this stranger to whoever had the thought to explore this entrance after me.

I reached a door at the end of the tunnel shortly afterward and stepped out into a flooded cellar. Broken wine casks rotted in knee-deep water. Moonlight spilled in from steps ascending on the opposite side of the room. I was almost relieved to see the light until I remembered I was an intruder.

I stepped out of the water, onto the dry landing. My legs shook on solid ground as if I'd swum for days. I took stock of my body. It was good to be out of the damp. I'd survive the pain in my jaw, but my left shoulder was a hindrance. Stripping off my gambeson and my shirt, I confirmed it was dislocated, not shattered. My right side, from my ribs to my hip, was already beginning to purple.

The last traces of dusk light spilled in from the top of the cellar's steps. A door at the top landing had collapsed along with a portion of the ceiling. I heard no voices, no shuffling of feet overhead. If there were guards in this manor, they did not seem to concern themselves with this flooded route.

I popped my shoulder back into place and collapsed against the wall. My head lolled back against the stone grit. The brightest stars were beginning to canvas the sky.

There was a soft kind of peace to be found in abandoned places such as this. Dark water lapped rhythmically against the stairs. Frogs vocalized from the dense clusters of sedge and milkweed that'd flourished on top of collapsed stonework. The rest of the manor might hold a counsel of fifty-six knights ready to behead any invader, but in this cellar, I lay in a pocket of time when they ceded their claim to nature's slow grasp.

How strange it was to see her grip so strong. Here, the soil was not salted. I would like to think that in a decade, maybe two, the water would come up to the ceiling, the grass and moss would grow thick, and the only hint that man's hands had touched this place would be tool marks on a stone buried beneath feet of silt.

That tunnel rat had spoken of gratitude for the privilege of extended life. What a blissful thing it must be to be so credulous. Outside these lands, hollowed buildings stood like gravestones. Stunted grass withered in the blazing sun. The world had been unmade by servants of ungrateful gods. The great cities they had sacked for their patrons' hunger had crumbled into dust in Morthia's palm. If I had been born in their time, I would have grown a garden on the soil left to me.

The House of Oghir

I did not wake the next morning so much as the sun startled me out of my trance. Flat black water had faded to a deep blue. An hour or so later, the sun came in and illuminated the backs of minnows circling below the water's surface.

I donned my gambeson and rolled my shoulder. The sword felt twice as heavy in my grip, but I'd rested as long as I had the patience for. Even if this had been a ploy by Theodoulos to collect a few teeth, the lady's reputation preceded her, and I was eager to make my own judgments.

The cellar steps lead to a charming demonstration of nature's persistence. The high fence surrounding this yard was overgrown with rich tangles of ivy. The daylilies had escaped their plots and flowered in a multitude of orange and maroon bushels. Grass and bluebells crashed against wide stone steps that led to a back entrance to the House of Oghir.

A guard stood at the top of those steps. He wore full plate, but the armor itself was mismatched. The pauldron on his left shoulder was a different metal from the one on his right. The backplate didn't align with the front of the cuirass.

When he saw me, he advanced, and I noticed his suit was incomplete. No gauntlet on his left hand. No back to the cuisse armor on his legs, no vambrace on his right. No cloth nor gambeson covered those bare patches, as if he were naked underneath the metal.

My gambeson sleeve had all but torn off from my skirmish with the tunnel rat, but it was incomparable to fighting in unpadded metal. He bore no shield, just a sleek halberd that would do its best to deny me the opportunity to come in close and strike him. If I hit him at a joint, the armor might do the work for me and crush and cut his bare skin.

He didn't call out to others or retreat, which boded well for me. Perhaps his companions were too few in number to aid each other or too far away. Or he did not consider me a threat.

He advanced, and we locked into a dance.

On his first swing, I needed only to step back. He followed up with a clumsy thrust of the halberd's point. I breathed easy then. I was faster than him. I could not be careless, of course. The garden was walled, and he could force me into a corner if I allowed him too much leniency, but I could control this fight. As he recovered his grip, I circled around him, aware of how much space I had between myself and the wall.

His attacks were not unskilled, but he was impatient. It would have been better for him to stay close to the door and force me to come to him. Since he chased me, I controlled where we went.

When he drew back to swing, I took advantage of the dexterity of my gambeson and rolled into his attack. I came up to his side and drove my arming sword straight through that gaping space between his breast and backplate. The encounter had not lasted long, but I thought it strange he made no sound when he died. No strained panting, no gurgles for breath. The spasm of lungs rattled my blade but produced no sound.

His last breath still slipped into me, but there was something feeble about it, as if I'd only killed the canary's pheasant. I stabbed into that gap again to be sure. There was no change, but he was surely dead. I withdrew my sword, and I plucked up his halberd, appreciating the weight and the make. I expected the garden door to be locked, but it took the slightest pressure to push it open into the House of Oghir.

Beyond a sitting room was a large, open hall that could serve as a receiving room or a ballroom. Both, however, would require the house to be in a better state of repair. The damp smell of the swamp drifted in through the broken windows. Dried leaves tumbled across splintered wooden floors. There were no guards, but there were creatures huddled against the far wall.

If I had not seen the bulging whites of their eyes, I would not have thought they were human. They squirmed under scraps of clothing pulled tight against their bodies. Each creature was flayed from foot to chest to neck. The whimpers that escaped them were the only release they had for the pain seizing them. When I stepped into the room, one reached out to me.

"F . . . finger," one of them said. "Gi . . . give me one. Give . . ."

They'd left it with its tongue. Its hand had been cut down to the lone palm. The other two gnawed on a femur bone too tough for their toothless mouths, but their fingers remained attached. It seemed, even in misery, alliances had been made.

On the opposite side of the hall, as far from them as possible, was an open doorway. It led to that flooded courtyard where the alligators dozed. I spotted a sparse few resting in the shadows of the house, under a low table, against a fallen bookshelf. They rested their bellies on molding rugs, and their teeth spread in patient smiles. The drag marks on the marble floor suggested that they had their pick of a meal when they were of the mind to hunt.

I inspected the other rooms of the house, finding my way into parlors and the remnants of a library, but most offshoots from the central hall had been destroyed. The collapsed wing had been left to the elements. The only way deeper into the manor was to follow the rooms east of the grand staircase. I imagined the kitchens, the servants' quarters, the pantry, and the storerooms would be on the first floor. I'd likely find the lady of the house in one of the second floor's quarters.

A crest of a whip-tailed raptor with a snake in its talons sat above almost every door. I passed servants' stations, private offices, and receiving rooms. I met more soldiers like the one outside in the garden and dealt with them using the halberd. I choked up on the weapon's pole, using the tighter corridors to my advantage. Though they were all in heavy plate, none of them had a unified set of armor that fit. We used to call these men "quilted knights"—usually they were poor squires or mercenaries.

There was one famously scandalous rumor that the quilted knight who'd won the Six Cup Tourney was a woman in disguise, and that's why her breastplate didn't buckle in properly. Never mind that breastplates were popped and curved at the front to begin with; the thought of a woman in armor had been the height of gossip in the time before the wars of earth and water—before the Young Gods.

The novelty of such an occurrence wore thin for me within fifty years, but of course, it had been a rarity to see a woman in armor for some time. I'll never forget the first one I killed. A Silver Tongue on the Krezta Plateau. She'd been dexterous and competent, but I could have had her five times before our duel was over.

I had been defending one of the last human fortresses in foreign lands. She had been an invader seeking to pillage their stores and flesh like any other brigand. It was the moral and good thing to kill her for the survival of that bastion. An outdated sense of chivalry, however, had made me hesitate.

I carried with me no such concerns for Lady Alanus, but I wondered if I would hesitate all the same. The devotee had been for spite's sake. When it came to the Lady, Theodoulos had sent me to kill her with a reasoning as thin as silk. The politics of the Green Castle were still obscure notions to me, but some things were beginning to take shape. If Alanus had fled the Green Castle and its own knights had followed, I could not help but wonder what scales I would tip if I killed her without question.

First, I had to find her. I breached what must have been the livable wing of the manor. Here, the furniture was well-maintained. The smell of damp was replaced with thick incense. The windows were boarded but intact.

As soon as I entered, another quilted knight appeared—but the armor on him was fitted and well-paired. The war hammer in his hand was held with confidence. Before anything, his hand went to his hip, and he pulled a bell from his waist. Three piercing rings echoed around us.

He then tossed the bell aside and took on a fighting stance. His first swing was fast—remarkably so. The flat head of the hammer slapped against my left arm, sending my shoulder flying back with my halberd. The force of the blow knocked the weapon out of my sure grip.

I moved back to recover my stance, sure that his windup would take too long to catch me. But a whistle pierced the air. A soft breeze prickled against my skin. By the time my hands were secure on the shaft of my halberd, he had taken a swing at me. The drapes fluttered, and loose paper flew up under his feet. A gust of wind blasted against my face as the hammer narrowly missed my nose.

This was not the speed of a man. I reared up with my halberd and staggered back for space. To my surprise, he let me and took up a defensive stance.

Then I heard that whistle again. I felt the cool air on my neck, and I *saw* the wind gather around him. I stood there in awe. Whatever power this man harnessed over the air was pulled taut like a bow and snapped. With incredible speed, he was upon me.

There was no time to move nor to correct my stance. With no other option, I swung my halberd. I felt the impact of my strike against his helmet as his war hammer punched into my right side. The helmet caved in, and the quilted knight dropped like a stone. The whisper of his death prickled through me, as dulled as the other guards had been, and the blow to my side lost its momentum. A sharp crack in my ribs traveled up to my teeth and burned hot through my body in that second. The quilted knight's follow-through would have crushed my ribs against my spine, but his death had driven me to the floor instead.

I lay there, sucking in breaths between my teeth. Every inhale pushed my lungs against tender, perhaps broken ribs. I could not catch my breath. Staring at the lump of armor that would have smeared me across the floor one second earlier, I knew I had not earned that victory. His speed has created the force that crushed his helmet. His limited vision through the slit of the armet was what saved me. The better fighter is not always the victor, but I hadn't felt the euphoric hand of luck in decades—and suddenly this House of Oghir was a terrifying place to be. How could I kill a knight that harnessed the wind?

How could a man accomplish such sorcery to begin with?

My hands reached for the quilted knight's armor. I wanted to search his person for answers. When I unbuckled the clasps, the metal did not slide off. I pulled on the breastplate and the bracers, but they were stuck, as if sealed with wax. Even the visor of his armet wouldn't rise. That was impossible. It *had* to open. The knight would need to see, to breathe, to eat. But I could not fathom how it would be removed.

The clatter of armor approached from somewhere deeper in the manor. Though my ribs screamed and my breath was shallow, I had to fight. However, a sudden, forceful gust of wind crashed through the room, and I was surrounded.

They made quick work of me.

THE GRAVE ROBBER

I had never fallen victim to a Flayed before. Pain had walked with me countless times in the past, but never like that. The less spoken of it, the better. Morthia took me to that ashen horizon and threw me back.

When I next breathed, it was almost as if I'd woken from a terrible nightmare. I convulsed at the bottom of the cellar steps, feeling the fresh shock of pain in my repaired body. Birds sang somewhere overhead. Water lapped gently beneath me. Late sunlight warmed my cheek, though the sensation felt tight and tender, almost burning against my skin.

I knew not how much time had passed. I knew not how I'd gotten back to the cellar. I did know I woke up with company.

A man was repairing a length of chainmail on the steps above me. His hands were small and had suffered amputations. Two fingers on the right pinched metal links with a set of pliers while he steadied the piece with the three remaining on his left. A line of gauntlets was laid out in pairs by his feet. Dappled sunlight illuminated his moss-green hood and cloak.

I had seen that coloring of cloth before in the graveyard. This was the robber who had startled me at Leoric's Temple.

I cast a glance at his hip, and there was the telltale pouch of a servant of the Seven Hands. I checked my own hands and counted all ten fingers attached, but they were strange.

My umber skin had a raw, pinkish hue to it. When I curled one hand into a fist, the movement felt tight, and I could see the strain on my knuckles, as if I were stretching a glove. I did not care for the sensation of new skin, but the itching discomfort felt like a hollow echo of what I'd endured before.

I suspected the hermit on the steps might have taken the opportunity to steal my fingertips, but I would have no way of discerning that from the sensation of regrown skin. Beside the pouch of fingers on his hip was a threaded chain of eyes looped over his right shoulder. A similar chain of tongues dangled from his left. When he stretched to pull another scavenged piece of armor from his collection, a patch of thin skin inside his elbow peeked out: dark and raised against his natural warm brown. I could not tell to whom he pledged his loyalty. It seemed he was prepared to take the communion of every god.

I could not even tell if he was loyal to the House of Oghir. He looked to be a weather-beaten thing that had crept in from the swamp rather than lived walled against it. Mud stains on his wrapped feet and burrs on his cloak appeared as natural to him as slime was to a toad.

I sat up, and the man stopped his polishing. His hood inclined in the slightest, turning his ear to me and his profile into the light. His eyes were covered by a linen blindfold, but he knew I was awake.

He took a bundle beside him and tossed it down to me. A pile of folded linen landed with a heavy thump on the bottom landing. It was then that I noticed my bare arms and legs for what they were. I'd been stripped from head to toe by the House of Oghir.

"Those should be big enough for you," the grave thief said. The voice was odd.

The stranger had workman's hands and the slender coils of muscle I'd seen on many laborers over the decades. There was a kind of uniformity to their lithe frames I'd not considered.

The stranger hummed. "Humor an old woman and take her hospitality."

When the stranger sat up properly, I saw how her tunic sat against her chest. Another blind woman? Was this where they were stored? She had fooled me at a glance, dressed in men's clothes.

Taking my silence for hesitation, she insisted again. "Consider it a gift in good faith."

I could not recall the specifics of my death, but I wondered if I had been dragged away from the House of Oghir instead of discarded. This awakening seemed too clean and secluded otherwise. No gesture of charity truly was free. Nor did I think anyone would know to wait for me to wake again unless they were familiar with my kind.

The thief seemed unsurprised with my resurrection—prepared, even.

"What brings you to the noble House of Oghir, Deathless?" she asked, a tint of derision in her tone at either the House or me. "I thought your kind killed each other off in the Old Country decades ago."

When I did not answer, she leaned forward on the steps and breathed so deeply her nostrils flared. A hint of graying, tight curls spilled down from her hood.

"I don't smell Morthia's madness on you. You can hear me, I'm sure."

"What does madness smell like?" I asked, disarmed by the description.

"Sweet. Like rotting fruit."

"Not so common these days."

She smiled, and a scar that cut her full lips in half stretched. A line of pink flesh extended past her upper lip, across her flat nose, and up to her bandaged eyes. But—that wasn't correct. I remembered eyes black as night staring up at me from a grave below.

"I haven't seen a fruit tree in thirty years, not since Konstantin walled the Gardens and bred his pigs. But smell has the longest memory."

"And how long since you've smelled a Deathless?"

She pointed again to the folded linen—too confidently to not know where it was. "Dress. Be at peace. I have no immediate designs for you if you have none for me."

I reached for the clothes as if they were a snare. "You watched over me with some purpose in mind."

She said nothing to that, but I gave in all the same.

I could not feel the coarse texture of the shirt under the pad of my thumb. I hoped the numbness would wear away in a day or so. The musty pair of workman's breeches fit well enough, but I did not have the dexterity to fasten the ties.

Every shift of movement made me *aware* of the clothes brushing against my new skin, as if I'd wrapped myself in heated bark. I looked with remorse at my bare feet, mourning the good pair of boots I'd had for five years.

"Were you the one to strip my corpse?"

"There was nothing to strip once Alanus' men were done with you. But I wouldn't rob a Deathless." The thief scoffed. "Knowing you'd wake again?"

"That's what you did for the others."

Her brow furrowed. She didn't remember me. I *had* been wrapped in armor at the time.

"Leoric's graveyard," I told her. Her lips thinned. "What happened to your eye?"

She dragged her thumb casually along the route of her scar. "Ambush, I'm afraid."

"No." I touched my left cheek, ignoring how my finger felt as if it was separated from my face by leather gloves. "The other one."

She thumbed the bandage over her left brow, revealing a hollowed socket. "Traded it to an Acolyte a decade or two back."

Traded. Not *lost.* I looked at the missing pieces of her again, my eyes darting even to her grin, which had a few gaps along the teeth. She may be the first person I met in this land that was as weathered as I expected in the Barrens.

"It's the other one you have, or had, not that long ago. Will you lift your bandage?"

"Such a fascination you have with my person—"

"I know you can see me. You know I'm no Acolyte of the Eye. There's no need for the pretense. Lie to me any longer, and I may bash your skull in with one of your gauntlets, and whatever designs you have for me will be for naught."

The two fingers on her right hand rubbed together. She thumbed up the bandage entirely. There was the eye I'd met at the graveyard. She tilted her head, asking with a gesture if I was satisfied.

"I'm here to kill Lady Alanus," I told her. "What's your business with me, grave robber?"

"What has Lady Alanus done to deserve a death sentence from you, Outlander?"

"That's my business."

"I suppose so."

"I asked what you wanted from *me*."

"That depends. I was here to make my usual exchange when I saw you lying in the receiving room like a fish drying in the sun. Seemed that when you woke up, you might need some new arms." She kicked at the satchel beside her so the metal jostled. "Anything you like for a reasonable price, of course. You seem to be lacking, but we can come to an arrangement. Armor. Weapons. Traps. Even the toll back if your motivation has sapped after this noble attempt at assassination."

She shook dozens of tiny teeth from a small pouch to demonstrate. I assumed the thief paid the tunnel rat with that collection. With four more, I could walk out of the swamp with no need for a sword.

Yet, this thief did not only offer me escape but also arms that would make me a threat to the House.

"Are you concerned for your lady?"

"*My* lady? Little Alanus? Don't misunderstand me. *My* ladies never wore circlets or silks. Their hems were short, and their hands were rough. The Lady of the House of Oghir has plenty of loyal dogs, but I don't count among them. A scavenger like me needs to have a good sense for business. You seem like you would be good for business."

"Selling to me or scavenging?" I eyed her strings of flesh on her person.

"Her guards made a meal of you. I left you as I found you. Though it is an odd thing, your would be invaluable to any servant of a new god if they ever thought to pen you like a pig. An endless banquet."

"You should keep such ideas to yourself, don't you think?"

"I have no interest in that application of your immortality, Sir . . ." She held the final syllable. I gave no answer. "Sir Deathless, then. I'm Minthisha. So, what will it be? Freedom or Lady Alanus' head?"

"I've been told she cannot be killed."

"You don't believe that," she said. "Only the Deathless are immortal. Lady Alanus has closed the door to death, but it's not locked. If you're determined, like Lollond walking his thousand roads or the White Knight's five-man army, with time, you will reach victory. It's a matter of putting you on the quickest road to that victory."

"For the right price," I echoed.

Her head tilted, amused again. "Usually, flesh pays for steel. But, if you're a man of honor, one life for another will do. I will suit you up now with the intent to collect later."

Up those stairs was a chamber where five knights had surrounded me with the power of the wind harnessed at their heels.

"Will your stolen suits do anything against that unnatural force they wield?"

"Unnatural?"

"Their manipulation of the wind."

"Ah. You haven't been here long at all, Outlander." She grinned, but it felt like a sneer. "I should have expected as much."

Minthisha dug a hand into her satchel.

"Young nobles were tutored in sorcery in courtly times. More than three centuries ago, when the Hallowed Lands weren't so hollow and the Evar

Kings had not risen, lordlings, knights, and the like demonstrated magic alongside their singing, diction, and religion. They used to bring gold by the wagon to Lorenial and beg on the streets for a Yew Mother to teach them anything at all. Though, it was used as often as jousting outside a tourney for all the practicality it had."

"It seemed common in that house."

"*Now*, those nobles made deals with cannibal gods and hung the Yew Mothers. Times were that a cool breeze could leave an unpracticed man bedridden and feverish for months. It was quite an event for a lordling to snuff out a candle with a wave of his hand. *Now*, the children of the material reach into the beyond from a shorter distance. It may as well be that their patron reaches for them. It's no longer practice; it's a price. They're limited by the terms of their bargain, so to speak. Fingers and eyes on their chain do more than sustain the body. Alanus gives me a good price for skin to feed her army of metal mosquitoes. They buzz this way and that all day."

I'd seen many wonders in my time, perversions of nature and law that could not be, yet were. However, my understanding of Rivialt's gift had come from meeting Flayed on a battlefield. An impressive endurance for pain was different from summoning a tempest. If it had a tax of flesh paid for sorcery the same way it did for injury, then the quilted knight's power must have been sustained by those shivering wretches in the ballroom. Sustained by *me* when they skinned me. If that was the case, then the use of that accursed wind must have its limits.

Minthisha righted herself. "I'm sure that your persistence can outlast their boon. It may take some time, but you have that in abundance. Of course, you could also leave Alanus' squabble with the Green to them and save yourself the effort. Whatever quest you choose, I offer you this protection."

Minthisha pulled what she wanted from the satchel and presented it. Judging by the length, it might have once been the hilt of a great sword.

Faded leather clung to the grip but peeled at the cross guard. It was rather ordinary, barring the pommel, in which a purple amethyst sat in the center of a snake consuming its own iron tail. A hilt with no blade did not feel protective.

"All I ask for is reciprocity when we are done."

"What's the name of this reciprocity?"

Minthisha's teeth flashed, and a soft, satisfied purr rumbled through her. "Luthor."

"And what has he done to deserve death by my hand?"

"You're here to kill the lady of a house you do not know. He's a man. I want him dead. It does not need to be more complicated than that, does it?"

I know not if it was her false benevolence that irritated me so or the slightest of smiles, but I had no patience for her proposal.

"There's no more vile gift than one forced into your hands. So instead, I'll offer this: give me what pieces I choose from your collection, and I'll allow you to live."

Threats brought simplicity to matters. While Geocelin had been flustered and Theodoulos fidgeted, Minthisha hummed.

"Have I wounded your pride by not confiding in you, sweet boy?"

I leapt to my feet, ignoring the strange lightness to my body that came with resurrection. It'd be easy to crush her against the wall. But, three steps up, there was an eruption beneath me, not of flame, but of force. It felt as if I had crashed into water. My body slowed on impact, falling through some dense space in the air.

I tried to lean out of it, but it was truly as if I was falling. There was no way to redirect. I had taken a step forward, and my body would complete that step. Attempting to break away now was like a fly trying to wrest himself from a spider's web. I had to wait for this trap to release. Struggle would only tangle me further.

Minthisha, my spider, watched me struggle in her web. When she was satisfied, she picked up her pliers. She positioned them just so. The tapered point of the hand tool hovered where my neck would fall at the end of my inevitable step. "Careful, Outlander. The rabble have the same tricks as these noble houses, but ours were never for show."

Witch. I tried to say it, but I could not open my mouth. All this time, and I had not, could not, finish my exhale. All I could do was watch as my body tilted itself into its own impalement.

"How many more do you have in you, Sir Deathless? If Morthia takes you now, will there be some of you left? Or will you be rabid the next time you wake? Perhaps I'll dress you in armor after all. I could push your corpse into the water and watch it flap. I'm told that broke men like you back in your day. After, I could watch the famous bloodlust of the immortal war dogs tear the lecherous House of Oghir apart."

I tried to speak again, feeling the lively shock of discomfort as the point of the pliers pushed slowly into the hollow of my jugular.

"Is this the road you'd like to take?"

If given the opportunity, I would have lied. I would have agreed to Minthisha's truce until she released me. I would have drowned her the moment I was free.

I suppose she knew that as well when she punctured my throat.

THE LADY ALANUS

When Morthia shoved me back into my body, the thief was gone.

A shield and mace were set by my side; chest and backplate were fastened over thin linen. Metal panels of a gauntlet scraped against the stone. Four teeth folded in a kerchief had been laid at my feet. I sneered.

Not only did she stab me, but now she pretended to be generous. In time, I would repay the presumptuous thief with myriad torments. Perhaps I'd push a sharp blade down her throat, let her feel the tip of it split that bitter tongue in half.

First, I had business to attend to. What did it matter who Lady Alanus was? Young Theodoulos had told me this place housed traitors to the Green. What's more, I could indulge in a bit of vengeance for my bitter greeting.

The *ache* purred in me.

My new instruments were unfamiliar, but there was no better courtship between a man and his metal than when he put them to use. I climbed back up those stairs and found another guard had replaced the first in the garden. To my amusement, he was just as easy to dismantle. The mace and shield rang out beautifully as I bludgeoned my way into the backrooms.

Blood stained the sitting room where I'd been overwhelmed. Books lay shredded on the floor. The door had been thrown off its hinges. The only missing evidence of my skirmish was the body of the one quilted knight I'd defeated.

I wondered what had become of him. Had they picked him apart like a pack of wild dogs, or had they buried him in the garden for grave thieves to repurpose?

I noticed the fireplace for the first time—the masonry. A slab of carved stone covered the firebrick in the back; it showed a boy playing a flute with three dogs jumping at his heels. My brother and I used to have a mosaic of that same scene painted over our shared room. It was one of the old tales I was not versed enough to recount. I knew the version my brother whispered.

"That's Rafa. He was the eldest of four brothers, but none of them would listen to him. One day, he turned them into dogs so they'd do as he said. If you don't listen to me, I'll turn you into a mutt, not even a hunting hound."

It felt oddly comforting to see that same boy here, worlds away from my home. The fixtures over the fireplace were warm and domestic. Three simple wooden figures, a man, a woman, and a child, were set on the mantle beside a bouquet of fresh-cut milkweed. A brass kettle hung on an iron mount. Quilted knights drank tea in this room. They *lived* here. It's not as if I hadn't realized, but I hadn't quite . . . remembered.

Barring the obvious destruction resulting from my last visit, the books were well-maintained. I inspected a few titles and browsed through tax ledgers and maps. I imagined a young lord of the manor scowling over this business in the late hours. An even younger lord would stand on his toes to reach a thin, tattered book that'd once been used for a child to practice their letters.

My sons had books like those. If they were to be the men of the house, I had said, they had to know their letters at least as well as their scribes. That was before I was pledged to Morthia and my sons' legacies died before I did.

The spines of some titles referred to histories of men and nations I did not know. How many did the Lady Alanus and her guests read in their ample time? A room like this would have been the study of fathers and uncles—heads of the house. Which relation had sat in the chair closest to the hearth? Who had lived in the House of Oghir before it had become this ruin?

I could not help but wish the stone floors were glazed tile. I stared at the dark, rustic furniture and longed for the orange sofa that'd occupied my own study. Out the window, the curtained branches of a weeping willow dripped where sturdy oaks and heathers should have stood.

Then I heard the distant clang of armor and was reminded of my cause. The first quilted knight rushed into the room. I knocked him back with my shield, but two others pulled me away before I could finish him.

They had me.

I shivered through the torment again.

I woke again.

I felt the burning parch in my throat, the twist of the *ache*. The tether to my mind was stretched and frayed to a thread. I could feel the thing with teeth inside me gnawing for control. At the base of those steps to the cellar, I was outfitted in a new patchwork assembly of armor. A maul had been left for me this time.

I went deeper into the House of Oghir on that third attempt. I climbed to the second story to another grand reception room before I was stopped.

I do not remember the next attempts, only the ravenous haze.

I always rose alone at the bottom of those stairs.

I always had teeth.

I always had scales.

There was no more thought. The House of Oghir greeted me like a giant with its mouth stretched open, poised to devour me once more. Over and over it ground its teeth down and chewed. If there was pain, her touch was numbed by my hunger. If there was satiation, it was less than a sip of water to quench my thirst. Sometimes golden sunlight tinted the radiant halls. Sometimes they were suffused with silver and blue shadows.

It might have gone on for days, months, a year. I know it only ended because the Lady of the House deemed it so.

One day, indistinct from all the others, there were no guards to meet. I climbed to the second story hall and found a banquet at the top of the steps; a line of offerings bound to one another by collars of rope knelt in a pretty row. They nearly strangled themselves trying to escape me. There were twelve in total. I hardly understood they were men until the blood beneath me pooled down my arms.

Morthia feasted. His whisper-soft touch brushed against my mind.

Even then, the ecstasy of inhaling their final breaths was dulled in my haze. It only came into focus when *she* spoke.

I do not know what her first words were, but I beheld her. Sunlight radiated off of her as if she were burning in Amivia's own heart. Twelve men lay dead at her feet, and I knew this gift had been hers.

I collapsed to my knees, supplicating myself the way I would have in days long dead. The melodic chime of mail and plate echoed like choir music in that vast room. Light danced in twisting patterns over her form.

"Well met, good sir."

With sublime ease, I raised my head and gazed at the face of Lady Alanus. She was cast in gold. Her lips were full, and her nose was pointed and long like a doe's. A jeweled snake curved down her forehead, like a stray curl of hair, to rest at the furrow of her brow.

Behind her splendid mask were eyes that shone like steel. Aside from that, there was not an inch of her bare. Her suit was overlaid with gold. The workmanship was delicate and sleek, molding the glittering armor perfectly against her legs, arms, and fingers like a second skin.

She removed my helmet.

Those eyes raked over me, and I felt the scrutiny of my years. Though my skin was new, there was no hiding the old bones beneath. The age I felt in all aspects of myself showed through. I looked back at the youth, so aware of how different she was in posture and manner.

"An Endless," lips behind the mask said. Lady Alanus' voice rang like a bell. "Where was the Green hiding you?"

The haze of the twelve had not passed over me yet, and I was only just beginning to focus when she abandoned her question.

"I am Lady Alanus of House Oghir, Widow to Evaright the Good, Shield Maiden against the Withering Blight, Mother of the People, and Rightful Queen of the Hallowed Lands. Tell me, good sir. Who are you?"

"Sir Darl of Rugenmont, my lady."

"Rugenmont . . ." She considered me. "An outlander. You may as well be Luthoron the Thereman resurrected."

The hall erupted into laughter. I suddenly noticed five men in full plate around us. Their laughter confused me, and I looked back to Lady Alanus for reassurance. Her golden face gave away no secrets.

"You've given my men a great deal of trouble, Sir Darl. Whether you've come for my head or my hand, I am sure you seek an audience." Lady Alanus unfastened the strap of a pauldron bound to my chest and the clasp of greaves on my wrists. When the metal clattered to the ground, I felt grateful for how she had unburdened me from its weight. "Tell me why you have come to my family home, Sir Darl."

The lady rested one hand on the pommel of her longsword. The other traced over my shoulder. "A man asked me to kill you," I gasped. "He says it will declare my loyalty to the Green Castle to Evarund, but . . . I . . . " I did not know what else.

I'd known this answer once, hadn't I? I was not on campaign. I was not fighting back barbarians to rescue my lands. But I had my reasons. I did. Why had I come here? Not only to the House of Oghir, but to the Hallowed Lands? I'd walked for so long and so far from home. All that time, I'd been following a trail. I had vowed to kill one man. The murderer. I hadn't seen him in years. I did not know if he'd fled to these lands, yet I'd come. For what?

For the boy with the mop of hair and the toy horse clutched in his fist.

I panted against the ground, my chest tight, my vision hot and clogged with tears. It was the Lady Alanus who saved me, who hummed and set those smooth, cool hands against my cheek. She traced my jaw and hushed my weeping.

With a soft click, she removed the burden of my chest piece with one hand. There was something in the coolness of the air against my soaked cotton shirt that sobered me. My heart fluttered, unable to find a steady rhythm, and my whole body jolted to attention. This was euphoria, not the lady that made me weep and question.

"You will find nothing worth the dedication of your body and soul in the Green Castle. Evarund's line has bred cowards. They are wolves gorging on penned sheep. They kiss the feet of a fraud and call him father just so they may be given what toys they scream for," Lady Alanus said. I could hear the faint metallic echo of her voice behind her mask. "Tell me, are you loyal to your god?"

There was no loyalty to be given to Morthia. The King of Flies was not a man paid but a beast slaked. *Thee or me, Morthia shall feast.* I almost said it, but a new reservation made my lips stretch tight. It was not new at all but a habit, centuries old, resurfacing.

"You were a man of honor once. I can see that in you," she said to me.

A clatter disturbed us. A knight in a full, well-fitted suit of armor stepped closer. There was a slight stiffness to his walk—his kneecap was dented inwards. The knight beside him rested the blade of a great sword on his elbow, as if prepared to take swift action if I stepped out of line. Three other soldiers to my left held spears.

"These are my loyal vassals. Men of honor dedicated to the righteous and good House Oghir. Evarund is rotting in his den of old men. The Green are stale, petrified of change, and they will petrify these Hallowed Lands with them. They've closed their doors to the outside world. Closed the door to the gods. They cower away from a Blighted city and leave their fields to the beasts. The Green Castle festers with cowards.

"Nothing is offered. Nothing is planted. Nothing grows. Every man covets their dwindling stock instead of hunting for themselves. They'll bury enough bodies to fill a giant's grave before they submit to the true meaning of their pact of immortality. But not us. We carry the true blood of this country, and we keep the bond with our god sacred, as it was intended. We have given all. Self-sacrifice has led the way to our metamorphosis. We have ascended. Our skin is steel, our lives are long, and we will be unstoppable when we march on the Green. We are Rivialt's children, resplendent and perfect."

She turned into the radiant light. Sunset poured in from the swamp through large windows, casting golden light onto a dais on the far end of the hall. Above the dais loomed a statue of Rivialt the Cretinous Flayed; the torsos of a man and a woman sprang away at the hip from a base with four legs, their faces withered with pain and age.

Time had snapped off the nose and hands of the woman. The arm of the man lay broken at his feet. I thought of the statue I'd seen in Leoric's temple, the one in front of the mural of Young Gods tearing apart the Old. Alanus offered her skin to her god not as an act of devotion, but as an exchange.

"You do not seem to be submissive to any, my lady," I said.

Light-stained portraits of these noble Oghirs glowered down at me. Blood soaked into the cracks in the tile from the twelve men, common unarmored men, she'd sacrificed to tame my bloodlust. And it was then that a gleam in the sunlight caught my eye just so. A small pile of discarded armor—pieces bent, warped, or rusted—cluttered the wooden dais. Among those discards sat the broken hilt of a sword. The purple amethyst at its top gleamed mockingly across the hall.

"You may not be a man of my god, but you understand sacrifice. You've given your body over and over to a dead god and received no recompense. Allow me to offer you the reward you so deeply deserve. We shall change the world and bring our abandoned brothers and sisters in the Green here to take the oaths they've been barred from. Noble blood will be washed of brown swill and returned to gold. We will grant them the privilege of immortality. The honor of a life well-lived as an ascended being will be theirs. And together, we will thrive and conquer the barbaric lands beyond our wall."

She dropped a weapon at my feet. I recognized the distinctive wide curve of a flaying knife. Realizing now my nakedness, dressed in cotton and trousers, barefoot, empty-handed, I picked it up.

"Accept kinship with the House of Oghir. Draw blood from your palm. Speak the words. Pledge yourself to me and my patron, Sir Darl of Rugenmont, and we shall use your gift granted by an eternal god to change this world for the better. We will save hundreds—thousands. Pledge yourself to me and let me guide your sword to its noble purpose."

I studied the eyes beyond the delicate mask and knew I had heard this story before. Her face had been her first sacrifice, but there had been more to come afterward. There had once been a boy in rags who had followed a war camp. He had cut out his brother's heart to escape his pain. And he transformed, not into a man but a Heartless.

The gods demanded their tolls. Alanus might spout ascension, but she was as beholden to her gods as any. And she would bring more into the fold, killing more and more to feed her precious benefactor. The devotee had the same misguided pride in her god. Lady Alanus of House Oghir, Widow to Evaright the Good, Shield Maiden against the Withering Blight, Mother of the People, and Rightful Queen of the Hallowed Lands was not any of those things. She cut them away on the day she pledged to Rivialt. All she would ever be from that day forward, all she could ever be, was a Flayed.

I felt the coarseness of the knife in my hands.

"Pledge to destroy your enemies in the Green Castle," I said.

"Pledge to bring forward a new age in which humanity will dedicate itself wholly to a higher power that may grant us eternal bliss and youth!"

The pledge she asked for was still a pledge of mind and spirit—a gesture that asked to be bound by my honor. Such an old-fashioned offer. Like Minthisha's gifted armor, I recognized the hypocrisy of this choice. Join, or the cycle would begin anew, and I would find myself stripped to the pink muscle in that ballroom once again. I was gifted with grace, asked to honorably serve, and threatened with pain. It was a tempting offer. Almost as tempting as the grave robber's had been. But I'd made my choice half a century ago that I would not rest until I saw Lambskin dead, and I saw no reason to make an exception for someone of his ilk.

I had no illusions about surprising the lady. When I struck out with the knife, Lady Alanus shoved me back before I could so much as graze her plating.

I let myself fall. It was no matter.

My point was made, and war was declared.

The Sunlit Hall

There was a certain rhythm to the phrases when facing a single opponent, an intimacy developed from the conversation between your blades. Conversation died in a crowd.

In a room of enemies, a single man had three friends.

Distance. Draw. Discourse.

Each of Alanus' soldiers wore full plate, and I had been stripped to my linens. There was no room for mistakes. I kept my phrases short. In an open hall, it is difficult to limit how many men can surround me, but I tried to allow no more than two to cluster near. And I could not commit to a kill, only distraction and incidental injury.

With only a knife's reach against their polearms, I spent most of my energy controlling my position. If they surrounded me, that would be my end.

I drove myself forward instead of retreating from wide swings and swift prods. If a man took a step, I caught him on unsteady feet. I was light. I was quick. The haze of bliss from slaking Morthia's ache made each step of my own feel intentional, yet untethered.

The smallest details came into focus: the rusting pins in their armor, the scratched layering of their plate, the mistakes in their posture. Two of the spearmen could not thrust fully; their elbows locked where the plate had been dented.

It occurred to me that this might not be the first time I'd met them in a skirmish. I might have given them more trouble than Lady Alanus was willing to admit.

In the hearth room, I'd smashed a vassal's helmet into his skull. If I'd killed one, why not the others? They'd overwhelmed me but had paid a tax for each instance of sorcery it took to do so. In my rampage, I would not yield to pain or sense that otherwise limited me. The little dents in their armor—damages that the soldiers had taken and had not had the time or ability to repair—restricted them. There were five men present now. Hadn't there been more in the halls before this?

Had I chipped away at them, man by man? Five men now, but perhaps ten before. Perhaps twenty. Maybe all fifty-six of the Green's banished knights had kissed Alanus' feet and cut their palms to pledge themselves to her house.

Now there were five, and they were not riding tempest winds with wild abandon.

The lady herself stayed out of the fray of battle, content to let her vassals swarm me. She'd taken a deliberate stance, straight-backed, her sword clasped in both hands and pointing up. The flat of her blade followed the line of her nose—a ceremonial position.

I thought I could ignore her until I'd finished her guard when I heard another strange sound, like the hissing of a snake, echoing across the room. Finally, a soldier had reached for the wind. I cast about for the source. Two men at my back parted, and the one with the great sword in front of me cleared away. The answer to why was forthcoming. I turned to see the whites of the lady's eyes, bright as pearls beneath her mask. Her steel flashed in them just before she struck me.

Forget the elegant conversation of sword masters; this was a bellowing scream. She might as well have taken a club to me for the little I could do to contest her strength. I did not deflect blows with my knife, but instead used the touch of metal to metal to push my own body out of her way.

I survived the first two swings, but a sudden thrust forced me to deflect or be skewered. In my position, I could only extend my unarmed left hand instead of my right. My palm met the flat of her longsword. My force redirected her own but could not stop it entirely. The point that was supposed to puncture my belly buried itself into the marble floor with a violent crack.

In the still breath of our mutual recovery, I felt something biting at my palm. I thought there was a barb on the blade pricking me. It was not a fixture, however. It was heat. The longsword was *hot* against my hand, as if it were a slab of metal left in the summer sun. I released the blade, but Lady Alanus did not. She tried to wrench it from the crack in the marble.

When her first attempt did not free her weapon, and she did not move away, I recognized an opening. I hooked a hand around her sword arm. The cool metal plate bit my scorched palm. My right hand followed, stabbing my knife into the hollow of her armpit where the mail would give—only it did not.

I'd killed men a hundred times with that simple maneuver. A puncture under the hollow of the arm, a stab to the groin. The undignified weaknesses guarded by only mail were the best way to kill a suited knight on the field, short of crushing them. Lady Alanus, however, did not suffer such vulnerability.

The knife clicked and glanced over the mail as if I'd struck plate. The skin above my thumb scraped against the side of her cuirass as my arm overextended.

Alanus could have grabbed that arm and pulled me down. If she had, I would have been shambling through her halls in tender, stripped flesh within the hour. Instead, I heard the telltale whistle of gathering air. One of her vassals rode a gale wind and attacked from my right.

A solid punch of force struck against my back and knocked me off her. The vassal did not stop, but instead skidded past me until the tempest fizzled out behind him. He held a spear, but there was no blood on its point. I guessed that meant he'd done little more than throw his weight against me. My ribs stung, though, like something might have cracked.

Just as quickly, another vassal—the arming swordsman—was upon me. I twisted, narrowly avoiding the thrust of his sword into my heart. The glancing blow still caught my left side. Without mail or gambeson, the blade slit through my shirt and cut my forearm like butter.

Before he could rip the blade free from my bicep, I stabbed low, cutting into the groin of the locked leg through a slit in the mail.

Unlike with Alanus, this underpadding bent, and my knife sank in.

Something felt wrong about the skin underneath—it gave too easily, like old meat. There was no twitching flutter of pain. The blade came back stained by a brown substance that did not ooze.

We pulled away from each other like two wild dogs after having gnashed teeth. We reoriented ourselves and began to circle one another. Blood trickled down my left arm, and my right side protested at any sudden movement. As for the vassal, there was no difference in his gait after I'd stabbed his leg. If these quilted knights didn't bleed and didn't feel pain, I couldn't resort to my usual habits to kill them. They had to be crushed, like beetles in their heavy shells. To do so required a blunt force weapon.

The sun angled low. The armor and weapons of the vassals of Oghir flashed orange. It was irritating to see that each of them carried cutting weaponry, no clubs, no war hammers—not a single heavy slab of iron on their person.

Alanus remained by the window. Her longsword glowed as if it had been forged from white sunlight itself. The air warped around her as if the blade should be burning, though not a single flame licked the air. Another enchantment?

Dancing between the phrases of the vassals with my pitiful knife, I thought of the heat that still tingled up my left hand. Was Alanus' sword as hot as fire now? Enough to pull a glove of blisters up from my skin if I tried to catch it again? My skin might burn just trying to deflect it.

The great sword vassal tried to close in on me. I let him and pushed closer to stab his neck. If he breathed, I did not feel it catch. He stood as tall and easy as he had before I cut his throat. All my precise stabbing did was trap me in place with my knife in his chin.

Another vassal came from my left in a fury of speed. I leapt back, abandoning the knife in the other's neck. My repositioning, however, allowed a second to rush in on the wind, their spear angled straight for my stomach. My hands came down to catch the shaft a finger's width from where the blade would puncture my skin. We skidded backward on his momentum.

The force of the gale wind buffeted against me as the knight tried to drive the tip of the spear through my stomach. I could not gather enough strength to push *back*. We were moving too fast. All I could do was hold on and wait for the impact. Some slab of wall against my back, some solid wall that would negate my efforts and allow the spear to slip between my fingers and into me.

But then there was a sudden moment of suspension, as if the spearman and I had crashed into water. We watched one another as the air caught us like flies in molasses. I knew this space. I had been trapped in this dizzying, extended fall before. I had seen Minthisha slowly guide a knife point to my chin. But the spearpoint was still closing its distance to my stomach.

Despite our suspension, I knew we were still moving, and I wondered if we would collide. Would I watch that spear point sink into me and feel it slice through every layer of fat and muscle until it ripped open and let its contents drip inside me? But then, it was over, and the vassal and I dropped from our suspension, sapped of all momentum. The noise of cicadas, clinking armor, and sharp wind pounded against my ears as if I'd surfaced from a lake.

The change was so sudden I staggered on uncertain ground. My legs knocked against the hall's dais. I fell flat on my back and met the wild eyes of the male aspect of Rivialt as he screamed for separation above me. The spearman who had attempted to pin me had collapsed just beneath the dais and seemed to be more confused than I.

Had the grave robber been bluffing on those steps? Had the suspension trick been a temporary measure, like a ricochet from a shield? If she had waited just a few seconds longer, would the magic have collapsed and left her vulnerable to me?

I jumped to my feet in preparation for the other four vassals to come charging in, but they all seemed to stop and observe. I did not know enough of this land's sorcery to guess what made the grave robber's suspension possible, or if it was unusual, only that it caused the others to hesitate.

I was not granted much reprieve. Once I showed I could stand on my own two feet, Alanus' vassals moved to close the distance. Two spearmen ran at me from either side. They did not use their charmed wind as they approached. It seemed they knew less of the grave robber's time snare than I did.

My eyes searched across the dais for escape, for anything to use to my advantage. I took the smooth marble forearm that'd once belonged to Rivialt's male aspect. It had a heft to it, so much so that I rested it on my shoulder like a great sword. I latched my hands along the statue's wrist, my fingers idly tracing the veins and wrinkles an artist had carved decades ago.

A spearman stepped onto the dais and attacked. I hoisted the heavy, marble arm and swung up from my low position. I didn't care so much what I hit so long as it connected with *something*—his shoulder, in this case. The pauldron on his left side dented in and back with a satisfying crunch.

The momentum brought me up, the slab of marble locked in my grip. I followed through, swinging the arm back down on his helmet. The spearmen dropped. The soft breath of death blew lightly over my face before rushing into me. I heard the second behind me, but I didn't step away in time. The spear connected with my hip. The sharp pang of metal on bone reverberated through my entire body.

Experience kept me from collapsing. I dislodged myself from the spear-point as quickly as possible and fled the dais. I'd staggered ten paces when I heard the wind hissing at me from three directions. A spearman and the two swordsmen hurtled across the hall. One nicked my thigh. The other tore across my rib cage. A red flower bloomed across my stomach. It was deep enough to cut into muscle and chip bone, deep enough to kill me from blood loss.

The vassals darted about the room like mayflies. I kept my steps short, learning to listen—to see the moments when they grew still—and breaking out of the circle when their spells were building. I whittled five to three with a great effort, only by luck, crushing the chest plate of a spearman and denting the joint of a swordsman badly enough to render his left leg useless. I found myself in the center of the room when I suddenly heard the shattering roar of glass.

The last spearman had been carried too far when trying to skewer me and had slammed into one of the windows, breaking it. Chances were he would have fallen out if another vassal had not been close enough to grab him. Alanus used the distraction to close in on me.

When her blade met Rivialt's marble arm, it sliced off his shoulder. My skin seared as the sword passed my face. I rolled under her next swing. Just as she completed her phrase, I brought the remaining marble down *hard*, connecting with the side of her helmet.

Any one of her vassals should have gone down. Their helmets would have dented, at the least. For me, the blow reverberated through my hands and sent my arms flying back as the force was deflected. Then, Alanus turned to me and thrust. I smelled burning skin before I could understand the white-hot pain searing into my upper thigh.

My back slammed into the sun-heated windows. My burnt leg quaked under me, raw and red, begging to collapse. I adjusted my stance, but I knew my movements would be too slow to make a difference now.

Alanus could have killed me again if she'd only followed through. Was she toying with me?

She'd ended me. Why not finish me off? Her vassals were cutting off bits of me without ever truly killing—maybe until I began begging for it to stop—begging to join them? Or maybe they would enjoy my misery regardless. If I stayed in this room, I could see the long, indulgent fate that awaited me.

I could move very little with my leg, so I would not be able to break out of the circle. But here, against the panes of glass, the men could not use their magic against me. The power of the storm would send them shooting out into the swamp. Of course, they didn't need to pick at me with speed now.

I was cornered.

Alanus stood victorious. "Shall it be another round, Endless? Or do you finally understand? Your resolve is wasted. You could be using your sword to better mankind. You could clean the filth with a flood and bring in the new. What have you done with all your years other than burrow in your own slime? Cast aside your pride. Open your eyes to this new world. You have been bested. Yield to me and pledge your loyalty, or I will carve you up another fifty times before I let you taste sanity again."

Submit to her new world, she meant. A new world where there were no men left, only slaves to gods. A world of strength and inhumanity. A world she would carve into my skin for eternity if I did not submit now. There was no other world in this House of Oghir, and she knew it. She knew I feared the pain again. She knew I would be brought to submission when threatened with the cycle of death. However . . .

I was not the only one who had to fear such an ignoble end.

I smashed Rivialt's arm into the window behind us. Glass rained down in a glittering cascade. I dropped the arm, and I charged the suit of gold. Alanus might have sunk into her stance to deflect me, or she might have been trying to back away. I reached her as a consequence of either decision.

She tried to bring that burning longsword down onto me, but I was already under her, throwing us both out through the broken window. The surreal weightlessness of falling stunned us both. I looked from the striking greens and blues of the swamp rising to us to Lady Alanus locked in my arms. Her placid gold mask did not hide the wild whites in her eyes.

We plummeted, falling past the stone and grass, into the murky water. The cold shocked my body. Bubbles swarmed around us. After the harsh crash of impact was a surreal drift down to a soft, muddy bank.

The sword boiled the water around us. I could feel the heat rippling up my arm and hear the bubbles churning. The moment I felt solid ground beneath me, I pushed off Alanus and tried to stand. I did not have to go far before I surfaced. At my full height, the water was only waist-deep.

Green coils of algae whirled away from where we'd landed. Alligators hissed at our intrusion.

A sudden, brutal squeeze on my ankle brought my attention back to the water, and a searing pain nearly sent me back down into it. Alanus was under me, touching her sword's blade to my skin. She pushed at my other leg, trying to shove me off of her and right herself from under me. It was then that my position pinning her truly registered. I had her.

Though my body felt heavy and ragged, I felt a new urgency and dropped my weight down onto her sword arm. With two hands and a foot, I pushed her wrist and shoulder down. The weight of her armor held the rest for me. Bubbles escaped from the eye slits of her mask as she screamed. Blessed or not, she needed air.

She struggled against me, her iron grip reaching for my arm, my hand, my shoulder. The water hindered her movements, making speed and leverage almost impossible. She twisted her palm, bringing that burning blade up to touch it to me. Since I could not release her, I stayed and watched as the flat of burning steel inevitably glided onto my shoulder. Our movements grew frantic, and there was a moment where I did not know which one of us would give in first. Then the sword's burning ceased, and lukewarm water began to cool.

Alanus' body twisted, and she kicked out at nothing, and then she was still.

I pushed off of her, keeping one foot on her wrist as I surfaced. The water was too thick with mud for me to see beneath. I imagined the mask of Alanus staring up at me. Evening sunlight danced on the murky surface, reflecting my own features in gold. The alligators bore witness as a final trickle of bubbles burst from the water, and Alanus' last gasp of life slipped into me.

The Exchange

I felt aware of myself in a way I had not been in a long time the next time I woke from Morthia's domain. Aware of the broadness of my shoulders, the rhythm of my steps, and the pull of my lungs. I was not ten steps from the water where I had narrowly outlasted Alanus, face-down on the swamp bank.

Not since the days of war had I run through so many cycles of death and renewal at once. My undead brothers and I would chip through stone and steel until we had conquered. Morthia's nails had dug deep into my chest day after day at the muddy bases of high stone walls. In the silence after the screams, we left the fortress to our lords and shuffled back to camp. Centuries later, I was still seizing castles. Only now I dragged myself out of the swamp water with no lord nor army to report to and no war camp to rest in. I was Endless, but not ageless. I felt worn.

I thought of the House of Oghir, a great family's manor that had been dead long before the lady. It was a shell of the grand fortress it must have once been. The sitting rooms went unused, and the garden was overgrown. Alanus had been all that kept the swamp from consuming it. Now that she was gone, its carcass would rot. I wondered if I should feel some kind of loss. I'd not only killed the lady but also her legacy.

My own family's villa must have suffered a similar fate. The mosaic of Rafa and his dogs must have flaked away tile by tile. The chessboard my brother and I used on rainy nights surely turned black with mold. The toy horse I'd left in the nursery would have been kicked to some forgotten corner.

Alanus' devotees would not carry on her vision for an ascended mankind. Fighting those men, I'd seen the truth of ascension. If they had ever been men at all, they had been hollow shells of ones by the time I'd come knocking. None of them had come after me. None had shouted their lady's name in despair. I don't think they even peered out that broken window to see what happened next. Something in their spirits had been taken.

Theodoulos had said the boar creatures we'd encountered in the fields had not quite been alive, and I wondered if bodies in suits of armor could be the same. Perhaps they would rust in that sunlit hall until it collapsed.

I inspected Alanus' sword—her only surviving legacy. The steel was of excellent make, well maintained, and well balanced. There was no decoration along its flat nor on the chape and cross guard. The pommel had no indulgent rune nor a house insignia. I was disappointed with how plain it was.

Yet, the sword had burnt hot as if it'd been lifted from the forge. Was the magic that ignited its steel a cousin to the kind that harnessed the air? The grave robber had said something about the limitations of the nobility's spells. I wondered if the sword mattered at all or if that magic had been Alanus' alone. Was that a boon she'd gained from submitting wholly to her god?

My god seemed to only bother to stretch out his hand to cross my path with unpleasant strangers.

I had not walked far in the swamp before I saw *him*. In the wealth of the swamp's greens and browns, a canary-yellow hood stood out. If there was any chance of missing him by sight, his voice carried far, and I'd caught him in the middle of an argument.

"What does it matter who they were?" Geocelin demanded. "Blight take them, as far as I'm concerned."

"You make conversation with your mice before you eat them." I knew the second voice at once: the grave robber. I should not be surprised that the two vagabonds had dealings with one another, but it was uncanny to see them together, like watching a weasel and a fox share a meal. Minthisha sat across from him with a collection of armor stacked between them. Her moss-green hood was up, but her posture expressed her impatience well enough. "You tend to know their titles."

"They were a Heartless and a Toothless. That's all I care to know. If you're so superior, I could always give such nice pieces to the Green bastards. They've paid double since their last smith died."

"I heard someone has come in from the Barrens who might be useful."

"To whom? The only useful people to me are dead." He crossed his arms and draped his body against the low branches of the tree they'd settled under.

"When did you get so secretive?" she asked. "Times were that you'd be eager to tell me we had a Deathless in our walls."

"If I had been told he was a Deathless, I would have pushed him into the ravine. You think anyone from out there is going to do any good here? They're competition. That's all."

"Luthor wasn't."

Geocelin balked. "That cad was nothing more than another lord with a worse accent."

"Is that what you believe?"

"He killed the right men for a time, I'll admit that. But he was always the Green's man. I know you wouldn't have wanted him to go to Lorenial. I know his foreign magic did your coven more harm than good. Blight take him and all the Theremen, I say." Geocelin cackled as if he had surprised himself with a rather impressive joke. "It already did, didn't it?"

"*Thyremoin,*" she corrected.

"Learn that from your foreign saviors, did you? You'd kiss their feet as much as they kissed the Green's if they let you. And you ask why I don't tell you everything."

"You're the one who left us for the Green."

"*Us?* You're not my people," he said. "I whispered the right words in the right ears because that's how a boy grows to be a man. Gods know no one else will feed him."

"Yet, you came back. Belly full. Those golden halls starved something out of you."

"Don't start moralizing my soul, *Mother Clay*. You're worse than *my* mother ever was. I dined with the pigs, and it was the best I ever ate. Now, do you want this, or shall I take it to my wealthy friends?"

Minthisha's hood tilted to inspect whatever armor they were negotiating for. The canary paced and cast his attention out into the trees, narrowly missing me.

She reached for something then and brought it to her mouth. Between deliberate chews, she made her decision. "Two eyes, four squares, six fingers for this pile here. A man's heart for the better set. An eye and a square for the coat."

"Save the eyes and the squares. I'll part with it for two fingers and a heart."

Minthisha paused, a knowing grin pulling at the scar on her lip. "Something happen to your friends?"

"My need is greater than theirs, is all," Geocelin said curtly.

Minthisha smiled wider. "Of course. But I asked if something *happened*."

"An old woman like yourself should know better than to stick her nose where it doesn't—"

Like a hare catching a scent, Geocelin froze and straightened a fraction. Perhaps I'd crept too close, or he'd spotted my frame in the corner of his eye. In either case, he turned toward me. I wondered what I must have looked like to him, half-soaked in swamp water, stripped down to linens. He bolted away as if I were a hunting dog ready to race.

His flight caused Minthisha to cast about in alarm. She pushed her blindfold up against her mane of curls. When she recognized me, she leapt off her crate. She might have been tempted to follow the canary, but a moment later, she settled back on her outpost and waited for me to approach.

She sat under the shade of a bulbous old yew. The roots that coiled out from its trunk sloped around her like little hills and had been covered with grass and brambles. The result was a solid blind that had covered her and most of Geocelin until I'd been close enough to hear them. The crates she'd stacked under its base suggested this was her cache.

Minthisha let me run a hand over a half a suit of armor she had been negotiating for. I searched around a bit for a coat among her steel collection and found a stack of padded shirts, but nothing resembling fleece. If Lambskin *had* come this way, Geocelin had not sold his personal effects to the grave robber. It was almost comforting to think the Heartless Geocelin referred to had not been the man I wanted dead. The clever war rat had evaded the snares set by this land's inhabitants.

"Have you finished your business at the House of Oghir, Sir Deathless?" Minthisha asked.

"Lady Alanus is dead," I said.

"Oh?" Her surprise was perhaps not unwarranted, but no less insulting. "And so ends the House of Oghir . . . "

"Don't pretend to be indifferent. You outfitted me for the task."

"I've outfitted you quite a few times. I thought of bringing your business to a swift conclusion, whatever it might be. There was always the chance you'd submit and agree to be her unkillable dog. You could have gone on to ravage the countryside in the name of Oghir. I would have preferred it if you had given up your stubbornness and left. It would have saved my inventory and our time. All the same, it felt dishonorable to let you repeat the cycle naked."

Dishonorable. She grinned in a way I found too innocent for someone who had played a part in setting me on that cycle. Yet, I humored her more than the canary. I couldn't help it.

It'd been a long time since I'd spoken to a woman not primed to kill me, and some juvenile part of me vaguely remembered I was a man who enjoyed the fairer sex. It must have been decades since she was a charming beauty with soft skin and oiled curls, but there was still something novel about the conversation. Though I knew she had fangs, they were the teeth of a cat, not a viper.

"Don't think for a moment I consider myself in your debt," I said, with just as easy of a grin.

"Pity that. I heard from my favorite Toothless in the tunnel that you're already bound to that page, Theodoulos. I'm told you killed Lady Alanus on his behalf. I wonder if it'll be just as surprising to him to hear the news. You should be careful with that one, Sir Deathless. Nothing's more dangerous than a novice who thinks himself a scholar."

Her words begged me to ask for more about the boy, but I could see that tease of information for the tactic it was. I should expect she would know about him. She seemed to know quite a bit about everyone. I wondered if she knew anything about Lambskin. If Geocelin bargaining with her moments ago was any indication, she would be the woman to ask.

"He's ambitious, perhaps overly so, and prideful about it."

"Like does draw to like."

I ignored her jab. "He has his uses. Do you think Theodoulos was unjust for asking for the death of the last heir of the noble House of Oghir?"

"*Noble,*" she scoffed. "It's fitting. Hers was the family that declared any family that had lived on Evarund's lands for less than five generations was to be considered foreign and banished from the Green. This was when the Undead War was a mere whisper on the horizon. Many born here were dragged from their homes and banished to the old country. That is to say nothing of the ones who had every right to stay and saw their houses burnt and their families hanged regardless.

"I don't pretend to know the ways of the courts, but even I know the Oghirs' prized daughter became queen consort to Evaright as a reward for their slaughter—for *blood purity*. She carried on her family legacy well. So ring out the sixteen bells; the House of Oghir is no more. I doubt Theodoulos appreciates the poetry that she has died at the hands of an outlander."

"But you do?"

Minthisha sank onto her crate and surveyed the blanket before her. "What say you to new armor suiting your station?"

There was steel, yes, but my eyes drifted to the clumps of moss and herbs that had been carefully bundled and set before her. At her side was a tiny wooden bowl where I expected there to be the communion she'd eaten—only to see it writhing with fleshy, pink earthworms.

"For this set here, I can offer a fine discount," she said. "No more than six fingers and an eye, or that reciprocity we discussed before."

She gestured to the armor laid out on a cloth before her, and I inspected the distinct cut and shape of *my* greaves and pauldrons. My helmet sat proudly stacked over my breastplate. This was my armor, not the armor I'd left in Theodoulos' care, but what I'd walked into the Hallowed Lands with.

"What do you charge for information?" I asked.

"That would depend on whether I know it already or not."

"I'm looking for another outlander. A Heartless in a lambskin coat. Your brigand friend may have told you about him arriving before I did. He's missing his right hand."

"What's his name?"

"He doesn't share it."

Minthisha hummed at that. "I can find him. You need only cut out the heart of a man for me."

"Luthor, wasn't it?"

"You remembered," she teased.

"What did he do to you? Steal your daughter? Raze your village?"

"It's not what he did to me, but what he's done to us. All of us." Minthisha pinched a worm from her bowl and watched it wriggle. "There was a time when immortality was an act of self-sacrifice and transformation. They've made it into a commodity. They don't pray to gods the way we did. The children of the Young Gods have overstayed their welcome, don't you think?"

"We all have."

The witch smiled. "Kill Luthor, and we'll be free of them."

Barring her suggestion that one man's death would somehow throw the children of the Young Gods into some kind of reckoning, she was far too amiable in making her request. All this talk of *them* as if she did not count.

"We'll be free? And what does that make you?"

"I'm an old woman."

"But you're not a Deathless."

"I'm older than that." Minthisha tossed the worm aside. "People used to come from across continents to study in Lorenial. How do you think your priests learned Morthia's name?"

I thought of the mural in Leoric's temple again. The temple marked as Amivia's own house now displayed her usurpers, but there was a time when she stood with her hand outstretched at the entrance. The Old Gods had lived here once. There was truth to Minthisha's words, but also an arrogance. These were the self-proclaimed Hallowed Lands that claimed to be ruled by the All-Father himself. She scoffed at blood purity, but she still held sacred the circumstances of her immortality in this dying world, as if she did not belong among the beasts.

"I'll take that armor and be on my way."

"And what would you pay for it?"

"It'll be the end of days when a man pays for his own armor. There was a time when the selling of stolen items, regardless of circumstance, was punishable by a fine, a flogging, and the loss of a hand. But we are in this new, lawless age. I'll forgive the offense if goods are rightfully returned and you tell me what enchantment Alanus imbued into this blade."

I tossed it to her, and the longsword caught in the air. It spun slowly with that same molasses-like lethargy I'd fallen into on the steps. The effect surprised neither of us. Now that I knew what to look for, I spotted the three gemstones she had fixed into the ground around her supply that were somehow linked to this catch. They were half-covered in dirt but placed deliberately. I'd recalled the pin with the ruby resting on the step by her hip; another had been in a crack between the stones of the cellar wall. At least the sorceries of this land seemed to have limitations.

"Your country makes good use of this strange magic. I wish I'd had it in my time," I commented. I counted five seconds, and the sword was still suspended.

"Did you find the present I left for you in Alanus' reception hall?" Minthisha asked. She waited a moment, then extended her hands. Just as they slipped into position, the longsword was released from its imprisonment and dropped straight down. Ten seconds in total.

I said nothing, collecting my armor—which would be an uncomfortable burden to strap on without gambeson and boots. She inspected the blade with the efficiency of a smith. It shouldn't have surprised me, considering she was in the business of scavenging and selling armaments.

"I sold this to her twenty years ago. It's Steelhand Cyrus' work. Evarlyn the Confessor hung him until his bones bleached in the sun not a month after he forged it."

"For what reason?"

"Treason or some such," she said distractedly to the blade. She traced her two fingers along its flat as if caressing delicate skin. "They needed him out of the way. Nobles enjoy that kind of simplicity. This sword is a complicated piece; it returns the heat of the forge that birthed it back to the metal upon command without warping the steel. The spell requires little from the user aside from an incantation."

"What's the incantation?"

"I wish I could say, Sir Deathless," she said. "My debt is forgiven upon telling you the enchantment. How to use it will cost you."

"This reciprocity you're so keen on."

"I want for little else."

She tossed the blade back up, and it caught in the pocket of suspended time. I reached for it slowly, but my hand caught in place as if I'd pushed into a wall of sand. Ten seconds later, the sword dropped, and my hand was free. I took a step forward, feeling the edge of the ruby-set hairpin under my toe, and recovered the sword.

"It's not reciprocity when the exchange is uneven. What do you really gain if I kill your Luthor, Madame Clay?" I asked, holding the sword away from my estimated limits of the time pocket.

I set my heel against the front of the pin.

"*Mother* Clay," she corrected, her tone harsh and reactionary. As soon as she said it, her mouth fixed into a hard line.

"Whose mother are you?"

"No one calls me that except the boy when he's feeling impudent," she dismissed. "You wouldn't consider yourself a father anymore, would you?"

I recoiled. "I had heirs."

"You outlasted them. It's as if they never were."

I thought of a grave plot I'd visited only once. I thought of brown eyes I'd known as my own. I thought of sunflowers withering in the shadow of a ruined house.

"What do you get?" I repeated.

"I can assure you he deserves his death."

My foot pushed back, and I felt a cool rush of air fill a space that'd been clotted by magic. Minthisha jolted in her seat, but I snatched her by the shoulder and held her in place. She was so small under my grip. Her frame felt so light and brittle.

She gasped at the sensation of cool steel pressed along her cheek. I'd nicked a piece of her right ear off with my advance. It would take only the slightest adjustment to remove her working eye.

"You're the worst of them," I said. "All of you want *something*. Alanus *asked* me to join her cause. Theodoulos all but begged for his favor. Gutter rat or king, no one lasts this long without wringing everyone else for what they're worth. You dressed me in armor regardless of my answer. You'd as soon pick me clean as you would dress me, if it served you. There is no exchange between us. You see a dog, and you'll bait him to hunt a rabbit."

I felt her shaking under my shoulder. I saw her dark eye turn black from fear. And yet, she did not placate.

"We can make an arrangement—"

I pulled the blade of the longsword back. A line of blood splattered her neck. She shrieked and clutched the split skin on her cheek. There was a moment, I'm certain, she thought I'd turned her blind. I'd considered it, but this sufficed. Bare skin seemed so vulnerable after the House of Oghir.

I caught the ropes of eyes slung around her torso. I fingered along the ring of skin and the bag of teeth. I brought the sword to each of them and cut the lines.

When I had each stash bundled in my hand, I threw all but one of each communion on the ground. With her options arrayed before her, I pushed her off the crate so she might more easily choose her salvation. However, she did not reach for any of them. Instead, she kept her hand pressed to the cut in her face. If pride prevented her from accepting my generosity or fleeing, that was of no matter to me.

I opened the crate, revealing the cache of goods I'd expected. It took a glimpse to understand the wealth of stores she had collected from looting corpses in Leoric's graveyard and trade deals with bandits.

"Outside these walls, I would have cut your throat and taken everything of use to me. I'm feeling merciful, but that won't last long. You should be gone by then."

At last, I saw her hatred laid bare. What a dog I was, and how she'd love to chase me away if only I didn't bite. If she had some magic to strike me down where I stood, she would have conjured it then. Instead, the inept witch sniffed and looked away in shame. Without another word, she left me with the spoils of the swamp.

I took my time selecting the best pieces among the gambeson coats and boots. Once I strapped on my old armor, all that was left were the three stone pins and the lines of sacrificial flesh. The ants had already come for the fingers and eyes.

The rest I threw to the alligators.

THE HIGHLANDS

I was not looking for Theodoulos. I could say I didn't seek him out for the sake of solitude, but I'd had enough of that. It was only that I thought, as with most things, our brief acquaintance would have lost its relevance. I might have spent weeks or months in the House of Oghir. It seemed best not to give the whole affair too much thought.

Even if the entire endeavor might have been nothing more than a ploy by a cowardly boy to collect a few teeth, I'd lost nothing from the diversion. With Lady Alanus' sword at my hip, I'd come away richer. If I learned a bit of this foreign land's sorcery, perhaps I could use its magic to boil Lambskin from the inside.

Minthisha had gotten nothing out of dressing me in armor. The tunnel rat had my teeth but was exposed to the next stranger who would come along. Lady Alanus was dead by my hand. My body had been restored by Morthia. I could leave all that behind me, no poorer for having diverted myself for a fraction of a moment.

Then Theodoulos *did* find me. He came running down a path through the swamp. He shouted my name as if the shock of bright blue on his tabard wouldn't make him obvious. He looked ridiculous with his sword slapping at his side, helmet twisting on his hip. He skidded to a stop just in front of me, eyes shining. "I was sure you were dead! I searched all over that manor and couldn't find a hint of you! Look at you, Sir Deryl!" I didn't bother correcting him. "You're . . . quite a sight. Are you . . . alright? It seems you're quite ashen."

"No worse than usual."

"Well, that's not quite reassuring, but . . . gods be praised." He made an aborted movement as if to jostle or slap my shoulder. He brought his hand back to his neck. "She's dead then? Alanus?"

"Yes."

"Truly? How did you do it? She's supposed to be invulnerable in that armor."

"Skin of steel doesn't do much good in water."

"*Ah*. King Evarund will be delighted to hear that she's finally fallen. You have her mask then?"

I lifted her sword, presenting it on the palms of both my hands. His smile faltered. Those wine-dark eyes flicked up to inspect my face.

"I—er, I don't understand."

"This is her sword."

"Oh. Well . . . that would be a fine token if it . . . what about her mask?"

"Buried in the swamp."

"Oh." Theodoulos' expression crumpled. "Do you think we could go back for it?"

"Would you like to?" I gestured behind me, making it clear he could do so alone if he wanted.

"You know, sir, this is"—he pushed the blade down—"a true victory. You should be quite proud of your efforts. But . . . a sword is . . . well, one like this is a bit mundane. Frankly, *anyone* could claim the credit for our efforts in killing that traitor without her mask. Are you sure you can't . . . ?"

I shook my head. Theodoulos groaned.

There was something so juvenile about the noise that caught me off guard. Immortal as we were, time still took its toll. My slim-faced childhood had passed before my pact with Morthia, but I'd seen young men pack on the bulk of age over the decades. Unless I suffered an amputation, my skin would wither and sag. Sections of gray coils tangled between my fingers when I braided them back, though I'd had none when I first pledged. I had not seen a man who had looked properly old in decades, and none that looked young acted the way Theodoulos did.

"Well, it's a good thing you have me. If an outsider like you brought something as plain as a sword to those gates to prove your mettle, they'd turn you away in a heartbeat. At the least, if I claim I was there when you issued the final blow, it'll add some legitimacy. I wouldn't want to leave you in the dust after our efforts. This . . . this is not a total loss."

He babbled to himself like that as we made our way back north, heading to the Green Castle.

We cleared the edge of the treeline by midday and stepped into the abandoned farmland. From there, we trudged up the same rolling hills we'd come from perhaps months before. I had yet to ask how long I'd been trapped in the House of Oghir. The wind whipped at our faces. Wild blades of grass swayed by our elbows. As I watched the sunset blot out all light in the swamp, engulfing it in bruised purples and blacks, I felt as if we had ascended out of some cold pit where the soulless and corrupted lay.

Theodoulos bid it farewell with a clumsy kick of a rock. "It was absolutely miserable waiting for you in that cesspool. Let's make a point to never visit again."

I was half-convinced he'd fought Lady Alanus alongside me with how he went on that night. When he did settle down, and I was standing there, looming above that dozing boy, stripped of his armor and bundled in a tattered woolen blanket, the strangeness of the entire day struck me. I could not comprehend the boy. How long had he waited for me? *Why* had he waited for me?

I could slit his throat now and set out to find Lambskin. Yet, he slept so assured that I would be there when he woke. Assured I would protect him from all the things that slithered and crept in the night.

In the clear air of a new morning, I waited for him to come to his senses and find the quickest excuse to abandon me. But he sat up and flashed me a toothy grin like my sons used to when they were inspired to mischief. "Sir Darl! I know what we should do!"

Disarmed, I could only humor him. "Oh?"

He crouched beside me conspiratorially. "Your sword is a brilliant trophy. No one will deny that. The Green would relish in its return and the news of Alanus' death. But I can't help but feel as if you wouldn't be satisfied. It all strikes me as unfair."

"That's the way of things, isn't it?"

"Well, Sir Darl, we did have an agreement. I've read that Deathless come from a time when men were noble in character and honored their word. In the spirit of that, I'm sure I could do more to help you find your Heartless friend. You see, I'm sure the Green would not have taken him in, but I do know there were others sympathetic to outlanders who were eager to recruit. If he'd been sent on his way, footpaths from the fields would have led him west, and if he'd missed Leoric's Temple, then he would have gone into the highlands. I know who would have taken him in—or, at least, tried to."

"Who would that be?"

"Well, I can show you."

"Why would you? You got your teeth out of this agreement."

"I . . . Darl, I don't know what you mean."

Liar. "Take the sword if that's what you're waiting on. You'd never be able to kill me for it."

"Darl!" The boy looked shocked at the suggestion that he would try. "We had an agreement, didn't we? You've fulfilled your end, but I owe a debt to you. Let me help you find your man. Besides, when you're not such a grouch, you're the most pleasant company I've had in some time."

That reflected more on others than my own charms. All the same, I saw no reason to reject his offer. So Theodoulos shaved, ate his tooth, strung a few unruly coils of hair with beads, and named our heading and the next man I was tasked to kill.

Sigmund, as Theodoulos would explain, was one of the important soldiers among the banished fifty-six. He was an Acolyte who had sacrificed his right eye for his immortality and served for a century and a half as a gateman before Theodoulos' birth. When the fifty-six had been cast out, he'd had a hefty following of older soldiers who had left with him.

The Green knew where he and his sizable following had settled, but they had been left alone so far. We walked west, across overgrown pastures and abandoned villages. The trees seemed to thin completely by the time we started a slow and steady climb into the highlands.

Theodoulos stopped to string his bow and pulled a hollowed arrow from his pouch. I did not wonder why for long. We came across a bloodied leg trapped in its greave in the middle of a rocky outcrop. Hoofprints too large to belong to a boar had stamped all around it, and the splatters of blood on nearby stones left little to the imagination. Leadswine.

We walked cautiously then. With so few trees about, we prioritized climbing high instead of in the exact direction we wanted. An hour or so later, we spotted a leadswine below us. It was in the process of crushing a plated torso between its jaws when it stopped and turned suddenly, snout raised to the wind. Theodoulos nocked his arrow, and I wondered how effective that distraction would be in this more open space.

We did not have to learn. The beast caught a different scent and turned away from us; another of its kind that was coming down from the west. The two of them stomped their hooves, sizing one another up with twitching ears and flicking tails. Both leadswine bellowed aggressive growls, and when neither surrendered, they charged each other. They clashed with a terrible heft to each strike. One of them was thrown to the ground with such force that it sounded like a tree cracking in half.

Theodoulos circled us around the pair, but we were not far off when one of the beasts cried out the distinct sound; the agony of death had a distinct timbre to it that unified all variations of that sound. We saw the victor collect the corpse it'd been defending and trot off north. Away from us, I thought with some relief.

"We should make haste before another one comes to collect it," Theodoulos said, nodding to the dead leadswine.

"Why would they?"

"Konstantin sends others back for the ones that go missing. You'll see more leadswine dragging other leadswine than anything else. They stop moving if they're away from High Mound long enough."

If it were a matter of distance or time, that explained why they kept so far from the Green, but not this behavior. "Yet, they gore one another."

"It's a remnant of their nature before they were made into . . . whatever they are now."

We saw three more leadswine before sunset that day. One dragged the rotting carcass of an alligator with it. Theodoulos had to use an arrow to divert another, much to his chagrin.

"It feels like there's more of them every year," Theodoulos grumbled.

"I thought they weren't alive. How could they breed?"

"They aren't alive," Theodoulos said. "They *were* once. According to older texts, they were a kind of wild boar, but the giants took their skins and conjoined them with a kind of old magic. They're as much metal and stone as they are flesh now. Forged, not born."

Oh yes, this giant business, again. Did the Hallowed Lands have every myth incarnate within its borders?

"The giants are creatures of old magic. The kind of magic that built Lorenial and the Thousand Hands Wall," Theodoulous said, naming the immense barrier between the Hallowed Lands and the rest of the world peeking out of the horizon. "Konstantin sends them to kill indiscriminately. There are hardly any animals in this area because of them. The Green hasn't had a proper deer hunt in decades. If only we knew how to harness old magic, the same kind of necromancy could be used to our own advan—"

"What do people in the Green Castle eat?" I asked, more intrigued by the notion of a deer hunt. Theodoulos' lip twitched the way it always did when I interrupted him.

"Same as they do out here. Fingers, eyes, skin—"

"No. *People.* What do *they* eat? None of the fields are being worked, and the livestock's dead or feral. There can't be enough room for more than a vegetable garden behind the walls."

"You mean the *unaligned*?" Theo asked with just the slightest hint of resentment in his tone. "Noble families are fed from the king's private stores. Beans and wheat from the garden. It's not a culinary marvel, but, considering the alternative, it's suitable."

"No one farms this land?"

"No way to defend it. As I said, with Konstantin's leadswine about here, and outlanders pouring in from the gate, there's no reason to risk it," he said. "No one will bother trying to make anything of these highlands until the giant dies and his magic with it."

"Except for your Sigmund."

"Well . . . his pack of traitors had no other choice. They were unaligned but . . . you see . . . the night before their official exile, Sigmund and ten other traitors stole twelve noblewomen. Feeding twelve unaligned is vastly different from feeding the entire Green's worth. They wouldn't need much land at all, and I don't think they would have risked it anywhere near the Green. They fortified themselves in an old baron's estate. Given the danger of the leadswine, our captain made the decision to abandon any attempts at a siege and leave Sigmund to his settlement."

"If he's locked away in a fortress your men couldn't break, how will we get in?"

"You, Sir Darl, are an outlander. Kept as they are, they hate it out here as much as we do. They would rather take the Green from Evarund, but they need numbers for that. They'll take kindly to you if you pretend to know nothing. Might even let you strut right in through the front door."

"And I'll be able to collect another trophy for you to show the Green." I understood and finally felt peace.

Theodoulos showed his teeth. "It's a beneficial partnership, is it not? Your friend may even be there, and you could both come back as heroes who returned the Green's stolen daughters."

"Perhaps," I said. "What do Sigmund's men eat?"

"What?"

"They're barricaded away, and they need to consume flesh to please their gods and maintain their life. If they can't go out to hunt or trade for the body parts they need . . . " I trailed off, hesitant to crush the boy's naive ideals that the daughters of the Green would be in a state to be rescued. Theodoulos looked at me like he couldn't quite puzzle out what I was getting at.

"Do *you* eat?" he asked, missing the point of my question. "I know you please your god with the act of killing, but you must take communion of some kind?"

"No."

"I have to swallow a tooth every few weeks. It's disgusting. I'd chosen Deiviknot because it was promised to be the *least* vile. You've seen how the others mutilate themselves.

"Still, I wish I'd chosen an eye. They can go a long time without feeling hunger—the longest, aside from the Heartless. I've seen them perform extraordinary feats of magic without exhaustion. At the time, I thought there was no need if I was not to learn, but I should have asked the holy man to pledge me to Koroe. But killing a man every year or so . . . it's as impractical as it is difficult. Not for you, I suppose. Is that why you chose to become a Deathless?"

There hadn't been a choice for what I would become. Barbarians had been invading from overseas. If there had been no one to meet them, there would have been no country to defend, no survivors after their rampage.

My country had needed monsters, and I had agreed to become one for it. Choice was for the young men who would come after me.

"It was better than death."

Theodoulos scoffed. "Anything's better than death."

The deeper we traveled into the highlands, the closer we were to Glenmore Hall, Sigmund's fortress.

In the heat of midday, we'd stop and rest in what little cover there was, armor stripped, eyes squinting. In the nights, crickets sang, and bats flitted overhead. When the moon turned the grass silver and gray, and the distant mountain peaks faded to obscure shadows, I could almost imagine I had somehow been dropped back into the wasteland on the other side of the Thousand Hand Wall. I braided long lines of grass to distract from the terrible, childish notion that the sun would rise to reveal a barren horizon, that I would hear no bird songs or boar calls, and that I would be alone in Morthia's wasting fields for eternity.

Theodoulos noticed the discarded tail of grass one morning and started staying up later to braid his own. He'd lie on his back and babble on for hours about anything. His favorite topics were the stories of heroic deeds of the All-Father and his knights, some of which I knew better, and the histories and cultures of countries he'd read about but never seen. I'd corrected him when the lies he repeated were egregious, and he never took offense. On the contrary, he seemed only too happy to let me speak of kingdoms long buried and mythical kings long altered. Sometimes he'd be so tired, he would repeat the same thoughts over and over until he trailed off to sleep.

It was such a strange impulse of his, and I couldn't imagine what he thought the benefit was. Surely, he didn't remember half the nonsense we discussed, and I warned him I would only let us rest at camp for so long, but he insisted.

THE BROKEN FORTRESS

The night we saw Glenmore Hall on the horizon, Theodoulos told the story of how Sigmund's men had crept into a fabled nest in a tower. He spoke of lustful men with grubby hands stealing pure noblewomen of the Green from their beds. They were carried across the fields like spirits, white shifts fluttering around their willowy limbs, their breasts heaving in panic against loose linen as they disappeared into their wedding night. And while Theo was angry during the telling, it was not a true story. Like the tales of the All-Father, this was a story told to him and relayed to me.

I had seen the rape of cities. It was not such a moody picture. The theft was never so poetic.

Yet, whenever we told these stories, we spoke of them with such romance. We had sacked the city. We had shown the women what real men were like. We had conquered a kingdom of treasured virgins to be plundered. There was an ugliness to it that made us call screams "moans" and stillness "submission." The songs we'd belted had us all howling in laughter. There was a rightness in the words that had settled us.

But when we'd heard of barbarians from afar coming to take our land and take our women, we had not thought of those softer words. Our memories had been what had conjured the fires of rage in our hearts and what had sent us out to kill those animals for what they would do. I hated those stories now as much as their scandalized telling.

"What'll we do if the women are there?" I asked in the middle of the story's climactic chase.

"What do you mean, Darl? They're *going* to be there," Theodoulos said. He pulled too tightly and frayed a strand of grass. "I don't doubt the Green would be grateful and generous to a noble knight such as yourself returning them home unharmed and intact."

Something in how he said it felt more placating than usual. He spoke with a good-natured tone, but there was a plea underlying it all. I was about to infiltrate his enemy's home on a whim, and he was not quite sure what I'd do.

It was not as if I would find it difficult to believe Theodoulos was afraid of me. But being intimidated by what I could do was different from him thinking that I would harm him. Of course I could. Perhaps I'd considered it before, but I thought we had an understanding. We were not strangers in the wastes. He had been so vulnerable this entire time that it was off-putting to imagine a part of his confidence was limited. I was, perhaps, growing attached to the idea that he put too much trust in me.

So I resolved to be a model soldier the next morning. I would greet this Sigmund at his wall and behave amiably as I took careful stock of his company and captives. When all were tallied, I would kill Sigmund first to expedite the fight and treat whichever nobles of the Green we met with grace and dignity. All those plans and more were thrown away as soon as I was near enough to Glenmore Hall to see that the front gate was ajar.

A cloud of crows circled its high tower and chattered along the ramparts. There was no other movement on the wall, nor even the silhouette of a guard. When I crossed their wall to the inner courtyard, I was not surprised by the bodies. Morthia's flies feasted in droves on the carnage scattered about. From the decay, I guessed they'd been dead a week.

There were eight bodies in the main courtyard. Only two appeared to be men of the Green, judging by their tabards and the beads in their hair. I recognized Ceylot armor, and one man had the piercings of a soldier from the Silver Coast. The guardhouse had caught fire and burned one man beyond recognition. There were also the telltale drag marks of men who had been near death but, taking their communion on time, were able to crawl away from the aftermath. Yet, if anyone had stayed, they had not come out to meet me.

I stepped back out to wave down Theodoulos. He slipped in behind me, still wary of being seen, though it was obvious from the stench alone that there would be no one to recognize him or care if they did. I was more worried that the opposing band responsible for this might have an ambush waiting for us akin to the one I'd set at the Splintered Hills; with each room I inspected and each corridor I cleared, I began to worry we would find nothing at all. Someone had beaten Theodoulos to his plot, and they seemed to have absconded with the kitchen stores, the tools in the armory, and whatever other treasures had been hidden away.

A portion of the fortress's face had collapsed. What was left was little more than a stone wall buffering the wind. I looked around for the offending projectile that must have been launched from some far-off trebuchet, but it seemed so strange for there to be no other pockmarks on the walls from other attempts. It also seemed ridiculous to think their men might have had the time or means to move war machines.

Suddenly, Theodoulos startled. I drew my sword in time to see him leap back from a figure sitting above the rubble. If his gambeson had been another color once, stone dust had stained it gray. His hair was gray and braided back in four neat rows that met at his shoulders.

A thick chain of metal around his neck flashed in the light. I recognized the ascending bird and the three burning roses of the All-Father. This knight's medallion, however, had been scratched. The bird was beheaded, and two roses were scraped flat.

The spear in his hands seemed to be little better than a support for him to lean on as he sheltered in the shade. Eyes that flashed the same red as Theodoulos' trailed over something in the rubble with keen interest.

"Elioth?" Theodoulos gasped.

The stranger lifted his chin a fraction but did not acknowledge us. All the same, Theodoulos averted his eyes, casting about in desperate search of anything—anyone else. The stranger returned his attention to the rubble. I half-expected what he was looking at, but I still checked.

With all the fresh stone dust about, the tower must have collapsed recently and suddenly. There were bodies crushed inside. Legs and arms, powdered sickly white, protruded from a few dug-out sections. Perhaps they had been dead by the time they'd been found. Some must have suffocated before they could be dug out.

Theodoulos followed me and stumbled over the rocks. The change in his face aged him a decade. The mild excitement buzzing under his curiosity flattened to dread. His mouth hung open as he took in the delicate shape of what was definitely a woman's hand.

"I . . . This . . . " Theodoulos tried to catch his words, but they escaped him with each breathless pant. "Darl?"

I hated that look he gave me. I was *not* the villain of his tale, but something far worse. I was the man he looked to to make sense of what was before him. He had the same lost look as a boy no older than fourteen covered in the gore of strangers.

"I think Sigmund's moved on," I said. It wasn't the comfort or assurance he wanted, but I didn't know what else I *could* say.

"Sigmund's a feast for the mice now," the man in the rubble muttered.

"Elioth," Theodoulos said his name softly, as if he expected the man to spring into action. He went on, his voice low and cautious, his head slightly bowed. "Sir, where is everyone?"

Elioth kept his gaze on a checked tabard laid out a short distance from the rubble. It took me a moment to realize from its shape that it covered a body, the only one that had been dug out in full. The tabard twitched, as if the corpse beneath was taking shallow breaths. Then I heard the squeaking.

Theodoulos noticed Elioth's attention and vaulted to my side. He tore the tabard off the corpse, and chaos erupted beneath. Hundreds of the little vermin clambered over one another to chew fingers to the nub. Tails wriggled in eye sockets. Little claws tore at what flesh remained in the throat from the inside. Theodoulos groaned in disgust.

"Vicious little things," the knight said. "The mothers eat their young when there's no food. Won't let their pups grow up in a world that can't keep them. Yet, when you lay a body like this before them and give them plenty, the fathers will eat the children if they see them."

A mouse nipped at its brother's ear to steal a flap of skin. Theodoulos crouched beside the body, into Elioth's line of sight.

"Sir Elioth. . . It's Theo. Do you remember me?"

The knight tilted his head back a fraction, deigning to look upon us for a clouded moment. "Which one were you? Leoth's boy? No. Ludo was he. Methodius' boy. You have his face. Erasmus, then? Pink snouts look the same."

"We're exiles of the Green," I lied, hoping that'd provoke his attention.

"Ah! Another defector!" His dark eyes crinkled with glee at the notion. He swayed on his spear, taking us in with more consideration. "Nothing but defectors now, after we've taken the great leap, eh? You've come to your senses! We did not pledge our bodies for generations to have our sons and daughters bred like pigs and sacrificed in our stead."

"I'm sure your convictions serve you well as you rot here alone." Theodoulos' lip curled with a surprising ugliness.

Elioth hummed in consideration. "I've been watching the nature of mice."

Theodoulos scowled at the mound of rodents with flat disinterest.

"No longer than a fortnight," I said. The decay of the corpse told me as much. "You were attacked?"

"They sabotaged us in the night."

"Who?"

"Red Guard, who else? You should have come earlier; we could use a spell-slinger or two. You're of the age for it," Elioth pointed to me.

I did not know what "Red Guard" referred to, but Theodoulos seemed to have no trouble understanding.

"Did they take any prisoners? Any of the women?"

Theodoulos' questions might as well have been a buzzing in Elioth's ear. The old knight kept his attention set on me. His fist curled around his staff, twisting an obscured spearpoint into the dirt.

"You're not one of ours. I don't know you," he said. "What are you?"

"Sir Elioth!" Theodoulos interrupted. "Do you remember what happened here? What happened to Sabrin? Remember her? She had a scar on her chin. Did you hold them somewhere else? Sir?"

He begged with a delicate earnestness I had never seen from him.

"They knocked the tower down," Elioth said. I looked about again, still unsure of how. The damage was too concentrated to have been done by a distant war machine, but there was no force a man could muster on his own that could crumble stone.

"They can't have all died here," Theodoulos said.

Elioth hummed in such a way that could have communicated agreement or annoyance. His eyes, however, did not move from me. "Why can't you just leave us alone? This was a good land once. Then your lot brought in waves of corruption. You tainted everything.

"I told Sigmund—I told him not to let them in. I could never understand why he took in strangers. Why would we share our weapons, our communions, or our women with strangers? To taint our own blood? This was meant to be the start of paradise again."

I wrinkled my nose. "Here?"

Theodoulos scoffed and returned to the rubble pile. He inspected the protruding hands with a clear marker in mind. When that didn't work, he dropped to his knees and started to dig stone by cumbersome stone.

"They were the future," Elioth said, watching Theodoulos in the rubble. "We had our first whelps. We raised them here in the fresh air. In the sun. Now, the mice have that luxury."

"If the Red Guard stole your future sons away, I could seek them out and reclaim them for you," I offered. At least, he might have another lead on where to find another refuge camp Lambskin might have taken shelter in. At best, perhaps whoever Theodoulos was asking after had survived the siege and had merely been kidnapped.

"I'm all that's left. It ends with me."

"If only that were true," Theodoulos muttered. It had been an impulsive comment. On his knees in the rubble, he was only half-listening to Elioth's ramblings.

Elioth, however, leapt to his feet. Quick as a viper, he choked up his grip on his spear and advanced with a soldier's posture.

There was a fraction of a second where I could have stepped in. I stayed back, thinking the man might cuff him in the back of the head or scold him for his disrespect. I thought it fair when Elioth closed in on Theodoulos and kicked the boy off balance, flattening him on his back. But then, the old knight stabbed his spearpoint straight into the boy's chest, into his heart. It had happened so quickly I could only look on in disbelief.

"I remember you," Elioth murmured. "The runt."

Theodoulos grabbed the spear. His boots scraped across the rubble, and he whimpered and squirmed, but it was all in an effort to get away, not to fight back.

"Not man enough to earn your place, you stole it. They never would have let you join. You're going to die out here, and all your sacrifices will have been for nothing."

Elioth twisted the spear deeper, and Theodoulos shrieked. I drew my sword, and in five steps, I had my hand on the knight's shoulder. It was the simplest thing to drive the point of my sword up into his kidney from beneath his gambeson.

The man hacked and gulped. I took the spear from his hands and threw him to the ground. Theodoulos looked up at me from the spearpoint, chest fluttering like a bird's wings. I pulled the blade out quickly and gave him a moment to recover. Only, he didn't. He clutched at the hole in his chest in panic instead of reaching into the pouch on his hip.

"Theo! Theo, your communion!"

The boy did not listen. He wheezed and gasped as he kept pressing his chest as if he could staunch the blood through sheer will. Terrified, bulging eyes fixed on Elioth gurgling his last. I knelt beside the boy and took a handful of teeth from his pouch. I set it in his shaking hand.

The texture startled Theodoulos back into his body. He cupped his hand to his mouth and swallowed them between gasps. Then he sat there, wide-eyed and shaking.

"Theo. Boy, look here. He's dead." I cupped the back of his neck. Theodoulos' hand latched on to my wrist on instinct, and finally, he ripped his gaze away from Elioth.

"P-promise?" he wheezed.

"Yes."

"Promise!" His hand tightened around my wrist.

"Don't let it knock you down, boy. He's dead. You're here. You're going to be alright." Soothing another man down from their panic was not something I had done often. Yet, on the occasions it had happened, I had given and received the same assurances.

"I'm bleeding." He was. I doubted his heart or lung was punctured, but he'd lost enough to kill a normal man. Yet even now, I could see Deiviknot's work clotting the blood. Within an hour, the skin would mend, and the puncture wound would be little more than a scab.

"It's mending." I took a deliberately slow breath and waited for him to copy me.

"Promise," he pleaded again.

"I promise."

We sat there on that rubble with Elioth at our feet. Theodoulos clung on to me, and the mice ventured out from beneath the blanket to explore the untrodden plains of the old soldier. By the time Theodoulos felt well enough to stand, a swarm had begun to chew through Elioth's clothing.

"Did he have a grudge against you?" I asked. Theodoulos answered with a grunt. He crouched down beside Elioth's body, watching the mice nip at each other. "But you knew him."

He nodded.

"And the others you were asking after?"

"They're dead now, aren't they?" Theodoulos said. He yanked the medallion from the defector's neck and drew away.

"Is there another fortress around here? Rivals that would have wanted to sabotage this place? Perhaps they could have taken prisoners."

"If there is, I don't know of it," Theodoulos said shortly.

"Does Red Guard mean something to you? Perhaps they would have taken prisoners?"

"I don't know, Darl!" he snapped. Then, he seemed to take me in for the first time, and his dour expression broke into a wry grin. A terrible little cackle escaped him. "I don't ever know what any of them will do. I *do know* this"—he raised the altered medallion in his fist—"may be enough if we say it belongs to Sigmund."

THE WANDERER

Theodoulos lay down like a stone that night. I braced for him to babble on about something for his own nerves while he braided, but when I offered him a few blades of grass, he waved them away.

"I can't keep you company tonight," he said shortly.

Company?

"Don't despair, boy. We can search for your woman on the morrow."

"My . . ." Theodoulos snagged his lip in the corner of his teeth. "She's dead. Or, she's not worth the trouble."

"It may not be so difficult—"

"I'm *tired*, Darl. Please."

He was as sullen the next morning as when we left Glenmore. Once he marked which way was east, he collected his things and walked on without another word.

I couldn't understand. Some men were shaken by their near-deaths, but there came a time when this was all a part of the routine. But perhaps, for Theodoulos, there was no routine. Was that the first time he had to take communion to save his own life? He had a whole bag of teeth, and I did not know how he collected them. My guess left the task of the harvest in another's hands. I was beginning to think he'd never so much as dueled another man.

The boy was young and naive. Delicacy like his had no place in a world like this. The Hallowed Lands were dense. I used to go years without seeing another person; here, there was a new stranger every few miles. If he truly had been a soldier, I doubted it had been for very long. All of his stories of campaigning out to defeat his enemies painted him as a part of the action. Alanus would have gutted the Green if their soldiers were only as competent as Theodoulos, and that was to say nothing of the strangers we met outside its walls.

It was in my best interest to split off. I had no leads for Lambskin, and the boy was little more than a nuisance. Yet, I resolved to see him home before returning to my own hunt. Ploy or not, he had put his trust in me since the swamps. Theodoulos was useless, but he could learn. He had spirit, at least, and a bit of bravery to him that could be molded into something worthwhile in the right hands.

There was an impulse in me that wanted to live up to the boy's expectations, unfounded as they were.

So when a creature appeared as a shadow in the dark on our third night, I played my role as sentinel. The stranger descended upon us like a black dog of misfortune, nearly silent in his steps but obvious in his intent. In the open hills, the grass was short, and the rocks were flat. If he had company, I would have known, and if he had company, I might have drawn my sword.

He walked right up to our camp, letting the flames lick at the tips of his boots before speaking.

"Share your fire with a stranger, Stranger?"

A dark scar ran down his cheek, cutting out his eye and a part of his ear. He covered neither up. His dress was simple: a padded jacket and hunting boots. That did not mean he was a man of simple origins. Spots of luxury flashed on his person: a velvet pouch on his hip, gold beads braided in his curls. There was a hunting knife tied to his belt, but the bow on his back was unstrung, and the quiver was wrapped.

What would be the harm? I had to pass the long hours until sunrise somehow, and Theodoulos' sullen mood had left me craving a bit of conversation. If this ended in blows, I would win.

"If you behave, so shall I," I said.

"Ah!" He grinned, showing off a sharpened, silver canine. "The most commonly spoken and broken contract."

I had read that phrase once somewhere. "A scholar said that, didn't he?"

"If one did, I don't know them. It was a favorite saying of my father's, but I never read the books he favored. Philosophies. Histories. Seemed a waste."

He settled down across the fire. He gestured to Theodoulos' feet beside him and hovered with a question unspoken. Theodoulos slept on, oblivious to his presence. The stranger inspected me again and seemed to reconsider. For now, it seemed reasonable to leave this moment between us. The boy was exhausted as it was, and remeeting another potential acquaintance from the Green seemed far from ideal for his mood.

"What did you study instead?" I prompted.

"War and weaponry," he said with an almost dreamy dismissal. "Also a waste. I didn't think so until I pledged, but that's the truth of it. You know, we used to till these fields, shepherd sheep, build cabins, spin thread. I can fletch an arrow and shape a bow, but once this jacket falls apart, that'll be the end of it. I'll be taking shelter naked under a tree sooner than I'll need to kill another man."

"Are you a Heartless?"

"Many would consider that a rude question. But no. I am not. There's a witch who trades flesh for armor and bugs. It's not a banquet, but it's enough."

"You're one of Sigmund's men, then?" I guessed

The stranger shook his head. "I didn't consort with his brigands."

Didn't. He knew about the fall of Glenmore.

"But you are from the Green?"

"Who isn't these days? I served King Evaline and his son, Evaright. My name is Diethell of Lorenial. Most people call me Hill. You . . . are not." He seemed to take in my face instead of my armor as he came to that realization. "I don't know you at all."

He had a youthful openness to his expression, but unlike Theodoulos, it was not naive, simply uncaring. If I were to guess his age by the weathering on his face and the gray in his hair, I'd say he and the canary must have pledged within a decade or two of each other. I could always be wrong, but there was something to how he held himself that convinced me.

"Darl of Rugenmont."

"Doesn't sound terribly unfamiliar. Seaside country, isn't it?"

"Mountains. Rugenmont is the area. Varlemont, my village. Bevelon is the country."

"Ah. I've heard of Bevelon. Stone men and wine. Don't know much more."

"I've heard a bit about Lorenial. A city of sorcerers, from what I understand."

"It was a giant's city first. The sorcerers came after to study the magic they left behind, but no reputable sorcerer would lower himself to live there by the time Evarlyn was king. I was born in the Green, and my court tutor gave me a better education in magic than I would have had there."

"You've visited?"

"I've seen it from a distance. I know it's in my name, but I feel no kinship with it. What about you, Rugenmont? You're a long way from home. Ever seen it?"

"I may be the last man who remembers it."

"Are you attached to it?"

"I was in my youth. By the time I came back from my first campaign, things had changed."

He nodded as if I had said something particularly sage. "Always wanted to do that—go on some long adventure. You start to fantasize when your world is three rooms. When I pledged, I thought it was an honor to go as far as the Elder Wood's borders on scouting parties. Bah! Outside the fortress was staggering at the time. I could go farther now that I'm not stuck in the

Green. I sometimes think about just sticking the bard and his little gang in that tower and walking into that misty unknown. But . . . here we are."

"Can't bring yourself to go?"

"Not with things the way they are," he said. "A group of us—we had an idea, you see. Perhaps a foolish one. It *was* a foolish one. We were exiled for it. We thought. . . How are the men who have no patron treated where you come from, Darl?"

"They're dead."

"Ah. Ours aren't yet. I saw this one grow up." Diethell pointed at Theodoulos. "He was a sweet boy in those early summers. They all were sweet boys—*I was a sweet boy.* Sweet boys don't earn their patrons. I wish they did. Or, no. I don't wish that. I wish they could have some land. Farm it, somehow—*Seeds.* I'm surprised you're traveling with him, given what he is."

The man rambled so quickly, it was almost lost on me who he meant. Diethell hadn't been about to ask to wake Theodoulos when he'd first sat; he'd recognized him. What, exactly, was Theodoulos to this man? Perhaps a craven thorn in his side or a sniveling child. Given my own experience, neither would surprise me.

I could see the man was hedging at something, but the incident with Elioth demonstrated enough for me. I could only offer Diethell an impartial shrug.

"If he'd known about our plans, I'm sure he would have ratted," Diethell continued. "I wasn't the planning man, but even I knew to leave the pups out of it. The idea was good. If we'd stuck to it, it might have been different. Sigmund stole away with his child-wives. Vernon split off to try and stop him. The Reds left to ponder in the mountains. The youngsters abandoned us for Alanus' self-aggrandizement. The cowards tried to sell us back to the Green once their feet got cold."

I was half-tempted to ask for specifics. Division in leadership was common enough in rebellions. Men could agree their leaders were incompetent, but not on what superior changes must be made. The Reds he referenced may be the very ones that knocked down a portion of Glenmore Hall. The Green stood unblemished while its enemies on the outside mangled one another like street dogs.

Diethell rubbed his hands together, fingers clicking over rings. He watched the fire as if he could see soldiers in armor dueling in its dance. I knew how an unpleasant memory could entrap a man. It was best to let the moment pass like a breeze.

"What's it like?" he asked. "Outside these walls?"

"I don't imagine it's what you would be searching for. Lorenial may have more to offer you."

Diethell snorted and bowed his head. "The witches took it over. They rigged the Elder Wood with death traps. Not too long ago, they infected every inch of that land with the Blight. Say what you will about the Green, but they've preserved good, strong numbers for a long time. They aren't set on ending the world."

"The world's already ended, Diethell. It's waiting for us to end with it."

Diethell chuckled. "You're the second one to say that to me this week."

"Who was the first?"

"An outlander, like you, in fact. One-handed. You know him? Javen. Javohn? Avon?"

My pulse quickened. "Lambskin coat?" I asked.

"He wore a peasant's coat. He gave me this."

Diethell pulled a signet ring from his middle finger that had a distinctly foreign style. The geometric pattern was one favored by countries in my region, Bevelon and Prethion.

"He *gave* you that?"

"Traded it. For information. Sweet boy. So lost. He needed a bit of direction, and I'm never one to refuse."

"What did he want to know?"

Diethell was suddenly silent on the matter. His unfocused chatter was replaced with an anticipatory grin. The airy simplicity he'd begun with faded. I reviewed the seeds of knowledge he'd tossed about. Half-answers and vague summaries. He had been fishing to see what would catch my interest. I knew these kinds of men. In the wastelands, they'd point out a bastion of surviving mortal men on a map in exchange for a strip of skin.

"What do you want?" I asked.

"A finger. Pinky or to the second knuckle would do. Doesn't have to be yours. You have stock right here, don't you?"

Whatever compassion Diethell had had for Theodoulos as a sweet boy inspired no sympathy now. Then again, my own pity for the boy was locked in a losing battle with my temptation. This would be more than a minor inconvenience. One of Theodoulos' fingers against Lambskin's neck was a good price. Still, it seemed a little cruel to use the boy to pay for my information.

"Alright."

I was just about to suggest my own hand and define our terms when I saw Theodoulos flinch. His breathing, which was often soft and even, was shallow and near soundless. He was awake. How much had he overheard?

Diethell went to kneel by Theodoulos' side, and yet the boy didn't spring up or make a fuss. No doubt he heard what I had agreed to do. I followed Diethell, waiting to see if Theodoulos' hand was shifting beneath the blanket to draw a sword, if he would sit up, scream, fight, or anything. Nothing.

A new irritation gnawed at me. Why wouldn't he move?

"Hand me your knife," I said to Diethell. "It'll be easier to cut."

I said it clearly so the boy could not possibly mistake what I intended to do. Diethell seemed to think better of trusting me with his weapon. "You hold him down, and I'll cut."

"Good," I agreed.

I stepped over his body to reposition myself. Theodoulos' breath hitched as my shadow passed over him. If he wanted to knock me off balance, he had an opportunity. He could push me to the ground and make his escape, but instead he remained.

I knelt by the boy's head, listening to Diethell circle around to where I had been. Theodoulos would be able to smell the stranger, feel the coolness of the air now that a man crouched between him and the fire. I laid a hand on his shoulder and felt it tremble against my palm. I listened to the knife scrape from its sheath and knew Theodoulos heard it too.

"Wait," I said. Diethell stopped just over his right hand. "He's an archer. Take from his left."

Diethell had to twist to accommodate the change. Just as he leaned to adjust, I braced against Theodoulos and pushed Diethell into the fire.

The man yelped as he toppled back, more startled than burnt. By the time he'd crawled out, I had drawn my sword. I kicked him off balance in the middle of his scramble, sending him flat on his stomach. Once there, I pressed my knee between his shoulders and laid my sword down by his pinned hand.

"A pinky, you said? Or to the second knuckle? Which one should I take?"

"Wait! Wait!" Diethell shouted. "You—you! We had an agreement! There's no reason for this!"

"You understand your life is in my hands, Diethell. All ten fingers are now mine, aren't they? You can earn them back if you tell me what I want to know."

"Anything, anything," Diethell wheezed.

"Where did the outlander go?"

"I don't—he wanted somewhere safe."

"Where?"

"Sigmund."

"Sigmund's fortress is a ruin. What happened to Sigmund and his men?"

Diethell groaned. "It was safe when I sent him. I could have sent him to the Green. I didn't. Wouldn't do that to him. He was safe when I sent him."

"If you sent him there, you're the reason it fell. That man is a parasite, a weasel, and a traitor. Every man and woman in Glenmore Hall is dead because you pitied that vermin."

"Fine! Fine! I won't help him again! Let me go!"

"You've only earned back two fingers, Hill. What happened to the captives at that fortress? A man like you must know."

"The Red Guard took them. If they're not in the ground, they might as well be."

I sneered at that. Lambskin was too tricky for these men. He'd survived decades as a war rat. He knew how to escape a bloodbath, and he would not be caught on the losing side of a siege.

"I already know that. Where can I find the Red Guard?"

At this, it seemed Diethell had lost his wealth of knowledge. The man bit his tongue and pressed his forehead to the ground. He knew, but he would not allow himself to say. Now would be the time to persuade him. But Alanus' sword was less than ideal for this job. It would be awkward to try to cut with such an oversized instrument.

"Theo." I did not need to look behind to know he was watching. "Find his knife."

"Y. . . yes," he whispered.

There was some commotion, and then Theodoulos slid in front of me. He held out the knife.

"No. You do it. He wanted your hand. You repay him in kind. We can start with the pinky."

Theodoulos' grip tensed. He looked between me and Diethell's hand, as if I were asking him to pet a viper.

"Scared, boy? Why?" Diethell hissed beneath me. "You've killed brothers for less."

There was no warning before Theodoulos dropped the knife, but when he did, it landed within Diethell's reach. The slick man snatched the blade out of the dirt and slashed back at me. I reared back, and Diethell bucked me off. He took off, racing down the highlands like a rabbit. I started after him, sprinting across the rocky terrain, but the moon was low and the stars were blotted. By the time I was at the bottom of the hill, I had lost sight of him.

I stood there, knowing my efforts in the dark would do nothing. Yet the temptation to chase thrummed within me. Lambskin was still here, alive, dancing on the corpses he had left behind, always just a few steps ahead of me. I should have let Diethell take the boy's finger if he wasn't going to fight for it. I could have proven his fears for me true and taught him the consequences of being so spineless. Instead, I saved the worthless child and lost a viable lead.

Damn Lambskin. Damn the boy. Damn me.

I cursed out all my frustrations and composed myself again. I climbed back uphill to camp, ready to lick my wounds and end this miserable night, when I saw Theodoulos kneeling. He had reset the fire and thrown in a few more bushels of grass to rekindle what Diethell had scattered. His blanket was folded, and his belongings were arranged in a neat row. My armor and gambeson were organized across the fire. When I was close enough, the boy sat up straight with his hands clasped in his lap and his eyes fixed on the middle distance.

"What is this?" I asked, sneering at the obvious display of servitude. I walked over to his side and kicked him lightly in the knee. He wobbled but did not move from that pathetic position. This is what he chose to do with himself in the face of betrayal? Grovel? "What are you doing, Theodoulos?"

"I'm sorry I dropped the knife. It's my fault he escaped."

"Then you should have gone after him," I said.

Theodoulos' eyes flicked up and back down, straight ahead. I couldn't stand that nonsense. Who was he pretending to be? There should have been a long string of uneasy, half-hearted questions that ended with him assuring himself that I would not have let harm come to him. To watch this boy crumple into such a small, meek thing—

I cuffed him in the back of the head. "Get up!"

He did. There was no argument. No curse or complaint. He stood, eyes lifeless and detached. I was wrong. I wanted him angry. Outraged. Anything. He'd been honest with Elioth in the tower. Why not me? I slapped him, and he let me. I made to hit him again, and he scrunched up his face and braced, and that ugly little face, so small and accepting—

Damned pathetic. I was almost sick with disgust to see those eyes water.

"Fight, damn you! Can't pick up a sword and slay your own whore! Can't keep yourself alive. You won't even tell me to stop? Do you want to die? Go lie back there like a corpse in the dirt if that's what you want to be. What are you good for? Tell me. Why did I bother saving you?"

In the great emptiness of the pause, I felt the ugliness of every word. I reveled in it. I was revolted by it. The longer the boy quivered, the worse the silence became. He was supposed to push back. You pushed, and they pushed back. My boys shouted, they bit, they spat, and they were disciplined. I had died for them. And this was what was left?

"I'm sorry," he said, his voice lifeless.

No. That wasn't. . .

And another silence collapsed on us. And this one was too heavy to break. I went to my side of the fire and waited for it to be over. Any moment now, he would leave. He would grab his few belongings and start up the hill and into the dark, and I would never see the boy again.

When he knelt down once more, I wanted to scream. I wanted to kick him back onto his feet and chase him away—and I wanted him to stay. I wanted him to be here but be different. I twisted blades of grass until they snapped. I tore out row after row to distract my attention. If he was waiting for a moment to speak, he would not have it. I would not give him permission to be pathetic. He had to learn.

Eventually, Theodoulos lay down. I heard him recline and settle on the bare earth. I listened to every counted breath as he lay there awake. Maybe his eyes were closed, but I imagined they hollowed to plain black, reflecting nothing but the flickers of orange light until it muted to red.

The Storm Mason

The fire smoldered to white ash, and the sun seeped in on bloodred tendrils. I'd seen more gruesome mornings. I had woken on hillsides with nothing but the wind lashing at my face and fog whipping around me. There had been the mornings when a passing storm threatened to wash me away in a flash flood. The war camps the day after a siege were always miserable, clotted with the scent of blood and manure. But today, the skies were clear, and the golden sunrise spilled over the hills in mockery of my dour mood.

It wasn't as if it would be any loss. When Theodoulos woke, he would walk off without so much as a goodbye, and we would be two strangers again. It wasn't as if the boy was of any value. If he stayed, I would hear nothing but his indignant whining now that he'd had time to collect himself. There was no reason to suffer his presence.

"Should we be off, Sir Darl?" he asked.

"Farewell," I said without tearing my gaze from the sunrise.

I heard him sigh and shuffle about. Then, I felt his shoulder brush mine as he settled down beside me. We both looked out over the sunbathed hills.

"You know, Sir Darl," Theodoulos said, "when I was a boy, I used to wait by our window to watch the sunrises. I believed it was hiding just underneath the hills, somewhere below where I could see. I imagined it rested in a lake of molten metal, like a smith's oven. Think of my disappointment the first time I summited these hills and I found out that the sun would just keep sinking no matter where I was."

What was I supposed to do with that nonsense? "And?"

"And . . ." Theodoulos drawled. "I understand the way of things."

False sunsets weren't the way of things. Men hunted one another for sport and for sustenance. This world was starving, and Theodoulos had to learn that or die. "You better grow a spine, boy, or they'll bite you in half out here."

"Yes, sir." Theodoulos' tongue traced along his teeth. "Should we be off?"

Without another word, he turned and started down the hill, trailing north. "The Green is east."

"Yes, but your Heartless is this way," Theodoulos said. "I was lying before. I know who the Red Guard are and where to find them. I just . . . was too afraid to risk it."

So this was repentance.

I sat feeling overwhelmed by yet another apology from the boy when I had given none. I should have found the words then and there to rectify this imbalance. I would have met his eye and told him something poignant and true.

In stories, the knights serving the All-Father composed ballads to inspire others. Laevourt the Just offered mercy and forgiveness to wretches who did not deserve it. Preu the Wise reassured the meek and young. The soldiers in stories all acted with such grace and composure. They knew what to do and say, and what a beautiful lie that was.

I had not slain the beasts they did, but I had destroyed many evils as a warbreaker. I had kept the cruel and bitter world at bay to my last breath. I had held the line in countless shield walls, I'd defended many cities, I'd sacked every fortress asked of me. I was a good soldier, a good knight, but I never learned how to wield words like Laevourt and Preu.

So there was nothing for it but to let Theodoulos take the lead and hope that, with enough distance, this ugly night would be left behind us.

The Green Castle's walls were designed by skilled masons, all straight lines and square-cut stone. Walkways, battlements, overhangs, and guard towers had a purpose and intention to them.

The fortress we approached had no such intention in its design. From a distance, I'd mistaken it for an extension of a mountain crest. Stones as large as houses were layered over one another in uneven links like a farmer's wall. Moss and trees sprouted along its windward side. Rivers spilled out of its cracks, quenching the valley. The perimeter wobbled along the earth's natural contours, not stacked on a dug-out foundation.

"This place is called High Field on the maps," Theodoulos explained. "It was named, of course, when there were three giants sleeping under the stars. I remember my mother used to tell my sister and me that the thunder we heard was the stones they threw at one another from their nests. It was only after I pledged that I learned that it was just the one nest, and the only giant inside never threw any stones. This is High Mound."

"The leadswine's home?"

"Among other things. Vernoth, the oldest of the soldiers, had built an outpost here. He's made no secret of returning here with his men since, but obviously, the Green didn't stick around to challenge him."

"I thought leadswine killed indiscriminately."

"They kill anything the giant tells them to, but Konstantin has had a truce with Vernoth since the beginning of the Undead War."

Theodoulos noticed my uncertainty. "When your countryman's crops began to rot and seized cities were sacrificed to your patrons."

"Earth and water. Wars of earth and water," I said. "A hundred and twenty years at most, then."

"That's a rather quaint name for it," he said, his voice chipper for the first time in days.

His eyes were bright and lively, and the impression of wrinkles had started to show from his smile. It was good to see him back in better spirits.

"What?" he asked, that smile faltering.

"I forget you're a young man, Theodoulos." That wasn't quite right, but it didn't upset him. In fact, he snorted in amusement.

"That means nothing coming from a Deathless! You must be older than even the witches! The last temples of the dead god were destroyed a hundred years before my birth. The last of the priests who could make your kind were hunted before that. You, at the least, have two centuries behind you, don't you? In fact, how old are you?"

I wouldn't know. How old were most of the men of the Hallowed Lands? Perhaps more than a century, ninety at the least. Alanus, as a novelty, could have been a youthful sixty. Was Theodoulos much younger? Knowing the exact number felt strange to me.

Once a man knew who he was, the years did little to him. My body had weathered a long life, yes, but I still felt quite distinctly *myself*. Theodoulos was different. Youth was moldable and shaped by many hands. A man my age was hardened, set like baked clay. We did not change at our age, we chipped.

"So where is this Red Guard?"

"There's an old path, but the leadswine nest in it," he said, more hesitant than before. "It's not ideal. In fact, it's horribly dangerous, but I know of no other way."

The rocks could be scaled, but they stacked high as a mountainous peak—too cumbersome to justify a climb as our first tactic.

Maybe within the stretches of mud-packed earth there would be one place where the gap between the stones had not been filled in. The breadth of the structure, however, deterred me from such a search. It could be days—weeks—before we found a possible entrance, and weeks more if we started exploring crevices that proved to be little more than elaborate alcoves.

I focused on the bent grass and the ruts in the soil. The leadswine already had their path in and out. If Theodoulos knew the clear way, it seemed a waste of time and effort to avoid the most obvious answer.

"Where's the path?" I asked.

Theodoulos frowned. "Darl, are you sure . . . Who is this Heartless to you, really? He can't be worth this kind of risk."

"I have unfinished business with him."

The lines in his face deepened. "He must have done something terrible to deserve being hunted across continents."

"He took advantage of my mercy. We'll leave it at that."

The boy knew what was good for him and relented. Within the hour, he brought us in front of the leadswine's nest. The House of Oghir had primed me to expect layers upon layers of the beasts in a massive congregation, but the gathering beneath High Mound's face was sparse.

We'd encountered leadswine so often, I'd imagined an army of the beasts, but there seemed to be no more than twenty dozing by the mouth of their cave. Theodoulos said they were corpses resurrected by magic, but I was glad to see they seemed to rest like any other beast. Fighting my way through a drove of these creatures was not feasible in my most generous estimation of myself. One swipe of their tusks would send me flying across the field. A stomp from their hooves would cave in my chest with more force than a mace. Though I had it in mind to sneak past them, there was no guarantee that would be possible without a distraction.

"How would Vernoth's men come and go?" I asked.

"I can't guess," Theodoulos said. "He was a powerful sorcerer—a Heartless, in fact. He's been living quite comfortably there, and most of the elders suspect Konstantin taught him the magic he used to influence them."

"Could he influence them to storm a fortress?" I asked, thinking of that lone collapsed tower in Glenmore Hall.

"For a Heartless . . ." Theodoulos shrugged. "What are their limits in your country?"

"My country didn't have conjurers."

"Oh. Strange, that."

"Can you tame them in that way?"

"It's giant's magic," he repeated, as if that were the end of it.

The den seemed as obvious a route as any.

"If we wait until they're asleep or gone," I said, "we may be able to sneak into the tunnel and see where the cave leads."

Theodoulos nodded timidly. He squinted at the drove of pigs in the sun.

"What if they smell us?"

"We divert them."

Theodoulos had those hollowed arrows for a reason. He looked as unsettled as a deer in an open meadow, ears sharp, eyes searching for the nearest hunter and the quickest way out.

"Don't lose your nerve now," I told him.

"This is a dangerous place to be for too long," he said. "The wind could shift. We should fall back deeper into the grass."

I doubted the few hundred yards we walked would make much of a difference to a leadswine's ability to perceive us, but we went. It seemed that so close to home, however, they were sedentary creatures. They must have gathered at midday to escape the heat. Like most animals, there had to be a time of activity and a time of rest. Even Deathless, tireless as we were, had our sedentary periods. All Theodoulos and I would have to do was sit low in the sun-yellowed fields, keeping the wind to our faces, and wait.

Theodoulos sat as still as a vulture—petrified or patient, it didn't matter to me. I tore up some grass and braided a loop. When the sun began to set, the leadswine had thinned somewhat, yes, but less than I would have liked. There were only twelve of them by nightfall, clustered in tight sleeping piles on the rocks. The pigs all slept at once, the idea of a guard beyond an animal's comprehension. I sharpened Alanus' sword and donned my helmet. With a waxing moon overhead and a brilliant studding of stars, we had enough light to see shapes and investigate a little further.

I could see how it pained Theodoulos to even begin to approach the dozing leadswine. His spine threatened to slip out of his skin with every step, but shivering and pathetic as he was, he did not flee. Once I started forward, he followed. He was not going to give me the satisfaction of disappointing me again.

When we were in the thick of the nest, the smell of the leadswine, rank with sweat and rusting iron, saturated the air. Labored, shallow breaths shook their bodies as they slept. We crept past them to the mouth of the cave and were met with a wall of darkness. Theodoulos gawked at the formless shadows, fingers pinched on a hollow arrow, bow clutched in his fist. The fact that we could make out shadows at all, however, was a good sign for us.

Though we couldn't see it, enough light leaked in from the back of the cave to give texture to the darkness. If we walked for long enough, we would find an exit, our entrance. Given that the leadswine were not particularly agile, it couldn't be difficult to walk to.

I knew not to trust the placid appearance of such places. A trap could be waiting for us at such an obvious marker of safety. For now, however, there was our answer as to how to slip into Konstantin's garden.

I regretted leaving our only moonstone at the feet of that hermit in Oghir's cellar. Soundless, heatless, dim light would have been perfect. Theodoulos seemed to recognize that as well, judging by the low groan he allowed himself when I asked if he had another. I didn't know the spell to bring heat and light to Alanus' sword, but such a trick would be little more than an invitation to attack.

A leadswine snorted and turned over in his sleep not an arm's span from Theodoulos. The man scurried to me, practically hiding himself behind my back—as if that'd do any good if the creature did wake.

"Stay right behind me," I told him, regardless.

The frantic little nod that followed took a great deal out of him. I tapped his shoulder twice and turned back to the cave.

Once I stepped inside, the sound muffled as if I'd closed a door on the world behind me. The evening wind that'd been wailing through the grass faded to a whistle. Gone were the cricket songs and the shrieks of owls.

There could be nothing in this stretch of stone, I reminded myself. It was too dark to see into the shadows. Too quiet to discern if there was something sleeping nearby. If there was, it could be as few as one or as many as twenty. I could not know. All I could do was focus on the light seeping in from the opposite side of the cave.

My every step ruptured the contained silence. Theodoulos' steps echoed as if he'd stomped in full plate into a marble temple. I had to stop him, hold him still for a breath as newer, quieter sounds began to fill my ears. There was that same low rattle of metal and muscle.

There were leadswine dozing inside the cave as well. The breathing did not sound dense, but in the dark, even one other boar was an added risk. The wet heat of their breath moistened my sides. My concern was stepping on a wayward tail and waking the whole drove. Theodoulos slipped out of my grip. His shoulder sank low as he crouched. When he next moved, I could still hear him, but it was a far more silent affair than before. I forced myself to slow as well. My boots scraped just above the floor.

As with any pressing task that must be done with care, I felt as if we made less progress the deeper we went. That sliver of light we walked toward never seemed to grow much larger. About halfway, I wondered if we *would* make it to the other side before morning. I couldn't hasten my steps and risk the noise waking these things. I couldn't take wider strides for fear of knocking into a beast obscured by shadow. So, achingly slowly, we crept closer and closer.

When I could feel the warm breeze from the exit, I allowed myself to feel some relief. A familiar scent, rich and ripe, perfumed the air—trees. I heard the creak and rustle as they swayed against each other.

I stepped close enough to see the moon bathe an orchard in pale blue light. The topmost leaves took on a faint white glow, while the lowest were cast in the deepest black. Fruits grew plump on their branches. Better yet, I saw a way down, a dirt mound that'd been smoothed out and well-trodden. Though it might have been narrow for the leadswine, two men could walk abreast with no fear of slipping down into the gloomy, formless dark on either side.

The angle of the rocks beyond the path suggested a sheer drop that I was sure we would not be able to scale if we tried. I could not relay as much to Theodoulos, who still was making his way through the darkness.

I waited at the entrance, but he did not emerge. His steps had faded as well. There were only the snores of the leadswine. Theodoulos must have stopped somewhere in the mouth of the cave. I peered into the pitch black, knowing it would do me no good to charge in after him. If I had to creep my way back into the tunnel in search of him, we might as well flee back to the highlands for all the time we would lose. I waved grandly toward the exit, sure he would be able to see me. Still, I heard no steps. Had he frozen?

Then, a sudden, shrieking whistle pierced the air. The sound bounced off the tunnels. It came to a musical halt when a hollowed arrow bounced against the stone wall and clattered at my feet. The sound repeated, a second whistling arrow shot past me, as loud as noonday bells.

A squeal erupted from the darkness. Then a chorus. I heard the clamor of many hooves scraping against stone—coming toward me.

I stood there too long, staring into the black as if I did not know what had just happened. As if I expected Theodoulos to be surprised as well. Of course he was not; he was hidden in the cave, out of harm's way.

If I died here, and the leadswine disposed of me, would I wake with my mind intact? I'd been unsteady since Alanus. In all likelihood, I would return as a beast. I would not give Theodoulos or the pigs that satisfaction.

I sprinted out of the tunnel, onto the dirt mound. Behind me, I heard the thud of hooves charging. They knocked tusks, half-goring one another in their haste to reach me. And they *would* reach me.

At once, I threw myself off the side of the mound, feeling the sharp drop of earth under my heel. The squeals did not follow as I plummeted into the black pit below.

THE MAZE

A bitter cackle escaped from my throat. I could not think why. Nothing was funny. Yet, there I sat, feeling a fit of giggles convulse through me. Then it stopped. I clenched my fist. My jaw locked. Every part of me flexed, curled into itself like a spider.

I sat at the bottom of a void in a cloud of dust. The canopy of stars overhead was the only break in the pure darkness surrounding me.

There was no fortress of men. No hint of one. No Venroth. Nothing but the bottom of a ravine and leadswine squealing overhead.

What cause did I have to be—I should have expected exactly what had happened. I'd had no reason to think for a moment—I'd seen it in his eyes. A coward's eyes.

Theodoulos had sent me to the dogs before. Why was this different?

It wasn't.

It wasn't even a surprise. He'd been terrified of me since Diethell. Before that. Elioth. This had been his revenge.

I had allowed it.

I had watched it happen.

Like a pathetic old man who couldn't stand to be—

I screamed.

Not in pain. Not with tears. I was not upset, only flushed with so *much* that I had to kick it, shake it out of me. My fist pounded down on the ground. My feet stomped as if I could crack the earth beneath them. Then it was over. My voice was hoarse, and I was spent.

I'll kill him, I decided. *I'll find my way out, and I'll kill him.*

I sagged against dirt and stone. I felt the bloom of a new rash on my back. The scabs crusting on my skin itched. The stars faded into a pallid sky, and I envied them. Untouchable, indifferent voyeurs.

In the morning, two walls on either side of me, stretched out like a hall, revealed themselves. Smoothed lines of dried mud towered to triple my height. With a steep, unclimbable dirt mound behind me, forward was my only means of progress. I drew my sword. I listened for steps, for squeals, for the intake of another's breath. But I was alone. Nevertheless, I walked carefully until I reached the end of the corridor.

At the end, the path split. A vine-cracked corridor ran to my left and to the right. They were equal in length, but I could see the shadows cast over a darkened, abrupt ending on the right. The left must have extended into a longer hallway after a turn.

I passed two more corridors before reaching the end of the left passage. Those corridors branched into further corridors. At the end of the left hall, my choices were the same obscure options: left or right.

A maze. I'd fallen into a maze.

I could almost laugh at the absurdity. Of course, the winding corridors never brought me where I thought they would. I could see High Mound's outer wall when I looked up at the right angle to orient myself, but that proved useless. I lost sight of the wall by midday when I tried to push further in toward the fortress, and yet, the next night, I found myself sitting close enough for it to darken my skyline.

The next day, I tried to walk toward the wall, following the sun as my guide from east to west. Again, by that next night, I felt as if I'd made no progress. Trying to make one turn only was difficult when there were so *many* halls I had to ignore and remember. On occasion, I could swear I was repeating corridors, walking back on paths I'd seen before, watching the same flowers bloom, stepping on the same patches of grass, only to turn and realize I was nowhere near where I'd thought.

It didn't help that this land was distractingly lush. Purple, pink, and yellow flowers sprouted in thick clusters. Waxy, thick leaves I'd never seen before spread like a canopy over my head. Plump fruits rotted sweetly on the ground and hung from overburdened branches of juvenile trees. Thick-capped mushrooms spotted the floor. Birds sang and flashed their bright feathers. I saw nests everywhere. Bees, butterflies, and ants thrived—all the tiny creatures of nature that conform to no limits marked by men.

By the fifth day, I'd grown used to strolling through narrow gardens. Short of scaling the vines—which would never support me—there was nothing to do but move forward . . . *any way forward.*

The pattern was hypnotic. Walk until dark, doff my armor, sit, and light a fire if I had tinder. Who would care or see now? When the fire burns out, wait for dawn. When dawn comes, don my armor and walk.

On occasion, I found a tiny marvel: a corridor where only yellow flowers bloomed, a crack in the wall that leaked a continuous stream of water, one entire section overgrown with thick bramble. Blackbirds congregated between the thorns of that last one. There was almost a prideful satisfaction to it, like discovering a monument in a sprawling city. So, when I came across a person, I thought of it as a novelty before I remembered to be alarmed.

The corridor looked no different from the others, just as lush with greenery, pelted by the mid-morning sun. I was halfway through, deciding which new path to follow, when he jumped out from a mass of ivy. He held an arming sword in front of him, and I raised my hands instead of fumbling for my own weapon. I felt no need to when I saw he only wore a linen shirt and trousers. His gloves were tucked into his belt, and a helmet and breastplate were stacked by his feet. He was more than the sword's length from me and content to keep that distance.

If he did swing, I could grab the sword with my gauntleted hand and rip it from him. But he didn't move.

The look in his dark eyes was still somewhat glazed over. He tilted his head, tossing aside a cascade of black hair that'd been twisted into thick locs. From his disheveled appearance, I guessed I must have caught him sleeping.

"Ah! Well, you're new," he said wryly. His dark eyes squinted, examining my hands and visor as if he could peer through it. "Adryane? Is that you?"

Everyone in this country was so talkative, yet I was often on the *opposite* end of the sword. Now that I wasn't, I found myself at a loss. It was tempting to close the distance and disarm him. Before I could, however, he continued.

"No. You're not from the Green, I'm sure. Outlander? Beven?"

I had not heard anyone refer to me as a countryman of Bevelon in decades. My eyes drifted back down to his armor. A red cotton surcoat lay folded neatly beside his helmet. A weather-dulled insignia of a feathered snake had been stitched into the top left and bottom right quarters. His boots were of good make and used but not worn.

Scars on his neck and forearms marked a long resume of battles hard survived, if not won. His face was marked with one scar across his forehead, but his eyes were both intact. His left hand, however, was missing two fingers, and his grip did not quite seem to accommodate the loss. I peered back to the gloves. He hadn't stitched the flaps to the palm—a recent amputation.

A chain and heavy medallion rested just on his sternum. A bird and the three burning roses were engraved on its face. Like Elioth's, his had been defaced.

"You're one of the fifty-six."

He tilted his chin up, defiant and regal. He was a knight, if not a noble. "And how do you guess that?"

"Your kind is easy to catch unawares," I bluffed.

"Yet, I'm the one holding a sword."

"I could change that if I wanted. It's no difficult feat to strip an already unarmored man."

"Ah, well." He looked almost sheepishly to his armor, rightfully embarrassed by the distance. "Hasn't been much point in wearing it, especially in this heat. You're the first man I've seen in months. Don't think I need it to put you in your place."

"Of course," I humored, but I wondered if I should be wary of him. His feet were in the right position. His hold was steady. If he was quick enough, he could close the distance between us and try to put me on the defense. But he had no armor and I did. We could make this ugly quickly.

I did not have the desire for a scrap. Not now when I'd rather be making my way out of the maze. I lowered my hands, letting them hang below the pommel of my blade.

"It is hot. I'll see myself to a shaded corridor."

I took two steps back and then turned fully. Part of me wished to take the helmet off so I wouldn't have to turn to catch him attacking from behind, but he did not.

Just before I rounded the corner, he called, "Keep on your way, stranger! I'll stick to mine!"

That could have been the end of it. It should have been the end of it.

Two days later, I had been walking through a corridor when he stepped out from one of the middle pathways. He had strapped on his armor, but the helmet still hung from his belt. Wordlessly, we both turned and walked straight back the way we had come.

The third time, I was the stationary one. My helmet rested under my arm, as I wanted to breathe in the scent and take in the color of the flowers before me—and escape the damn heat. I'd found a bushel of pink azaleas.

My mother used to grow them in pots in the courtyard. Four or five anemic branches would flower in the scorching summer under her care. My sons removed them after her death. Here, a brilliant mass taller than me had stretched out over half the width of the hall.

The knight caught me but did not leave. We both seemed to realize we had circled too close to ever truly lose each other in this maze again.

"Admiring the garden?" he prodded from a cautious distance.

"Nothing else to do, is there?"

"I suppose introductions are in order. This is our third meeting, after all. Unless some other Beven is here with the same armor."

"Go on, then," I told him. I'd spoken my name more in these few weeks—months?—than I had in sixty years. I was still not keen to be the first to do it.

He obliged. "I am Sir Peregrine Rostam of Cilean. It's well . . . it was a beautiful place once, just north of the highlands, but the Blight took it. I did, however, venture beyond the wall in my youth to answer a summons calling for bannermen for my mother's cousin's house. I served Lady Raphaelle of Stormsumnt in the Salt Wars, if that means anything to you."

Indeed it did. It was the fourth generation after my time, when all my lords were dead and we were assigned as dogs to their pups. The Salt Wars came from us salting our enemy's fields to make them useless to their soldiers—a counterproductive measure when we were all trying to avoid famine. The wars of earth and water arose from those campaigns.

I looked at him again, at his clipped ear, at the scar on his chin. A piece of taut skin disappeared under his collar where the start of a scar knotted his flesh. He'd been on a battlefield; I could be certain of that.

"Sir Darl of Rugenmont," I announced. "Knight in service to Lord Forestier at the Bear's Stronghold."

We would have been on opposite sides in the Salt Wars. He seemed to realize this as well. A small, exhausted laugh escaped him. "I didn't cut off a piece of you twenty-three decades ago, did I?"

A bare pang of relief seized me when he said that because he was smiling when he asked. Because he recognized my liege. Because he wasn't lying.

"There's a chance," I said, with no shortage of mirth. "I may have taken that clip off your ear."

He reached up as if he needed to touch the scarred flesh to remember it. "No. That one was the fault of a night of heavy drinking and overconfidence. A friend of mine wanted to demonstrate his skill with a throwing knife to the duke hosting us. I nearly lost an eye that night."

"His aim was that terrible?"

He leaned forward to draw me into a joke. "My temper was when he clipped me. I almost threw him out a window."

"He almost had an enthralling experience," I said. "There's nothing quite like the weightlessness before the plummet."

"I'm sure he resents me for denying him."

The knight turned back to the flowers, and I followed his lead. I stared at sun-caked mud, waiting for this sense of ease to seep out of me. He could be on me with a sword at any time, and I couldn't let myself forget that.

"Do you ever wonder about that?" he asked. "If someone you've forgotten a century ago still remembers you? Still hates you and is hunting you?"

"I don't often leave people with a grudge behind me," I said flatly, vaguely aware Minthisha made that declaration a lie, more than aware that I was still hunting Lambskin. Theodoulos . . . I would remedy that. I knew I should go, but I couldn't bring myself to move.

"Oh, don't be so serious now!" Color assaulted the corner of my eye. I jumped back too late. A soft blow landed against my cheek, and petals rained down my shirt. The man had thrown a stem of azaleas at me. "You were just proving to be fun. I haven't seen an outlander since the Thyremoine. When did you arrive?"

"Not long ago. When did you trap yourself in this maze?"

"Not long ago," he echoed. He stared at the flowers, but I could see his lip quirk and his shoulders shake. He smiled a lot. His head rolled lazily against the wall to meet my gaze. "Darl, was it?"

"Yes . . . Peregrine?"

"Perin if you're impatient."

"What are you doing here, Perin?"

"News of the fifty-six has gotten to you. I assume you know the gist. Since exile, a few brothers and I regrouped to try and establish a little outpost."

I balked. Had the weasel told the truth? "There was a Venroth with you?"

"Venroth? Gaheris?" Peregrine frowned. "No. He was a . . . perhaps not a good man, but a dutiful one. A loyalist. He died the night before the exile. He was a guard to the tower, and a defector killed him to break in and kidnap some of the children. Where did you hear about him?"

"Your country is full of gossips."

"I suppose there's plenty to run into out there. Heard anything about the Reconstructionists?"

"Unless you go by a more colorful name, no."

"I don't know what you've heard about our larger exile, but my men weren't interested in power, just what was right. We accepted exile as a consequence of disloyalty and were happy to settle away from the Green's shadow. Of course, settling has been the trick. Half the land's been ravaged by the Blight and the parts that aren't have damned leadswine sniffing every corner. We thought it'd be easier to come up to High Mound to deal with them directly.

"Since Konstantin's the sorcerer who's given life to the pigs, we thought it would be better to meet him in his garden. We were overambitious and scattered into this maze when he proved to be too much for us."

"This is Konstantin's garden?" I asked. I knew Theodoulos had told me as much, but he'd told me plenty of folk nonsense.

"Yes."

"The giant?"

"Yes."

"And the leadswine hunt for him and bring their spoils back here."

"I take it you had a different impression of this place?"

"None that matter," I said. "We're trapped all the same, aren't we?"

"Yes, that is the rub. Trapped indefinitely. Unless you, perhaps, have some brilliant means of escape?"

"Find the exit to this maze. Kill Konstantin if he's in the way. Leave."

"I like it, quite Beven, leaving room for improvisation."

I couldn't help but enjoy his little slight against my countrymen. It was warm in its light, familiar sting. "If you're not useless with a sword, maybe we have some cause for cooperation."

Peregrine's smile waned. "I'd call myself an asset. I've seen the gate that bars this place from the inside. It's sealed by giant's magic, and I know its counter. But it's not such a simple effort. I warn you, I came with a band of five men, all skilled knights, and they were crushed into mulch before I could open it. Another three came later; they're also dead."

"Any by your hand?"

I could see in his eyes that he debated lying to me. "Konstantin took the five that were my brothers within the first year. The other three saw a stranger as a meal when they realized they'd be just as trapped as I. I wasn't fair about it. Didn't challenge them to a right of single combat or anything of that nature. I understand if that sours your offer."

On the contrary, the admission was comforting.

"I'll do my best not to hold your allegiance to Stormsumnt against you."

I enjoyed his answering smile far too much—like we shared a secret. He'd throw me into the beast's jaw when the time came. Whether or not we'd seen the same corner of the earth, we'd both lasted long enough to be *here now*. And, if I knew anything about these famous Hallowed Lands, it was that the honest and pure did not survive. In the interim, he might be of use before I would have to push him into the dirt.

The Checkered Knight

During the Salt Wars, king and country still had meaning, but the Deathless were no longer the unified legion it had been in its conception. Those of us who'd survived our original purpose in the defense of the Greater Continent of Tyrmore went our own ways, sought out new lives, served new kings, and made new fortunes. I answered the summons of the great-grandson of the first Lord Forestier I'd groveled to in my youth. Many others just as easily took up arms for men they'd sworn against a lifetime ago. I found myself shoulder to shoulder with strangers.

It was a lonely grouping until another soldier noticed my cloak's colors. "Didn't realize they were letting in Nor'men. Isn't the air too thick for you down here?"

He had a shaved head and an accent from the other side of the little mountain range I came from, but he was Beven. The farther a man is from home, the less such a distance means. He was Deathless, like me, and he asked if I was any good at dice. I told him I wouldn't be playing the backward rules Loplanders like him used. We played draughts on a cloth-patched mat; that game had the same rules on both sides of the mountain. We were friends for decades afterward. Lifetimes. I would even be the last man he dueled.

I hadn't thought of him in decades, and yet, I felt that same pull with Peregrine. There's a terrible kind of magic that weaves itself around certain people, the kind that makes acquaintances feel as if they're decades old.

Echoes of the future are made physical and bind men like steel. It was a dangerous spell.

The knight of the Green could attempt to kill me at any time, and, unlike Theodoulos, he stood a chance. Peregrine had the skill to match me if it came to blows. I could tell that alone from how he watched me the same way I watched him.

But then he would turn to me and ask something so innocent. "Were you at Dianete's Field during the rains?"

And I would grimace at the memory of mud, slippery grass, and incompetent children making calls over their generals. We'd commiserate over nonsense. The long marches through the Erhaven Desert. Winters where we settled in the homes of strange lords. The retold misadventures we'd fine-tuned for years to create the biggest laugh. We didn't speak of the darker memories we wrapped in aloof words, just the good parts.

"How did you know I was Beven?" I asked once.

"The grass braid tied to your belt," he told me. I looked down, almost surprised to see it there. Of course it was there. I'd braided beside Theodoulos on the way here. I hadn't given it a thought until now. "It's for luck, isn't it?"

Grass is the same wherever you go. Weave a piece of home and keep it with you. I had lost the first braid centuries ago. "In a sense."

"We all have little traditions. I always thought those hanging fixtures Raughen men nailed to their doors were a nice thing to do. The Thyremoine said it was odd that we kept flowers and carvings of our families on the hearth mantel."

"When was that?" I asked, thinking of the guard on the Green's wall.

"It was Evarlyn's time, so . . . ninety years ago? Maybe eighty? Five of them came seeking amnesty; they carried a holly branch and laid their swords at the gate. King Evarlyn was hanging any man who so much as whispered treason at the time. Outlanders were turned away in the day and slaughtered at night. It took the damned mandolinist interrupting all the shouting to prompt any real deliberation."

"A musician was posted with the guards?"

"Not posted, but no one stopped him from entertaining. Baseborn men like him were talented jesters. Geocelin the Swamp Toad. You might have had the pleasure of meeting him. He's stationed at the Thousand Hand Wall's gate these days."

We shared a pained grin.

"He was young then, more concerned with being a nuisance than a diplomat. Because of his antics, however, I was able to get a word in. I was one of the few men who'd met Theyremoine before and knew they were not half-reptilian ogres. This was in the early days of the Undead War, you see? Not twenty years since the Ingohelm Massacre."

Not a man in the world hadn't heard of Ingohelm, the first devoured city. Stories of bisected torsos left scattered for the vultures had been a horror, a distant one each fortress had reassured itself was too far to happen to *it*. With time, Ingohelm was only unique in being the first city to fall prey to such violence, and it would be more of a novelty if a city hadn't gone the way of Ingohelm.

"My brothers weren't considering such things. They know most of the world from books, and not ones written to flatter. Blow on them, and they'll bend one way or the other. Weak men like that don't make good knights, and they should not have been entrusted with oversight of so much in those days. Cowards don't belong at the gate."

"Some had conviction, though."

"Conviction."

"I heard any man whose loyalties were divided between their god and king was exiled."

"Ah." Peregrine's jaw worked as he contemplated. "Things were tumultuous before the fifty-six were exiled. A man could serve Evarlyn and Evaline loyally for the greater good with a torn heart. But, upon King

Evaright's death, after his traitorous wife tried to usurp the throne, you had to live by your convictions or accept the new order. Pledging loyalty to Evarund, however, was asking us to pledge to serve a new Green, one I could not tolerate. Only the cowards remained loyal. It's a shame there were so many."

"Do you know anything about a knight named Theodoulos?"

Peregrine shrugged. "Must be the youngest generation. He's one of us? An exile?"

"I don't believe so. He says he's a part of the Green."

"If you spoke with him, and he's outside their walls, I wouldn't count on it. I do pity those boys. It's not about loyalty for them, not in the same way. I know they pledge their lives to the Green all the same, but you can see it in their eyes; they don't believe in it the way we did."

"What did you believe you bound yourself for?"

"And you finally ask." Peregrine smiled as if he'd won a game. "I, myself, am curious about you."

"I'm wondering if your reasons were practical or philosophical," I evaded, somewhat guiltily. I did not want to explain what I was. Theodoulos, Minthisha, and Alanus had found me useful upon learning I was Deathless. I did not want to invite that interest.

"Both, in a sense. But, in my time, Evarwight was king, the world was green, and men who ventured outside our walls took on pacts to survive campaigns as much as they did out of a sense of pious duty. I loved my country. I recognize little of it now, but at the time, I was willing to lay down my life and personhood for it. Now, I see these boys talk about pacts with such reverence. Alanus thought it was ascension. To a child like her, it must seem that way when she's seen so little of the world. Evarund waves it around like it's a reward for loyalty. He's breeding a den of devotees there."

"They can't all be fanatics."

"That's all that's left. The rest were exiled."

"Yet they kept a foreigner? There's a Thyremoin posted as a guard at the Green."

"Damovanor?" Peregrine asked. "He's a Deathless. Exceptions are made for useful beasts, so long as they can be controlled. He was a part of the mercenary company. King Evarlyn made it seem like a favor, though we all knew how desperate he was to reign in dissent. It was an unsteady time when we were first hearing about the decay outside our borders.

"He offered to grant the Theyremoine citizenship and knighthood if they captured strongholds in the Hallowed Lands we'd been struggling against for three decades. It was a suicide mission. Knights of the Green Castle knew it was an impossible request.

"Yet, two years later, they returned with seven heads on pikes—Earl Isolde of Drewent, Inquisitor Badrick Narcourt, Baron Glenmore the Blackheart, Vagrant Kings Javel and Jean, Earl Olivien Tergis of Brighthome, and Consort Lathelous—names now, but dangerous men in those days. The Thyremoine presented the heads and flags of each fortress sacked. They were knighted and sworn to the All-Father with all the ceremony of our most esteemed nobility. Each of them was Deathless."

I listened closely to how he said that word, *Deathless*. There was something bitter there. I wondered if he resented my kind. I resented that it would matter to me if he did.

"So a band of Deathless Thyremoine lives in the Green Castle?"

"It's only Damovanor now." His voice carried less deference then. Peregrine took my silence as a request for explanation. "In Evaright's last years as king, ignorant peasants that'd been strangling each other for decades sought out forces older than the gods. They employed the witches and dug up the deathbeds of the first giants in Lorenial. None of them knew how to make a pact with the Young Gods, so they were seeking the secrets to the giants' long lives. They instead unleashed an evil that corrupted half the Hallowed Lands, including my homeland, and would have extended far into the Old Country.

"Evaright sent the Thyremoine to stop it. Two threats were managed that year: the Blight was contained, and all but one of the Deathless were destroyed."

"How?" The only hand that could destroy a Deathless was another Deathless. Neither water, fire, nor stone could break the pact made between us and Morthia. We were made to be reapers of souls, and our only escape was to be reaped ourselves.

"I don't pretend to understand the foreign magic they used to stop it," Peregrine said, misunderstanding what I had asked. "Somehow, they survived their journey into the Elder Wood during the height of the Blight's corruption. Deathless have unusual limits, and they lasted long enough to do what was necessary. Damovanour won't speak on it, but whatever happened wasn't enough to restore everything to what it was, or else I would have gone back home. The witches are all dead, so perhaps what remains is simply like a burn scar. You can still feel the Blight in the Elder Wood and in the highlands."

Only the witches weren't all dead. But, more importantly, one Thyremoine in particular wasn't dead either, not if the witch was to be believed.

"Luthor's still alive," I said. The witch would not have asked me to kill a dead man.

Peregrine frowned. "Where'd you hear that name?"

"Damovanour mentioned him on the wall," I said. It was a part of a lie, but explaining Minthisha's deal would explain that I was Deathless. If Luthor was one of these five Deathless, Minthisha *needed* me to ensure he met his end. "He said I should duel him."

"Ah, well, I assume you two didn't part on good terms. I suppose it's subject to debate. Deathless are especially durable, and magic cannot extend beyond its caster. Either the Blight was sealed and the effort killed the Thyremoine, or they're still there, holding back a storm that will destroy us all. The damned troubadours find the story of an eternal fight romantic, and that's the one that's caught on when it could be as simple as they killed the hags that were summoning that plague. It makes little difference what caused the Blight to stop. It's been stopped for decades now, and the Thyremoine never returned."

And Minthisha wanted vengeance for her sisters' deaths, perhaps . . . or she had meant what she said when she offered to be free of the servants of the Young Gods.

"They died well. That's all I'll say for certain," he added. "And they'll be remembered so long as the Green carries on."

"That's all a man can ask for," I said out of habit more than belief. My words used to be *for sons and daughters,* and there was a certain pleasant romance to such a notion.

"I remember being in the Salt Wars and afraid no one would find my body," Peregrine mused. "I was far from home. No one would know me if I fell. No one knew me as more than the outlander. I walked past the stone heads that had been weathered to smooth rock. It's terrible to think your body, your life, is no more than space in a ditch. Nothing after."

There are children, I almost said, though that was a false start. I'd outlived my sons. That little wooden horse I'd hidden in the rafters had watched my boys die in their home. They'd never taken the pledge, and they had been guided to the After by Morthia. Their names had died with me.

Orphaned boys pecked through fields of bodies like crows in the shadow of my war camps. I had taken pity on one. When he begged, I gave him bread. I had left out blankets and good shoes for him, and I had let him sneak bowls of stew to his brother. I had paid him for knives and tools he came across, and he was offered a squireship because of me. He had lived because of me.

"Deeds are remembered."

"I envy them that. The Thyremoine have us as their legacy. I'm grateful for that. Not many men can say they *have* a legacy."

I never saw Peregrine eat. Not fingers or bones, at least.

I saw no pouch or chain on his person, but he did stop one day under the shade of a fruit tree and cried out in delight. He shook a branch and brought about a hail of yellow fruit.

"My family home had this tree in the garden, right above a nest of fire ants. When I was a boy, I'd have to climb and pick the best ones. My sisters would catch it in their skirts before they rolled into the river." He took an eager bite and tossed me one. "I used to throw some down and try to hit them. It's good. There may be worms, but that's flavor."

I scowled at the fruit in my palm, baffled by the feel of its skin against my fingertips. The sweet fragrance that wafted from its cracked flesh was no more pleasant than a flower's.

"Why?" I asked. Neither of us needed it.

Peregrine studied his own fruit as if he hadn't considered it. "*Because.* It's easy to forget now that things have withered so thin, but food is still a pleasure. Our pledge allows us to extend the little joys of this life. What did you take yours for?"

"We were called to protect our lands from neighboring invaders." It was not the whole of the truth, but the truth would tell him I was Deathless.

Peregrine's grin widened. "I knew you were older. It's hard to tell now that we're all gray, but I had an inkling. All the old men called it a duty."

"Did your brother's children call your rationale old?" I asked. Peregrine studied me strangely, waiting for me to explain my question. "If you saw the Jillianus wars, you're a second son, at least. They wouldn't have allowed you to pledge to a god or go off on a foreign campaign without heirs."

"No, they would not," he agreed. "I was fourth. It'd be a scandal for the only son of a family as noble as mine to take the pledge and forfeit his fertility before he had a wife and whelps. Of course, that's when lands mattered, long before the Master Physician left and sickness took my grandnephews. Alignment was a *privilege* after that. For only the descendants that showed the most . . . *promise*, we'll call it.

"It's a shame I survived them all. For *them*. For me, I am free to enjoy the fruits of my heresy. Take a bite, Darl. And, for my sake, savor it."

My teeth broke through the skin into the yielding, sweet meat beneath. It was a foreign sensation, one that took many steps to remember. If there was pleasure in it, it was second to the look of satisfaction that lit Peregrine's eyes when I did as he asked.

He didn't ask about me until that evening.

"Were you the only one in your family?" Peregrine unstrapped his armor. His dark eyes reflected the fire's licks of orange flames. "To pledge?"

"I expect so."

"You don't know?"

"My sons refused. No need for them to become monsters."

Peregrine grimaced, "You're a father?"

"My older brother answered a summons meant for me when I was young. He went to war. I married and had children."

Whatever witty remark he had ready faded, and he considered me for a long while.

I expected him to ask more—to pry Mica's name out of me. I *wanted* him to ask me for my story, to take my shame piece by piece. And I was terrified to tell him. Instead, his attention shifted, and he pointed to my hip. "That's not a family heirloom, that sword of yours. Where did you get it?"

I felt my hand drift to the pommel, and it was as if the scalding sunlight of Alanus was back, however briefly, before me. "The House of Oghir," I said with ease.

"Oghir?" Peregrine sat up. "What were you doing there?"

I sought to end this topic quickly. "Bringing an end to an overextended line."

Peregrine smirked. "And how did you know that applied to the House of Oghir?"

It was too playful to be condescending. I would ask the same if he'd come to my homeland.

We both knew I'd be lying if I said I'd sought her out of my own volition. So, I swallowed and told him what I could tolerate. "Theodoulos begged me to kill the Lady Alanus for him. I saw nothing better to do and thought I might win a worthwhile boon from the effort. I was right," I said, drawing the blade to let it flash in the firelight.

"I see . . ." Peregrine watched me instead of the blade. "This Theodoulos . . . he's been your guide in these lands?"

"More a pest that hasn't left my side. He followed me here, stumbling in the dark and squealing like a piglet. He alerted the whole burrow of leadswine to his presence and mine by extension. It'll be miraculous if he survived."

"What were you both doing here?"

"A man I knew from outside may have come here looking for shelter. I went to investigate. Theodoulos was afraid to leave my shadow." There was no need to explain to him the lie the boy had tried on me.

"I hope he's doing alright without you."

"I'm sure he's skittered back across the hills to the Green by now. I may kill him for the trouble he's caused me if he isn't already dead."

"Have pity on the incompetent; they've only just found their legs. That sword had a good smith, if I'm not mistaken. May I?"

He did not hold out his hand in expectation, as if denial would surprise him less. I slipped the plain sword from my belt and offered it to him. Peregrine took it with reverent care. He smiled like a young man handed his first knife, a look of pride and awe illuminating his face.

"Beautiful. Cyrus of Drewent made this. You can tell by the spellwork. He was a brilliant man, far more than his birth. The peasantry squandered his talents on nails and horseshoes in their muddy little village for years. He had the soul of a nobleman. Then, Evaline hanged him on his daughter's wedding night. Hung the bridegroom too."

"Why?"

"He'd been in hiding sometime before that. He was too immoderate. They sought to make an example of him and his family."

"What happened to the bride?" I asked, though I knew how such things went.

"The witches took her." That surprised me a little, both the fate of the girl and how short Peregrine was with the telling. He cleared his throat and presented the sword back to me on both palms. "It's a beautiful piece."

"Show me."

Flames danced along the steel's face. Peregrine went remarkably silent.

"Nobility such as yourself can harness spells, can you not?"

Peregrine nodded. "Yes, but its use comes with a hefty toll. Given that there's only you and me here, I would prefer not to."

"What are the words, then? Of the incantation?"

Peregrine debated for a moment, then stood. He settled himself down beside me. He described a texture to the sword's magic that was as legible on its face as an inscription would be. With a stick, he traced symbols he described as the Elder Language in the dirt and explained the spell's strange, antiquated tongue.

"My tutor was a wasp about pronunciation, though these words were long dead before any of us thought to manipulate them. The Yarim Scholars, after the giants, are supposedly the last who spoke this tongue. So, what does my tutor know of how it *should* be said? I always thought it was more the evocation itself that mattered. This translates to '*Sire of the flame.*'"

"And how did magic words translate to sorcery?"

"With a good deal of care and work. If you possess such a power, Darl, we can practice it after our escape when you come to live in our new settlement."

"A settlement of one, isn't it?"

"Two now." He said it without hesitation. "Plenty more that will come stumbling in every year. I still have friends and other Reconstructionists in the highlands. And there are the outlanders. I have my own world to build with my own hands. That'll be how I'm remembered. You can't say you don't want the same—to be remembered."

He squeezed my shoulder before returning to his side of camp. The curtain of fire dwindled to embers between us as a tangle of many things twisted through me. Many worming, writhing things I'd laid shrouds over long ago.

Unlike Peregrine, I had hoped to uphold my family's pride and honor until my sons could carry it for me. Perhaps they did in their lifetimes. I was not there to see much of it. There was a point where it seemed I returned to that manor just to read the new headstones on the grave plot. The strangers inside had my surname and knew my armor, but they thinned and withered like everything else. My family line had ended with the indignity and obscurity of a peasant's.

I could not even find the stone monuments where their bodies lay. When the armies decayed, it was only Clement and me. Then, I ran through my brother in arms, and I was alone again. When I buried Clement, I buried him with the funeral rites of a man of Bevelon, and he might have been the last man in this world laid to rest in that fashion. Somewhere in the Barrens is a grave marker for the last Deathless I killed, my last true friend, and the next stranger who sees it will think it is only a mound of stones.

THE GIANT

Late in the night, I felt a pain in my gut. A tiny pang roused me from my passive watch of the fire. I waited for it to subside, but it grew. And grew. And grew until I was convinced some small creature had trapped itself inside of me and was trying to pull the walls of my body together and gnaw its way out.

I stripped out of my gambeson, hoping the shed layers might relieve me. It did not. This thing, like a plant with gnarled roots, spread and twisted tighter. My skin was unmarred. Old scars were puckered in the same place they had been before. Still, the pain grew. Poison?

The fruit. I saw through Peregrine's design: kill me with a local toxin and cut the pieces he needed off of me. The scavenger. The *rat*. He slept without armor—dreaming in blissful peace as I withered in agony. I refused to allow him such an easy victory. I leapt across the fire and pinned Peregrine beneath me. I grabbed a fistful of his shirt and disarmed him in quick succession.

His eyes burst open just as my sword met his neck.

"What did you give me?" I hissed.

"Darl?"

I shook him by the collar. His fingers scratched at the dirt, tearing little ruts into the earth. Finding no purchase, his hands slid to his sides and fumbled for a weapon. He'd find none. I'd pinned his sword beneath my foot and tossed his knife aside. When he realized that, his bare hands shot up and grabbed my fist.

I pressed Alanus' blade down until I could feel him swallow against the steel. The skin broke. His head fell back, and he breathed out a deep sigh, relaxing under me. It was not submission, but a pause. Plenty of men had taken my measure over the years, but to see it from Peregrine when I held a knife to his throat was as insulting as it was amusing. The sheer ego of him.

"Get off me, Darl," he said, his tone low and serious. *That* was the voice of a man who could kill me. "I'll make you regret it if you don't."

"The fruit. There was poison laced in it. Tell me what it is, and I'll let you live."

Peregrine huffed. I thought he'd admit to his cowardice, but then, he did something worse. Without warning, he released my fist. One hand grabbed the sword on his neck by the blade; the other clasped around the back of my head. He pushed up, and my grip on the sword faltered—and then soft lips met mine, and his breath was on my cheek.

A thousand other kisses, softer, smoother, shyer echoed in my mind. The lusts of my early youth, the conquests of my knighthood, and the obligations of my marriage trampled over me like a procession of ghosts that gasped and moaned.

Suddenly, I was on my back, and Peregrine was kneeling over me. My breath came fast, angry, flushed. My skin felt the sharp bite of the cold air; already it mourned the loss of warm skin.

"What have you been doing these past centuries?" Peregrine gasped. It was then I realized he'd wrested my sword from me. The blade's point now sat on my sternum, hot blood dripping from its edge where it'd slit his hands. "Ring the sixteen bells! You're hungry, you fool!"

He released Alanus' sword and relaxed, sitting back on top of me. "I think I finally understand you—why you're so dour, why you're so eager for a fight. You're *starving*, Darl."

"That's your fault!"

"Mine? On the contrary, you starved yourself. You're a man so thirsty you've forgotten you're parched. Oh, my friend. A life without passion—life is music, it's poetry, it's song and sex and food and laughter and you—you haven't had a taste of anything but violence to make you feel alive in all these years?"

"You don't know what I've had!"

That was the wrong thing to say. His lips curled into a smirk, and he leaned forward, lying flat so we were chest to chest. He braced his arms on either side of me. His nose brushed mine. Lower, he shifted, grinding his hips against mine in such a way as to make us both gasp.

"I know what you haven't," he smirked.

I shoved him off me, and he tumbled back like an acrobat. I recovered my sword and raised it to him, as if the threat of steel could keep him at bay. "I should kill you."

"You should *thank* me. Do tell me, Darl: you're going to kill me, then kill Konstantin, then find that worm Theodoulos and kill him too. For good measure, you can clear out the entire Green Castle, and then you'll have done it. You've rid the world of us all. What'll be left?"

"That's all this bargain is. You dream of settlements and newcomers. From where? The lands beyond these walls are ash. There are no new persons that will carry beyond us and our patrons."

"You're talking like a dead man, Darl."

I hated how he said that, like he was schooling a young boy on the obvious. My arms dropped, the sword heavy in my grip. I would cut myself continuing this absurd threat before I harmed him. Peregrine clasped me on the shoulder as if this were some harmless squabble.

"We're still breathing. Nothing extends beyond us, but that does not mean we lie still and grow moss like stone. The old world is dying, but we are not dead—here." Peregrine reached to his hip and tossed something to me. I caught that same fruit that had started this. He slapped my shoulder and sat back. "When we escape this place, you'll be master gardener in our settlement. Keeping you away from provisions, I think, would prove deadly. You'll be in charge of pruning and all that nonsense."

"And what'll you be doing?"

"Ruling, of course."

I shoved him, and he laughed. While I ate, he wrapped his hand with a tearing from his shirt. I could see he had pouches that could have stored flesh. He did not reach into them, only binding the cuts without so much as a salve.

"You should take your communion. I won't look if it's such a private thing."

"No. No need to fuss."

"I'm not. You'll need your hands to be of use to me."

"I don't have any left," he said with an unsteady laugh. Quickly, he added, "I'm not starved, of course, but no reason to strain myself."

"What do you need?" I offered.

The words spilled from my tongue but clotted the air once they were spoken. Blood hammered in my ears. Peregrine watched me as if he wanted to discover some deception. When he found none, a heavy breath stuttered its way out of him.

"No, Darl. Thank you, but no."

"It—" I bit my tongue. It was a presumptuous thing to offer. "If you change your mind . . ."

"Thank you," he said shortly.

I sat back and wiped my sword clean of his blood, then continued to run the ragged cloth along it until dawn light seeped into the cavernous maze.

◆

I had not expected things to be the same the next morning, but I had not expected them to be so easy either. Peregrine quipped I must have felt exceptionally miserable if I had taken both watches. He slapped my back, warned me not to fall asleep standing.

Whatever resentment we could have harbored for one another for threats or humiliation had dissolved and left behind a clean foundation. A kind of ease came over us, as if something rusted over and clogged had been scraped clean.

"Do you know how to garden?" he asked.

My mother had kept a personal one in the courtyard and liked to tend to it with a steady devotion. I had wanted to plant peppers with my sons the way my mother had with me, but I hadn't had the opportunity. What little I retained could help me raise a few basic herbs. I told Peregrine as much, but we still planned lines and lines of plant beds that would be seeded in the walls of his new settlement.

"Trial and error would be fine enough teachers," he insisted, and we had plenty of time to learn.

Peregrine had a whole street planned; a garden house, a chicken coop, and a great hall would come first. We'd build and restore a half-ruined fortress that the Thyremoine had sacked in Evarlyn's name. He knew how many trees we'd need to fell, where he'd collect them from, and how they would stack. Having raised a few houses in my town when I was a young man, I had my own input, which would be imperfect until I could see the state of this crumpled little settlement he described.

And it seemed that we could have gone on for much longer if the exit had not suddenly been sprung upon us. We turned one corner and fell into silence, seeing the wide, light-flushed gap where the walls parted ways for a line of lush, green trees.

I looked behind us and took a step back as if we'd come to the wrong place entirely. This was what we should have been hoping for. Yet, I couldn't help but feel as if it'd come too soon.

The maze parted like the unclenched fist of a great beast, releasing us into the vulnerable forest. It was dark out there. The trees had grown tall, thick-trunked, and dense. They'd been spaced in their youth but had since outgrown their beds and tangled. The roots of one tree would strangle the other in time, and the tallest leaves would cast deadly shade on the others. The procession of a war that would span decades was taking place before us. At first, we were skittish children, toeing out into the open, one hand to the wall, as if it could curl around and protect us from danger.

Fearful or not, we could not go back. The maze, though tempting, could not serve as our eternal refuge. Peregrine would starve without a communion. But with the most to lose, he still lingered at the gate. I smothered my hesitations and stepped out first.

When Peregrine followed, he kept close to my side, shrinking into himself as if he hoped to disappear into my shadow. We walked in silence through the trees with the maze's wall always within sight. Though we were in an orchard, we felt exposed. Rows and rows of trunks that stood like pillars to an endless hall. If there was something here—this giant or his leadswine—we would be easy to spot.

It was not long before we reached a second wall that jutted out perpendicular to the maze. This one had been constructed from square-cut stone instead of smoothed from the earth. At a glance, I could tell a skilled craftsman had shaped its face. Each stone locked into place with no crack or uneven pattern to the facing. It was far more elegant than the clay maze.

"Who made this?" I asked, feeling along its face.

"Konstantin, I'd assume."

"I thought giants couldn't use tools."

"Who said that? The door will be only a half-mile from here," Peregrine said sharply. "We should hurry."

His expression was pinched as he surveyed the orchard again.

"Where did it happen?"

"In the field," Peregrine said, nodding distractedly to the line of trees that extended to our horizon. "I expended most of my reserves trying to open the door, but I hadn't been prepared. I heard them behind me.

Konstantin swung his arm down, and that was all. He'd grabbed one of them, lifted him to his mouth, and just . . . They were good men. Now, they're the bedding for the orchard."

"How long has it been since you've eaten?" I asked.

The sweet rot of the apples wafted their taste in the air. If only the replenishment of his soul could be as simple as reaping the wasted harvest. I half-wished there was a leadswine about, dragging in a victim we could scavenge from like vultures to take the communion Peregrine needed.

He leveled me with a pointed look. "I have enough to do it, Darl. I know what's required this time. I won't ask that of you when I don't need it."

"I'd rather lose an eye or a patch of skin now if it means we avoid the giant altogether."

"We will avoid it," Peregrine said. "He toils in the sun all day and sleeps like a stone at night. He will hardly have time to wake before we're free."

We followed along the wall until the orchard ended. The grass field Peregrine spoke of was here. It extended for a short while before it was closed by another, distant tree line.

The land directly in front of the wall had been tilled. The smell of fresh earth and iron struck us. And a figure not five hundred yards away, slow and silent, tended to the soil.

The giant was as tall as four men. His legs were as thick as a man's torso, ending in flat, stumpy feet. The skin on his head and face was thick, hairless, but wrinkled. He was crouched low to the earth, inspecting a row of budding plants with mud-caked fingertips as thick as a dog's snout. When he turned in our direction, I caught a glimpse of his eyes—enormous and blue as the sky.

I had expected him to be larger. I had pictured a being so massive the divots in his shoulder blades would one day become the hills and mountains. Konstantin resembled a tree more than a mountain. When he walked, he did so bent over, leaning on a broken, dried tree trunk for support.

He moved slowly when he knelt and slower still to rise. A great creak, like the snapping of many branches, followed his labored movements. Though he was enormous and his body rattled with the chips of old age, he didn't speak, nor sigh, nor whistle. I hardly heard him breathe. A squeal from the distance interrupted his silent work.

We watched Konstantin stomp up the orchard to meet the leadswine. Peregrine and I hid ourselves in the orchard, though the pigs did not wander far into the field. They stayed a near league away, at the edge of that walkway I'd fallen from. From a distance, we could not see the exchange but heard the clash of tusks as they fought over the giant's prize.

Konstantin returned with a torso swinging from one fist like a plucked chicken. The remnants of the man had been crushed by his armor, the chest pieces and helmet nearly flattened in their rusting glory. Peregrine's hand tightened around my arm. When Konstantin tossed the man into a mound of dirt, rot, and weeds and began to churn, he looked away. The sharp snap of bones made his shuddering breath stop.

I pulled him deeper into the trees. Exposed as it was, it felt safer than staying within earshot of that creature. We walked up and down the orchard to soothe his restlessness until night set in.

We waited longer for the giant to bed down. Konstantin attended to every sapling in his path with a patient delicacy. When he was finally finished, he uncurled from his hunched posture and took in the night sky like a child, mouth agog and head tilted back. He swayed like an old oak and toppled down onto the open field with his eyes set on the stars. He fell asleep not ten yards from Peregrine and I, yet we could not quite tell. In the right circumstances, his prone form could have been mistaken for a hill. He did not snore, nor breathe deeply, nor make any sound that would alert a creature of his presence until it was too close.

Peregrine and I toed into the field with our shoulders pressed to the stone wall, unwilling to delve any further into the giant's range than required. Standing in the open, before the giant's gate, my mind was not on the giant resting behind us but on Peregrine. He traced along the stone for some rune or marking he needed for his magic trick. The gate was not a traditional fixture of hinges or chains. Instead, a patterned group of brighter stones, as abstract to me as the enchantment on Alanus' sword, was identified by Peregrine.

His lips moved soundlessly as he mouthed invisible words from left to right. He stopped, having made some discovery that satisfied him.

"This," he said, gesturing to a segment of stone three feet above our heads. "I have to start here. Darl, the spell will be taxing. Do not interrupt me. Do not touch me or move me if I don't respond. If you hear leadswine, or if the giant stirs, run. It should not take so long, but . . ." His forehead creased and his jaw locked. "This will be our only opportunity." He spoke as if he were afraid to disappoint me.

I should have quelled whatever anxieties he had with words. Yet, I could conjure none. I pulled my gloves from my belt and began to strap on the bracers that likewise hung from my belt. "We'd best be suited, then."

Peregrine tried to tie back his locs with a strip of leather. His hands shook so much that he couldn't quite secure the knot. I swatted him away and tied it back for him.

"Keep your helmet on. For outside," I told him. "When the way is open, we'll have the leadswine to worry us."

He reached up and rapped the side of my own helmet with his gloved knuckles. The cross-guard went slightly askew.

"You should find yourself a proper helmet." He strapped on his gauntlets and laid his great sword before him. "Protect your best feature, Darl. Can't have you getting scratched up."

"Darlington."

"Hm?"

"Darlington Ezia Maumont Lavereaux of Rugenmont. For when your ridiculous settlement starts taking a census."

Peregrine's terrified expression broke into something more mischievous. "Suits you."

"If I fall, leave me where I lie," I told him. "Don't try to collect me. *Run.*"

It felt important to give him permission. He winked and lowered the visor of his helmet. Two stars ascended on both sides to his forehead. An engraved feathered snake speared up the middle of his visor.

Peregrine laid both palms flat on the stone. At first, it seemed like his enchantment was nothing more than a slow whisper, almost melodic in tempo.

He kept his eyes straight ahead as if he could peer through the stone. I had almost grown accustomed to his muttering, blending it with the chirp of crickets, when he spoke a little louder. The words of his incantation took on an urgent speed, his whispers crackling in the air. I knew not what he said, but he repeated some strange phrase until it felt like noise.

Then something *changed*. It was like a wave that burst from where he touched the stone and rippled outward. There was no flicker of light. No cool breeze on my neck. No ripe odor in my nose. No metallic taste on my tongue. A sense beyond those of the body stirred inside of me. And I was not the only one that felt it.

Then came a deep groan that shook the earth. The black hill that had been the shadowed giant had woken. I looked back at Peregrine; still muttering, forehead pressed against the wall, palms flat.

The ground shuddered. The giant approached. I drew Alanus' sword and stepped into the field. Grass grazed my hip, but it only brushed this giant's ankle. The closer he came, the less like a man he looked.

His face was as gnarled and knotted as the base of a mulberry. Mud flaked from his skin like cracked bark. He smelled like blood and the earth. When he pulled back a single fist, a creak like the twisting of trees in heavy winds sounded from his body.

When the fist hurtled down toward me, it was slower than I expected. I had jumped away and safely brought up my sword before he touched the ground. But the force of it when he did! The might of the blow cracked the earth beneath us. My knees buckled inward, surprised by the sudden strain. When he raised his fist a second time, I had to scurry away to keep from being knocked over again.

I ran like a rat between his legs, slapping my blade against his ankle. I tried to cut the flesh, but I did not have enough force to break through skin as tough as leather. So, I ran and I whistled, drawing the giant's attention toward me. Konstantin turned, his pale, blue eyes eerily dull and clouded.

Standing across from each other in that grand field, I felt like a mouse armed with a needle. I would not kill him. We both knew this. But I did not need to. I only needed to be the only mouse he noticed creeping out from his walls.

It was a game of distraction, like goading a bull in the ring. The giant was no beast, but he was not a man of complicated thought. If that were the case, he'd have noticed my clear attempts at distraction as I whistled and waved my arms. I circled him, never quite attempting to cut, only to draw him to me. Whatever Peregrine's spell was, I could see it working, stones shifting, trees shaking, but I could not discern how close it was to completion.

I thought that might be fine if this was the pace of the giant. When Konstantin crouched low and swung like a child, I could dodge his clumsy fists. However, I kept having to dart in close to him to keep his focus on me as the rumbling of the wall grew louder. Though I was quick, a single miscalculation would be enough to trap me between his feet or in the path of his hand.

And when it happened, the worst part was I could see it coming. I'd darted to his ankle to avoid his fist, and he kicked out violently. Just a toe caught me, but it had been enough. I was flat on my back before I could feel the impact, gulping my breaths. My ribs kept pushing against metal; my plackart had been crushed inward.

I scrambled to undo the buckle at my shoulders to remove my chest piece. My lungs burned. I could feel the ground shake with the giant's steps; he would be upon me at any moment. I saw his shadow. I smelled the dried earth on his skin. I fumbled with the clasp, freeing the strap on my shoulder, then the one at my waist. I gulped shallow breaths as I tore at the next buckle. Konstantin was at my feet—and then he was lumbering past me.

He hobbled toward a growing split in his garden wall. The stones were pushing outwards, restacking themselves like blocks. Peregrine was on both knees, hands on the floor, still muttering his strange words as the giant approached.

Don't let him die.

I was free of my plate and running. Alanus' sword was in my hand in the wrong grip, but it seemed not to matter so long as I had it. I was faster than I'd ever been, shouting, screaming, making any noise to warn Peregrine—to goad the giant—anything.

The ground shook. Konstantin raised his fists to the sky. I passed under the shadow of the giant, and then I was there, at Peregrine's side, and then I had him by the shoulders and shoved him back. I turned in time to see a fist the size of a carriage barreling toward me.

It happened with too much force to be painful. I was aware of wind on my skin and weightlessness. Then I stopped. My back and my helmet snapped against the wall.

There was nothing for a bit. Then an uncomfortable throbbing. The helmet had gone askew. The nosepiece cut into my cheek. My first instinct was not to rise but to wonder what it would feel like to be bitten in half. Would I come back if he swallowed me? I'd never been eaten whole before.

I thought of Alanus and her impenetrable skin. I'd assumed I was doomed to eternity as the last Deathless and here lay before me the possibility that I would simply cease to exist if enough of me was picked apart. It made me smile in the drunken way the injured do. Then there was a strong grip digging into my shoulder, bending a snapped collarbone further.

"On your feet, Darl!" shouted Peregrine.

He tugged my arm, but my body was heavy. Peregrine swung my arm around his neck and tried to lift me. I raised my head enough to see Konstantin's eyes glittering like twin stars in the sky.

Peregrine's curses echoed in his helmet. He pulled mine off, and I felt the cool of the night air. My shirt stuck to the hot blood trickling down the back of my neck. I followed the shaking movements of his hands, untying his pouch. "What's your communion, Darl? Come on! Darl! Whom are you pledged to?"

He was searching for flesh. I shook my head.

I tried to explain. I needed to explain, but I couldn't speak.

Peregrine's helmet turned. He muttered something, and I realized how much I disliked his helmet. I couldn't see his eyes. "Stay awake."

And then he was gone. And the sky was black, yet pale in the starlight. A cloud drifted over the moon, and there was a scream that rumbled through my chest like the moan of an old oak. Then there was nothing.

THE DIRGE

When Morthia wrested me from death, it did not feel like a sudden tug into consciousness, but a gentle waking. Cool air stung my cheek. Ants crawled on tall grass, and beetles climbed my knuckles. A fly buzzed by my ear. And then there was the strum of a clever hand on strings and a lilting tune drifting through the air. *A song.*

When was the last time I'd heard music?

A voice, rich and melodic, hummed in place of words to a popular tune. "The Soldier's Goodbye." In ale-sweating halls, the troubadour would close the night with a man's final lament to his sons. We'd stagger out bellowing the chorus or weeping in each other's arms like children.

I did not want to open my eyes. If I kept my eyes closed, I could imagine the soft echo of stone walls and the warmth of a fur draping against my back. Thick beer souring in the air of the only place I was human. The heat of a crowd, red-cheeked and beaming. They did not dream of home; that distant land was the world, a place teeming with strangers who would not understand. I wanted to stay in that tavern and feel alive for just a verse longer.

But the verses did not go on forever. My eyes opened to gray sunlight and a cold dawn. I sat up. My bare hands fisted into the earth and I breathed in the sweetness of the garden air.

Before me sat a mandolinist with a canary-yellow hood. Behind him lay the giant, face down in the grass, dead. The garden had wasted no time reclaiming him. Vines stretched between his fingers and wrapped around his toes. Little budding flowers bloomed white and yellow from his mouth and ears. Had this been the work of hours? Days? Weeks? I could not tell.

How long had I been asleep? Where was—

I cast about, looking into the trees of the orchard, searching the tilled earth for some sign of red and black.

"Sir Deathless!" the yellow canary sang. "Welcome back! How was the bleak and endless After?"

"I'll break your neck if you're not gone when I stand," I warned.

"After I serenaded you in your sleep?" Geocelin asked, plucking a few errant strings on his mandolin. "I don't think you found it so offensive. But forgive me the indulgence. There hasn't been much of an audience to entertain outside of the Green, and those old men didn't like anything but what they heard as boys. I could strangle the next man who asks me for 'The Tin Knight,' I tell you."

I made to stand but had to stop before I could get my feet under me. A sharp pang pierced my chest. I bared my teeth, refusing to wince in front of Geocelin, but my hands fisted into the dirt—fingers clumsier than they should be. Numb. That little parasite had cut them off as I'd dreamt. I'd strangle him with my newly grown fingers once I could stand and my heart stopped spasming like it'd burst.

"Don't go straining yourself, friend. Can't have you keeling over on me again. I don't have the patience for it."

"What are you doing here?" I snarled.

"Playing at caretaker," he said. "They never told us how long this part takes—your resurrection. When they tell stories of your kind in battle, it's all grand acrobatics and the strength of ten thousand men. 'Slit your throat if you see them coming up over the walls,' they told us. The Theremen almost had me believing it. You had me believing it. After this business with the giant, it's good to know bards were liars in your day too."

I lunged at him, but Geocelin darted out of reach. I might have run after him if my head hadn't spun at the sudden rise. My heart writhed like a worm impaled on a fishhook. The sudden weight of this *body* over-whelmed me. I sank to my knees.

"Trouble catching your breath?" Geocelin asked.

The mischief in his smirk was too self-satisfied. I wanted to deny him the pleasure of my admission, but he already knew exactly why I couldn't get to my feet. "You cut out my heart."

He frowned, like a boy realizing his toy was broken. "I thought your kind renewed when you came back from death."

"I know when something's been cut out," I hissed.

"Don't snarl at me. I only took my fee. Fingers have nothing to do with breathing. Noble Rostam was the one who dug your heart out of your chest."

My breath shook at the mention of Peregrine. How long had this vermin been following me? Even now, he loomed over me like a vulture. Peregrine should have kept him off of me. He would have stopped this thief from picking at my corpse as I drifted with Morthia.

"Where is he?" I asked.

"Dead."

"Liar."

"You didn't see him on the other side with you? Perhaps not. I don't know exactly where men like Peregrine Rostam go." Geocelin said the name with contempt. Those lips stretched again into his thin, false smile. "I can only hope it's cold and dark for all eternity."

The slick glee he displayed couldn't be true. The troubadour wanted to torment me for the sake of provocation. In spite of that, there was a pain in my chest that was no use to the vulture but would be vital for a Heartless. Peregrine had hidden his patron in the maze, perhaps not out of shame but for fear of losing my trust. There was only one way to feed his patron, and he didn't know—he *couldn't have known* about me. He must have thought I was dead, taken my heart, and left me behind unknowingly. That was the truth of it.

Peregrine had survived. He had been right beside me before I'd died. Konstantin lay slain in the field. Peregrine had been victorious. He'd survived since the Salt Wars, and there was no possible way he would have given up on his life now. "He took his communion."

Geocelin's long fingers strummed a few notes to fill the silence. "I thought he would. He looked like he was thinking of doing so when he dragged himself to you. I think he expected you to be dead when he cut into your chest, but you gasped your last when he drove in the knife, and he started crying. He didn't know you were a Deathless, did he?"

"What would that matter?"

Geocelin pressed his lips together and looked past me to the damned orchard.

Life has its myriad cruelties. The worst of them are the ones that happen without grandeur. There's no great cry before a moment of bravery, no resounding clash of steel that shakes the earth, no rattle of spears or the sobs of brothers. There is an end so small that it goes unnoticed, swept away like dust in the wind. There is no release. There is only the sudden, blunt awareness that something has been lost, and it cannot be brought back.

I curled my fist into the grass, feeling the numbness of my fingertips, and turned. The orchard was vibrant and green in the sunlight. Broken apples ripened in the shade, and the leaves fluttered together in a great whisper of air. He lay there with his back to one of the trees, my heart in his hands, uneaten. Was it so peaceful when he had died?

I laughed. What else was there to do? Immortality was a consistent teacher, yet I refused to learn. My father had been no loss, but my brother had been a humiliation. I had buried my mother; that had been expected. My wife was a stranger in a veil when they laid her down, and by then I'd had others to replace her for decades. It was my sons that should have been my lesson. They had not been boys in their mounds, but old men with wrinkled hands and white hair, and I'd wept as if they'd been born still in my hands. I had outlived everyone. That was the way of things. I was the beginning and the end. I was my own eternity.

Peregrine was wrong. I was not a man starved. I was full. Bloated. I'd eaten my fill and a thousand others', and I was still here. I would always be here to bury those who should have been burying me.

"When I was a boy," Geocelin said suddenly, "I told myself things would be better when men like him finally died and let the rest of us go about our lives." He crouched close to the corpse to gaze upon it. His yellow liripipe trailed behind him like a beast's tail. "Now, here he is dead, and the rest of us . . ."

My first instinct was to throw him to the ground and break a few of his teeth under my fist. If I could have moved, I would have scorched him with all my rage. But my heart spasmed, and forced me to watch the canary's smile turn to a strained clamp of teeth. I watched him bow his head in supplication and dig his nails into his arm. It was not mourning or grief on his face, but there was a pain coursing through him that shook like a sob.

I sat back, reminded of my place. What did I think I was doing in this land of strangers and giving them one ounce of my grief? There were centuries behind me. I knew what monsters we all were. I had seen kings stripped and hung from rafters with only their crowns. Great walls toppled and crushed the citizens they guarded. Women lay in mass graves with broken nails and split skirts. People died every day without cause or spectacle, and I had seen it all before.

Why did I want to bury Peregrine, a man no better than a stranger to me? I'd met and killed countless like him before, yet I wanted to dig every little insect out of his skin, to push back his hair, to lay him down in a bed of dirt with a sword wrapped in his hands. I wanted there to be some dignity to this routine, a ritual or a marker to remember him. I wanted someone to remember the last few days I'd had with him, but I didn't remember him the way Geocelin did.

The last man I'd buried I had killed, a Loplander Beven named Clement who had cheated at dice and sang so prettily. Somewhere in the barren country, there was a mound of stones to mark his grave, but no one would know his name. Give this land a decade, maybe two, and the same would happen here. The world would change, and I would be the only one left to remember how it had been.

"It's time we moved along," Geocelin said.

I couldn't understand him. Where should I move along to? How would it be much different than here?

Why not sit and watch the beetles burrow into Peregrine's neck or the flies lay their eggs in his cheeks? There seemed to be no point to anything else. All these squabbles of the fifty-six and the Green would burn themselves out like a melting wax candle and snuff out to nothing in half a century. Theodoulos would be eaten by the pack of wolves he could not contest. Scavengers like Geocelin would consume their friends and then themselves. The witch would strip everyone's corpse bone by bone. I would outlast them all. There was no need to concern myself with a world that would not outlast me.

"Come now," the canary said. "I think we've both had enough of this gloom."

"Leave me be," I told him.

"Well, I can't have that."

"Why?" I sneered.

"Don't think I've grown sentimental, Sir Deathless. I'm paid to act as your shadow. The longer you linger, the longer I linger, and I don't care to linger *here*."

"You were told to follow me?" I repeated numbly.

"Yes."

"For how long?"

Geocelin shrugged. "As long as I'm paid to."

He didn't seem like the type to wonder why, which left only one relevant question. "Is it the Green or the witch?" I asked.

That earned an impressed little pause from him. "You've caught on to how things are here." Someone had designs for me.

"Which one?"

"You'll have to come with me to find out."

"Or I could mount your head on a pike and enjoy my solitude."

Geocelin whistled, and, suddenly, an arrow burst from the trees, grazing past the tip of my nose. "You'll find my friends disagree with that arrangement."

The arrow had come from the orchard. The archer hid himself well among the shadows and the apples. Unlike last time, I hadn't the faintest guess where he was. There was nothing to see but Geocelin, the mud, and the rotting giant.

"Is this a threat?"

"An understanding."

On a different day, I might have fought him for the pleasure of it. I might have taken my chances running down his pack until I had them all lined up in a grave or I was gutted under those same trees. On that day, I stood and walked on sluggish feet to the carcass of Konstantin.

Skin blistered and blackened where the burning sword had cut. Muscle had been split and cauterized in one stroke. Peregrine had slashed off the giant's fingers and torn deep into the meat of his legs. Alanus' sword lay discarded in the grass only a few steps away, its face bloodied and abandoned after it'd served its purpose.

I cut out one of the giant's eyes and tied it to my sword belt. For how impressive it had been in the night, holding it now, it was no bigger than an apple and not much heavier wrapped in cloth. I thought of going back to Peregrine's body and taking some piece of him with me, a scrap of fabric, a lock of hair. Maybe I would fold it in cloth and tie it around my neck.

Such fantasies lasted only a breath. His death was no more special than the thousands that had come before and the hundreds left to come after.

Geocelin and I walked out of the garden without any ceremony. We passed fields of gold where leadswine were lying in the sun. They smelled like iron and carrion. Their still forms buzzed with clouds of flies so thick around their muscled hides that it was only by the occasional pulse of the insects that I realized their bodies must be breathing, or mimicking it, as they rotted in place.

"They haven't moved since Konstantin's death," Geocelin told me. "The flies flocked to them like open sores. Give them a month, maybe, and they'll be nothing but bones and wrought iron."

At night, Geocelin whistled and hooted into the darkness to speak with those hidden friends of his. I counted perhaps two distinct directions, but I could not guess their numbers. Despite being surrounded, they were not the reason I felt unsettled. Their interest in me, unlike the last time, felt impersonal. They were not wolves out for a hunt, but shepherds. Geocelin slept ten yards away from me with a knife in his hand, and a ghost in the shadows hummed to signal his presence and attention on me.

One of them knew an old marching tune I'd often heard on campaign and no doubt chose it to mock me. Stars glided across the sky with the bitter echo of a time striking right up against my mind. Clement and Peregrine's ghosts wouldn't leave me as those war camps danced in the air.

We returned to the lowlands where the Green Castle sat comfortably on the horizon. When Geocelin veered down a byway through the southern woods, I knew we'd be meeting the witch.

However, we did not go to the swamp. We arrived, instead, at a small clearing where the blackened bones of a hamlet now stood. A modest collection of ten or twelve houses had been put to the torch and abandoned years ago. Roofs had collapsed, leaving only the stone foundations to mark most of them. Little vegetable gardens were overrun with choking ivy.

There was a dead yew, gnarled and deep-rooted, that had been burned black in the middle of this homestead. In another life, it might have been a place of gathering and honor. Children would climb on its low, sloping branches. Young men and women would wear garlands of the flowering nettles in the spring. Now, singed ropes hung from cracked branches. Below were the bones.

I imagined the terrible display one dark night. Bodies kicking as men dragged them by the neck behind their trotting horses. Gleeful laughs as they were raised and dropped and raised again. Then the fire. The screams.

Geocelin tossed a handful of wild buttercups to the base of the knotted tree as we passed. The act was too quick to be a performance, as ritualistic as handing Amivia her bread before entering a temple. He took us beyond the gallows branches to a slanted shack just outside the hamlet's borders.

A mark of white ash circled its low fencing. Bird bones hung from the trees, tied with twine into symbols I did not know. Carved stones lined a puny herb garden. A ruby hung above the front door, with two familiar hairpins stuck into the dirt on the walkway to it. Before Geocelin could approach, we heard voices around the back of the house. I grimaced, recognizing the first.

"I am begging on hand and knee!" Theodoulos whined.

Geocelin and I rounded the house to see him standing just outside the back garden. The boy was leaning over the small property fence, hands clenched on the wood until his knuckles were pale. Minthisha lounged on a stool on the opposite side with her cloak hung up on the door and her wild curls free about her shoulders. She darned a shirt by the feel of her fingers, head up, blindfold secured.

"I've laid those men to rest, boy. They're not to be disturbed. I have what I have to trade, and nothing more. If you're so pressed for armor, why not go off and find another fortress to storm? Play at soldier for a bit longer?"

"Have I not done what you asked?" Theodoulos balked. He waved about in a grand display that was juvenile even for him. "I brought you the flowers. I chalked the homesteads. I collected the bones."

"And you have the gall to come back here every time. Have you learned nothing?"

Theodoulos groaned and flopped onto the fence. "You can't shock me with your riddles, witch. You want me to see the graves and think that men are cruel and the world is evil? I already know it! I don't need to count the bones of the dead to know it. I've wasted a decade out here with you miserable cretins. Now that I have a real opportunity to leave you, you deny me? Why? You can waste the next decade showing me the line of corpses that carpet Evarund's hall, or you can point out one grave for me. If you give me as little as a pauldron, I'll gladly proclaim you dead to the Green. What do you care what happens to their bodies? They weren't a part of your covenant. You hated them! You despise *me*! It benefits us both if you give me Alanus' armor!"

Geocelin covered his mouth beside me. Either Theodoulos' temper or his defiance toward Minthisha amused him to the point of laughter. Minthisha did not so much as slow her stitching as she spoke to the boy. "I'm old, Theodoulos. Gray as a mouse. These wrinkled hands pried armor from the fleshy muscle of thirty young men who rusted in their cages. I laid boys seduced and consumed by Alanus' false promises to rest. I buried her legacy. With that, her armor. There it will stay."

"I could just take your head. They'd grant me a prince's welcome for that."

Minthisha stopped her needlework. The change in demeanor was so sudden that Theodoulos flinched. She approached the fence, stopping with her hand on the hinge of a small gate.

The top of her head only reached his shoulder, but Theodoulos shrank beneath her gaze. "You haven't been on this side of the wall very long, princeling. Let's see you in another decade."

Minthisha's posture straightened, her head tilted a fraction toward Geocelin and me. Theodoulos spotted us over her shoulder. Those eyes, wine red in the afternoon light, looked to my sword and my arms that'd since fallen to my sides.

"You—You're alive! I was looking everywhere for you!" he said, his voice high and reedy. "I—I thought you might have been torn apart by the leadswine!"

"If I was, I would have had you to thank for it," I told him. My words had little bite to them, but he flinched all the same.

"I—I don't know what happened. Venroth should have—"

"Theodoulos, stop."

His hand twitched at his sides, fingering the knife he knew he had no chance of besting me with. Part of me hoped he'd try. I wouldn't stop him. I'd wake in a week or so after they'd scattered and finally be left alone.

"What are you doing here with him?" the witch asked, incredulous. The question, however, wasn't for me.

"I thought I might entertain us both." Geocelin grinned. "Sir Deathless has been eager to reunite with his loyal apprentice."

Theodoulos' first instinct was to anger, but the sight of me terrified him into stammering submission. "I-I didn't—"

"Leave him for dead?" Geocelin goaded. "Now, Theo, this isn't the tower. Batting your lashes doesn't wash the blood off your hands."

The mandolinist enjoyed Theodoulos' discomfort, but I felt no satisfaction. I thought I'd be angry if I ever saw the boy again. I thought I would have to manage my temper to even allow him a breath. In truth, I felt exhaustion and pity more than any kind of hatred. Geocelin wanted the rage of a Deathless. I wanted to pick a direction in the forest and start walking.

"I don't have patience for your plots, Goss, not now," Minthisha said. "What is all this?"

"The Deathless had nowhere else to be. I know the stories. There's no worse plague than an idle Deathless. I thought you'd be eager to set him on your little hunt before I introduced him to the Green."

Theodoulos found his resolve then. "*You*? You're not introducing him to anyone! *I'm* the one who found him!"

Geocelin ignored him and addressed me. "If you wanted to strangle him before we go, I wouldn't tell anyone. You deserve a little satisfaction after what he did to you."

I laid a hand on the canary's chest, and, friends in the shadows or not, Geocelin moved back.

"You brought me here," I said to him. "Find something else to mock, or I will find a better use for that tongue."

"Goss, leave and take your pack with you," the witch said, gesturing vaguely behind herself.

Geocelin set his teeth on top of his lip. A sharp whistle cut through the air. The sound of feet crunching on leaves startled Theodoulos. He cowered behind the witch as flickers of cloaks and hide coats passed through the trees. When they were gone, the boy didn't even have the nerve to look me in the eye.

"You paid him to retrieve me," I said to Minthisha, eager to get on with it.

"No," she sighed. She tapped her three fingers against her fence as if she was puzzling out why as well. "But the Green might have ordered him to do so. It's my good fortune he's been defiant since he was a babe. What happened to you?"

"Killed a giant."

Minthisha hummed, low and unmoved. "If you're here and staying, perhaps we should revisit our negotiations."

"I'm tired of killing men for the ambitions of others."

Minthisha pursed her lips. "What ambition? Do you think I aspired to this merchant's life? I could have hidden away in the woods, far from all of these warring children, content and free. Instead, I'm here, mending shirts and armor to trade for flesh. Do you think I care for steel and bones?"

The sunlight caught the pale scar on her cheek, puckered from stitching. She had not used communion flesh to mend it.

"You wouldn't ask me if you didn't want it. You wouldn't want it if you could take it for yourself. At least the boy knows when to beg."

Theodoulos averted his eyes. Of course he'd hide in his shame now. What good was cruelty against something so cowardly? He couldn't even face me like a man.

"I'm not begging you for anything. I made an offer, and you think me to be much cleverer than I am," she said.

"Not clever. Deceitful. You're hiding why you want him dead."

"And if I said revenge for a personal dishonor?"

"I wouldn't believe you."

The witch could claim benevolence, but I saw her character. She was a shrike with molting feathers, too weak to do more than pick at the corpses left behind. The gray in her hair did not sprout in the blush of innocence. The scars running across her face and the patches on her skin did not belong to a woman who had no will to survive. The dead wanted for nothing. No one lasted this long without feeding off of someone else.

Peregrine had been right to leave the Green and all this squabbling behind. The Hallowed Lands were peopled with gluttonous creatures, greased in the fat that trickled from their toothy grins. The sooner I was rid of them—of all of them—the better.

"Which fortress do you want?" I asked her. "The House of Oghir is empty. Glenmore Hall, perhaps? Which ruin will be yours to call home? The glorious Green? It'll be a pile of rocks in a century. Have you lived long enough to understand that? I have. Tell me. What is yet another death going to do?"

She looked very much like a beast with her teeth bared and that single black eye, dark as beetles' wings, dark as Morthia's realm. "I want you to kill the one man whose death could change this world for the better."

"That's a lie. The man you want dead is the only reason this world is still living. That's it, isn't it? He stopped your coven from destroying it all, and you'll use his death as leverage or a threat or whatever best fits your designs. People will have to listen to you if you can reignite the end of the world. I've collected heads for Morthia. I've cleared the land for him to rule when all of you—all of this—is nothing but dust. I'm his soldier. Not yours, Theodoulos, and not yours, witch. With one man's death, I'll change nothing. I'll save nothing. I've never saved anything."

I drove myself to another fit of laughter with the sheer hilarity of it all. I'd killed Alanus, and I did not know why. I sacked cities, and I did not know why. I disciplined my boys, and I did not know why. What did I think would happen after I killed Lambskin? How many centuries have I spent killing for nothing?

"Theodoulos!" I snapped. The boy jumped to attention. "Let's be off. We've wasted enough time here. Now!"

He scrambled to my side.

"Off to where?" Minthisha asked. "To the Green Castle? You'd pledge to serve the tyrants?"

"What difference does it make? If I pledged to you, I'd be serving the brigands."

"I serve the people."

The scorched houses and cut nooses creaked behind me. "What people?"

THE WAY THINGS WERE AND ARE

Before time stood still, when the soil was rich and the world was gluttonous, there'd been a need for my kind. Lord Forestier rallied his men to answer the king's call to defend Tyrmore.

Barbarians from the west brought their spears and their shields to our countryside. They were coming for our livestock. They were coming for our sons and our daughters. These monstrous men who grew horns from the sides of their heads would dock on our shores, burn our farms, and drink our blood. They kept their tails bound to their hips and cloven hooves hidden in their high boots. These barbarians, who had no language, no culture, and no mercy, were coming, and they were winning.

It was in such an uncertain time that our holy men sought out a pact with a higher power. There were many Old Gods in those days. My father prayed to Wroungemout, the Worm, during the harvest for the seeds of our vassals to take and grow strong. My brother, Mica, went to temple once a week to pay respects to Sibdeot, the Twelve Hands of Ambition. My mother and I consulted with Fuemog the mornings after my father raged. Through faith we found strength.

I was sixteen when my brother was conscripted into the war. Lord Forestier had called upon young, virile men willing to die for the freedom of our lands. I was the second son and unmarried. Forestier rightly asked for me, but Mica insisted he take my place. I was too young, he said. He went in my stead, and dead or lost, he never returned. A decade later, I would follow him, but to a different front. The war I saw was not the one that took him. His war was one of battles between men. I was dragged into the wild to join the beasts.

I was the last of my father's sons, the last Lord of Bevelon after his passing and Mica's conscription. Legally, I had been safe. But I could not hide away in shame while my brother rotted under me.

Holy men divined a greater purpose.

They spoke to the god we did not pray to, the nameless one we begged away each year. The thief that sicced death on the young and prolonged the suffering of the old. He dwelt in the sky where the stars and moon could make no light and in the pits of men's hearts where their evils dwelt dormant. And he had the power to reach through us and slaughter the parasites ravaging our homeland.

We waited in the dark, locked in a cellar and chained to the wall for three days. No food. Water was squeezed into our lips from a rancid bucket once a day. I festered in a cell of ten, stoic and devout. Suffering would yield to strength. Strength would lead to victory. We would survive. We would conquer. We would defend.

Then, the harvest moon was over us, a sickly yellow beaming down on the black fields. We were brought into the night air, our toes curling against frosted grass. Our bodies were anointed with oils. Lavender and poppy pulsed on our skin. A noxious concoction, thick with honey to mask its rancid taste, was pressed to our lips. And then our steps became dreamy, our path a haze in the flat moonlight.

A man in dark robes stood at the base of an altar where Amivia's endless circle of death and rebirth, a snake eternally consuming its tail, lay broken at the base. The nameless god had no icon of his own, only the defacement of another's.

The man in the robes held a serrated knife in one hand, and something squirmed in his palm. A scorpion? A rat? I could not tell. The shadows were too deep that night, the light too sharp. Cold hands cupped my throat, and a wet voice whispered the name of a god into my ear.

I felt no pain when my throat was cut.

I collapsed into the embrace of Morthia, King of the Flies. I woke unattended with seven others. Three lay where they'd fallen, their pact rejected. We, the chosen, thrummed with a hot-blooded thrill; our tongues tasted iron and desired more. Newly alive, we were ravenous and could only think of sating it. We would have torn into each other had the priests not abandoned us beside an enemy's camp. We were naked, barefoot, and armed with the crude instruments left scattered by our masters.

I remember not what happened. I was not a man then.

I recall waking in the morning, feeling a bliss and satisfaction I never knew before in life. The morning sun sang to me as I walked the field of twisted bodies I'd created. The terror and nausea would plague me later. Then, I looked to the north, and the thought of home brought me comfort.

For sons and daughters were our words, and they cradled me on the nights I shivered with blood cooling on my skin.

From that day forward, I was a hound of war. Skirmishes, ambushes, the final push. When violence and pure power tipped the scales, I was the hammer. Sometimes I was lucid for it. Sometimes I fell mid-battle and would wake with renewed hunger, attacking from the flank any man in sight—ally or enemy. We were the Warbreakers: unkillable, unstoppable.

And we won the war for Tyrmore.

And we were still alive.

And we were still hungry.

Tyrmore was free from foreign invaders, but what was our king to do with us now that there were no forts to hold and no cities to sack? War dogs are sent to farms when there is no more use for them. What *could* they do with us? We couldn't die. We didn't starve. We could go days without rest, and we were *restless*.

We were given land and titles and shoved into discreet corners of the world to fight barbarians on the border of our civilized world, from the

White Sea in the East to the western Jillian Coast. We moved often from one front to the next, rotated like cows in a pasture. Too soon, however, there was no one left to subdue. No peasant revolts. No foreign caravans.

On the long nights, I'd trace the stars to home, but I never asked for leave. What would I do there?

Within a few years, the lords who gave us land and titles expired, and we kept on living. Who did we answer to then? The orders of their sons were the commands of soft children with too little experience to respect. Some of us went back to enjoy retirement on whatever novel property we had been given. Others realized their leashes were so rusted they'd break off with a little tension.

And then that little war whispered about from far off crept closer. Great-grandsons of the men who'd commanded us sent out messengers across the world to round up their sires' discarded dogs. Many of us answered not for loyalty but satiation.

For sons and daughters, I said, the words a banal habit.

A new battle was fought for earth and water. We sowed chaos, raided villages, and burnt down castles. This time, however, we were not the only hounds on the field. New gods had long since come into this world and sent out their pawns. Children promised salvation if they only sacrificed a token of the body to their patron had spread like dandelions.

And like us before them, their masters died. The wheat and barley withered with their castles. The water went rancid. What little food did grow was bitter. Within a generation, all that was left was us and our hunger.

There might have been a moment, a year or two, where we could have rebuilt. Where the decay and rot could have been reversed—farms rehabilitated, water cleansed. But there were more things than men in the world now.

The hounds were hungry, and it was easier to eat a meal that didn't bite back. We pillaged our own countryside. We salted our own crops. We raped our own kin.

It wasn't until much, much later that we turned our arms on each other.

I looked behind me one day and realized I did not know the way back home. All that was left was to walk on and see what was ahead. What else could I be expected to do?

Lie down and die?

THE HOMECOMING

Theodoulos was useless for most of the day but docile enough to not be a hindrance. When we were back in the grasslands, and the Green Castle stood less than two miles away, he stopped, shaking with nerves. There was no comfort to be found in the open field or the Green on the horizon. Each new detail seemed to vex him until he was staring at his hands with a kind of awe. "Why am I alive?"

"What good would it do me to kill you?" I asked. I tossed Konstantin's eye to him. He shrieked and let it drop.

Ants crawled in the shadow of the orchard over Peregrine's corpse. Lambskin was lost to the highlands. Here I stood with a boy afraid of his own spoils.

"It's my fault for expecting you to be better, but you'll be of use to me," I told him. "If not, I can always change my mind at the gate."

"I'm sorry," Theodoulos blurted.

"You wouldn't have been if I had died." We both knew it to be the truth.

"It's not a matter of guilt," Theodoulos said. "I know the way of things."

"What is the way of things?"

"I don't pretend to know your Heartless, Sir Darl. But if I knew you were hunting me with little reason . . . I'd want help."

"You think you helped?" No. This was about that night with Diethell. I'd failed the boy and he'd wanted his revenge. What was this nonsense? Betraying me for Lambskin? "You don't know anything."

"I'm not sorry, but I apologize."

He must have thought himself brave. He was standing up to a beast. How quaint. What did I care if he felt remorse or if he couldn't understand his own mistakes? If they ever crossed paths, Lambskin would skin him from toe to nose. Until then, he would imagine some poor victim of circumstance he could save. I put it behind us.

When we arrived at the Green, the same audience awaited us on the wall. Knowing what I knew now about the Thyremoin, I observed the Deathless with a new curiosity. Though his armor was not outdated, I wondered if his woven pattern was one of his own invention or if I would recognize it from the Jillianus Wars. His cloak fluttered between the battlements, but it sparked no memory.

He peered down at us, all but his smile hidden behind his helmet's visor. "Young Theodoulos! Returned from the wilds again, have you? And with a boar!"

"I've come with evidence of my loyalty to my bloodline," Theodoulos announced. He unwrapped the bundle as if it held a newborn babe and raised the giant's glittering blue eye. The Thyremoin whistled. "Tell his exultant Lord Evarund that I've returned with the blood of the Green's enemies and tales of deeds unparalleled!"

Despite his claim to the credit, the Thyremoin was unaffected. "You'll impress me with a cow's eye next, young Theodoulos. Don't think I'll be lenient just because it's a feast day. If that's the best you have, you'll have to wait for the next. Evarund has made his terms for your induction clear, and you will do yourself no favors bringing an outlander in tow."

Induction? So that was the truth of it. Theodoulos, knight of the Green, was not a knight at all. What was he, then?

"Ah! See, Thereman, that's where you misunderstand. This man here," Theodoulos said, "is a part of my deeds unparalleled. I have a Deathless sworn in loyalty to me and only me. Go and tell the Green I wish to pledge his service at the blessing of mine to my All-Father."

I did not miss the clear interest my announcement garnered. The archers on either side of the Thyremoin leaned over the battlements to peer at me.

"What was your name, sir?" the Thyremoin asked me, digging respect out of a trough.

"Sir Darl of Rugenmont."

The Thyremoin's tongue danced along his teeth. He left the wall suddenly, and Theodoulos and I were made to wait with the archers. Perhaps an hour passed, or two, but the Thyremoin did not return. Instead there was the call of relayed orders, a loud affirmative, and the click of a heavy metal lock being undone.

Theodoulos grinned like a cat as the gates groaned open. "At last, our just reward!"

"You hardly needed the eye. A collar around my neck would have saved us both the trouble."

Theodoulos turned to me, aghast. "What good is a scythe without a harvest? I've been dishonest with you at times, Darl, but I told you this benefited us both. I could claim your merit all day, but they would turn you away if they thought you hadn't been put to good use. Let's put our grudges behind us. In the end, we never have to see these vile lands again unless we're nostalgic for the view."

Never was too long a time, but I considered his invitation. Another castle and another fall awaited. Why not spend my nights on soft beds, drinking and eating as I pleased until the wolves came through the fence to feast on the lambs?

Men marked with the ascending bird and three burning roses stood at the ready inside the Green; they looked well-fed and clean.

A clotted red heart was clutched in pale hands on some far-off mountain, and it should be nothing to me.

"Darl?" Theodoulos stood before me, one foot toeing under the open threshold.

Let the gates close. Let the world behind me fade.

Our reception was the quiet, careful affair one might expect for a stranger and a long-suffered burden. Theodoulos beamed like the sun, his bright eyes flashing with pride. He marched unaccompanied along a well-worn route/

The central courtyard was muddy and sparsely peopled. There was a stable, but I could see no horses, no casual games of dice or knucklebones. With fifty-six men exiled, how many were left in the Green? A dozen? Not enough to staff the place. There was no one to chop the firewood, no one tending to the garden plot, and no one sweeping.

We walked up the steps of the great Green Castle to an oak door. Theodoulos opened a smaller wicket embedded in its face. The inside was warm and pleasant to smell from the pine burning on three strong hearth fires. Dozens of coats of arms flooded the hall with color. There was a buzz of conversation, drums, and flutes. I had not seen a crowd so densely packed, nor so many eyes on me, in decades, longer still since they had been giddy and wine-flushed. Someone had brought the news of Theodoulos' return ahead of us.

"Konstantin is slain!"

"The leadswine with him, I hear!"

"What a grand day for the sons of Evarund!"

Men clapped him on the shoulder. They asked him to show them the giant's eye. They cheered at the sight of our gory prize.

Curious looks were tossed my way, but I, for the most part, was treated akin to a hunting hound: something to be wary of outside the shadow of its master. The mob and I were both the better for it. I had not been around such an abundance of men since the Splintered Hills.

My hand twitched by my sword; they had not asked us to surrender our arms. Wearing steel in the reception hall would have been an insult to a host in anyone's time.

I knew some of the coats of arms the men wore on their tunics from stories in my boyhood: the purple unicorns of the Indomitable Auclairs, the bell and star checker of Laevourt the Just, and the twisted braid of Preu the Wise. Each man slayed monsters in the countryside and saved the peasantry with distinguished brows and noble grace. I did not know if these were those knights' descendants or if they'd taken on the decoration after their admiration for the myth. Many were old and gray, but I doubted any could match mine or Peregrine's years. None were armored, but most carried a sword wrapped in ceremonial canvas. Rings clicked on their fingers, and bare golden chains hung from their necks. They smelled of rosewater and other perfume oils.

As the crowd absorbed Theodoulos, I kept my attention rotating between the strangers out of habit and above and around me at the edifice out of desire. Wealth coated the hall. Above us, murals decorated the heavens. Dead kings, perhaps? Not gods. Each figure appeared uniformly human with two arms and two legs, gazing down with dust-clotted eyes. Their paint was fresher than their backgrounds'. Marble statuettes of children, round-faced and full-lipped, wrestled the severed heads of malformed fiends. Carved liana leaves spiraled down the pillars.

The murals on the walls depicted stories of the great king Evarund and knights slaying mythical beasts on perilous cliffsides. The wonder in the array of colors, the smell of wine, and the sheer *noise* of it all engulfed me. Music echoed in the hall. In one corner, on a small wooden platform, a flautist and a drummer played a lilting melody. They each performed with the practiced indifference of servants set about their task.

And then, just as quickly as it had erupted, a hush fell over the room. A man as gray as I in a servant's dress scurried out from a side door. All eyes turned to him.

He passed under a massive stone altar, climbed a set of steps that led to a raised end of the hall, and stopped at the base of a closed entryway. The page made a gesture with one arm, directing four men who'd stood at attention to reach for the bars holding the doors in place.

The entryway groaned open like the horrible moans of Konstantin. And then, as if a great wave had passed over the hall, each man fell to one knee, hands clasped above them.

From the recesses of the dark, a man hobbled forward. In his youth, he must have been tall, but now he stooped like a crane. He balanced on two legs thick like tree trunks, purple with clotted blood. His skin was wrinkled and ashen gray, his hair white and sparse. When he approached the steps, I felt the urge to go to him and catch him before he fell. At that same time, Theodoulos grabbed my arm and pulled me down with surprising strength.

"Get on one knee," he said. "Do not look him in the eye."

He clasped his hands before him in supplication to his god-king with the rest of the hall.

THE GOD-KING

I stood in a crowded court glittering with sunlight and gold, and there sat a king who claimed to be the All-Father of legends. Evarund was beyond the naivete of boyhood, beyond the boastful pride of an aged man seeking immortality through legacy; he was beyond memory. He looked about the room with eyes so milky they were almost white. His once proud nose drooped with age, and his beard fell in a tangled wisp. I wondered if this shambling corpse could see half of his reception.

He moved to the stone slab I'd mistaken for an altar and collapsed upon it with a belabored gasp. He smacked his lips together, taking one great breath before slumping forward. Kneeling just by his bulbous knee were three men in green brocade robes and hoods that dripped over their faces. Positioned on the step as they were with a tower of shields stacked by their feet, they looked like an opulent counterpart to Minthisha with her tattered cloak and sack of armor.

Evarund wheezed out a long, pained breath, and his hand extended to the hall and then pressed back on his forehead.

"His Grace Evarund asks what children have wandered into his hall seeking shelter," one of the hooded men said. I doubted His Grace Evarund even knew I was there.

Theodoulos swallowed beside me. He squeezed my arm tight and released. The boy then stood, his chest puffed, his chin high with the same confidence he'd feigned for me in Leoric's graveyard.

"My exultant forefather, Evarund, King of the Hallowed Lands! I am Theodoulos, son of Methodius and Sabrin, loyal descendant of the Great Blood. I was sent away to prove my loyalty and worth, and I have come before you today with the spoils of my victories in your name."

All-Father Evarund cast his gaze down at us through watery eyes.

"I come here today to tell you that Leoric, the once Master Physician, traitor to our home, progenitor of the white-capped plague, has been slain and dishonorably laid to rest. Pureblood Alanus Oghir, usurper, disgraced daughter of the noble House of Oghir, traitorous whore of the Steel Skin Army, has been slain and dishonorably laid to rest. Her mercenary forces are disbanded. Her house is emptied."

Evarund did not react to this news.

"The traitor, thief, and abductor Sigmund of Drewent has been slain and dishonorably laid to rest. His amulet is laid before you, reclaimed by your loyal servant. Konstantin, giant of High Mound, master of the leadswine, and ravager of the Gardens, has been slain and dishonorably laid to rest. His eye sits before you as proof."

The All-Father did not so much as tilt his head in the eye's direction, but the three hoods arched up in interest.

"And last," Theodoulos added hastily. "I bring before you, Sir Darl of Rugenmont, knight in service of the king of kings in the age of men's greatest need. A warrior of the unhaunted spirit, pledged loyal to me, I bring before you to pledge to your service, with only the hand of death to reign higher."

I did not know the exact title Theodoulos used, but I'd heard the like over the years when the courts exchanged words about me. *The Endless Man. Patron of the Ultimate God. A man of ultimate sacrifice. Half-man.* "Unhaunted" was a prettier word than "Deathless."

"A chosen hand of the dead gods," the middle hooded man said. "Come forward. Present yourself to His Grace."

On my knees, I looked between the apathetic king and his mouths. The leftmost one spoke next. "His Grace Evarund is pleased with these gifts. He invites the Endless to pledge loyalty and service to him."

"Accept, and all manner of glory in this castle will come to pass upon you," the middle-mouth said. He extended his hand past the formless drapery engulfing him and plucked a single white hair from Evarunds' head. A basin filled with sweet oils, dyes, and spices, a fragrant and extravagant demonstration of wealth, was presented by the leftmost mouth. The single hair was dropped into the bowl. "Wet thine sword and kiss its blade."

I knew this tradition. It had fallen out of fashion when I was a young man: a loyalty pledge to a monarch presenting all the riches he vowed to provide. Gold and silver meant less than cartilage and bone these days. To see this bowl, this hall, draped in all the markers of expense for trade routes that did not exist and craftsmanship that was long lost, felt less like a tradition reignited than theater. It *was* theater, and how many men would let it play on?

The hall looked upon this display with the utmost seriousness. The three mouths beckoned me forward, so I went. My reflection glowered back at me from that pool in their wrinkled hands. To accept would be to act my part in this farcical pageantry.

All this struggle. All this talk of Evarund, and *this* was the All-Father men rebelled against? Of course it wasn't; those three mouths were the All-Father Alanus fled and the fifty-six defied. Perhaps it was the three alone, or a cohort of many, or an alignment of all. I could reject any and all of them. I could walk out those doors and pledge to no false kings.

For what reward? So that I could live out in the open wastelands for another century with no warmth nor comforts? I could smell the wine and the oil. There was music and padded benches and woven clothes. All of it would disintegrate with time, but it existed now, and I could have it if I kissed the offerings of a man long overdue to expire and agreed that the words spoken from three mouths came from one.

In this hall, there was not a man who had not made that bargain. I stood where Peregrine, Geocelin, and Theodoulos once stood. They paraded in the costumes of men of legends and called this skeleton the All-Father to share in the act. Sacrificing comfort for pride's sake earned me nothing. I would not go back to the forest and serve as a hound of the swamps.

I drew the sword of two traitors, Lady Alanus and Steelhand Cyrus, and dipped it into the bowl. Holding the sword in both palms, I knelt and pressed my lips to the cold flat of the iron.

Evarund shifted, and the room fell to that uniform silence, waiting on baited breath for his reception of my capitulation. The god-king sat back and laid his hands on his knees. After a brief hesitation, the mouths proclaimed it a good sign.

"Such gifts of yours are rare, Endless," the middle-mouth said. "Take His Grace's favor, and know you are in the wealth of brotherhood."

The mouths then turned to Theodoulos.

"Welcome home, dear child of this grand house," the rightmost said. The middle-mouth presented the bowl the same as he had with me. Theodoulos drew his own sword and dipped it in the mixture; the point of his blade scraped against coins at the bottom. He quickly withdrew and kissed its flat. "Son of our sons, His Grace grants you not only immortality through your patron but the deserved spoils of our lineage. Rise as a man and take a seat and share in the wealth of brotherhood."

He listened with pride, wine-red eyes glistening. Rosewater dribbled down his chin.

There seemed to be an exhale in the room. The three mouths bent low, holding the basin with one hand each. A man, barrel-chested and wearing the purple unicorns of Auclairs, walked to Evarund's side and clapped once.

"What an auspicious timing fate has for us!" He looped one great arm around Theodoulos and ruffled his curls. The boy warmed to it immediately, beaming under this stranger. "Our young Theodoulos returns to us and becomes a man on our most prosperous feast day! Cooks, light the fires in the kitchen! Butcher, cut fresh meat. Roll in the ale. Strike a tune. On such an occasion as this, we, the sons of Evarund, prosper!"

When I turned, the hall had collected around the basin, men collecting trays of hot spiced wine from golden goblets. The band struck up again, and the room was alive with the clatter of breath and music. Men huddled close to the tables, starting games of dice and cards beside their empty plates. A sudden throng of strangers surrounded me and introduced themselves in quick succession with warmer smiles and thick, soft-pawed hands.

"An outlander, you say? Where from? Prethion? You have that manner about you."

"How did you ever conquer the leadswine!"

"I hope you left Sigmund dangling from a noose after what he did to our daughters."

"Would you say no to a duel, Endless? I'm eager to put my skills to the test against someone who's battled more than their wives on their wedding night!" That last part was to goad the rest of the hall into a makeshift competition.

The press of the crowd sparked the urge in me to retreat.

Theodoulos had wasted no time jumping into the chaos. There were men who looked only a fraction older than him tussling his hair and clapping his back. Someone shoved a cup in his hand and waved them off playfully. He looked so different across the room, among his peers, relaxed and confident. There were none of those averting eyes or strained smiles.

A goblet of wine was passed to me. I felt the residue from another man's fingers around the stem. The tang of cinnamon stung my nose. I stared down at my reflection in the dark liquid, and I marveled at how simple this seemed to be.

Peregrine spoke of enjoying life, but there wasn't anything *out there* to enjoy. The fifty-six had truly thrown their lives away over ceremony and principle. Whatever the old man withering in this hall was, he was not a divine human but an overripe thing that could be ignored. Perhaps he was truly the All-Father from the beginning of time, and perhaps once he fought giants; today he was nothing—a formality. His many children danced around his unseeing form in celebration of a grace they offered themselves.

The band played "The Tin Knight."

I am Sir Fantastik

Victor of great fortune!

My hat is tin—

My sword's a stick—

I'm stomping lands so foreign!

If I bound myself to Evarund, I bound myself to what? To this? Where else was there to go? Back to High Mound, to the orchard where the ants were crawling into and out of the holes in Peregrine's chest?

No.

There was a great stomp of feet and voices, and I was no longer in Evarund's hall. I was in Lord Forestier's as a youth of fourteen, watching my brother's heart swell with pride as he was praised as a promising young successor to our beast of a father. I was in the den of a Ristozin Duke with a half-dozen men who did not speak my language, but all knew this tune. I was in a tavern with allied Thyremoine in our newly sacked city, trading details of our swords. I was the eldest in a hall of youths of twenty and fifty, tripping over changes the next generation had made to the lyrics. I was in the Splintered Hills, humming softly to myself as the flies' wings beat sweet music in the bloodied hall.

I staggered back, watching these men weave together, removed from time. The tapestry of my life shone gold in the fire, stained red and brown, and was so much smaller than I thought it would be.

Theodoulos fabricated a story in which he'd driven his sword through the eye socket of Lady Alanus' helmet to a dense crowd. Knights whose coats of arms I knew from books I read as a boy bore the faces of unremarkable strangers. All around me was boisterous laughter, games, cheer—*noise*.

A buzzing.

A swarm of flies.

And then, a drum beat twice, and those gray pages brought out platters. The smell of glazed meat wafted through the air. Spice came alive over our heads, and dishes I did not recognize were laid on the table. I thought they might be roasts, beef or pork. And then I saw one man reach for a dish and come away with what was unmistakably a finger—and I looked at the platters with renewed awe.

Eyes spilled out from a goblet, strung on a line of twine to resemble grapes. There had to be at least three dozen. Sprigs of greens, roots, and vegetables tried to disguise it, but it all served for the presentation of the meat. Slabs of skin were laid out, crisped and blackened like bacon. Thirty hands must have gone to those fingers that had been molded to mimic a rack of lamb. Hearts, thick as a man's fist, had been garnished with herbs that were quickly picked off in place of the meal.

There was no silence. No prayers spoken, no toasts or demureness to their consumption. They swarmed, pulling their little pieces and retreating before someone else could grab them out of their hands. Grease shone on their fingertips. And they washed it all down with the goblet of rusted brown.

Theodoulos, of all the men in the crowd, was a point of stillness, watching with a perturbed look. He met my eyes across the hall, and I saw teeth that lay in a silver dish before him, shining with a glaze like candied dates. He reached in and took a handful.

None of these men had been cured of their affliction. Their binding to their gods, the flesh they must offer, still took hold of them. All of them ate.

I had seen men rip a piece of skin between their teeth, fighting bloodied for another breath. Acolytes had harvested the eyes from entire villages.

Corpses had been looted. Lines of flesh had been strung up and traded like sausage links. Why did this display, of all things, sicken me? There was so *much*, and it was spiced and dripping with sauce, ready to be indulged in. Was it the aesthetics I despised? Did I want shame and somber conversation?

It felt like gluttony. The hall felt ravenous, but they had to have collected from somewhere to prepare this banquet. From the charred villages we'd walked through to meet Minthisha? From a fallen fortress in the highlands? From any outlander who happened to walk through the Thousand Hands Wall into Geocelin's trap? In my wildest imagination, none of them combined would provide enough.

And where were the others? I had been promised there were humans in the Green, men and women who had not knelt before a holy man and tied themselves in ceremony. There were the mortals who had not cursed themselves with this eternal affliction. The ones who killed none to preserve themselves, who made love and song, and aged as their children did. The ones barred from seeing the ugliness of our nature were not here. Our sins had seeped in with us.

This was a hall of soldiers, and these things that we were supposed to suffer in our silent duty, to swallow in bloodied battles, were laid out on display. Where were the ones with no pact to a god? The ones that had sickly children and sat in cushioned halls? The ones that ate the fruits of this withering earth?

As if some malicious spirit heard my questions, one of the men cried out, specks of meat flying from his mouth. "Where's our entertainment? It is not a feast without the nobility!"

A roar came upon the crowd, their cheer drowning out the music.

A door opened in response. There were others in this castle. Small things with slender arms and legs, collarbones cutting like knives across their bodies, entered the hall. Their gowns were of a fine quality and make, though they hung limply off the children who wore them. The years had sapped the colors and matted their fur trims.

The nobility shuffled on bare feet. Their bodies were bruised, but they were not missing pieces. They had made no pact. Women—*girls* who had barely filled into their bodies. Young men—*boys* who hardly had hair on their chests. The eldest of them was perhaps twenty, but they had not grown into their bones after years with too little food or rest.

They were made to stand on the banquet table. "A poem, children! Give us a poem!"

"Which one of you is the Valliante boy! Which?" one of the knights shouted.

The leanest man raised a shy hand. The knights pounded the table. "He'll tell it well! He will! The Epic of Gwendyre! Go! Boy! Tell it!"

The Valliante swallowed, but it seemed he couldn't speak. He was too fixated on the display of human flesh around him. He looked to the other three in his group, but they were as horrified as he.

"Speak boy!" someone jeered. "Or we'll add you to the table!"

The crowd roared in laughter.

The young Valliante opened his mouth and began to recite the Epic.

"Lo! Hear me speak, great brothers

with the hearts of kings!

Lo! Hear me sing of the deeds

that brought joy eternal to—"

I knew this poem vaguely from a time after the Jillianus Wars. The crowd mouthed the words as they chewed. I watched, mesmerized by the boy's strained recitation. He seemed to relax into the telling within a few meters, and I could not help but smile a touch. But, then, something strange happened.

Villiante had not stammered or floundered his lines. He hadn't had a flat voice or an unnatural tone. But then one of the knights banged on the table and shouted.

"Wrong! That's not how he says it!"

Villiante flinched away. He tried to go on, but the table rattled again.

"Wrong again, boy! Villiante never told it like that!"

It wouldn't matter what the boy did next. His telling was an offense that could not be tolerated.

"Use the other one!" a man said. "You!" He pulled a young woman to stand on top of a scraped silver platter, and she continued where Villiante had ended.

I did not follow her telling because now I watched the boy tossed aside cast about in the room for a sympathetic eye only to find none. The crowd was so dense and violent in its movements that they knocked into one another like bulls brushing shoulders.

The boy was pushed into Theodoulos, who splashed a handful of wine on the floor. From the look on the boy's face, he knew Theodoulos. I saw him speak his name. I saw Theodoulos throw a punch so hard and quick it sent the boy to the ground—and a man took Theodoulos under his arm and cheered.

And I stopped. I stared at the writhing mass of flesh twisting together. This was the greatness of the Green. These were the noble men and women alive and protected in this final bastion: rabbits in a house of wolves.

THE THYREMOIN

I escaped to the ramparts. Cool air kissed my damp collar. I sweated out the poisoned heat of the hall but suffocated all the same. I breathed with my nose pressed into the battlements, my forehead grinding into the stone, as if I could crush myself and be done with it. My chest fluttered with the frail newness of its heart.

Waves of grass swayed against the Green's wall. They whispered over the ghosts that had once tamed them with scythes and seeds. The black canvas holding up the stars stretched out like Morthia's cloak. If I was not satisfied, oblivion was a vault away. I could throw myself off the wall and plummet back into the land of ash and bone. There, in the nothing that was to come, my sensitivities would not be prickled by the inevitable.

I had seen men holding their guts in open stomachs. I had seen boys too young to reach over their mothers' skirts beheaded. All my attachments did not matter in the scope of eternity. Yet it was Villiante's quivering voice that twisted like a knife in my chest, over and over again. Brown eyes like my boys'. The red gash across his cheek. I forced myself to move before I bashed my own skull into the wall. I walked along the parapet.

I expected to run into men dozing at their posts, but there were none. The guard towers were not only empty but abandoned. The bedshelves were stripped, and the dorms lacked the usual nesting human clutter. There was not a stray whetstone, sock, or deck of cards to be found.

There had not been a shortage of men in the feast hall, but it seemed none were to be excluded from the festivities. Was it a matter of rank, tradition, or a result of the news that their nearest enemies had been slain that led them to leave their posts unattended?

It wasn't until I was over the front gate that I met the lone remaining guard. He sat squeezed between the battlements, bundled in his green cloak. He watched nothing in particular as his slender fingers twisted a loose blue ribbon wound around his sword hilt. A rot, sweet and putrid, subtly tainted the air around him.

The Thyremoin looked so much more dour in the shadow of the Green's festivities. He did not turn to face me, but, no doubt, he'd already heard me approaching.

"Blue is for wealth, isn't it?" I asked abruptly. I had not started an introduction in decades. My skills were lacking.

Damovanor rolled his head back against the stone. I could see a spark of recognition as he took note of the braided loop on my hip.

"You've been to my country, Beven?" he asked.

I had met and lived alongside several Thyremoine in the Jillianus Wars. Our languages were different, but we had the same roots from the time of Emperor Jillanoxtus, and that made us brothers. In defense of the legacy of our fathers' fathers, as descendants of that great empire we had never seen, we'd fought together.

"I've met your countrymen before."

"And now you've met the last of them." It was strange to see his eyes, dark as coal and lined with crow's feet. Tiny scars spotted his nose and cheeks. "Blue is protection from evil when wrapped on a sword. Wealth, if it's stitched to one's sash."

Damovanor didn't wear a sash, but there was a red bit of thread tied around his waist and a tiny pouch of *something*.

"I thought I'd met the last of *you* long ago," he continued, referring to something else altogether that bonded us. "I know that rot smell."

"It's the same as yours."

His jaw hinged and flexed. Those black eyes puzzled me out quickly enough.

"Is that why you're so cordial after I spit in your face?" he asked. "Shall I kiss your cheek and call you brother? I had brothers. What am I to do with you?"

I was not naive enough to expect camaraderie, but I had not seen nor spoken to another Deathless since Clement. The Thyremoin had lost his brothers to stop this strange Blight. In the decades since, he'd been as alone as I, hadn't he?

"I'm told your name is Damovanor—"

"Piglet, I am not whom you are seeking," he said abruptly. "You and I have lasted so long alone in the world. It's best to keep it that way, is it not?"

"You're not alone."

"I'm not?" Damovanor shot a glare back at the hall. "Oh, you have a poor idea of company if that is it to you. I'm a man at his post. No better guard than a Deathless that needs neither sleep nor rest—never mind whatever else makes them objectionable."

He looked slyly to the orange cheer pouring out from Evarund's hall.

"A lone guard at night while everyone is drinking to the bottom of their cups?" I tried again.

"They think I'm enough. Even now . . . They're letting you wander around on your own, aren't they?" He swung his legs around, meeting my gaze with a contemptuous smirk. "What dust bowl did you blow in from?"

"Bevelon." He'd deduced that already. "Varlemont."

"Ah. The Little Mountains. You should start walking for them before their Evarund puppet puts you to work. You'll kill men for a better cause outside these walls than you ever will in them."

I did not want it to be this way between us. I could not stand the idea that *he*, of all the men of the Green, would not understand.

"There's nothing out there."

"That's what's so good about it."

He hopped off the battlement and brushed off his cloak. With practiced hands, he secured the ribbon around the hilt of his sword.

"Perhaps I'm being unfair, *brother*," he said. "Come. Let me give you a welcoming gift."

Abruptly, he started down the walkway. When I did not follow, he turned.

"What is it, Beven? Come." He whistled and clapped his hands like he was calling a dog. "Come! It's not far."

I fell into step. If not him, cruel and unpleasant as he was, who was left?

We circled the hall and entered the castle through a smaller door on the fortress' side face. He lit a candle and illuminated our path through narrow walkways and up curved steps to an open courtyard behind the Green's hall. There, he left the candle burning in an alcove and walked on with only the moonlight overhead.

A garden had been attempted here. Puny vegetables peeked out from the wrinkled leaves. Bitter herbs shriveled in their boxes. Damovanor stepped around the shrubs as he guided me to a second tower on the opposite end of the courtyard.

"The nobles tend to the rows every day with my oversight, but the soil's poor and the water's limited. King Evarund has a private garden on the balconies higher up. It fares a little better," Damovanor said. "Lady Alanus, good woman she was, cared for this one. It thrived under her touch, and she taught others the habits of each plant. We could have sustained the whole of the Green if any of them deigned to labor in the gardens in the peasant's districts after her banishment. If not for Sigmund organizing a hunt, they would have starved within the year."

"They have more than enough for a feast day now," I said instead of asking the question. I thought of the unburied bodies piled in the cellar of Leoric's den. There were the skirmishes in the highlands between factions that might have ended with enough bodies to supply what I saw. The witch had dealings in flesh, but they did not extend to here.

"A new tradition, ninety years young, though the choice of meat's changed," he said. Wistfully he turned and, for the first time, seemed interested in me. "Do you remember all the ceremony that used to go into that? Boys would go months on campaign waiting to choose the *right* body. They'd clean up that bloodied prisoner, dress in their best, and pray like men who had a god that listened. You'd think they were kissing the feet of their gods when they swallowed their pieces of flesh."

"I remember," I said. Then the campaigns ended and there were far less good reasons to capture or kill a man and cut off a piece of him.

"Morthia was never like that," Damovanor said.

Morthia did not desire our sacrifices for our own sake. We were tossing slabs of meat behind us, hoping to distract the beast pursuing us. *The hunt begins. Thee or me, Morthia shall feast.*

"Our gods were simpler."

Damovanor huffed. "There's nothing complicated about these ones. They're the same as Morthia, hungry mouths that need to be fed lest they bite into their pledged servants. That's how we lost the village."

He pointed below us to the dilapidated roofs congested in the shadows. Rows and rows of clustered box houses had once formed a little town with its own market square and central well. There was a temple and a graveyard that had since been churned into mounds of overturned dirt. The streets were cluttered with broken furniture and tattered canopies. How many people had lived in that walled town? Two hundred? Three hundred?

"Not all at once," Damovanor said, answering what I did not dare ask. "It started with the bodies in the graveyards. Outlanders like you came along in excess in those days, but we still supplemented shortages with a few plots and made examples when bodies were stolen to be reburied by locals. When we ran out of graves, there were the riots and organized escapes. The recovered ones were executed. Common men hung in that square at sunset, were served at dinner, and were nothing but bones by sunrise."

"And what do you butcher now?"

Damovanor snorted an ugly laugh. He stopped when we reached the base of the opposite tower. He untied a ring of keys from his belt and unlocked the door. He guided us up another, narrower set of steps.

My boots clicked against the stone. I could hear the hushed tones of soft conversation seeping out from locked rooms spiraling up. Damovanor continued wordlessly. He guided us to the top of the stairs, where he stood before a thick oak door. He lit a burning wick. The moment the orange light flickered to life, the noise behind the door went silent. The key turned loudly in the lock. Warm candlelight illuminated the side of his grimace. He stepped back, inviting me to look inside.

I did not understand until I pushed within. In any other circumstance, I might have considered this room to be a luxury. It had once been a king's chambers. The rooms, however, had become overstuffed with cushions, blankets, furs, and rugs. None had been washed in decades, judging by the reeking stench of the air.

In this excess, men and women had nested in the textiles like rats. They'd created pallets from broken chairs and table legs. They'd rolled up tapestries to serve as couches and headrests. Broken shelves had become dividers for beds or bits of territory they'd carved out for themselves. Little figures were folded from pages of old books and dangled from the strings to decorate a small child's tent. The space was not cramped to excess, but it was a set of rooms meant to accommodate far less than the village it housed now.

Men and women dressed in the same finery I had seen downstairs stared at me. The heavy velvets and wools hung limply on their lithe frames. They were all so small and young. Not one of them had a strand of gray in their hair. I saw two women with rounded bellies; one sat beside a young man who might have been the father. Some conglomerated around bookshelves, reading and scribbling with scraps of paper. Another group worked together to weave strings of many colors and thicknesses into a blanket. Most held bowls of black gruel that smelled as pungent as blood sausage but were as wet as a bean stew.

"What is this?" I asked.

Damovanor stepped inside, and I watched as these men in finery recoiled, as if the jewels woven into their dark black curls and clicking on their wrists were little more than decoration.

"Flies and kitchen scraps."

Damovanor pulled a bowl out of one of a noble's hands. They did not resist, and instead shrunk down as if they could disappear into the tapestries and slip from his attention. The knight tossed the bowl to me. Sticky gruel splattered at my feet.

"Oh, you mean the gentry?" he said coyly. "You know what this is."

"Why are you showing them to me?"

He smiled because I already knew.

The Barrens were not a thousand leagues away, crashing like waves against the Thousand Hands Wall. They were here, seeping in through the stone and the mud. The earth was sown with our rot, and all that had survived were these creatures, stored high and away in a castle tower until they were called upon for their final meal. Their dirge sang out in King Evarund's hall.

THE CHILDREN

There is a quiet kind of madness that grips men when they have nothing but phantoms to fight. It heats the chest and takes a firm hand and demands action. There were walls that needed to be torn down. Halls to be burnt. Throats to be slit. And I was here in a tower with chickens in an open cage. A young man in a faded blue robe shrank like a worm into his silks when my attention swung his way.

"Get up," I told him.

Pitiful eyes blinked past me. *Pathetic.* I grabbed his arm and pulled. He stood without a fight. He waited, eyes on the ground, trembling under my touch. I spat, and he cowered.

I turned to the girl next to him.

"Get up!"

She squeaked. "You already—" She stopped, smothering that plea as quickly as it escaped her. She stared unseeing at the floor like the boy—worshiping the flat, formless god of stone tile.

"What?" I snapped. "What? Speak!"

She bit her lip and kept those eyes down. I grabbed her wrist, and she didn't squirm or lash out; she went as still as she could and tried to blink back the tears in her eyes.

"I've already taken the ones I needed for this banquet, she means," Damovanor announced. At the sound of his voice, the nobles burrowed deeper into their coverings like maggots hiding in rotting muscle. "Do you think the hall is sated? Should I take her for dessert?"

All around me were bowed heads, turned away and ready to accept whatever punishment I would give her.

"They can't be here."

"Where else would they be? The Barrens? There's nothing but wolves out there. They'll be devoured in a day."

"They're being devoured *here*."

"Not to extinction. I wouldn't indulge you in taking the girl, for instance. She's still young enough to bear children. You can take the boy. Don't you look at me like that, Piglet, as if you're innocent. Ours is a price that demands life. Your hands smother. Mine prune."

I thought longingly back to that sealed hall in the Splintered Hills, wishing I could return to sleep among the corpses until the end of time. The nobles might as well lie down beside me—skin cracking, clothes crusted with blood, skulls hollowed by blowflies. That end, terrible and abrupt, would be more merciful, and Damovanor knew it.

It was then that I noticed a shadow in the doorway. The scent of blood and oils wafted into the room as a knight of the Green surveyed the scene before him. His curls were tousled from roughhousing, and there was a splattered stain on his sleeve. Theodoulos' wine-dark eyes almost seemed to glow in the dim light.

"Let go of her, Darl," Theodoulos said. "We should be getting back to the feast."

Damovanor cackled. "You followed us all the way up here, boy? Were you feeling nostalgic?"

"Shut up, butcher!" Theodoulos snapped. "Come, Darl. There's no reason to linger here."

He was deliberate in keeping his attention on me alone. Though he acknowledged the girl half-forgotten in my grip, he did not look at her nor any other pitiable noble in the room.

"Darl. *Please.*"

"You heard the little prince," Damovanor said. He sauntered back to the door, nudging it open with a touch. "We'd best be off. No good has ever come from lingering with the stock. Best to leave these poor creatures before they feel too much exertion."

Seeing Damovanor stand above them all, I was struck. I could not walk. I could not move. My hands shook. The weak flutter of my half-grown heart thundered in my ears. When I drew my sword, it excited no screams, nor the scattering of the nobility underfoot. Though some flinched, most watched with lethargic indifference. Damovanor smiled on the opposite side of the room.

"Darl!" Theodoulos snapped as if he was trying to bring a dog to heel. "That's enough! Let's go back to the banquet. Forget this room and whatever lies the Thereman has told you. You're still an outlander. There are things you don't understand."

Damovanor grabbed Theodoulos by the collar of his tabard and threw him into a nest of pillows.

"Sit quietly among your peers, boy," the Thyremoin said. "The men are talking."

He pulled the ring of keys from his hip and slammed the door closed. There was a shift in the air as he began to lock it. The men and women who had done their best to ignore us crept to the farthest walls they could manage while his back was turned. Mothers gathered wide-eyed children and tucked them into the shadowy corners. Older men took hold of curious adolescents and turned them away from the Thyremoin and me. With three clicks, Damovanor locked all three of us in the room, and I knew there was only one way it would unlock again.

"What are you doing, Thereman?" Theodoulos shrieked. A wave of Damovanor's sword quieted him.

"You're goading me," I said.

Damovanor gestured grandly to the room. "Of course I am. My brothers died for these pigs. There's glory in dying to protect the flock. There's nothing in being a swineherd." He unclasped his cloak and folded it neatly before setting it on the floor. "I thought I was the last of us. Perhaps you are a good man, Beven. Perhaps not. I would have hated to play at friendship in either case."

With a slight nod of his head, he tossed his key ring to me. I caught it and understood exactly how he meant for this night to end. This was his gauntlet. If I killed him, the way out was at my fingertips. If he died, retrieving the keys would be as simple as lifting them off my body. If victorious, Damovanor would continue to play loyal guardsman. If he failed . . . He did not care what I did.

He had no assurances and did not bother to request them. The safety of the lives in this room was inconsequential to him, a means to an end. It should not have disgusted me so. I had been willing to do the same not an hour before, hadn't I? The world would end, and I would outlast it all. What happened in between did not matter if we all died in the end. I had already decided to accept luxury while it lasted, and here I was, goaded to rage against it.

"Darl! Throw me the keys!" Theodoulos said. "I can run for the others!"

"Take my quarters and my cloak if it fits you, or don't," Damovanor told me plainly.

"I'll have your head, Thereman!" Theodoulos shouted. "This is a hangable offense. We're not barbarians here! We'll let you dangle and revive for months!"

"Shall I make it formal? Invoke the right of single combat you country-men are so fond of?" Damovanor asked. "Step aside, or I'll gut you first, boy."

Theodoulos turned to me, as if I'd be a voice of reason. His confidence withered when he met my eyes.

"Shall we?" Damovanor asked.

I answered in the only way left to us.

Our exchange happened in the quiet moments before swords touched. A shift of a foot here, a twist of the wrist. Each adjustment was a battle proposed and rejected until we found the positions that suited us best. One of us would be mistaken, of course.

The Thyremoin had good form. I had no doubt he had been an impressive swordsman in his day. We were both Deathless, and the danger such an opponent posed to me was at the forefront of my thoughts, but so was the temptation. Only another Deathless could kill a Deathless. A greedy part of me wanted what Damovanor was begging for: the opportunity to end it all. What *did* we have to look forward to? City after city had fallen apart like castles of sand between our fingertips. The Green would be no different. What good was watching another slow decay? In my weakest moment, I was sure we were both angling to lose. But then I looked down and saw hollow cheeks and reddened fingertips.

It was over in three moves. I clipped him in the thigh, then the throat.

Years without practice might have slowed his hand; I told myself that for both our dignities' sakes. My sword vibrated against his pulse. It was all so fast, but when I felt the cool, euphoric rush of that life slip into me, I cried out, screaming as mortality slipped between my fingers. My sword clattered to the ground.

I had decided to fight in earnest. That didn't fix the thousand drums thrumming inside of me. He'd slipped into Morthia's tight grasp and would be devoured into the eternal peace of blackness, and I stood here, in his blood, in his mess, with a hundred eyes watching. For a moment I had thought—what did I think? That I could not leave these children to Damovanor's care? How would mine be any better? Why would it be my care?

What now?

It was all the worse to look around and see a room of velvet creatures all waiting for me to answer that very question. I started with the lock. When the door opened, I thought some sense of urgency might drive the room to action—to my detriment or benefit—but no one moved. They blinked at me owlishly. Such big, simple eyes.

I ran my fingers along the keys on the ring. From what I'd seen in that banquet hall, this could not be all of them. "How many more rooms are there?" I asked.

"You can't take them!" Theodoulos exclaimed. "Darl! Let's—let's go back to the hall. We can go together and tell them that you've killed a traitor. Evarund will be grateful to you. This can be good for you."

I was taking them, wasn't I? If I wasn't, what had I made such a fuss for?

"Are you going to try to stop me?" I asked.

I was tired the way a man is tired when he can see both horizons of his life as a featureless plain. No light left. Not a shimmer of another star in the vast expanse. Walking either way would be the same as staying in place, yet I could not remain where I was. I had to walk toward *something*, or I would have to *be*.

"I am trying to talk sense into you, Darl," Theodoulos said. "You—you don't understand. You are asking far too much of these simple creatures. They're—they're weak. Delicate. They haven't earned a patron. Out there, they won't do anyone any good. It's better for them here. They're protected. They're fed—*well fed*. They—they had a chance to ascend properly. They couldn't manage it. It was too difficult for them. Some people are meant to live simple lives." He spoke like a hare on the run. "You—you must understand this is the way of things. We each serve the Green in the ways we are most fit—"

"Get out, Theodoulos, or I will kill you here. The rest of you, get up."

They did not. Such wretched creatures, less than the men and women of the Splintered Hills, hardly human at all. There was one close to me, a teenager with hair as thick and black as Theodoulos' and big brown eyes that watched me like I was a god. I took him by the arm, intending to drag him out the door if I had to, when a sudden rush of hands grabbed his arm, his waist, his neck, his hair. A dozen bowed little creatures huddled around him, ready to resist if I tried to take the boy now. There was *something* left in them.

Theodoulos stepped in front of the exit and drew his sword. "I can't allow it."

He must have felt confident holding steel while I only had a set of keys. The fluttering sweetness of Damovanor's passing had me salivating for another fight. I did not try to arm myself. I simply walked up to the boy and grabbed his sword by the point of the blade. My strength overwhelmed his, and I pulled him forward, jamming the keys into his right eye.

He shrieked. I watched him drop and flail about on the carpeted floor like a salted maggot. I wanted to shout at him not to whimper, to face his demise like the knight he pretended to be. I held the point of his own blade on the hollow of his throat in an attempt to stun him into stillness, but he was too panicked to notice. He almost cut himself in all his wriggling.

I drove the point down through his right ankle. His scream turned guttural, and I could swear I heard the faintest whimper of "Theo" from somewhere in the room. Centuries of my life had been endured for this boy to reach manhood. I tossed the sword. Let Theodoulos nurse himself by the fire. Let him soothe his ego drinking deep from the cups of his king, ignoring the aftertaste of blood on his rim.

"Get up or I leave you like him," I announced to the room.

There was a moment when I feared they would not listen. There was a pause as they all seemed to take me in and then the door. Many eyes exchanged wordless conversations. But then, someone stood, and it set them all into action. Like worms coming up from the earth in a rainstorm, they slipped from their camouflage of velvets and silks. They walked in a line down the steps, some holding hands, others carrying small children in their thin arms. I stopped to unlock every door in that tower and emptied each noble pen I found. It was all so easy. A few barked orders and these children, so used to obedience, joined our haphazard parade.

When I was confident the tower was empty, I brought them out to the garden and down one of the old walkways into the abandoned peasant's quarters. The festivities inside the hall were still roaring with music and song. They were in the middle of a chant that required the stomping of feet and the banging of fists on tables.

I did not meet guards outside, but stragglers from the hall who had cut into the fresh night air. They were poor substitutes for the Thyremoin. Disorganized. Inattentive. Insultingly easy to kill with discretion. From there, it was simply a matter of throwing open the gate. The nobles herded themselves most of the way. Names were whispered as separated souls found one another in the dark.

They stumbled on with hands to shoulders, palms to palms, arms looping waists, as if they would lose one another if they did not touch. When I brought them to the open fields, they marveled at the feel of the soft dirt under their shoes and the grass on their skin. Some stopped altogether to gape up at the stars.

It was in the midst of this silence that the spell was broken.

"Where are we going?"

A woman asked me that. She did not look at me for long, as if she regretted reminding me of her presence. Yet, hers was a question that trickled through the mob.

I stood there, voiceless and frozen. I had walked this salted earth for decades in solitude, and never once had I felt so alone and lost. Never once had I looked up at the sky and craved divinity the way I did then. There, in that field, I thought of the Old Gods, the ones who'd ruled my father and mother, who were slaughtered by the Young, who had left me orphaned. No. Worse. I was the child of the one god whose attention I should not want.

I wanted Morthia then. I wanted to feel the *ache* deep inside of me that drove me to hunt. I wanted him to appear before me as a man in black with a dozen false promises and a path to tread. I wanted *someone*, anyone, to tell me what happened next.

I had pulled sheep from the pen and set them in front of the desert. What good did that do besides satisfy my pride? I'd liberated them. Now what? I wanted to cram them back in their pen and lock the door. I wanted them to stand and speak and look after themselves and no longer be my concern.

"Where are we going?" they asked. The question hummed through their ranks.

"We're leaving this place."

"To go where?"

"Move!" I ordered.

"That's not good enough. Where?"

Good enough? They would have been butchered if they'd stayed. Anywhere else was good enough. Never mind my own doubts, how could they have any in me?

I couldn't be angry. I had to keep my temper. These weren't the wandering souls Peregrine had imagined bringing into a new settlement. These were children. But Peregrine was dead, and so were his plans for a haven. There was nowhere to take them.

All I had was his ridiculous dream, an infectious little image of a few cabins and a garden—

And none of it was real.

"Where are we going?"

This had been a pathetic stint. What had I been thinking? There was nowhere to go. There was nothing left. They should turn around and walk right back to the Green. Maybe they'd migrate to the bridge and fall off the edge into the endless fog. What did it matter?

I didn't know what to say, so I walked. To my horror, I heard some following. I thought they might break away when I said nothing, but they carried on, clumsy feet tripping in the dark after me, so I had to choose *somewhere*. I did not go back to the Barrens, where they would be picked apart by vultures and I would waste away with the land. I did not go to Leoric's Temple, where bodies rotted in the shadow of the Young Gods. I did not go to the swamps where the alligators feasted on the carcass of the House of Oghir. I did not go to the Garden, where the apple trees shaded petrified leadswine.

I walked into the charred village, to the overgrown shack where precious gemstones embedded in skulls glittered back at me like teary eyes.

I knocked on a splintered door, and the witch emerged. She scowled at me in the lamplight. There was a single word tempting my lips, a plea I had not asked of anyone in decades. It was not my place to ask as something less than human, so I stood there in the dark and let the witch pick out the figures huddled behind me like goslings.

A shadow passed over her features, and she looked so *old* then. She'd been gray before, but now the lines that'd been no more than traces were deep-cut wrinkles. Split lips flattened to a frown that spread across her whole face. "What have you done?"

"You claim to serve the people."

Minthisha sank against the door, her mouth agape.

That was all the permission I waited for. If I hesitated, I feared she might come to her senses and shut me out. Even as I stepped inside, I did not dare glance behind me to see how many had come. There could be an entire mob trying to cram in behind me as I rearranged the shack. I tossed another log on a small fire the witch had been keeping and pushed a table against the wall. There were three straw-padded beds covered with furs, and by the time I'd inspected one, my little gaggle had crowded inside with me. There were only eight of them, but it still felt like far too many. Their gaunt faces were pinched in worry as they took in the lopsided rafters and the dirt floor.

"It's not a palace," Minthisha said suddenly with a warmth that refused to betray anything other than welcome, "but there are worse things than dust on your pretty feet."

They crowded to the beds of straw that were clearly designed to pen goats and chickens.

In the light, it was easier to tell how gaunt the nobles were, where shoulders jabbed out at sharp angles and bones pushed against skin. They were clean, if a bit musty smelling, like worn carpet. What little skin I could see was invariably bruised. I did not know if that came from their delicacy or a history of being handled.

Minthisha retrieved dead men's clothes from a cache to serve as blankets. She crushed oats, an apple, and a few herbs into a cauldron and boiled it until it was fragrant. There were not enough bowls, so she ladled the concoction into the one for them and had them pass it around. They all watched her as they drank, as if waiting for her to snatch it out of their hands if they broke an unspoken rule.

There was one with a long, doe-like face and dark eyes. She sat last in the huddle, watching me and the door as the others drank their fill. When the bowl came to her, I could see her temptation as she licked her lips, but she refused. Minthisha looked at me as if I had something to do with the girl's distrust.

When the group was settled, the witch ladled out another portion, grabbed a stool, and ushered me outside. She took us out into the garden and sat us down by a chair and table she had left some time before.

"Sit." I obeyed, and she sank down next to me, laying the bowl between us. She did not look at me at first. I knew I had surprised her, but I could see the open shock working through her body. I stared at yellow fruit rinds curling on the table. There was no Peregrine to help the conversation along. "What is this?" she asked at last.

"I . . ." I looked at the gruel on its humble setting and almost balked with hysteria, comparing it to the grand golden plates of flesh and bone in that hall. I thought of men gorging themselves in harsh orange light. I thought of Theodoulos smiling under the arm of a compatriot as he popped a tooth into his mouth and licked the rim of his goblet. I thought of the nobility in their dark, velvet rooms and the black gruel in their stomachs.

"I'll kill Luthor. That's what you've been begging for. You had a plan. I'll help you leverage this Blight nonsense." My voice was *pathetic*, shaken, and small. I cleared my throat. "In exchange, I want you to keep them here, safe from the Green."

Minthisha balked. "The Green? They're from the Green?"

She waved me off when I started to explain.

"You think I can keep them safe? In a woodcutter's cottage with children's bone ornaments scattered about? The Green has known and raised this village already. You stole away with them in the middle of the night, and you think I can protect them? The whole of the Green will be after them!" she hissed.

"Find a way. That's my price. With Luthor dead, you'll have the Hallowed Lands in the palm of your hand, won't you?"

"No! Damn Luthor. Damn our bargain. What have you brought to my doorstep, boy?"

She craned in her seat as if she expected to catch one of the nobles spying out from the cottage window. I wouldn't put it past the doe-faced one. Minthisha groaned and pinched the bridge of her nose.

"They're so *small*." She sounded exhausted.

"They were all like that."

"All?"

"They kept the nobles locked away in rooms—cells. You can take care of them here."

"What would possibly make you think that?" she asked. There was another moment between us, long and ponderous. "Killing is all you're good for, is that it? You poor beast."

"Your coven conjured a plague that nearly annihilated the world. Neither of us has room for righteousness."

"It was not a plague, and it wasn't for leverage." She rubbed a finger along her brow and groaned. "It wouldn't have touched the men and women innocent in all this, the last villagers on the outskirts."

"They're innocent." I nodded to the shack.

"They're not!" It had been an instinct, and one she seemed to regret. At once her lip twitched, and she took a long breath. "All this time . . . I never imagined that. I can disappear with eight. I can hide them in the swamp and leave it at that. Don't concern yourself with Luthor. They'll need a guardian. You and I can manage eight."

For a moment, I thought about lying to her. Yes, these few daring children were all I had to protect. Never mind the lithe frames shivering without a fire. There was no need to think of the ones I'd left exposed to the night air in an open field. But she leveled me with an old and knowing look, and like a boy caught with a broken vase in his hands, the truth spilled out of me.

THE TOWER

In the sallow morning light, the ghostly impressions of bodies in the grass trailed down the valley. They were gone, plucked from existence in less than a night. The wolves had come for the sheep I'd left unattended.

If there had been a high place, then I might have walked straight off of it, falling into an unmarked grave. If we had been ankle-deep in the swamp, I would have waded into the water and let the alligators tear into me. There was no such route for release in the field, only the sudden hollowness that begged my spirit to wonder why it was latched to my body.

"Did they fall into the stars?"

A boy had spoken, one of the nobles, his voice soft and juvenile. I thought it a jest until I turned to see a teenager squinting into the sky without a hint of humor. One of the women beside him, too young to be his mother but close enough in the face to be related, whispered for him to keep quiet.

Minthisha said nothing, though I knew she could only think of what a useless wretch I was.

"Was it all of them?" she asked.

I did not answer.

Minthisha tugged up her hood and walked on with purpose. I followed. The goslings stumbled along just behind me. It was not long before I realized where we were going.

"I'll gut him for this," I said, glowering at the dilapidated guardhouse.

The trip took longer with the eight nobles in our company. They were heavy-footed and unused to walking for prolonged periods. Minthisha and I often slowed our pace for them, but we did not indulge in a rest. It was late afternoon by the time we stepped under the shadow of its stone facing. Fog had come up from the canyon, and the bridge was bathed in diffused, yellow light. The archway where Geocelin sat appeared to end abruptly in a bright void.

The mandolinist played for three birds chittering in the cage beside him, chin tucked into his chest, legs stretched out.

When he spotted me, he waved. "Ah! I wondered when you'd show." He nodded his head to an empty chair that was waiting across from him. "Left something behind, have you?" he asked me, eyes twinkling with mischief.

Geocelin tilted in his chair, catching sight of the children behind me. "Joy . . . you've brought more."

All but the doe-like noble looked to the ground under Geocelin's inspection.

"Where are they, Geocelin?" Minthisha asked.

"Corralled. The way all livestock should be." He winked at the eight. If he wanted to shock them, they offered little reaction in turn.

"You wasted no time harvesting them," I said.

Geocelin balked a laugh. "What else was there to do? Leave them to the animals like you? Yes, I know it was you. The whole of the Green knows it. Evarund's calling for your head, and it's already primed to be quite the hunt."

"You don't know that."

"I do, in fact." Geocelin thumbed the pendant out from around his neck. The king's crest dangled from his fingers. "A few months and you've learned all our secrets? You don't even know the names of the fifty-six. Rest assured, I was not among them. King Evarund's halls are open to me.

"Last night, my friends and I saw the mess you made, so I wandered back into that pigsty to see what damage you had done. To my disappointment, they were all alive and tucked into their debauchery.

"The next morning, they find the Thereman dead in the tower, a few others dead on the grounds, and the rooms empty. That yap, Theodoulos, had plenty to say once he swallowed enough teeth. He wasted no time telling some nonsense about how you bested him in a duel. Tell me, did the boy graze your chin with a spoon?"

"How are they, Geocelin?" asked Minthisha.

"You have no appreciation for the art of good conversation, Minthe," he chided. Geocelin settled back against the birdcage. "They're as good as fowls. You can see them for yourself. They eat and defecate and little else. They hardly speak the crown's tongue."

"But they do speak," Minthisha said.

"So far, they've been expending most of their energy barricading them-selves on the second floor. When they are moved to speak, it's to beg us to keep them hidden from the Green."

"And have you?" I asked.

Geocelin glowered. "Did the dead god make you this insufferable, or is it that rehearsed on your part?"

"Behave, Goss," Minthisha said. "I'd like to see them."

The canary held her gaze. His hesitancy surprised me. Despite his callous language, there was no hiding the tension flexing the line of his jaw. He gestured to the fortress door. "Iliesa's watching them. If they speak at all, it'll be a feat."

"Wuh—"

We all turned to the doe-like noble who had gasped a half-syllable. She wanted something, and for a moment, we thought she might ask for it. But the audience overwhelmed her.

"Yes, girl?" Minthisha asked. "Go on. You can speak here."

"May we see them?" she asked the collar of her dress.

"Of course. Inside, all of you," Minthisha said. The instruction seemed to relieve them, and they quickly filed in with the witch just behind them.

I tried to follow, but Geocelin extended his mandolin by the neck to block my path.

"Where are you going, Sir Darl?" he asked, looking down his nose. "Leave the witch to her business. I won't have you doing any more damage."

"You and every man in that hall feasted on them, and I am responsible for this?"

"You signed their death warrants," Geocelin said. "What a waste. Here I thought the witch would sic you on the lazy cowards. At the very least, I thought you would be less of a coward than your dear Peregrine and kill more than an old man on your way out."

The sting of his taunt flared up in my chest. "I should flatten you against the wall for letting him die."

"Letting him die was a more delicate revenge than that man deserved."

"He never—"

"Never what? Never disgraced himself as a knight? Never used his noble blood to his advantage?" Geocelin's smile was poisonous. You'd find more sympathy in a mask. "Age flatters us all with silver, but we are not treasures. You were here for none of it. In the Green, he was as *noble* as the rest of them."

I hated that he would dare suggest Peregrine could belong in King Evarund's halls. I hated that he could be right. The maze trapped a man who would never lower himself to taste that banquet. But I could not argue that to the canary. He wouldn't hear me, and I wouldn't tolerate the challenge. There was nothing to do but sit in bitter silence.

We waited the way children might, staring at one another, the wall, and our feet as long hours passed and the shadows slipped over us. Now and then, there would be a sound from inside: a bang, a shout, a collective storm of voices, and then nothing.

Finally, Minthisha emerged. She'd pushed her bandage up to expose her remaining eye. Geocelin could not stop staring at it. An uneasy grin crossed his features. "What is that look?"

"Did you feed them?" she asked Geocelin.

"More than they deserve," he said. "It's such a waste."

The few birds in the twine cage were no doubt what he referred to. Minthisha inspected the handful remaining. "We'll need to catch several hundred more to keep them on their feet."

"I wish you luck on your hunt. The sooner they're out of my hands, the better."

"Geocelin."

"Do you want them or not? Would you rather we walk them off the bridge? Save us all the trouble?"

"Don't say that. Not even in jest," Minthisha hissed.

"Should I lie to you? They're as good as corpses already. Damovanor the coward and our ignoble Sir Darl saw to that."

"Why did you bring them here?" I asked. "Why not return them to the castle?"

"Better they die here and now than watch another three generations become little better than pigs."

"You cruel boy," Minthisha said.

"Do you propose we send them back, Minthe? I'll slit their throats myself before I give them to the Green. I will push each and every one of them off the edge of this bridge. Let them fly once in farewell to their fate."

"They're children, Geocelin. Young enough to be your grandsons and granddaughters."

"It's a shame to see youth wasted," Geocelin said. "Your Deathless should have thought of that before—"

"Can you think of nothing else to do but moan?" I interjected.

"There's nothing else *to do*, thanks to you. We can't feed them, so they'll starve within the week. I don't see any holy men among us. We can't bind them in a pact to the Young Gods. Your death god is useless. Minthe's nymph mother of the wood is shriveled to dust. Even if we did pledge them, we'd be breeding competition. Tell me, how do we save them?"

I turned to Minthisha. There was a hand to be played here, power to be leveraged. "There's Luthor," I said.

"No!" Minthisha snapped.

"The Thereman?" Geocelin asked.

I pressed Minthisha. "With him gone, you'd be able to leverage the Blight."

"He *is* the Blight," Minthisha said.

Geocelin cocked his head. His face pinched as he tried to puzzle out her words. "What does that mean?" he asked.

"Gods of hands, hearts, and tongues? You think they're all so different? They all ask for flesh. You shook hands with a god whose face you didn't know."

"What does that—"

"It cut the strings that'd been stretched," Minthisha huffed. "It was a death sentence for you worshippers of flesh. The Elder Wood is as lush and green as it ever was, and not a blade of grass withered where it started in Lorenial."

"How?"

Minthisha sneered at the canary. "Didn't you know, Geocelin? It's a principle of magic taught to children. Your noble masters all know it."

He bared his teeth. "Now is not the time to be clever, Minthe."

"There is something like a door between life and death," she said. "Your bond to a god is a bond to the immaterial world that allows you to bring magic into the material. The thing you call Morthia makes no bargains; it is incapable of grace or favor; it simply *is*. When the first Deathless were made, they sacrificed men's lives, not to a god, but to a door sealed by the displacement of their souls."

She spoke with such a callous dismissal. Without grace or favor, perhaps, but I had been laid at the feet of Morthia too many times; I'd felt his ache burning in me too often for him to be a being without malice. "Perhaps in your country, witch."

"In every country, Deathless. It was old, taxing magic taken from the tombs of giants, and in the decades since, young sorcerers realized they did not have to sacrifice a man's whole body to seal that door. They could hold it closed for some time if they only offered pieces. Your immortality, Geocelin, is conditional. It lasts as long as your communion offering is sufficient. When you reach for magic, it tugs on that string and cracks open that door to draw from the other side. The Blight was not a plague—it simply opened that door."

"You conniving shrew," Geocelin said with a stiff smile. "Then the Theremen came along and he killed all your sisters in Lorenial, and they missed you. And you—you have been waiting to do this for years."

Minthisha frowned. "It's already been done. The door was opened. Cut strings that cannot be remended. I do not know what Luthoron did, but I know he sacrificed his brothers to sabotage us. From what I can guess, he brute-forced a barricade with his body."

"And you wanted me to kill him to release it," I concluded. "Konstantin's leadswine lie petrified. Alanus' soldiers rusted in their armor. Luthoron's seal will break with him."

"And it'd take all of us with it," Geocelin said.

"Goss, I—"

"All these years I thought you had stayed for some good reason beyond my comprehension. Sentimentality. Guilt. No! You wanted a man to clear out the rabble for you. Isn't that the rub, good witch? Your immortality is pure and of the trees, is it not? I debased my soul by taking my pact, but not you. You'd never *stoop*. If we kill Luthor, we hand you the world, good and pure as the day you found it."

"All things must come to an end, Goss."

"So long as they're on your terms."

"I didn't suggest it!" Minthisha hissed. "We have more important concerns now."

Geocelin sneered. "As if that is all there is to it. Don't think I don't know what this is. I remember what it was to live praying to you. Powders and ribbons and flowers all laid at your feet. We begged for scraps of meat, a sip of milk. When you denied us, we thought ourselves unworthy. If you deigned to cure one fever, we were *grateful*! And when soldiers came to burn our homesteads and corral us up to be butchered in those banquets, where were you? Any of your sisters? You'd come back when it was over and fawn and cry with us as if you had suffered the way we had suffered. Now here's a whole castle's worth of worshipers who are afraid of their gods and would be glad to pledge themselves to a new one."

"Goss . . ."

"Tell me I'm wrong, Minthe."

"Which way to Lorenial?" I interrupted.

"You can't be considering this!" Geocelin snapped.

Whatever the truth was behind this magic, if the touch of the Young Gods could be wrested from the soldiers of the Green, then one man's death would be easier than fending off an entire army for decades to come. "We're limited in our options," I said. "We can't feed them or house them for long here. We have nowhere to hide them—"

"Then damn them!" Geocelin said.

"We could send them back to the Green with you, Geocelin," Minthisha said. "You're a loyalist. Tell them you defeated the Deathless that stole them away and are returning them to their home."

"I would rather slit their throats," Geocelin said.

"Then it's Luthor and the Blight," I concluded.

Geocelin ground his teeth so hard I thought they'd crack. "Let's put aside how unwilling my men and I are to die for the witch's self-satisfaction. What if you fail? Darl, I'm sure you have been praying for decades to go out in some noble, glorious death, but put aside the romance. You're a Deathless, and so was Luthor. You're a good killer, but if I can nearly best you, you'll have little chance against the Thereman."

"I wouldn't need him dead," Minthisha said. "If he was distracted, I could try to break the seal myself."

"How would you do that?" Geocelin asked, his tone sharp.

Minthisha did not answer.

"Put your pride aside, you old goats. Success or loss, they'll still be sent back by the time you reach him, and they'll rot locked in those rooms one way or the other. They might even rot outside of captivity, given how useless they are. You, Sir Deathless, stole them away. What keeps this from being an extended execution?"

I'm sure we both hated to admit it, but Geocelin was right. Minthisha turned her attention beyond the shadow of the guardhouse. Fog rolled over the bridge to the barren lands.

Geocelin's canines bit into his lower lip. "A mass exodus? Just as everyone's fighting their way in here."

Minthisha's jaw clicked. She seemed tempted. Perhaps I would be too if I did not know what waited on the other side.

Crossing over felt like severing a tie between myself and the Barrens. Here, green grass flourished and strangers sang. It occurred to me that the witch and the mandolinist could only imagine what the splintered remnants of the world looked like on the other side of the Thousand Hands Wall. From the grim consideration in Minthisha's expression, I was certain they had no inkling.

"No," I said. "They won't last."

"What do you propose then?" Geocelin asked.

"Nothing out there."

"How useful," Geocelin grumbled.

"But *here* . . . " I thought of the pink flowers and towering walls of mud. Peregrine would get what he wanted after all, I thought wryly. "The garden. Konstantin's garden."

Geocelin balked. "Back *deeper* into the Hallowed Lands. May as well walk them into Evarund's mouth."

It was taking a great mental effort not to smash his teeth in.

"There's no better option."

"On the contrary, I'd take whatever lies beyond that bridge a thousand times over what lies in here. You barbarians are spread out. Find a secluded ruin, build a village, and breed like rabbits for a few decades. They'll starve in peace and obscurity."

"Food grows in the garden. Whatever safety exists out there would be one we'd have to search for. We *know* where we can feed them and settle them here."

"Tell me, when you send them there—*if* they manage the walk on their stick legs—what stops anyone from walking through that open gate *we* walked out of to take them back?"

"I can seal that gate," Minthisha spoke softly, almost to herself. "I know the magic that built Konstantin's hovel. The leadswine were forged from those tethers; I could try to revive them. That had been enough to dissuade the Green from marching on the highlands before. But . . . " Minthisha looked back to the tower. "How long does it take to walk to the garden?"

I turned to Geocelin only to find him already looking at me expectantly. Days, but how many? It had been decades since there was a need to reach any destination in a timely fashion. I had no provisions to ration, no one to answer to. The seasons were easy enough to note, and I could estimate the age of old tracks, but time itself was not something I marked.

"It'll take longer with them," Geocelin said, hedging.

Minthisha sighed. "We'll be pursued."

"I'll manage them," I said.

"Might as well be the White Knight himself," Geocelin mocked. "Dangerous and incredible as you are, Sir Darl, the appeal of your kind is that you rise up after being slaughtered. That's useful on a battlefield, but when it comes to defending sheep, you'd make a lousy shepherd."

"Don't we have a say?"

It's a testament to how quiet these noblemen learned to be that I didn't hear them until they were at the guardhouse door. Three ghostly figures stepped out into the sunlight. The smallest among them, the doe-like woman who'd followed me to the witch's, had been the one that'd spoken. She fought the urge to duck her head as she waited for an answer.

"And what would you like to do, little one?" Geocelin asked.

She took us all in but settled on speaking directly to Minthisha. "What's this talk of a garden?"

They were not striking representatives, but the little one held her own as Minthisha told her of Konstantin's den and the Barrens. I examined the poor things in the daylight.

What struck me most was the boy standing with them. He was a youth, probably twenty, and the tallest in the group. But his face was sharp, his skin a red-bronze complexion, with familiar wine-dark eyes.

The boy caught me staring and, to my surprise, did not shrink away. I could tell he'd wanted to, but he copied the girl and pushed up his chin, taking his inspection manfully. The boy repaid me with the same scrutiny I'd placed on him. He inspected my build, my armor, and my face with a candid mix of wonder and fear.

Minthisha had the attention of the other two. The little one who'd spoken first had quick eyes and danced her thumb along her fingers as she listened. She only interrupted once when Minthisha suggested they could pin the blame on me and retreat back behind the Green's walls.

"We're not going back there," she said, stern and resolute.

When Minthisha had told all there was to tell, the three representatives whispered among themselves for quite a bit. The girl finally announced, "We'll have to see what the others are willing to do."

"And waste more time?" Geocelin snapped.

"Go on," Minthisha told the three.

They slipped back into the tower. Geocelin and I exchanged a look, and by some unspoken understanding, turned on Minthisha.

"You shouldn't put it in their hands," Geocelin said. "They haven't so much as decided on their meals in decades."

Spare me. I had to agree with the canary. "They don't know enough."

"We'll see what they have to say. If we feel they've chosen wrong . . . well . . . First, *we* have to agree on what the right course of action is. Don't we?"

We were not left waiting long; such was the simplicity of youth. We overheard a few shouts and choired groans, but they had been conscientious enough to limit the length of their discourse. A new set of five squeezed down the steps with the doe-like girl in front.

Before she announced their decision, she looked back at the other for reassurance.

"We'll stay in our homeland," she said, certain to enunciate rehearsed words. "We know what grows here and when. We have maps, our histories, our names—this land was ours to inherit. We won't give it up."

Geocelin's face pinched, but he did not so much as glance in the bridge's direction. Despite his sour expression, he must have felt relief to not be responsible for the choice they'd made. They instead chose my suggestion. Minthisha appeared to be the only one unrattled.

She was quick to deal out instructions to wrap their feet and cut their dresses. The girl was assigned to formalize a headcount. The witch joined the commotion of preparation, directing and advising as she saw fit. She emerged again from the tower with the fledgling lines of these scarecrow nobles clustering like packrats shooed from a nest.

"Finally, I'm rid of them," Geocelin said. "Good luck on your quest, Sir Darl. I'll tell them you've gone to the Barrens when the Green comes asking. Beyond that, good riddance."

"It's a large flock, Goss," Minthisha told him.

"I'm sure they can herd themselves." His lips stretched wide in that unfriendly smile. "Don't ask this of me, Minthisha."

"I will ask this of you," she said.

"Minthe—"

"Geocelin, son of Cedella, I was there on the day you came into this world, and I have overseen you—"

"That's enough, Minthe!"

"—I have overseen yours and your family's lives until they were taken to the Green. You grew into a man before me. You are still that man today. If not, you would have left them to be found in the morning, and you know it. They cannot go back, and you cannot wash your hands of them now."

When we'd first met, Geocelin had held such a careless youth about him. Now, as he shrank under Minthisha, I saw all his years. More than forty, yes. They'd cut deep into him. They'd scratched his cheeks and burrowed into the hollows of his eyes. They'd sharpened his teeth and hardened his knuckles. In one look, the decades revealed themselves.

I would not know what he had promised. Those years, however many, were locked away in their history. I glimpsed their echoes singing their haunting refrain now as Geocelin submitted.

THE LONG WALK

In Varlemont, hundreds of hands arrived for the annual harvest. They clogged the streets with carts and flooded the docks. Moving them all into the fields took months of preparation. I had also traveled with armies in wartime. Convoys of noisy soldiers marched in step along narrow footpaths. Oxen hooves plodded over boards laid down by builders. Drummers pounded the rhythm of our steps.

Moving these people—children—*worse than children*—could not compare.

We had not considered ourselves overly ambitious. Geocelin and I guessed that our walk back from the Garden had taken us four days. For the size of our group and the sake of our route, we added what we thought was a generous stretch of time to our estimation.

Cutting directly west to High Mound meant walking in rolling, open farmland. While hiding in the southern swamps would allow us to take from Minthisha's caches as we went, we expected the Green to search there first. North was the Elder Wood, which was unfamiliar to Geocelin and to men of the Green. Minthisha knew the old paths through that wood and its resources, but it took some time to earn Geocelin's begrudging concession to use the cover of the northern wood to take us west. Minthisha assured us the Blight's effect was, for the most part, harmless, but that did little to ease his or, admittedly, my hesitations.

In all, eleven days seemed manageable if we kept the nobles hidden, moving, and fed. Their legs were untested and had already been strained by the walk to Geocelin's fortress. Not all of them had shoes, and the few that did were in silk and velvet slippers. So, when we set out that very sunset, it felt miraculous to see them last so long walking through the night, and we were only caught out in the morning light for an hour before we had most of the nobility hidden in the northern treeline.

In the meantime, Minthisha was tasked with obscuring our path. Like the vassals in the House of Oghir, she harnessed a burst of wind and sent it tearing through the grass. Geocelin and I took heart in surveying the fruits of her labors that morning. The effect was convincing enough to mimic the trail our herd inevitably left, but hers led in a dozen winding directions out from the open fields.

Seeing how well the children had kept pace that first night, we were confident we would reach the garden within a week. But the next night was all aches, blisters, and sore legs, and we hardly chipped away at five miles.

That was to say nothing of their fatigue and hunger.

I doubled back to meet Minthisha at a series of her caches. She had stored crates of roots and dried insects there for years. It was not difficult to find a handcart stored away in the dead farmlands. We caught a few feral chickens and stacked on jars of strange preserves and a sack of apples from Konstantin's garden. Geocelin had collected them for her, she said.

"It'll be gone before you realize," she said as we loaded a hefty bag of grain. We'd cleared out the third cache she'd had hidden in the shadow of Leoric's Temple.

"Surely not," I said, eyeing the dried bugs. "Mortals may not be able to eat what you do."

"I *am* mortal. They'll do just fine." She laughed when she saw the plain disbelief painted on my face. "Truly, I am. In Lorenial, there was a school of practitioners of the body, scholars. Evarwight burnt it down long ago, but times were that an apprentice learned the secrets of nature, from the toxins in baneberry to the workings of the heart, and if she were devoted enough, she could dedicate years to a gradual transformation. Little by little, she would become something other than human, slow and resilient as the trees, with healing hands and a mind unclouded. A long life was a part of our change, but not the purpose."

She rummaged through her stores with five nimble fingers, searched with one eye, and slid her tongue between gaps in her chipped teeth. The cut I'd given her on her cheek had scarred, healing from a scab to a puckered line.

My flesh healed anew when I was sent back to Morthia. How many scars would I have if it did not? How different would I have been if I knew I only had one body? Perhaps I'd have been more cautious. Quieter. A man who sent others to do the work that I could not risk. But also, a man who would not be harmed by severance from a god.

Some feature of mine must have betrayed me, because she caught my eye.

"I didn't ask for power's sake. I wanted it to be over. All of it. I didn't care what happened after you killed Luthor and the Blight spread. If there were any mortals alive, I knew they hadn't tilled the soil for eighty years. The millers, the hunters, and the fieldhands were long gone, and I was comforted by the idea that any children lazing in that tower would starve. It'd be our final revenge. Now, here I am . . . feeding the cuckoo birds."

She smiled at first, as if she'd intended to mock herself. But the bitterness crept in. Her eye, dark as the night, turned glassy with tears. She groaned and rubbed her brow.

"Why'd you have to bring them to *me*?" she asked.

"I didn't know anyone else who could help."

"Of course not. Who else *would*? I have been here for *decades—cen-turies*—screaming, and no one came to help until *now*, when *their* children were in danger."

"Their children" was spoken in such a way that struck me with a terrible familiarity. I'd seen the stern-faced resentments of mothers raising bastard sons and called them callow for their hatred of a child. It took Minthisha near tears for me to consider them again. It was not the child they hated, was it? I'd brought home no bastards, not out of love for a wife I hardly knew nor respect for our oaths, but out of my own neglectful indifference. A wife raised bastards out of duty, but it was a sour thing. They were forced to raise their husband's shame as their own.

What was I asking of the witch? I knew these nobles as the emaciated children born and raised in those towers. But they lived to see the end of the world because their parents and grandparents sucked the marrow out of the bones of everyone else before turning on each other. That shame was perhaps a notion to them, if they understood it at all. For Minthisha, it was a haunting.

"I'm sorry," I said, aware of how lacking those small words were.

"It's anger, Darl. It'll burn as it does," she said, composed and withdrawn. "I could have gone to a foreign court and been an advisor to kings, a *sorcerer*. I stayed here, where I'm called a witch, because I believed every man deserved dignity. That can't change now."

We regrouped with the rest of our company after two days. By then, the nobles had recovered enough to travel a short stretch. They walked like foals, heads bowed, legs stiff and easily tired. When they bedded down for the night, they depleted what food we had and whined for more. Geocelin and his band had been able to snatch a goat from the fields and cook it. He'd sent out two of his group to light false fires and covered our own. With the addition of Minthisha's stored goods, we could portion out enough rations to feed them for three days.

"They can't need that much!" Geocelin exclaimed.

"Unless you want to exhaust them, that's what it'll take." If nothing else, I remembered marching rations. On our first campaign, before anyone truly understood Deathless, we traded bacon and grain for extra favors around camp. Even with my most conservative estimations, we had four days before we starved them.

"Does anyone remember how to hunt?" Geocelin asked. "Animals, I mean?"

Of the five in Geocelin's group, the Flayed I recognized from the night in the tall grass, and a Toothless said they did. We wouldn't be able to wait for traps, though we could set a few snares at night. The time it took one man to set them would add another few hours of preparation to our day and drag on our journey.

"We'll forage wild roots and plants on the way," Minthisha said. Our efforts alone, however, wouldn't feed hundreds.

"Maybe we should take some along with us," the Flayed suggested, which surprised me. Geocelin's band tended to avoid speaking directly to us, but it seemed it wasn't for the sake of bashfulness or flat obedience. "I can't shape another bow in a day, but it only takes a stick to make a spear. If nothing else, they can forage. We split them into groups, one guardian per division. It'd thin out our numbers a little."

Though not a perfect solution, it would ease the burden. We thought it might be difficult to find volunteers, but one could always expect adolescents to throw themselves into labor if it was called an adventure. So Minthisha and I led the largest group, consisting of the slowest elders and youngest children, while the Toothless and the Flayed split off with a division of the more active youths.

The Flayed was a woman of few words, but her eyes were warm even when her answers were clipped. She kept her hair in neat, patterned braids and demonstrated the technique to her gaggle of hunters with a grim-faced seriousness. The next morning, half of them had their black curls woven in half-finished rows that mimicked hers. She made a great show about being annoyed but helped them finish the next night. She was a competent woodsman and always returned with a bundle of mushrooms or wild greens if not meat.

The Toothless wore a geometric-patterned scarf I recognized as Prethen and had a distinct limp. He was a good shot with an arrow and had no doubt worked with youngsters before. He made a show out of preparing whatever thin gruel we managed and made sure to credit each contribution by name. The young men would trip over themselves the next day to find even better offerings to win his praise. At night, the Flayed gave him a salve she mixed from the local flora to soothe a nasty scar on his leg.

In the meantime, the other members of Geocelin's band set about trying to divert the Green away from us. There were two new Acolytes of the Eye who wore the traditional veil and mantle but otherwise had no markers of a distinct country. Not since the Barrens had I seen anyone who practiced their worship with dress and prayer; they must have been older. One was left-handed and had debossed "wrong hand" on his short sword's scabbard. They disappeared for days at a time, laying down false trails and lighting decoy fires. They often came back bloodied, and I was sure the two of them were more eager to lure in new prey than to aid us.

The last new face was a Silver Tongue with a strange appearance: eyes green as pondwater and straight black hair that tufted like raven feathers. He didn't speak our language, but he shared a secondary one with Geocelin. He always came back with a few game animals hanging from his shoulder and gifted small, whittled birds out by the handful.

I didn't know their names. Given the circumstances of my last meeting with Geocelin's band, it seemed for the best that we never made formal introductions. They stayed on their side of the camp, and I stayed on mine. When Minthisha needed something, she asked Geocelin, and he delegated.

Despite our hunting parties and the success of a few snares, the nobles still went to sleep hungry most nights. Amongst themselves, they created a rotation for meals so that the ones who starved the night before were given the first portions the next day. It was easy to think we were doing quite well for ourselves, but our pace was still miserable.

It took us five days to pass Leoric's temple, an accomplishment that Minthisha and I had just managed in two. Still, with nearly a week without trouble, I was beginning to think we had been overcautious. Aside from a few avoidable scouting parties, the Green did not seem to be interested in a chase. But then came the night strange stars were shot across the sky, casting the grass below in sharp, pale light.

"Scouts," Geocelin said simply. Two more of those slow shooting stars appeared, one so far south and distant I mistook it for a piece of a constellation, and another a few miles behind us on the edge of Elder Woods.

I asked the obvious. "Magic?"

It was hard to determine from Geocelin's expression if I should be impressed with the power on display. I had no reference for the limits of its possibilities, but Geocelin looked more sunken than impressed. "This doesn't bode well," he said. "They're starting to take us seriously."

"They should have used those lights before if they were so desperate to find us."

"They thought they wouldn't have to waste the energy. If I'd been with them, I would have thought at least half of the brats would come running back by now. Now, they haven't, and it's not so entertaining anymore, I'd wager. Each one of those lights is three eyes, a tongue, three inches of skin . . . you understand?"

"They'll be hungry if they find us."

"*When*, Sir Deathless. They'll be using less obvious methods too. Enjoy the lights; they're for us. They want us to know it's come to this."

A number of children watched the sky that night. Hundreds of tiny lights glimmered in their eyes, and an uncharacteristic murmur passed through the crowd. Geocelin signaled for his group to watch the children instead of the woods.

"If anyone's going to run," Geocelin said, "it's going to start now."

"None of them want to go back."

"Come now, Sir Deathless, don't be dense. You don't kiss the feet of your king because you like him. Have you been watching them? There are loyalists among us. If we're not careful, they can grow into traitors."

When the nobles did converse, they kept to whispers and close-knit meetings that would trickle out to the less involved members during the day. That was how they'd created their food system and how they divvied up cooking and trapping in the evenings. I'd heard a few names repeated, and taking Geocelin's advice, I began to note the spearheads of the group.

The doe-like one, Lysiane, had a dominant place in those meetings. Most muttered complaints involved her. She seemed to be an enforcer of whatever systems they created, and resentments built among those who considered the structure unnecessary. There were a handful of petty grievances. Her critics tended to support an older counterpart, Gillianne, who seemed to speak for the more exhausted members of the group and wanted most labor to go to the young.

A man missing an ear, Rosaireth, was the least contentious speaker, and he often kept the peace, though it seemed he was there to deliver the same instructions as Lysiane with better reception from Gillianne.

And a wrinkled man with a shaved head called Scholar was dragged into conversations about history or geography whenever some reference was needed. I could not discern too many of the particulars; when I walked too near, they fell into a hush.

Minthisha was the only outsider whom they sought out for counsel. She checked them all in the evenings for scrapes and signs of exhaustion. The nobility rationed even that, sorting their struggling members into groups by complaint and sending a tally of each to her before they'd all settled.

It was clear by the ninth day that I had won neither their confidence nor their trust. I recognized the fallacy of the comparison. I did not need to know their names to patrol their camps at night. I did not need to know the history of their country to kill men from the Green who found us. This wasn't my land. These weren't my people. It was already tiresome enough in my time to return from long campaigns to a house of strangers. What was I to do with a mob of them?

Geocelin, however, was as removed from the group as I. The Flayed and the Acolyte, both foreigners, had become favorites instead. The Flayed's hunting party followed her around like a group of goslings, but she also was useful to the rest, mixing salves that soothed blisters and sores. Though most people preferred Minthisha's softer touch, they knew she was a quicker option, and she would explain the look and purpose of the ingredients she mixed. The Acolyte had gotten into the habit of playing card games with a few of the younger nobles; one hand was paralyzed, so he shuffled primarily with his left, but he was a quick dealer and knew a few card tricks that dazzled the little evening crowds.

All the same, Minthisha closed the distance they could not, and it was rare not to see one stray or another waiting patiently to approach the witch at all hours of the day.

"They probably ask her superstitious nonsense," Geocelin remarked one afternoon. "They're waiting for magic and blessings."

"And why would they expect blessings?"

"Peasant stories. Their heads were filled with them by the time I joined. Women who weave fate, heal the sick, guide the lost were more exciting to them than the tales of knights that shared their names slaying dragons. Some sap told them about the yew trees that sprouted from their backs after their death so that they would look at the old one in their courtyard and feel like someone was there to . . ." Geocelin bit his tongue, a habit I had started to notice. It seemed it was his natural inclination to go on for a long while if no one stopped him, and no one resented that more than he did.

I watched Minthisha sitting and speaking quietly with the Scholar that afternoon while a toddler tugged at her curls. She was smiling as she spoke and laughed on occasion, but I couldn't help but remember how she'd grieved at the idea of this.

"Do you think she's happy?" I asked.

Geocelin plucked a few stray notes on his mandolin, as he tended to do whenever we'd settled. "I'm sure she adores the attention. Why, Sir Deathless, are you feeling neglected?"

"I don't mean that. I brought this to both of your doorsteps. Neither of you were glad."

"Why would I be glad to see *you* at my front door? Better to ask if I'd be happy to see a wolf that maimed me once," Geocelin said with an inviting smile. It was bizarre to be cordial with the canary and glimpse what it must be like to be his friend. "Happiness is for the full. I'd rather not be involved at all, but this would have ended more pitifully if that were the case, and this is already pitiful."

"I asked a lot of you. These aren't your children."

"Ah," Geocelin reexamined Minthisha. "Is that what this is? Her first brood was no good, so this'll be the one she saves?"

"I didn't mean to suggest that."

"I do. At least she's trying this time."

"With the Green's children."

"Whose else's would they be?" Geocelin scowled. Then, a realization dawned on him. "That should be the least of her concerns, and it certainly wasn't yours when you started this."

"I'm an outlander. I've given my sympathies to men who don't deserve it before."

"You saw a den of starving children, Outlander. What do they deserve?" Geocelin asked. He let those blunt words hover on their own for a long moment. "If you reserve salvation for the ones who deserve it, you'll have very few cups to fill. Those were Minthe's words once. She despises me for joining the Green, but things were not so pure and innocent on this side of the walls. Yet, she loved us all the same. We live with things we don't deserve all the time. You worked for a lord once, didn't you? You understand."

Geocelin had such a talent for delivering callousness with an air of flattery. I knew exactly what he referred to. There was no better way to bring out the ugliness in a man than to trap him in a corner and offer him an exit that only damaged his pride. I had burned down strangers' homesteads far less often than they walked me to their neighbors' doors and named the enemies of Lord Forestier.

I had also been a man in a position to bring out that ugliness as a knight. My comrades and I took liberties and went beyond the bounds of decency. Even when I abstained, I allowed it to happen. Sometimes it was for the sake of speeding along the inevitable, and other times it was because we were tired and irate with our own masters, and there was no harm in a bit of mischief. We knew that when we sat at the table with a common man, we sat higher, and that brought out the desire and capacity to bestow great benevolence or great injury at our whims.

"For the nobility, preserving the Green preserved humanity," Geocelin said. "They had the resources, were true to their cause, and they won. Their reward was eating *their own* children last."

"Is that why you left?"

"Not at all. What did I care?" Geocelin cleared his throat. "Singing the same five songs every day was what did me in. I found my talents were of better use hunting wide-eyed outlanders at the gate. But I do wonder what you think will happen when we lock these children in their garden, and you kill every starving soldier of the Green, and me, one by one, to defend this new humane settlement. What happens when *you* get hungry enough?"

THE ACOLYTE

While we still pushed west, there was no denying we were lingering in the Elder Wood. Our estimated eleven days had come and gone. But when we had to answer the question of how to cross the highlands, the distance and exposure petrified us, to say nothing of the scarcity of food.

There was, however, the Blight, which we were growing eager to part from. The effects had not been as devastating as the Green claimed, but they had not been pleasant. There was a heaviness in the air that never quite relented. Geocelin complained of nightmares, and if that extended to the rest of his group, it would explain the frequent shifts in watch overnight. I had felt watched on occasion, and my ears had rung twice since we ventured so far, but these were not significant complaints. But then we finished one walk, and my feet were sore. The next night, I dozed off, not for long, not deeply enough to dream, but the Silver Tongue tapped my shoulder and startled me out of it. The nobles, however, seemed unbothered.

In fact, they had taken a liking to the forest. There was talk about starting a settlement here. It made the younger ones overconfident. The Flayed had a few in her hunting group dart off like wild foxes and lose their way. Some of the elders would find a particularly nice spot to rest and would conjure a wealth of reasons to stay just a day longer, as if this was a labor they could simply abstain from. I carried the persistent ones to save us all time and might have started a contest, of sorts, between them to see who I would take the next day. It was only with the interference of the likes of Lysiane and Rosaireth that the nobility kept to a regimented routine.

Once, a young man stopped to stare at the broken remnants of a hunter's lodge. I had to drag him away with both hands tucked under his armpits. He squirmed out of my hold like a cat and bolted deeper into the woods. When I followed him, we ran into two knights of the Green that had been just over a knoll.

"We're lucky most haven't held a sword in a half-century," Geocelin said when I handed him the insignias I cut off their corpses. "One competent scout must have marked us by now. No point in distant decoys anymore. They aren't following us into the woods. They must guess where we're going or be close to it."

"Shouldn't we have half of the Green in our shadow?"

"We should," Geocelin grumbled. "Yet we haven't seen too many, have we?"

It was either the pitiable lack of evidence that irritated him, or he knew something about the Green's capabilities that I did not. This was a country of sorcerers. In the end, we stuck to the Elder Wood, preferring the challenges of the forest to any risks we'd take walking the more direct route into the highlands.

For all the misery walking caused them, the nobles seemed delighted by the simplicities of nature. They were entranced by the call of a new bird or the sight of a squirrel. Sun-pocked leaves fluttered down like a soft rain whenever the wind picked up. Minthisha would pluck two similar cuttings from the woods, and the assembly behind her eagerly listened to her explain the difference between them.

I once overheard two young men debate whether a certain tree was a walnut or an elm, referring to texts in their home library as evidence. It was an ash, and I told them as much as I ushered them along. Instead of feeling scorned and moved to obedience, they crowded me to learn more, pointing at tree after tree for me to name.

And *their* children were all the worse. One early dawn, there was a sudden, violent screaming coming from the camp. The Flayed and I raced to catch whichever knight of the Green had slipped through our watch, only to find a swarm of children no older than six being chased by an older girl with a robe over her head, pretending to be a ghost. I hadn't heard children playing in a century, and their penchant for mischief resurrected soon enough.

They played games I remembered from my childhood and sang the same youthful tunes with different lyrics. They climbed trees as high as they could until they trapped themselves on flimsy branches and sobbed that they couldn't get down. Most were drawn to the allure of the shaded alcoves or abandoned outposts and would wedge themselves into the deepest, darkest crevices they could find in the name of sabotage, since we inevitably halted the group to collect them. There were so *many* of them. Thirty, at the least, stood no higher than my hip.

The older nobles often walked in Minthisha's shadow. She gave them wriggling bugs to chew and showed them magic: a gust of wind, a fire lit with no spark or tinder, a few gemstones stuck in the ground to create her air net. She would tell them stories of whatever mountain beast used to dwell in a cave we passed and what hero vanquished it with cunning and steel.

One group of teenagers flocked to the left-handed Acolyte's post at night to hear him talk of his adventures in the Barrens.

Most amusing to me was a youth of perhaps thirteen, who'd never quite left his father's shadow. Yet, one night, he crept up to Geocelin's mandolin, which the canary had left unattended, and began to pluck the strings. He set the instrument in his lap the way Geocelin would and placed his fingers along the neck in a clear mimicry of what he'd seen. I watched him strum a few disappointing notes again and again. He pinched and prodded the neck at different angles, plucked the strings, and braced against the instrument until it gave him one sweet note. He smiled triumphantly, and by then, Geocelin had returned.

"You'll have to harden your fingers before it'll sing sweet for—"

The boy dashed away as if a snake had lunged at him. His sudden terror seemed to strike Geocelin, who stood agog. His Flayed friend mocked him for it.

"It's your face, of course," she laughed. "Terrifying!"

Geocelin gathered the mandolin. He played a few strings, coaxing the boy back with the promise of the full melody. When he was close enough, Geocelin offered up his mandolin. He adjusted the boy's hands and told him the names of the positions. The youth's brow furrowed in monk-like concentration as he committed each instruction to memory. There was a delicacy there that I pretended not to see, lest Geocelin stop at the notice of an audience.

❖

On the thirteenth day, the Flayed warned us of our first ambush, and we went out to meet them.

Fletching whistled past me as I drove the tip of my sword through the throat of one man and bashed in the breastplate of the other. Two tried to run away. I would have given chase if the Flayed and an Acolyte had not suddenly sprung from the wood like fresh bloodhounds. They butchered the knights, stripping them of their fingers, their skin, their tongues, and their eyes within a half-hour. Nothing went to waste.

"There's another group ahead to the southeast. We can avoid them if we head northwest," the Flayed said.

"We're already too far north as it is," Geocelin complained. "We have to start climbing. If it's another small group, I say we cut through them and push back to the highlands."

I had been about to return to the children and await Geocelin's decision there when I suddenly noticed the Acolyte. The veil he'd worn, little more than a scrap of thin cloth, had fallen from his face. His nose was scarred, and his curling hair was long and streaked with gray. The moment I knew him, all noise fell away, all instructions were gone. I was walking, and then I was in front of him.

I grabbed Lambskin by the throat.

He locked his left hand around my arm, and the right pushed from the wrist while the glove bent unnaturally far back. A fake hand. I couldn't tell if I had thrown the first fist, but I did know he landed a punch that made my ears ring. My knuckles grazed teeth. Then, just as I braced for a left jab, we were pulled apart. There were hands under my arms and across my chest, pushing me back. The Flayed stepped between us, and the Toothless had a protective arm thrown around Lambskin. Someone was shouting. Geocelin was in front of me.

"Calm down, friend. He's with us."

He'd known? All this time, he had Lambskin in his company. He sent me to every corner of this damned country, and the parasite was with him the whole time! Had he been the fifth man in the grass? He was *here*, with the nobles.

I lunged for Geocelin, and another arm locked around my chest. The Silver Tongue shouted something in his language. Geocelin responded with a softer tone.

"Let's all compose ourselves."

"I should mount you on a pike!"

They held me back as I thrashed. My fury burned hot, and I raged.

"What is this?" It was Minthisha's voice asking.

The Flayed was walking her to us. How quickly had they gotten here? I heard the crash of voices; shouts imploring Minthisha to *do* something about *me*. The holds on my body were bruising. I didn't know what they expected me to do, but I knew they were afraid. And like that, the anger was shocked out of me. A terrible, cold embarrassment replaced it. What was I doing?

I stopped moving far sooner than anyone was willing to let me go.

"Are we calm again? Are we civil?" Geocelin repeated.

I promised Geocelin again and again it was over. Lambskin had been released. He made a show of stumbling about like a fawn as if he hadn't hit me back. Minthisha went to him, checking his neck and jaw. My face burned, and my heart thudded in a way it hadn't in . . . not long ago at all. I hadn't felt like this since I'd hit a boy in an open field for failing a test I improvised. I left the moment I was released.

Geocelin shouted after me. Eyes bored into my back. I walked deeper into the Elder Wood until I could see and hear no one.

I found a creek and washed the blood from my arms and face. I must be frightful: tall, hard-faced, and marked with a permanent scowl. I could slaughter every last one of them if I chose to, and it showed not only in my face, but my manner. I was not human. I was the cobbled-together scraps of plate and padding shaped into a man. A month ago, this had all been in my favor. This sudden onslaught of civility was jarring.

If they'd defended Lambskin with swords and fists, I could understand. But they held me back with soft hands and less than a threat. Two weeks ago, we could hunt each other to our satisfaction, but now it was a childish breach of an agreed truce. We had greater concerns, and I'd thrown it all aside.

"You look tragic." I recognized his voice. How had I not before?

Lambskin knelt by the water. He splashed his face and scrubbed off the last stains of blood from his lips with his left hand. He took his time, almost challenging me to finish what I started.

Was he gloating? Mocking me? We were both bound by a cause, or, at least, the desire to keep the peace with Geocelin. He must have known that, or else this would never have started with anything less than knives and fists.

"I should apologize," I said. It was an obligation. We were no longer two men in the wild. I'd made a spectacle of myself.

"That won't do either of us much good," Lambskin said. He undid a tie around his right wrist and removed his padded glove. He cupped a handful of water and wiped his right wrist before smearing one of the Flayed's salves on the scar tissue. "I know the way of things. You hunt me. I try to kill you. We've had a routine long before local politics came between us."

He smiled at me, hoping to share in a joke. The longer he looked at me, the worse I felt. I disliked that phrase: *the way of things.* Theodoulos had sounded so naive. Hearing it from Lambskin felt like a taunt.

"I, for one, was wondering when you'd notice," he went on. "I might have been looking forward to it. It is too bad Geocelin is so insistent on this fellowship."

"What are you doing with them?" I asked.

"Traveling . . . for a while."

"Why?"

"I get lonely. You never did, but I do," Lambskin said. Is that what he thought? He stopped to look at me, and I did the same to him. We had never been so close to each other without knives and killing intent. When he was finished, he sucked his teeth and turned away. "We'll see how long they last. They usually betray me one way or another. Then I'm alone again. You're my most stable companion, you know?"

"That's a pity."

"Well, I think we deserve each other." Lambskin sat back on his heels. His smile flattened. "It's a strange country, isn't it? Quite impressed with itself as it gnaws its own arm off."

I hated how he said it, reveling in the misery. I hummed, just to let the moment pass.

"You know, I imagined all the things I was going to say to you once I had this opportunity. I planned for this moment, even. It's not as satisfying as I wanted it to be."

Yet he was still here. "I'd thought about it as well. This can't be all you wanted to say."

"No. But you already know you took everything from me. You already know how terrible it is because you're doing everything in your power to keep *them* from suffering the same fate now. What am I supposed to say to that while we're rotting at the end of our miserable lives?"

"You could have had a good life elsewhere."

"I *had* a good life. I had a father and a ranch and a brother who was young and irritating." He dared me to counter him or offer some pitiable challenge. I did not doubt that if I did, we'd come to blows again. I let myself be whipped like a dog and turned my head away in deference. "I don't hate you for that, you know?"

"Why, then?"

He sighed. "You acted so benevolent when you did decide to offer me charity, as if you didn't make the mud that buried us, as if we were born filthy."

"Jav—"

"No. None of that. I think we're finished here," he said quickly. He stood and dusted himself off. With a whistle, he flashed something metal and tossed it to me. "You dropped this a few decades back, old man. I'll collect it off your corpse in a year or three, when this is over."

"It won't be like it was. We'll do it right this time."

"I'm sure you believe that."

I inspected the face of the ring he'd thrown me: the three-mountain crest of Bevelon. The boy knew how to pick his insults, didn't he? All this time, he'd carried my family ring. I remembered the night my father passed it to me, his expression hard as stone. I should not have been the recipient. He handed to me lands and titles meant for Mica and we both knew it in that bitter light. I was not the heir he wanted, but the one he had.

When I had my own sons, I didn't want them to feel that same cold dread. I wanted them protected and safe. I wanted their days to be prosperous and devoid of the evils I was raised with. I took vows, I fought goliaths, I clawed and scraped at the dangers I could see mounting on my horizon, knowing I was one piece on a board far larger than me, all in the hopes that one day I might be able to wrest a little good from my toils and give them a world, a country, a father they could be proud of.

I used to be a knight. Braids tight, beard trimmed, armor impeccable. When had that faded? When did the resentment build? When had I darkened their door? My presence struck fear into the eyes of my boys, and I hated them for it. They would always line up to meet me, feet shuffling, heads bowed, waiting for dismissal. I had been the man who had made an enduring wife shiver in silence. The man who had sent back money to keep a home he never lived in. The monster that raged and lashed out when the world of civility made me terrified and cold. To give my family legacy and status, I had gone off to war, and they had grown without me, apart from me, and that had been good. I was a part of it by being apart from it. Such was my role.

Still, I had planned to give this ring to my eldest. I had fantasized about that day when I could give the entirety of myself, and the men that came before him, to him. Maybe then, if I gave him all that I was, he would have finally understood, and things would have mended. I stared at those three mountains long into the night.

Geocelin found me when the children were bedded down. He sat beside me and gestured to the ring. "Present from the lad? You two made amends?"

"We'll be civil," I said.

"Good. We need that. My brothers were hardheaded as oxen, but they knew when to leave aside grudges. It's what killed them, in fact, but you understand what I mean."

"You had brothers?" I asked.

Geocelin licked his teeth.

"I don't have to worry about this afternoon repeating, do I?"

So he sought to discipline me like a child. "That's entirely up to him," I said. "He's . . ."

"Difficult," Geocelin said with the empathy of experience. "Mo keeps him settled, but he startles easily. I'll manage him if he falls out of line."

"How long was he with you?" I asked.

"Not as long as I think you expect," Geocelin said. "We met him in the highlands while we were following you. He tells me the hand is your doing. He won't tell me why, though."

"I doubt that."

"Well, he told a *story* meant to inspire my sympathies. It was a good piece of fiction, very moving."

"You'll not have the truth from me, either."

Geocelin hummed. "And I share so much with you. Fine. What's that he gave you? Can I know that, at least?"

"My homeland." I handed it over to him to inspect.

"Mountains?"

"Bepiv, Bevi, Kuri. Grandfather. Father. Son."

"I'm sure one of these bookish brats would understand, but I was raised in the mud. Is that its name?"

"It's our story. There's the All-Father, but in Bevelon, we have our own giants, and they're bigger. Kairos was a giant alone in a barren world. It's a long story. He creates a son to consume. The son hides away and overthrows his father when he's big enough. Kairos decays, and his body becomes a mountain with wildlife upon which his son thrives and grows even larger, and so on. That's how we have our mountain chain."

"Really?"

"It's a story, Goss."

"What do I know of the outlands? You could be riding on the backs of flying snakes out there and pulling women from the skins of animals. You should work on your telling, though. Dramatics like that need good timing, some indulgences in the details, not a half-muttered, embarrassed delivery."

"Goss."

"I like the story just fine," he said quickly, as if he were soothing my ego. "I thought about what you asked me the other day. About why . . . this."

He offered the ring back. There was still that lightness to his tone, but underneath, I knew he was leading us somewhere.

"This business with the lad had me thinking about how I treated you with Rostam." I flinched at the mention of Peregrine, and Geocelin noticed. He pretended not to and plowed on for my sake. "He's the last man I hated, but what does that mean to you? That kind of pain doesn't pass on to others. Minthe . . . has that same frustration with me. I know what she endured. I know what she's lost. But it's a story to me; it's distant, almost poetic, and I owe it no loyalty. I'm sure you have your own pains I can't comprehend, Sir Deathless."

He'd promised not to ask about Lambskin, but he knew there was far more than that. With so much time behind me, I thought there would be more to grieve. There were some losses that hurt more than others. Many were from the early days, from a youth I had considered too old to feel young, where the world felt the most frustrating and my passions came from a place where every matter was tied to my heart. As I grew older still, it was difficult to keep that attachment as the land shifted under me. But there were moments, of course. Perhaps it spoke to a selfish part of me that could guess at who Peregrine was to Geocelin, and didn't grieve any less.

"I endured the same as any other Deathless of my time," I said, feeling the inadequacy of that answer already. "We believed in a noble ideal of who we were to our country and our families, and we watched both fall away from us. I know my sympathies seem arbitrary, but I have a sense of what Peregrine must have been. I know you had your reasons."

"I hated Peregrine, and not the way I hated the Green, but I didn't hate him the way I hated the men I was raised with either. The Green was what it was. You don't expect sympathy from a bear. For forty years the man I hated the most was a miller who named my family as traitors to save his own skin. We used to play together as boys. His children grew into men and women, and mine did not because of him. But by then we were all Minthe's darling children who must all be forgiven. The Green was the enemy, and we must cast aside all else."

"You did not agree, I imagine."

"I am a man without scruples."

"That's untrue."

Geocelin leaned back, taking me in like a man waiting for some trick to be revealed.

"You don't eat in that hall," I said. "I'd wager you never did. You were a singer, not a soldier. And if Minthisha and I did lead this migration on our own, you would not have given up our names."

"You shouldn't be so confident in that," Geocelin dismissed.

"Betrayals are not clean things. This country was not the same for you as it was for her. Benevolent and pious self-sacrifice is an ideal that asks so much of a man, so much of a child. And as you said, we are not all treasures." And then something came tumbling out that should not have. Something I had kept locked in a chest and closed for so long I had no proper memory of it, only a wet tangle of words and moments, twisted like tree roots. "My brother, Mica, was a much more forgiving man than I was. He believed in the spirit of our family's name and legacy and held himself to a higher standard for it, though our father had smeared that name in the dirt for as long as we could remember. He wanted to bring honor to our family name. I wanted to abandon our name. I'd made plans to leave, cut myself out of the rot, and leave the little good and all the terrible behind. I would have if Mica hadn't died. But he did, and *someone* had to take care of the house and carry on the legacy."

For a moment, I thought Geocelin wouldn't say anything to that, and I'd made a fool of myself for nothing. I could hear him shifting as I toyed with the leaves beneath my boots. Finally, he spoke.

"Minthisha told us we were the children of the All-Father who tilled the earth and devoted himself to knowledge and good work. The Green also grew up as children of the All-Father. To them, that meant a birthright of kings and divine fortune. Every king wanted to be the All-Father Evarund incarnate, until we gave up the charade and settled for that."

"Given up the charade? They bow to a withered old man who does not know what room he is in and pretend it's not a hooded trio speaking for him."

"Well, of course. One man can never be the All-Father," Geocelin said, unfazed. "That trio isn't even a set one. It's a ceremony. Evarund speaks for the hall, and the hall speaks for Evarund. None of those men want a king. They want absolution.

"You should have seen the great-grandparents of these brats. You had the ones who truly believed the Hallowed Lands were exempt from the plague of undead because of divine mandate. Then you had the practical men, like me. When they ran out of the peasantry, around Evaright's time, those nobles found themselves next in line, and they had the gall to be surprised. Alanus wanted to push us *out* into the world to hunt and preserve our own. Conquer and conquest. The rest of the hall wanted a pigpen but had no right to usurp the wife and mother of the succeeding heir. So a woman was banished, a child was killed, and the pigpen was made by the decree of All-Father himself."

I recalled Theodoulos' almost gleeful telling of Alanus' betrayal. There were the practice books and the little shelf of flowers and figures in the House of Oghir. There had been a child on the mantle. And they chose to parade around an old man and kneel in deference to nothing. "They've gone mad."

"On the contrary, I think it keeps them civil. Men want to be connected to *something*. For men like us, that's tested in ways our parents never could have imagined. Mortal men had their family, their legacy, their country, their stories. All of them burn fresh and bright in their hearts. As we immortals grow older, those things get stranger and stranger to us; we watch other people change their meaning before our very eyes. Family dies or disappoints, and one day your closest relation is a great-grandnephew who's stolen your brother's eyes. What's left but to cling to a story, broad and clean and easy to latch onto?

"Perhaps we have our gods, but yours are dead. The Seven Hands understood what it was to serve many, so I thought they'd look after me. I don't care what Minthe says. I feel them. But boys who could be my grandchildren look forward to pledging and consider the gods only in terms of what they sacrifice, not what they'll be binding themselves to. It all becomes a bit detached, doesn't it? You would know better than I."

"That's time."

My youth had such different ideas about what the markers of my life would mean to me. As time went on, they decayed. My sons were strangers before they were dead. My family villa, once a place of warmth and love, had grown cold to the touch before its abandonment. I had lost my pride in defending Bevelon long before it collapsed. War changed. It was not that armor and weapons were innovated and the generals and countries changed. A campaign was a campaign. But war was supposed to be a sacred room, a place to go and shut a door. It was not supposed to be dragged back home.

Morthia's horizon of ash promised that endless decay. One day, even this place would dry up and burn in the sun, the Green would crumble, and the mountains would be blanketed with ashes because Geocelin was right. No matter what haven we made now, there would be a day that I would be hungry enough, and I would topple whatever bastion I made for myself.

Lambskin was certain we'd meet again. Plant a seed, watch it grow, watch it wither. It all ended the same. But I was *trying* not to believe that.

"The Green has nothing but time, and they do nothing with it," Geocelin said. "They host the same feast every month. The same party every night. Same faces. Forty years and they've only ever inducted three new boys into their ranks, but they pretend it can be more with a false ceremony and some menial training. There is no ending for them, but there is one for their children.

"The noblemen born in that tower are the ones who whispered about collapsing that stone and burning the men in their hall. They're the planners and the would-be usurpers. They're the young boys who try to earn their pledge for the chance at escape. They're the ones who crammed together in a little corner of their room to hear nonsense peasant stories.

"I understand Minthisha a little more now. I don't have a newfound sense of forgiveness, but when I see them, I don't see what was taken from me. I see children, brats at times, but children. Mo caught two deserters the other night, and I didn't punish them. Didn't tell anyone. Just talked with them and sent them back into the nest. They're all here now, drowning. They're all scared little fools, and to them, the All-Father is a man who will breed and butcher them so that he can indulge just a while longer."

We both had a restless night.

Two days later, the Toothless and the Silver Tongue returned with a deer, a beautiful, mature buck that took half a day to prepare. The venison did not last as long as we hoped. The nobles at last were each given their own portion, and they made quick work of the flesh, sucking on marrow and chewing the skin. Some made themselves sick on it, which irritated me when they came begging for more.

"Do you think they'll always have such appetites?" Geocelin asked, clearly as irked as I.

"You forget what hunger was," I said, though I shared his mood.

"I'm sure I've heard some of the brats whispering we don't feed them enough."

Fifteen days in, and we still dreaded the highlands. Food was becoming a larger question, as we knew there'd be less in the open rocks. The burning lights overhead had stopped, but it was wishful thinking to believe that meant they'd given up their search. More likely, they knew where we were.

"They'll complain when we're thirty years settled in the Garden," I said, so shortly it caused Geocelin to laugh.

Perhaps it was not a well-thought-out answer, but it was the only one I had. Peregrine had plans for his settlement I could transfer onto the Garden, but none of this would be without its difficulties. I wondered what the nobles imagined every night before they bedded down. Did they think of a clear blue lake stocked with fish? Did they dream of orchards bearing fruit more diverse and wondrous than a few apples? What would they think when they finally arrived? *If* they finally arrived. I wondered how apparent the impermanence of their salvation was to the noble lot.

That evening, a throng of young men approached me, all puny and boyish in the face.

"You're the Stone Knight?" asked a skinny one with a mane of black curls that was twice his shoulder span. He was perhaps seventeen. When I stared at him without comprehension, he continued. "Mother Clay says you can kill a man with your bare hands."

"It's one of my talents," I answered, feeling a little flare of shame remembering my incident with Lambskin. The boy had not spoken two words to me and was already cowering under my shadow. Yet . . . here they were. A smaller boy standing just behind him subtly nudged the speaker on.

"And with a sword."

This noble's interrogation would be amusing if he didn't look so grave. A sword for some. Mace or hammer for others.

"As you've witnessed," I said plainly.

"Will you teach us how to do the same?" another one asked.

There was no curve to the muscle on their arms. They twisted sticks they'd brought along with them as if they had expected my agreement. The fact that they were asking at all to learn how to fight perhaps should not have been strange. I recognized some as the young men who had gone hunting with the Flayed and the Silver Tongue.

"You're too skinny," I told the first, and all of them by extension. "You won't be able to lift a sword. Nor do I have any to spare for you."

"Knives, then. We have those," the first insisted.

"And they're of better use in my hands."

"Not forever," he said boldly. The audacity of it made me laugh. Clearly, he didn't understand what I was.

"Why ask me?"

"You're not doing anything else." As if it were as simple as that, though I could see him shaking. It was a rehearsed demand, no doubt, but it had a fleeting confidence behind it.

"What's your name?"

"Archelaus."

"Do you think you can kill a man like I can, Archelaus?"

"No, sir. But I can learn it better from you than I can from anyone else."

There's little you can say in the face of that kind of bravery.

"Find a stick, boys."

The ones who did not already have one branched off to do so. Archelaus threw his arm over one of his group members. "Mayrisha will be practicing with us today."

He'd announced it with a purpose, but he looked nervous that I would turn him away. I tried to discern the difference between Mayrisha and the others was before I realized she was a woman. It *hadn't* been permitted, had it? For women to carry a sword before the cities fell. That was a long-abandoned custom by the time we were all hunting each other, but in the Hallowed Lands, it was preserved behind that wall. The Flayed was unique to them, perhaps the only woman with a sword they'd ever seen.

"So long as she has a stick," I said.

I was no proficient teacher, but they were an observant bunch. I kept the lessons simple; what spots would kill a man in moments; how to hold a knife; how to twist out of holds. I expected it to be an evening distraction, little more than an exercise to be demonstrated and forgotten. They came back the next day, and the day after.

And, without warning, I had an evening routine.

THE DIVIDE

I woke to golden sunlight streaking through linen curtains. Mountain air permeated the cool, concrete room. I knew this room. My tongue stuck to the sides of my mouth. My chest was tight, and I couldn't catch my breath. I sat up, and the moment I did, a terrible, aching pain seized my back.

I cried out, then stopped, stunned. My voice was not my own; it was deeper and scratched, ugly like a buck's whine. A sudden stinging flared up in my fingertips. I yanked my hand away from the rat gnawing at it, but there was nothing there but wrinkled, gnarled fingers. Deep brown skin was mottled with purplish bruising, and dry, white lines marred my knuckles. I screamed at the sight of my sudden decay, and even that was a weak, foreign thing.

"I'm coming, Bepiv. I'm coming," a woman cooed. She glided through the door with a tray balanced against her hip. Her hair was tied up in a colorful orange wrap, the same way my mother used to bind it. Her face was the same warm brown, but her eyes turned wine-red in the morning light. She sat beside me on the bed and set the tray on the table beside me in a habitual manner. "I'm here with your medicine."

Bitter herbs mixed with hot wine were given to me to drink. Her thin, smooth hands rubbed a salve over the dry spots of my knuckles. I looked around, trying to orient myself to my surroundings. This was my family villa, my home. The red tiles under my feet were the same, down to a chip by my doorway. The mosaic detailing lined the same top section of the wall with the same greens and blues. The woman said something to me. "What?"

"Did you have a good night, Bepvi?" she said loudly, frustrated she had to repeat herself.

"Yes," I said, though it sounded too frail to be me speaking.

"Good. Everyone's in the garden today," she said again, slow and loud, but I could still hardly hear her, and she wasn't quite looking at me as she spoke. "Today's the party, remember? Your son is here."

"My . . ."

"Your eldest is here, Bepvi. He came to visit us. He's in the garden with his brother."

"No. He can't. He's . . ."

"Did you wash last night?" she asked me suddenly.

"What?"

She sucked her teeth. "Bepvi, I won't keep leaving the basin if you won't clean yourself. Either you do it, or I do it, but it has to be done. You are the father to a noble house, not a beggar."

She chided me like this was a long-standing argument between us, and I was irate. I wanted to wave her off.

"Come, Bepvi," she said, "let's get you dressed, and then we'll go to the garden."

I told her I could do it myself, but when I went to raise my arm, my shoulder locked, and another stabbing pain came. She undressed me like a child. She replaced my nightshirt with a red and green patterned tunic and a thick blue wool cape. She oiled down the frizz between my braids.

When it was time to go, she handed me a cane. The handle had smoothed from use under my palm. When I stood, the weight of my body pressed the air from my lungs. My ankles were as thick as tree trunks and purple with blood. I could not feel my toes. I threatened to topple over if I leaned too heavily on my numb feet.

"Fourteen steps, Bepvi," the woman said.

Three steps in, I wanted to forget the garden. I wanted to go back to bed and lie down. I had sprinted down this hall a thousand times as a boy. Now, my march was slow and laborious. There were the painted, wooden mules that my mother had mounted on the walls. There was the little alcove and the altar to our carved Amivia; her flaming heart was adorned with fresh flowers. Crossing every fixture felt like a milestone.

And then we were in the sweltering garden. The fruit trees offered sparse coverage on the front patio. Sturdy evergreen shrubs lined the walkways. Potted azaleas wilted under the sharp sunlight. The woman sat me on a bench in the shade and handed me a cool cup of sugar water.

As soon as I was settled, a throng of children surrounded me, each with thick black curls and eyes that flashed red in the sunlight.

"Morning, Bepvi," they each said, stooping to kiss my cheek, then flitting off. I could not place a single one of them.

The garden shaded a sea of faces I did not know. They cut into fresh apples laid out on a long wooden table as they waited for a pig to roast on the central spit. A small plate was set beside me in my lonesome corner, but I was otherwise ignored in this den of strangers. Where were my sons?

"Bevi! Finally decided to join us!"

There was Lambskin, smiling with sharp teeth. His black hair had been oiled and braided back in the fashion of a Beven man. He wore my family's colors. My signet ring gleamed on his finger. The garden of strangers embraced him as he approached. Children trampled the flowers and started digging into the dirt with their bare hands.

"What's that face, old man?" Lambskin said.

"What are you doing here?"

"It's still my home, Bevi. I've only been away a few years."

No. No, he wasn't . . . Where were my boys? There were only strangers here. Women laughed and kept laughing. The men pushed one another playfully.

"Where's my son?"

"Oh, Bevi, he's right there. Didn't you see him?" Lambskin cooed. He pointed to the children who pulled fistfuls of worms from the earth and stuffed them into their mouths. There was a boy in a blue tunic with mud-caked hands and thick black curls, the boy I had seen digging into the pockets of dead men on muddy battlefields in the shadow of his brother. The roasting pig began to smoke.

"Get him out of the dirt," I said.

"No, Bevi. He likes it there. Come, have a glass of wine. Enjoy the party."

The pig caught fire; sizzling fat sloughed off its skin. The laughter became as sharp as cries. A fist was thrown, and a brawl broke out. The fire flared high until the flames licked the tiles of our family home.

"Darl! Darl! Get up!" Geocelin woke me under a canopy of trees.

Tall trees. Dark trees. I smelled smoke, and leaves crinkled beneath my head. I gasped in *my* voice. My hands flexed in the dirt, and they were *my* hands, dark and strong. I was in the Elder Woods. It had been a dream. I had been *dreaming*.

"Darl!" Geocelin shook me again.

I sat up. "What's happening?"

"Fire. It's an ambush."

He darted away before I could understand. Orange light splattering against the forest bed and the furs and velvets tucked away in the underbrush. Sharp shadows of men darted between groups who were only just waking, shouting for everyone to get up, screaming "Fire!" as a wall of smoke encroached on them.

Purple smoke billowed through the air, smothering the children in its blanket. The fire had no distinct shape in the haze. It had a body of flame thick enough for each crackle of wood to crash together like cymbals and create the deep-bellied growl of a beast.

Opposite the smoke lay a clear, pale-blue path into the dawn light. The children were already running into it.

"They're here!" a man cried. "They're going to kill us! They're going to kill us *here*!"

I pulled him out of the smoke into the open air.

"No one will touch you," I said with all the authority and confidence I could harness. "Keep a hold of your friend here and head toward that break in the trees. Do not stop until you see a clearing."

He obeyed as if I had some remarkable foresight, but I was the one struck by his words. This was the Green, wasn't it? They had set fire to the woods. This was a trap. Was this supposed to smother us? To herd the children to the one clearing? What waited on the other side of the forest?

And just like that, the arrows burst through the smoke cover. Flickers of metal flashed in the air. One woman shrieked as her shoulder was grazed. The man behind her was struck in the side by the same arrow.

I drew my sword, but I could not see anyone. The haze was too thick for them to be hiding in those charred trees. They'd suffocate sooner than harm us. Yet more arrows flew from its depths, whistling overhead. Another wave of panic sent the children running. Geocelin's hood flashed in the distance. I rubbed my eyes, feeling the scalding heat of the flame. I had to go.

Then, suddenly, the Acolyte was beside me, the half-blind one who had been traveling with Lambskin.

"Would you watch my flank for a moment?" the Acolyte asked, his voice measured and calm. The man had never asked me for anything. Bewildered, I agreed.

"Which of you six . . . " he muttered, his single glistening eye scanning the wall of purple smoke as if he could count figures behind it. I realized then he could do just that. He was an Acolyte of the Eye, after all. A little smoke may sting his eyes, but looking into it was a different matter. He drew his bow, the wood groaned as it stretched, and an angled duck feather touched his lip. "You."

His finger released, and the arrow flew. I heard the dull thud and a groan of pain from someone much closer than I expected. The blazing wall recoiled for a moment, as if the arrow had stung the fire as well.

"How many are there?" I asked him.

"They're not the ones we're worried about," he said. "They're too busy keeping themselves from choking to aim. They want us out of the trees. Geocelin's up front. You should . . . "

The Acolyte raised his bow and loosed another arrow, but that did not stop the sudden lash of fire that whipped out from the smoke. The flame coiled like a snake around the Acolyte, singeing his clothes and burning his skin, his hands, his hair. Sorcery.

By the time I collected myself enough to try and push this living fire away, it disintegrated, but the Acolyte was hissing on the ground, hands blistered, raw flesh on his cheek. He cursed and fished through his pockets. He bit into a preserved eye and scrambled to his feet. I let him grab onto my shoulder and led us away from the smoke.

He did not want to flee; instead, he had us trail the back of the group. Geocelin and the Flayed were shouting ahead, and the Acolyte kept his focus behind us. He pointed out a man who had collapsed into the underbrush and rushed us both to his aid. Once the one noble was back in the clear air, the Acolyte had already marked other stragglers. We stayed no more than ten steps from the fire that crowned the treetops with laurels of flames and broke off charred limbs to rain on us.

Our controlled retreat hastened until we were nearly sprinting ourselves. We did not choose where to go; the flames herded us to where the forest thinned and the treeline broke against sloped, rocky land. We were being driven out into the open, but it seemed the nobles had realized that. The Acolyte and I were running to a thick-clustered mob, all huddled together at the treeline. Men and women squirmed against each other, fighting to dart into the open or hold one another in place.

Behind them all, Minthisha was on her knees in the dirt, bent over a bundle of cloth. She twisted a piece of string around her strong fingers, head down, thumbs pushing in whatever she had stuffed into a pouch still deeper inside. Geocelin was calling her name. The children were fighting. The fire came in like a rolling storm. Smoke flooded the trees.

Then Minthisha clapped, and the puff of air sent the nettles and leaf scraps shooting from the pouch's mouth. The fire died as if it'd been snuffed out by the force of her hands. Where there was once the crackling roar of a great beast, there was silence. The orange light vanished, leaving residual heat and the coiling wall of smoke.

Minthisha gasped as if she herself was shocked that her spell had worked. Geocelin turned to the Acolyte.

"Mo, they still in there?" Not our own, the archers.

The Acolyte peered into the drifting plumes. "All but two, but … they're not my worry."

He turned to the clearing we had yet to cross into, and I suddenly understood why everyone was so clustered, why even now they edged as close to the smoke as they could stand. Standing on the open ridge, banners in hand, regalia on display, was the Green. They were waiting for us.

It was an infantry line of generals and lords. Banners of that great bird ascending over three burning roses fluttered on the hillside. Each man was dressed in his best, waiting with his helmet under his arm and his sword at his hip. The gold beads in their hair glittered in the sun. Their eyes were hard, though they smiled, so satisfied to see us corralled. And there, in one of the far corners, I spotted Theodoulos in his bright blue, standing amongst his peers.

In front of the ensemble stood the Indomitable Auclairs, holding a blooming magnolia branch, an antiquated gesture of peace calling for a parley. They made such pretty promises with their dress and presentation, but out here, they'd have to contend with us in the mud. I could kill the ones on the rightmost wing first. The sheer number of them meant I would lose, but perhaps I could be a good enough distraction for the children to flee back into the Elder Wood.

Geocelin tossed a velvet robe over my head. "Keep out of sight. I'll speak with them."

I grabbed his arm. "They're not here to talk."

"They didn't bother with all the pageantry for nothing. Unless you're going to fight an army yourself and win, your talents are not useful here. They want to lose as few of their livestock as possible. Stay with Minthe. Someone might try to be clever while I'm occupied."

Like that, he jogged out of the forest, hands on display but speaking with an unaffected confidence, as if this were a planned meeting rather than an entrapment.

"Ermaine!" he called. "It's been too long!"

The Flayed, the Toothless, and the Silver Tongue walked into the open, showing themselves to the infantry with straight backs and steeled eyes. Some of the children pushed to the edge of the trees, watching as Geocelin sauntered up to the man in Auclairs' colors. Unless they had remarkable hearing, there was nothing new they could glean from the two men sitting on that distant hill. I felt that same sense of eagerness and dread in my chest. What was he going to say? What *could* he say? There was so little time for the group to discuss, and he went to speak for us all.

"Don't fret, old man," the Acolyte said. Unlike the others, he had taken a position behind the crowd, mended fingers skimming against fletching. "We planned for this."

When? They had sat through countless meetings among themselves, but that brought me no comfort if their decisions were hidden from me.

"What did you plan?"

"Why don't you go sit with our Lady of the Wood?"

His suggestion felt like an echo of Geocelin's. I found Minthisha where I left her, head cradled in her palm as she worked through whatever strain that last instance of magic had put her through.

"Was that difficult?" I asked.

"I just need a day to collect myself," she said. "Where's Goss?"

I showed her what everyone else was watching with bated breath. Geocelin's yellow liripipe was dull and haggard compared to the line of bright, bold soldiers.

"I knew this was a fool's gambit!" Gillianne moaned, taking in the knights of the Green. Her bundled gray curls were frayed from the smoke, and her lip quivered as she spoke. "Here we are: leagues from home, starved by these cannibal beasts, and what have we to show for it? We've marched with the wolves, and we'll be treated as feral! You can say goodbye to our books. Goodbye to what little entertainment they afford us. If they're feeling vindictive enough, they'll take away the boys' ceremony, and then we will be truly reduced to nothing!"

"What were we before, Gillie?" Lysiane snapped. "Did music lessons and etiquette in that pen make it any less of one? Do you think that band on your arm makes you any more married to Elrend Tergis than Annalise? You both bore the same bastards, and they were taken all the same!"

"If you knew your place, girl, you would understand! There are duties we must fulfill for the sake of the Green—"

"Yet you came along all the same!" a young man shouted.

"Well, what good has it done?" Gillianne sniffed.

Lysiane looked away, quaking with rage. Soldiers lined their horizon.

"Dear girl, do you think we lived without a knife to our throats?" Gillianne asked. "We had sons and daughters. My Talia and Sabrin were dragged into these wilds, and they were given no better treatment."

"Then go back!" Lysiane scolded. "I've heard some of you speak of it! Which of you sold us to them now?" She was a small thing, but there was a fury in her that commanded a mob. She pointed behind her to the display of banners as if she could thrust them all there on will alone. "Go kiss their feet and be welcomed home. Dream of your ascension. Maybe one day another one of your sons will be a man to them, but you will always be a sow."

"Better a sow than dead!" an older man shouted.

Tension rippled through the group. I caught the Acolyte's eye. His attention was divided between the children and Geocelin's negotiations; if this devolved into a fight, I would be the only one able to break it up.

We were saved, however, by a sudden laughter on the hill. The crowd turned, and we all watched the Indomitable Auclairs smile and clap Geocelin on the back. If one didn't know the circumstances, they may be mistaken for old friends. Or, they were, and I was watching the casual betrayal of the deceitful canary.

"What are they doing, Outlander?" It was Lysianne asking me, her brow furrowed with worry. It was the first time she spoke directly to me.

"Don't worry, girl," I listened to myself say. "He's a weasel, but he has his principles. He'd never give you to them."

"And what if he tries?" Gillianne asked, her tone incensed.

The Acolyte tilted his head to listen but tried not to be obvious about his interest.

"That would be up to you, my lady," I said, unwilling to conjure a real answer. There would be little I *could* do, and that was the bitter truth of it. We were here, alive, by the Green's will, and we'd have to wait to see what they wanted with us.

Their meeting lasted long enough for nervous anticipation to twist itself into exhaustion. Many of the nobles took their seats, and the youngest children went back to playing games. Minthisha would have busied herself restoring the others if the Acolyte hadn't told her to keep her hood up and her head down. I asked her about a plan, and she knew as little as I. I sat with the heaviness of the day, feeling it all there, present and sore in me.

My eyes drifted closed again. I did not want to fall back into that nightmare. I forced myself to my feet and took a short walk around the children's perimeter.

Peregrine might have been haunted by the same distortions when he visited the Blighted areas. Did he dream of rivals from a century ago forgetting his face? Had he been returned to some twisted version of his home? This *was* his home. These were his children. I should have buried his body.

"Sir Darl?" I turned. Archelaus stood behind me.

"Yes?"

"Are we going to fight them?"

What an obvious and juvenile question: Are *we* going to fight them?

What was I to say to that? Stories of boys whom I'd seen die in war or the fog of battle seemed too honest for now. Instead, I turned to that line of glittering knights and asked, "Which would you want to take on?" I sat with the boy as he rambled about defeating his favorite of the villains and tried to delude myself into thinking our victory could be as easy as he imagined.

When Geocelin finally returned, a hush fell over what little conversation had sprouted. His band surrounded him, insulating him from the children who swarmed him with questions. He pressed through the crowd until he found Minthisha.

"They'll leave a third," he said, nodding to the line of soldiers behind us. "If we give up the rest, we walk away unharmed. They want most of the young women and the children. If we want the older ones, they'll let us keep another twenty."

A low murmur went through the crowd. Little hisses of outrage were followed by wandering eyes. They had already conceded that *someone* would be chosen, and they were thinking of other names so they would not count amongst them.

"We're not dividing them like breeding stock," Minthisha said.

Geocelin shrugged. "We can always just cut their throats, take the pieces of them that are useful, and scatter."

"You wouldn't butcher them now," I said.

"Considering the alternative?" Geocelin asked.

"We can't concede."

"So we'll fight? You, me, and the army of children? Or would you like to take them all on yourself? You're impressive, friend, but even you can't match ten men. Three would be a miracle."

He wasn't wrong. And here, one death lost us everything. By the time I woke, they'd be on their way back to the Green with the children.

"I'm sorry, Minthe. We tried," Geocelin said. "That's enough."

"*Enough*?" Lysiane spoke up. "They'll butcher half of us in that banquet hall the day we are returned. It's not enough. You're supposed to fight for us!"

"They can't go back, Geocelin," Minthisha said.

"It's a wasted venture, Minthe. They're not ready. In another ten years, maybe, but not now."

"In another ten years, there will be less to save," I said. Both looked at me, eyes glassy in the sunlight. I twisted the blade of grass between my fingers.

"Less?" Rosaireth scoffed. "It's your decision when we are ripe for the plucking?"

"Against these men, yes," I said.

"Do you expect us to choose from amongst ourselves?" Gillianne asked, the insult clear in her tone.

"If that's the case, then take Gillie. She's already volunteered," Lysiane said.

The nobles erupted into an argument. Minthisha's eye, dark and infinite as the sky, took in the chaos. Despite its cause, their reaction was a stunning change. Men and women, slim as twigs in tattered robes, shouted and pointed where they had whimpered and submitted not so long ago. Rosaireth and his supporters, who had abstained from most arguments, ran in to break up the fighting.

"Enough!" Rosaireth shouted until the crowd simmered. "Have you forgotten why you're here? All of you? Throwing one another on the block is why we're here!

"We left because we knew anything was better than that tower! If that has changed, then our old captors are there, waiting. But I beg you not to take that offer, not to bend to their terms. We are not butchers. What you've endured, we've all endured together. We've taken this risk together. We've survived together. We stand together now. I want you here, fighting for this miserable blot of dirt we inherited, Lysiane, and you, Gillianne, if for no other reason than I don't want my children or yours to only ever see it from a window. I love you both deeply, and if these strangers will give us nothing more, then I'll give you everything I have. I know I can expect the same from you."

Rosaireth had enough favor to quell the agitated crowd. He spoke to the common sentiment. They'd had enough of controlled sacrifice, and already there was the rousing talk of fighting to the last, a poetic notion that would not see itself realized.

Suddenly, there was a hand on my shoulder and a weight that nearly sent me toppling. "We won't go back! Stone Hand's taught us how to fight!" Archelaus shouted with a hand wrapped around my neck. Half his cohort stood around me, chests puffed.

"Be serious, Archelaus," Lysiane groaned.

"You act as if you've never seen your great-uncle trip over his own sabatons!"

"Listen to her," I told the boy. "You're outmatched."

"Why are we discussing fighting when we could avoid confronting them altogether?" I couldn't pick the owner of that voice from the crowd. Someone else contradicted him, asking how, when the entirety of the Green was watching them. The arguments flared up again.

Some youths spat and threw themselves at us, only to be held back by Lysiane and Rosaireth's men. Scholar, a man who rarely spoke, stood with the help of his son and clapped once. The mob faded to silence with more obedience than we'd ever coaxed from them.

His voice was warm but crackling with age. "We will not wait for your ... verdict. Decide what you're willing to do for us. If this is where you will leave us ... then we *hope* it is amicable. You've done, as you say, enough."

Hesitant as it was, I knew a threat when it was spoken. I was rather impressed with them. I knew the sheer numbers of the nobles would be enough to overpower Geocelin's group if they set their mind to it.

The canary saw it too and cursed again. His band crowded forward like a pack of dogs. They had been markedly quiet through all of this debate, perhaps prepared to defer to him if things turned for the worst. I wrapped my hand around my sword hilt, eyes on the closest ones.

But then, Geocelin looked at Minthisha. "How long would it take to get to Lorenial?"

Minthisha's lips parted, but she seemed unable to summon the words.

"What do you mean?" I asked for her.

"You know full well," Geocelin said. "This Blight kills only the pledged, doesn't it? How long would it take to reach Lorenial, Minthe?"

"F-four—five days. Then there's—"

"Luthor, yes." Geocelin looked at me like he was inspecting stock cattle and groaned. It seemed to pain him as he turned from me to address the children, "Here's what we do: we give them the two-thirds."

There was an immediate uproar, and Geocelin raised his hands until they calmed a little.

"They walk *slow*," he said, loudly and clearly, and the mob seemed to catch onto the scheme hiding in his words then. "It took us weeks to get this far; it should take them weeks to return. The Green doesn't have enough to feed you either. They don't want to starve you. You aren't prisoners of war or barbarians; you're their children."

That provoked a lesser wave of outrage, but they were listening.

"We give them the young ones, the ones who have been hunting with Iliesa and Cecil. The ones who can endure that walk back volunteer them-selves. The rest of you will sustain yourselves here in the forest. On your way back, the rest of you offer to forage and to hunt, and you delay a while. If they're offered a solution to keep you fed for the way back, they won't fuss, especially not with their numbers. That would give us time."

"To do what?" Rosaireth asked.

"Minthe?" Geocelin prompted.

Minthisha gaped at the crowd, as if this was her first time among them. Weak, soft words slipped breathlessly from her lips. "Death."

"Kill Evarund and every man of the Green," Geocelin announced.

There was another shock of murmurs.

Minthisha looked only at Geocelin. "They're not ready."

"They say they are," Geocelin said. "Draw me a map. I'll need to know where to meet you."

"You're not coming along."

"Of course I am, but after we're finished here. Discussing terms is the most excitement they've had in years. We could take our time sorting out which of these nobles counts among the two-thirds, and that's another day right there. What do you say, old man? Ready to die in a blaze of glory?"

For all that we'd done to avoid this path, it did not feel unexpected. I had been walking on wet sands, turning over coral and brushing sand off rocks, and a wave had been building on my horizon. I knew the crash was coming. Now, it was here. When Geocelin asked me what would happen when there was nothing but the children and my hunger, when I thought of Minthisha's land of ash, I thought of this crash.

THE FLIGHT

The Green had given Geocelin the night to deliberate, and we would be remiss not to take advantage of that time. The realm of spruce, ash, and birch was one of loose leaves and thick underbrush that slowed the most agile traveler, and we needed every second. The smoke was still thick enough to cover our retreat. The Acolyte had marked the two spies in the haze and preferred to shoot them both when they thought themselves well-hidden.

Minthisha said hurried goodbyes with grace. I looked on, feeling inept in my own ability to relay any final sentiments. Though familiar, Geocelin's companions were strangers to me. Geocelin and I had little to say to each other, and we would not be parting for long. As for the children, I knew I was an intruder in their tightly woven nest. But as I made to leave, one reached out for me, brushing the frayed edge of my gambeson. Then another. And another.

Archelaus and his little group crowded around me to pat my shoulder and wish me well. A few of the older nobles I had carried from Gillianne's group acknowledged me as I passed. Lysiane, eyes bright and guarded as the first night I'd met her, handed me a loop of braided grass and walked off without saying anything. I recognized the troublemakers, the complainers, and the silent sufferers. Final smiles and soft goodbyes were whispered by familiar faces I wished I knew better. I thought of my boys the day I left to become a Deathless, when they'd grabbed my cloak just to keep me a moment longer.

So many faces, but it was the one I did not see that strengthened my resolve. Lambskin was gone. There was no way to be certain when or under what circumstances, but I knew how he expected to meet again. And in a year or three, I did not want to be trading blows over a ring.

Our flight into the Elder Wood was much swifter without the children behind us. We walked all afternoon and through the night. At daybreak, we could see nothing but the trees. A terrible, creeping thought came to mind as I rose that next morning. *Geocelin could be lying.* This could be little more than a trick to send us away, and he'd relinquish every noble back to the Green and wash his hands of them.

"They will be hungry . . ." Minthisha trailed off, swallowing the question as if breathing life into the thought might make it reality. Geocelin had warned us of the cost of the Green's magic.

"Five days," I said. That was all the time this trip would take. "They weren't butchering their own before. I'm sure they'll want to wait until they can hide it behind a curtain and ceremony. This will be over before they even see stone walls again."

Minthisha nodded numbly.

"When it's done, you'll be there to guide them through whatever losses there are."

"And Goss will be dead," Minthisha said, her words as somber as they were at Leoric's Temple.

I had no way to console her. This was my fault after all. I'd raised the blade of a guillotine over all of our necks, not just the children's or the Green's. Now, we were racing to end the world.

I was racing to Morthia's domain of ashes and the After I could not see. I was going to die, at last and too soon. Death, a true death, was difficult to imagine. Would there be a judgement? Would I walk unaccosted? No matter what happened, if I joined the ranks of Amivia's army of the fallen or was barred to some still, vacant place, I would be gone, and the rest would go to Minthisha. She had been right in taunting me. I was only good for killing, and I was too set in my ways to change them now.

I laid the burden on her to do the rest that I could not. She said none of it, but I sentenced her to years of new harvests and uncalloused hands working under her instruction—motherhood to strangers.

Geocelin must have handed over the children by the second day. He had not wanted this. He'd raged against his execution until now. Again, that thought returned. *He could be lying.* I did not know his companions' opinions or if they even *knew* what he'd sent us out to do. What reason did strangers like them have to forfeit their lives?

The trees were too dense, and we were too far off to hear screams or spot other signs of distress. If the children were being taken, we would not know it.

Minthisha carried on as long as she could, but she had to rest and, worse, sleep. I could carry her to an extent, but there was that weight in the air that tested me as well. I could no longer take the youth of my body for granted. My feet ached. My back was sore. *I* had to rest. In my dreams, I was a withering sack of bones. When I sat awake at night, *everything* felt so tediously suspended.

Minthisha seemed to hate our rests as much as I did. She cursed her legs, staggering before she stopped. My legs were stiff in a way I was not accustomed to, and it was harder for me to catch my breath. Though our progress felt too slow to us, I was encouraged when we started to pass the early signs of a city: mossy mile-markers, overgrown walls, abandoned towers. Frustrated as I was with my strange new exhaustion, we knew we were making good time. On our fourth day, however, complications came our way.

We heard them first.

Compared to the quiet chirp of the woods, our pursuers were obvious. Their chainmail rattled; their armor clicked together. Knights of the Green. It was then that I was sure Geocelin had lied, and the children—the ones that had not been butchered in the highlands—were being dragged back in chains. They had noticed our absence, and Geocelin had told the Green where they could send a few eager soldiers to indulge in a hunt.

I tried to count how many flashes of armor and bright-colored tabards appeared between the trees. Six? I was sure I saw two men with different patterned coats of blue and green.

Minthisha reached into her pocket and collected a handful of gemstone pins in anticipation. I drew my sword. Then the first arrow fluttered past my ear, and that was the snap that threw us into a skirmish. My first instinct was to search for the archer, but a knight in a green surcoat, armed with a battleaxe, charged in from my right. The weapon came swinging sideways for my torso. If I stepped out of the way, that would leave a clear path for the blade to cut into Minthisha behind me.

His swing forced me to close in. I stepped forward, one arm extending to grab the shaft of the axe while the other drove my sword clumsily forward. The point of my steel pushed against but did not break through the gambeson. I drew back, only for another arrow to brush just past my cheek. Hot blood throbbed in my ear.

A third shaft flickered close to the knight's face. He startled and tried to pull away, forgetting I had a hand on his weapon. I dropped my sword, grabbed the ax, and threw the entirety of my weight through my shoulder into the knight. He fell back with me on top of him. I righted myself, swinging the axehead down and crushing the steel gorget into his neck.

I oriented myself quickly. Minthisha was behind me. Three men to my left—two arming swords and one mace. Two men in front of me—spear and war hammer. No archer in sight.

"To the witch!" one of them shouted.

They tried to cut to my right—following Minthisha's flight. I sprang to intercept them. I focused my attention on the spearman, prepared to take a blow from the others when they suddenly froze in place. The knights of the Green were not petrified. They hovered mid-step, one in the middle of a thrust, the other wound up for a swing, but it was a slow act, as if they'd been dropped into molasses. Sunlight reflected off a scattering of gemstones unsteadily stuck in the ground. Minthisha must have tossed it behind her, giving me a precious few seconds to deal with the spearman.

Having seen what I had done with the axe knight, he was trying to retreat. Just as I had gotten close enough to catch him, though, his war hammer friend rushed in swinging. I brought up the battleaxe to block the hammer, and the spearman darted away. The force of the hammer's blow sent me flying back.

I couldn't recover my footing before he was on me again. He swung and aimed for my chest to crush my ribs and punch the breath out of me. There was nowhere for me to go, no way for me to block. All I could do was move with it. When the head of the hammer met my chest, I grabbed the shaft, dropped, and kicked myself back. The hammer's head was pulled into the cushion of my gambeson, leaves slid out under me, and the sudden momentum threw the knight's weight back with me.

Like that, he was forced to the ground, and I had wrested his weapon from his control. I panted as I righted my grip on the hammer's shaft, watching the knight start to recover much sooner than I could compensate for. Had it always been so difficult to transition from the floor to my feet? I was about to take a wild swing when the spearman came rounding back to us.

The point of his spear caught me in the shoulder, digging in sideways into the meat of my back. The knight beneath me began to crawl away, and the spearman pushed, trying to drive me into the floor. I felt my legs giving, my back spasming and recoiling from the pain. I was forced to my knees. My palms braced against the ground, the hammer slipping between my fingers. I could feel myself being driven further down when suddenly, a burst of concentrated wind shrieked behind me. The spearman's weight was thrown from my back.

Minthisha's green cloak flashed in my peripheral vision. The war hammer knight tried to right himself, and I threw myself at him. We struggled in the dirt, kicking and hurling leaves and dirt as often as fists, but eventually, I had a solid grip on the hammer shaft and swung into the knight's visor. I hit him again with such force I dented the metal plate.

I turned, ready for more, when a sudden, sharp whistle echoed through the trees.

"She's stuck!" someone shouted down from a hillock.

The spearman ran, kicking up leaves as he fled into the woods. The others followed, toppling against each other in their flight. I hadn't even touched the swordsmen, and they were retreating already?

A cascade of crunching leaves gave away a final band member, the one who'd signaled the others, but it was hard to pick out where he was in the trees. I took one step toward the noise and felt my knee buckle under a sudden, sharp stab of pain. My hands flew on instinct to the source of the burning in my leg.

Minthisha said something, but I did not hear. Her voice might as well have been like the rustle of the trees, as my thudding heart could only take so much in the aftermath of our skirmish. I recognized the fletching in my thigh.

Theodoulos.

"What?" Minthisha panted. I'd spoken out loud. I turned to see the witch standing just behind me, looking like she took the worst of her scrap. Leaves were tangled in the coils of her hair, and a new cut—a deep one—bled down the bridge of her nose. Had that been the spearman's work?

"You're hurt," I said instead.

"What?" To my horror, she looked down, and I followed her gaze. It felt like a dream at first, a terrible nightmare, as I saw a dark spot blooming against her shirt, just above the hip. When she pulled back her hand, her palm came away slick and red. "Oh . . ."

She swayed.

I caught her, but pain flared in my leg. Joint by joint, we collapsed. I froze with my knees in the dirt, one leg braced to support her weight while her feet splayed out beneath her. When had it happened? With the spearman? Before? I hadn't seen it. I didn't want to believe it, but there was the split skin and the smell of iron.

Minthisha pulled up her shirt. It was a deep gash, pooling with dark blood. "My—my pack."

I scoured the forest floor. Bodies. Gemstones. Hammer. Her pack lay just behind us, where the spearman had been thrown. I crawled to it and threw it to her. She dug inside, unrolling strips of leather with one hand. She found a vial of something and swallowed it whole.

"Darl, come here!"

I did, my pulse rippling through my neck, every movement too light. She gave me instructions, and I followed them, barely aware of the coarse cloth when I unrolled it. My fingers shook so badly I had to uncork a vial of yellow powder with my teeth. It tasted bitter and numbed my tongue. She brought out a bone needle and catgut for stitches and took over that work despite my feeble insistence. She sucked in loud breaths with each pull of the needle.

I stormed around, feeling a need to kick out the pain, to hit something. I shouted for the knights to come back. We had a fight to finish. No one answered. I kicked the man with the battleaxe. I stomped on the chest of the war hammer knight. My leg gave out under me, and suddenly, Minthisha was there, hand on my calf.

"Sit still," she grumbled. Her hands were steady, but her bottom lip quivered as she extracted the arrow and bandaged the wound. She wrapped my shoulder, sprinkling it with a powder that burned.

"Cowards couldn't even follow through. They'll stick us with pins before they have the courage to skewer us," I growled.

She shook her head. "Good thing I'm not the one killing Luthor."

"You're only unleashing the Blight."

She tried to smile, but it became a pinched thing as a new wave of pain rolled through her. She let herself fall back, her gray hair splayed out all around her as she braced her hand on her wound.

"Will you die?" I asked. It was a ridiculous question, but she was still so composed. Perhaps it looked worse than it was.

Minthisha huffed, a strained little laugh escaping her. "Not yet. Can you walk?"

Not well. "If I died, I could . . ." I couldn't. We didn't have the time. If I died, Minthisha would be injured and unprotected. I dreaded to think of what a few days exposed to the elements alone would do to her. I was trapped with a bad leg and a limp shoulder.

"We can't have that," she said, understanding our predicament at once.

"What happened to you?"

"I threw the spearman off of you. He tackled me." Minthisha stopped to swallow. "He had a knife. It's not so deep, I think. Will *you* live?"

"I should be able to last."

"Three days? That's how long it'll take to reach Luthor from here."

"I thought only one."

She looked at me helplessly. We both had been trailing at less than our best, and now we were heaving labored breaths on the forest floor with injuries that would kill any other man. Three days seemed to be a generous estimation. If the knife wound didn't kill her, the strain of the trip *would*.

She exhaled a long, pained breath. "They didn't stay for long, did they?"

"No."

She's stuck. The knights had all gone running after her, not me.

"They know."

How much, I could not guess, but they knew enough to want to stop us. They knew we were headed for Lorenial. Theodoulos had known about Luthor, if not the purpose behind her commissioned hunt. I thought of

Geocelin shaking hands with the Indomitable Auclairs and trading over the details of our plan in exchange for clemency.

It all seemed so far away and so suddenly unreachable. The noose of time tightened around my neck, choking.

Minthisha watched the sway of the treetops. "They don't *know*; if they did, the whole of the Green would be after us. They know I'm involved, and they overestimate me as much as you. They think that without me, you'll be useless. We're close to Lorenial. We can be there by tonight."

"No. You need to rest," I told her.

"To do what?" Minthisha asked wryly. "Time's not my friend now, Sir Deathless."

I fell back, letting the weight of my body sink against the earth. A twig poked into my hip and rubbed against the shoulder wound she'd just covered. But the trees swayed, and the sky was so gray it almost looked white. I felt the thrum of my body against the earth. I listened to the little snapping shifts as the crawling things beneath the leaves that would gnaw me down to the bone. It'd be the simplest thing to stay here until we breathed our last. If only Morthia's domain could be so bright.

Our steps were heavy, unbalanced things. We collected her gemstones, the battleaxe, and my sword and continued onward. Minthisha could stand and walk for a few steps on her own, but we found she did better if she was able to put some weight on my arm. My leg didn't seem so terrible at first, but it devolved into a limp that had me half-collapsed against Minthisha in turn by the evening.

It was nightfall by the time we saw the outer walls of Lorenial: blocks of white marble, aged and mossy. Part of the structure had collapsed, making it more akin to ruins than a grand city's entrance, but Minthisha warned me it would not be a humble walk. The city spanned miles wide, and the bulk of our time would be spent navigating the labyrinthine streets.

We took shelter in a stone building that overlooked the city; the stables and lofted beds suggested it may have once been a roadhouse. There was a comical hunting scene chipping off the wall: a man being chased by boars and rabbits armed with maces and arrows. Minthisha was more mobile than me, which I took to be a good sign. She winced as she cleared out a little space for us and checked on both our dressings. I was given another vial of something tacky and sour, and she went out a little ways behind the house and set a snare in the hopes of catching some breakfast in the morning. When it was time to bed down, however, she was shivering even wrapped in her cloak. I tried not to think about it as she curled up to sleep. I watched shadows shift in the trees and tried not to think too much about how still she was.

I peered out from the narrow door, listening to the night crickets and the crunch of leaves under boots. My hand flexed and relaxed on the grip of my sword. I expected another arrow, the flash of a bright blue cloak in the starlight. Instead, I watched the empty dark until it faded into my dreams.

I watched my villa burn and buried my sons in my sleep. I watched Clement be picked apart by crows and decay under the shade of an orchard tree beside Peregrine until their bodies were nothing but compost for the roots. I watched my fingers, withered and brittle, break off of me piece by piece as all my years ripped me apart, and I collapsed to dust.

When I woke, there was a terrible, rattling breathing in the room.

◆

Minthisha was slow to wake, and when she did, she couldn't stand on her own. We'd caught a rabbit, and I stripped and cooked it for her, but she only swallowed a few pieces of the meat before waving me off. I tried not to worry, even as she uncovered her oozing bandage and fresh blood trailed from her stitches. I pretended not to know what the terrible, swollen bruising and smell were. She sighed and asked me for my arm, and I gave it to her without question.

It was not a mile to the wall, but by the time we reached it, I had to carry Minthisha across the threshold into the ruined city of Lorenial. The gate was a work of heavy iron and timber. Black scorch marks, splintered hinges, and warped ironwork were the scars of a siege that had defaced it. There were no bodies nor tools of war.

We walked through a peasant burrow similar to the one I'd seen in the Green Castle. While nature promised to reclaim the House of Oghir, Lorenial had already been overtaken. Where stone once towered, nature stood taller. Mature trees sprouted from the windows and caved-in roofs. Thick roots wrapped around leaning homesteads, and moss coated wide city streets. Everything was large here: the doors, the windows, the archways.

When we sat back to rest in the sunlight, Minthisha beamed. "I missed these little designs. See the animals carved there? They loved snails, of all things."

"The giants?"

"What do you mean by that?" she asked, tracing the pattern on a step.

"I heard they built the city."

She hummed. "There was a city here before Lorenial. We came after. Builders laid down tile and remodeled the streets and houses to their liking. The snail was ours, our little gardeners. This was a place for architects, craftsmen, arcanists, and mathematicians. Giants did not know half of what we learned from them, and we built libraries and taught anyone who asked in the hopes that the same would come to pass for us." She traced the spiral shell with her nail. "Expanding out eternally."

"It might still come to pass," I said, though I'd tried not to mention the nobles directly since we'd left. Theodoulos always referred to his books, and I'd overheard many a snobbish debate by the children that used book titles to settle their arguments. The smile Minthisha gave me was too polite to challenge me. "I'm sorry you won't see it."

I wanted her to counter me, to dismiss my worries with a scoff, but she didn't.

"I didn't expect to," Minthisha said instead. "I counted on the effort killing me. Luthor's sorcery created an imperfect seal. If we're fortunate, it might be simpler than it was the first time, like unclogging a stream. But it'd be easier to kill him. I didn't invite you for the company."

"Assuming he doesn't kill me first."

"Well, I expect you to do what you can to draw out your defeat if that comes to pass. It'll be your last death. You should savor it."

My last death. The thought of it shouldn't sit in such an uneasy place in my heart. I had lived for an eternity, as close as any man could understand it. I was older than my great-grandfather and had seen more of the world than even the kings of my time would have ever dreamt. I walked through the end of the world, and some childish part of me wanted more. It felt like stepping out of a banquet hall just as a party was striking up again. But I'd already been up all night and endured the boring lull. I wondered if I had aged the way I did in my dreams, if I had lived to watch my sons and their friends strike up the band, if I would toast my last cup and eagerly shuffle on to bed.

"And it'll be your first," I said, more shaken by that.

She hummed in agreement, and then it was true. She would die. They'd killed her. "Is it supposed to be terrifying? Even as old as I am?"

"Perhaps. I don't know," I admitted.

Aside from the expansive wall, there was no clear sign of where the heart of the city lay. There was no grand fortress, no great hall, no structure built to intimidate and show power. Instead, we navigated through lush meadows that might have once been markets. We walked through old homesteads littered with old furnishings. We found a small pond in an open plaza where the street had collapsed into its well source. Little golden fish circled in the dark water.

I put Minthisha down for a drink. Her sable skin was slick with sweat. The fever had come so fast.

"Are we close?" I asked, unsure how much longer she'd be coherent.

She nodded. "Not far now. Do you need to rest?"

"I'd rather be there sooner."

"I do need you to *attempt* to win," Minthisha said. "I don't know if—"

I raised my hand to quiet her. I heard it, the soft footfalls on the stone and moss. Armor. Mail. I drew my sword.

"Come out! I can hear you!"

They were somewhere in those streets, hidden in the overgrown homes.

And then, like rats, they emerged from the alcoves of the city. One came in from the streets to my right. Three to my left. Two archers at my back. The plaza was expansive, and they'd have no trouble using distance to their advantage. The two swordsmen, the mace, a new knight with a polearm, and the war hammer. I'd smashed in the knight's visor, but someone must have shoved communion down his throat.

Some had come forward without their helmets. The heat must have gotten to them. Seeing them now, they mostly appeared to be as slim-faced and youthful as Theodoulos. Unless the Green had made a habit of pledging such young men much earlier, it seemed the novices had been thrown at us. Perhaps their elders did not want to risk traveling so close to the Blight, and either logic or pecking order had decided who hunted us.

Any other time, this might have been nothing. If I were overwhelmed, I could toss down my sword and let myself be killed. But now, I could not die and leave Minthisha unguarded.

Theodoulos looked resplendent in his laundered tunic and cloak, his hair oiled and beaded with gold. His legs seemed to be working fine, and though he had a new scar on his brow, his right eye had been saved. He pinched the fletching of his arrow between embossed leather gloves.

"We can do this here, Sir Darl," he said. "I had hoped there'd be no need for these theatrics and the witch would die in the night."

"I'm right here, boy," Minthisha said.

"I've come to extend an invitation," Theodoulos went on, addressing me alone. "Whatever business you have in these ruins, it stops now. Surrender the witch and come with us. She has conspired with Geocelin of Pulrodge and other barbarians against the king. You were caught in the middle of this frightful upset, and if you prove your loyalty now, you'll be welcomed back to the Green. We'll dress you in proper armor and give you a sword that isn't stained with a traitor's blood."

"And then what?" I asked.

"Then we'll drink in Evarund's hall as brothers and feast and forget your transgressions."

I wished some part of me burned with well-founded anger then, but there was only a bitterness that coated the back of my tongue. This is what Theodoulos had wanted, because the alternative was far worse, and he knew that.

"You can't take them back to that life."

"We already are, Darl. I know things are different where you are from, but your sympathies are misplaced. We take our communions to survive, not out of some gleeful malice. There are those of us who will continue the great legacy of our fathers and those who serve us in other ways. Some people are not meant for greatness. I would rather meet you as a friend than as an enemy. Whatever this witch is asking of you, it will do us no favors. This is not the time for division."

I hated that posturing talk, the same kind he used on me when we first met in the graveyard. "You don't want that life, Theo. If it doesn't tear you apart, you'll lose all sense of the harm you do, and you'll become something less than human."

"What do you want, Darl?" Theodoulos snipped. "Please, this is exhausting. What is it about this stand that matters to you?"

"Theo, it's not for my sake, and it's not for yours. I wish it was for yours. I truly do. You've made your choice . . . I don't blame you, but you have to let us go."

"Don't pretend to have scruples just because no one ordered you to do it! You didn't protest when I told you to kill Alanus. You *would* have killed

Sigmund. The men and women of the Green are treated better than any of the barbarians you met out in the Barrens. They live better lives under our care, and if it upsets you that young men have to earn their place in that hall, then you're more naive than I. Hunting men in the wild does not change the fact that a life is lost for your own sake."

It did not, and that was the crux of the problem. Minthisha sagged against me.

"How many will you bury in your lifetime, boy?" she wheezed. Her voice was soft, just barely reaching Theodoulos. "How many will be enough? I know what it's taken to stand where you stand now. No child should be forced to pay such a price."

"I don't want your pity, witch!" he said sharply. "I want you to stop poisoning Darl with your false ideas of righteousness. Mourn your glory days in the swamp, but we live in a new world. I did everything right. Why must I be punished?"

"Why does water wear away at rock?" she asked.

"I know her schemes better than you, Darl," Theodoulos said. "Her people are the reason the Green is all that's left in the Hallowed Lands. The Blight is her doing. You may not like how things are now, but we are alive. The witch just wants death for all of us."

"Just *us*!" Minthisha snapped.

"Then take the traitor's sword and drive it into your throat, and leave the rest of us alone!" he snapped. Theodoulos pulled the string of his bow taut.

I lunged in front of Minthisha just as the knight to my left gave a great cry. I swung with enough force to send him staggering back. Before I could advance, the polearm knight intercepted. An arrow fluttered past my hip from behind us. I pulled Minthisha to my back and clumsily deflected the stab of the polearm with Alanus' sword.

My hand was not ready, and I was stuck in the hip. I stepped back only to feel the thud of a blunt weapon making contact with my tender shoulder.

There was nowhere to retreat. I couldn't create distance or retaliate with Minthisha, and they were using that to their advantage. I felt something nick my heel.

Minthisha yelped and collapsed behind me. We were surrounded, and each knight was primed to skewer us. We had to run. I reached for Minthisha, ready to face the consequences of showing my back.

Two swordsmen were primed to take their swings. One suddenly reared back; an arrow slipped under the collar of his helmet. The other was thrown on his back by Geocelin's Flayed. She had driven her sword into his heart in the time it took for him to scream. Behind her, the polearm knight was thrown into a dance of heavy swings and tiny cuts with the Silver Tongue.

The skirmishes that broke out around me ended as quickly as they had begun. Theodoulos' company retreated. The Acolyte sank a final arrow into the mace wielder's back, and the rest fled, intimidated by the slightest show of force.

"What state have you two found yourselves in?" Geocelin asked, all smiles, though there was a nasty new cut in his clothing at the shoulder and a gap in his bottom teeth. He fished a finger from his pouch and blew the blood from his nose.

"You're here."

"Yes. I'm told this is where I'm to meet death. You two, however, were supposed to wait for us."

Though I knew it had not been too long, I had doubted him from the start and was never more glad to be proven wrong. "Don't start crying on me, old man."

Then I remembered myself.

"Minthisha!" I said. "She needs . . ."

"Yes, I see. Iliesa!" Geocelin called. The Flayed arrived and began to pull a collection of herbs from her satchel.

"What'd you do to yourself, Minthe?" Geocelin asked.

"Are the children alright?" she asked.

"Have you no confidence in me? Lie back."

I wanted to leave them to her and walk the perimeter with the Silver Tongue and the Acolyte, but Geocelin all but pushed me down.

"You're staying right here until Iliesa can take a look at the mess you made as well. I was getting worried when we were following more blood than tracks. It's a good thing that little rat shouts so loud."

"Where's the rest of your band?" I asked.

There was another aside from Lambskin missing, but Geocelin took my meaning. And though he knew I wanted to know why, his answer was measured and diplomatic. "Everyone who wants to be here is."

"And the children?" I asked.

"We left them four days ago and came after you as fast as we could manage. They did well. No little revolts. No screaming. As far as the Green knows, they're returning quietly."

"Theo. He might—"

"Yes, yes, old man. I know. Stop squirming. Let us take care of things for an afternoon. Arms up, let's see about that cut." Geocelin stripped me and cleaned the worst of my wounds. The Flayed ground together a few salves for myself and Minthisha. The two of us were set side by side like patients sharing a medical tent. She was given as many instructions to twist and breathe and drink as I, all the while the Flayed glowered at our injuries like we'd wanted them in the first place.

They set a fire and made camp around us. The Silver Tongue made two bundles of cloth and grass to support our heads while the Flayed boiled a tiny dish of water and twisted strands of her own hair to make thread. Minthisha found that fascinating and plied her with many questions about her methods as she worked. The Flayed brought out a hooked needle about the width of a cat's tooth that both Minthisha and I recoiled at. I went first, biting my tongue through the burning flare of thread being tugged through skin. I had not missed this kind of slow healing. Minthisha critiqued her stitches, which sparked a spirited argument about medicine I did not have the foreknowledge to follow. Despite their argument coming to a good-natured end, the Flayed looked only more dour by the time she finished. She pulled Geocelin aside, and they whispered in the shadows out of our earshot.

"She's telling him I'm dying, isn't she?" Minthisha said, her voice grainy and melodic. She watched them through her half-lidded eye, seemingly moments from a dream.

"Tonight?"

Mithisha hummed. "Did I have any other commitments?"

"Luthor."

"You'll take care of him for me. I have visitors."

She tilted her head like she was gesturing to someone, but there was only empty cobblestone beside us. She twisted to watch Geocelin and the Flayed from a better angle; their bent heads and careful glances in our direction did not suggest good news. When they spoke, they did so with the shadows of their faces turned away.

"You think they'll tell us?" I asked her.

She smiled, but I knew by now she was too exhausted to laugh.

"Might think us too fragile. We'll see, won't we?"

"We'll see," I repeated hollowly. I didn't want to fall asleep again, though my body was hot and exhausted from the strain of our long walk and the Flayed's manipulations. What if I fell asleep and Minthisha was gone by the time I woke?

"Do you think . . . tonight?"

"You heard the children are alright?" she asked, sounding so soft and melodic as she ignored my question. "That's good. They were clever little things, weren't they? You had all your overexcited warriors. Hopefully they're not too much trouble. They'll be alright."

"They won't even see the Green," I assured her.

She smiled. "And they'll be walking in the Garden in a fortnight."

I thought she'd be angrier. Her bitter tears had dried at Leorcis' Temple when she'd found them useless, but that did not mean he had no resentments left. For the children, I knew she would not show them that ugliness and treat them with kindness, playing her role with serenity. Perhaps she was serene and had taken to them as quickly as they had taken to her. If it was obligation or redemption that blotted out her anger, as Geocelin suggested, she offered me no more than that glimpse, and I would not demand an answer now.

There was something, however, that dampened her smile. Geocelin cast a nervous glance in Minthisha's direction. He turned away as soon as their eyes met.

"You'll watch him for me?" Minthisha asked.

"You should say goodbye."

"He wouldn't want that." She adjusted herself, sinking deeper against the bundles. "There was a time when he looked at me as if I brought out the sun. Then the soldiers came, and I hurt that boy, Darl. I'd lived so long, and I thought it would pass like a storm. I left him behind. Now, here we are, and I'm leaving him behind again."

"I think he's forgiven you for it."

"You're mistaken."

"He came all this way for us."

"In spite of me. He won't let my mistakes be repeated. Where I failed for him, he won't for them."

All this talk of failure from a woman who had lived among and wept for her children. A woman who had known them. My house was a strange place, foreign and uncomfortable to me. It was suffocating and tense, and I resented it for that. The only relief I felt was when I was packing to leave for war or had brought half the camp with me to my front door. War made sense. I knew what my place was there. But fatherhood? A husband's and lord's duties? I fumbled through those expectations as they came and begrudged their hollow reward.

But there had also been the ones I thought I'd done the best for. The ones I thought I knew how to save.

"There was a boy in the war camps," I said, moved to a sudden confession. "He was a starved little thing that scavenged the battlefield for a living. He was one of dozens, but he had a little brother, and the two of them looked so much like my sons that I took a liking to them. I did what I could within my rank. I fed them. When they had no shelter, I found them a tent. When they were sick, I paid for the medicine. I told the boy he could act as my page and make a good living in war. And he hated me, and I did not understand it. I thought it was pride.

"Of course he hated me; I'd burned down his homestead, I'd stolen his family's horses, I'd robbed him of his father, and I told this boy who'd only ever wanted to raise horses that he should aspire to war. He did terrible things, and he was monstrous, but I didn't understand what I was to him. I regret that I spared him so little and thought it a fortune. I regret that I kept my distance out of a sense of . . . " Preservation? Pride? Fear? "I don't know. But you are not like that."

"Oh, I am. I was. You have caught me in a good century, Sir Deathless," Minthisha said, flashing me a grin that could have belonged to Geocelin. I doubted she was ever anything like me.

"You made mistakes, but I think you've done well."

"Then that's one of us. We could have done better if we had more time," she mused. We were speaking of greater things now. "Perhaps we shouldn't have given them a choice. We should have taken them into the Barrens. There, they wouldn't have been chased, and we would have had time. A year. We could have had them ready in a year, maybe two."

I thought of my boys. Little Justinian and rebellious Valorant. Once, they were slapping one another with sticks in the yard, mimicking the postures and forms I practiced every morning. Small hands that fit in my palm with smooth skin. I set that toy horse on their rafters to look after them while I was away.

Then, I left for war, and I brought it back with me. They learned to endure. When I next left and returned, they became men. Calloused hands and sharp jaws. Justinian bent over the villa's account book. Valorant led the men of the village in every harvest festival. They had built a life without me, and I was a guest in my own home.

Maybe if I'd stayed for another year, I could have mended what I'd broken, or maybe it would have been worse, and I would have only been rot festering in old wounds. Some of it was wishful thinking. I wasn't the man I was a century ago, a month ago, and I would not do as well then as I imagined. But I also knew it was all fantasies, imagined stitches on wounds I did see and could not mend when I had the time, and someone else had to take up the needle.

"We had the time we had," I heard myself say. "We can't change our mistakes. They'll just have to make do with what we left them."

"That's still terrifying."

THE DEAD CITY

Minthisha did not pass away that night, but she was gone by morning.

She had slept for a while, and I sat up watching her ragged breaths strain her chest in the silver moonlight. The muttering began as something soft, almost peaceful, but then it went on. Its pace quickened, cramming between breaths. The embers of the fire crackled and hissed. The wind picked up, moaning from the hollow bones of the city. Black water lapped at the plaza's tiles.

She started coughing, and it kept going. It grew thick with phlegm and strained the back of her throat. Then it muted, and she was choking. The fire flared a blistering white, the wind raged, the water crashed in foamy waves.

The Flayed dug into Minthisha's mouth and pulled. She hooked something like hair at first, then a clump of it, and it thickened and tangled as the Flayed wrapped more of it around her hand and tugged. Something snapped, and Minthisha vomited and went slack.

The fire snuffed out. The wind died. The water stilled. The old woman's eye reflected the stars.

In the morning, she was different. Her movements were slow. Her expression did not change when the Flayed, or Geocelin, or I addressed her, but she heard us. She would turn her head if we said her name, and when the Flayed offered her a strip of rabbit, she took it and chewed without complaint. Even as she blinked, I knew it was to see something leagues away.

"Minthe? Remember me?" Geocelin cooed. "Minthe, do you remember where we're going? Why we're here?"

When she found words, at last, she spoke with a richer voice than I'd ever heard from her. "There are stars in the ground. Earth black as the sky. He's buried there. We're waiting there."

Geocelin swallowed. "Iliesa . . . You can . . . you . . ."

He was on his feet, retreating to the water's edge with that fragment of a thought. The Flayed took over. She cleaned the brown spittle from her chin and neck. She braided frayed strands of her hair and secured them in place with a leather thong.

"Hello, Mother Clay," the Flayed said. "I'm not one of yours, but I've heard stories about you. Are you coming with us?"

That, Minthisha acknowledged, and she readily agreed with a firm nod.

Despite her new state, the limits of Minthisha's body had not changed. Geocelin refused to carry her, and I could not. The Acolyte was their marksman and needed both hands, so the Silver Tongue took up the responsibility. He bowed at the waist and said something in his own language before reaching for her. Minthisha responded to him in kind, speaking that strange series of consonants and nasal sounds before extending her hand. The Silver Tongue responded with a showman's wink and kissed her hand. He wouldn't tell Geocelin what she said.

The Flayed gave me a vial of something to numb the pain and revitalize me, but that could only compensate for so much. My leg could bear my weight again, but the Acolyte had fetched a sturdy branch from one of the city's overgrown trees. Overnight, he'd fashioned a makeshift cane for me. I knew it would be best, but I could not help the fear that taking it would somehow connect me to that lumbering, pruned creature in my nightmares. I accepted the gift. In the end, I preferred to walk on my own rather than collapse onto Geocelin's shoulder.

We moved on with muttered instruction from Minthisha. Geocelin and his companions exchanged a few words and strategy, keeping a lookout for Theodoulos' party, but when I offered to help, they all exchanged that same look.

"We'll take care of it. You just keep up with Feras," Geocelin said, pointing to the Silver Tongue.

It was not an outright dismissal, but something slightly more unsettling: I was being coddled like the noble children had been. Here I was, no less Deathless, but with a limp and a cane, and put under the attention of four caretakers. I could tell the Silver Tongue was slowing his pace to match mine. The Flayed and the Acolyte scouted ahead but never went out of earshot. They had better reasons to assume we were being followed, and they seemed hesitant to leave us unattended. Geocelin guarded the rear, making a show of admiring the architecture and taking his time so I wouldn't rush.

We were deep in the heart of Lorenial, where the city showcased the height of its ambitions. We climbed hillsides worth of steps where monuments carved from marble spiraled up over our heads and were topped with the sprouting of wild trees. While admiring the view from the top, we spotted a cluster of shadows trying to hide under overhangs. We had a solid lead on Theodoulos' group, or they weren't trying to close it.

"They know she wanted Luthor dead," I said.

"If they know why, it's too late for them to send for anyone else," Geocelin said. "Who knows? Maybe they'll let us try our luck. Luthor might do their work for them."

I understood that Geocelin could have his reasons for changing his mind, but after all those hushed conversations, I wondered if the Acolyte or the Silver Tongue even knew what we had set out to do.

"They all agreed to this?" I asked, keeping my voice low.

Geocelin turned to his company. "Gentlemen!" he belted. "How are we enjoying our last day alive?"

"It's rapturous," the Flayed deadpanned.

"I was overdue for a good walk," the Acolyte said.

The Silver Tongue and Geocelin exchanged a few foreign words, which ended in the Silver Tongue laughing.

We continued to a city block where the facades had been decorated with impressions of sand and seashells. Pillars of another had been carved with hundreds of symbols none of us could discern. Little copper statues of ducks, rabbits, foxes, and mice, now green with age, marched along the railing of an old bridge. Seeing them, I realized how few gods I'd seen set in alcoves or carved into the walls. I had not expected statues of the Young Gods on display, but there was not even Amivia's circle to be seen here.

Mosaic tiles the size of my thumbnail covered an entire street in blue and yellow geometric patterns. The Silver Tongue scraped away clumps of dirt with his heel to marvel at the colors, faded oranges, and deep blues. There was one mechanism in front of a massive building that we stopped to inspect. Spinning pieces groaned from their perpetual movement, but there was no face nor decoration to suggest their purpose.

We turned into one sunlit square canopied with fruiting trees. Pale yellow fruit lay split in the street. The Acolyte scooped one up and offered it to the Flayed, who took a bite and handed it back. Geocelin tapped me on the shoulder and offered a broken half to me.

"Careful, there's worms."

I broke off a piece and offered it to Minthisha. She had reacted to little all day, but she reached for this as soon as I extended it to her.

"Poor man's apple," she said in that strange voice. "They should not be. A man came on foot, trading seeds. Too cold. Roots too shallow. But look how she digs. Here she is. Watch her bloom."

She twisted the flesh between her fingers until they were tacky with juice.

Geocelin cleared his throat. "I-I'll go look ahead. Theo and his miscreants must have something planned."

I let him go. There was no comfort I could offer. Whether it was for his sake or hers, they had no parting words. Minthisha lay against the Silver Tongue, and her eye looked out into eternity through me.

I wished she had given me some sentiment to pass along, perhaps a memento only they would understand. But it was a fantasy to imagine she'd be able to mend the years between them with a tearful goodbye, that she might have on her person some mythical token to express all that was left unsaid. I twisted the ring of the three mountains on my finger; that's all the farewell I ever got, and he didn't know that was all there would ever be. Imperfect and bitter as it was, it was better than nothing.

We moved along through the city at an unhurried pace, which I was sure was for my benefit, but we still came to the end so soon.

Minthisha pointed us to a final street where the trees were thick-trunked and old. The sunlight leaked through translucent leaves in golden tendrils, catching the pollen drifting through the air. "He is buried there, deep in the roots where the rot is cold."

The six bodies lay scattered on beds of grass. The bloodstains had been washed away by years of rain, but the marks of their violent ends could be read on the building's facades. A man had been crushed against a wall here. Another had been impaled in the street. An arm had been torn off. A tattered green tassel fluttered around a discarded blade hilt.

Minthisha raised two trembling fingers and pointed to steps extending just beyond the courtyard. At the top, an overgrown archway beckoned us inside. Heavy footsteps echoed from an unseen stone floor. He was there, so close.

Though I knew we'd been walking into the Blight for some time, I had not felt a distinct change until now, looking at our final door. Death waited there, one way or the other.

It was then that our shadows made themselves known. Theodoulos and his pack walked into the courtyard after us, hands at their sides, weapons sheathed.

"Sir Theodoulos!" Geocelin called. "Come to grace us with your presence once more? Good, I've been meaning to return your arrows to you."

"It kills us, doesn't it?" Theodoulos said. "You want the Blight to happen. If you want death, Sir Darl, all you need to do is walk through that door alone. You, Toad, I don't know what you want but to spite us."

"I live for the opportunity," Geocelin sneered.

"Theo, it's not what you think."

"What is it, Darl? I thought you said you were done killing for other men's ambitions," Theodoulos said.

"This is for your sons and daughters," I said. "Any man granted immortality will die. The rest continue on. We'll bring an end to lives overextended, and we'll give this world over to them."

"Overextended? I'm hardly as old as my father was before he was butchered. That was his fate, but his alone. Don't drag the rest of us to the flies' kingdom with you. Enough people have died for nothing."

"They have," the Acolyte said.

"And what do you know of it?" Theodoulos sneered. "You've killed more men than I've met, no doubt. Now that you're suddenly so concerned, why not come back to the Green? If you object to how the unaligned are treated, then perhaps you should be putting your efforts toward that change instead."

"Change has already happened," Geocelin said. "My brothers were thirty-six when they were hanged for treason and conspiracy. They freed fifty-three prisoners from the Green who were recaptured and butchered within the year. *Your* brothers died at fifteen, and the Green didn't have to do a thing to add them to their banquet but promise you dignity and a title. That's change."

Theodoulos bared his teeth at Geocelin, but chose to hold his tongue. He sought me out instead. "Darl, *please*. This isn't fair."

It wasn't. "I'm so sorry, Theo."

Like that, it sparked. Swords were drawn, arrows were nocked, and a whip of fire lashed about us. Geocelin had a hand on my chest and was pushing me back. "Through the archway! Now!"

A line of fire burst beside me. The Acolyte drew back an arrow as a swordsman charged him. I didn't see how it ended. The Silver Tongue and Minthisha raced ahead of me. I heard heavy boots catching up from behind us. Arrows struck the dirt. Swords clashed and rang just as I crossed under the arch.

The courtyard was wide and flooded with sunlight. What had once been an open market square had flourished into a wild arena. Moss, ferns, and wildflowers covered the work of exacting stone masons. Rooftops were overgrown with lush ivy and trees. In the center of this open field was a yew tree, thick-trunked and stooped low with age. Its roots had ripped up half the earth, coiling out to grasp the edges of its city.

The Silver Tongue made for the tree and intended to follow him when a sudden hammer of force crashed straight into my back. I didn't so much as exhale before I was on the ground. My breath hadn't been knocked out of me, but the fall had been hard.

A knight of the Green cursed behind me, and I heard encroaching footsteps. The next strike was coming. It had been a mace, hadn't it? He hadn't hit my spine, and the blow must have been barely out of his reach for the force not to shatter me from the inside, but he'd have no trouble bashing my skull in if I didn't move *now*.

I heard Geocelin shouting and the shriek of metal on metal. The knight of the Green was right above me. His foot pressed on my shoulder. I reached for it, desperate to throw him off of me or to distract him from his blow, then suddenly he was gone. No. He had been ripped from me.

An armored man in tattered white stood on top of the crumpled splay of limbs that had been the knight moments ago. A sword, a slab of metal chipped with age and use until its edge looked like serrated teeth, had been driven into his back.

The courtyard went still, beholding the sudden slaughter before them. The mace wielder gasped beneath a rusting knight, too stunned to scream.

The white knight curled down in his armor in a strange, lupine fashion, as if he did not quite understand what he'd killed. His mouth was open in a snarl, peeking from beneath the low visor of his helmet, but he said no words. Long fingers flexed over the grip of his sword and twisted. A final gasp escaped the boy trapped beneath this white knight, who seemed to sag and shiver with his last breath. And I recognized that euphoria. This was our Deathless.

A stained ribbon swayed softly around the hilt of Luthor's blade.

Suddenly, he struck out again. This time, he lunged toward the Flayed, who had been locked in a close-quarter fight with the war hammer knight. The speed might have killed them both if not for her reflexive swing that redirected the white knight's strike into the ground. She dropped her sword, her hands shaking from the shock of the force. The war hammer took the opening and swung into Luthor's opposite arm, crushing the mail.

"Stop!" Theodoulos scolded. He and the rest of his group had chased us into the courtyard, but they all halted in awe of this armored creature. "We need him alive!"

The Thyremoin paid the blow no mind and wheeled back on the Flayed. With one quick thrust, he skewered her through the thigh.

The Flayed stared down at the blade, maybe as surprised as the rest of us to see what had happened. The war hammer swung for Luthor's opposite arm out of instinct, or fear that he'd be next, but Luthor did not flinch at that blow either. Instead, he ripped his blade out of the Flayed's thigh and decapitated the war hammer in one swing.

The Flayed collapsed, screaming. An arrow suddenly punctured Luthor's backplate. Another embedded itself into his uncrushed leg. The Acolyte had collected himself enough to start shooting. Luthor staggered, bracing one hand on the floor and one on his sword, but then that helmet shifted, and his attention turned. He launched himself at the Acolyte, closing thirty yards in half a second.

I knew that fury. I knew that speed and danger. That was a war dog, resurrected again and again. That was a man of Morthia, with nothing left but the ache, the hunger. I could see the pauses where he sagged in relief over the Acolyte's corpse, where the gasp of death sighed into him. His body, first stiff and efficient, began to sway with euphoria.

Then he turned to me.

At once, I reversed my grip, holding the point of my sword down in both hands, and raised the cross guard to align with my chest. The white knight straightened and slowly brought up his sword, returning the old salute.

A show of respect and honor from the days before the wars for earth and water. So he was not completely lost to his hunger. He'd have enough of a mind to strategize. That was unfortunate. If he had been a mindless beast, he would have been an easier opponent to manage. As he was now, I would not be able to delay him for long.

I looked for Minthisha and the Silver Tongue; in all the commotion, I'd lost track of them on their sprint to the yew tree. Geocelin was in my line of sight, near Theodoulos. Both men had watched the beast make quick work of their friends.

I stepped forward. I could feel the numbness of my leg fading. Pain humming fresh. The new blow to my back pulsed, and my breath caught too shallowly in my chest. It might be a miracle if I survived the first counterstrike.

Luthor took a step, and his crushed leg dragged behind him. The right arm that had been crumpled hung at his side, leaving the left to pull the bulk of his sword's weight. Perhaps he wasn't as immune to pain as he first appeared. If we were two broken things about to put the will of our bodies to the test, this might be better odds.

I released the salute and took my position, expecting him to copy me. Instead, he threw his sword down, embedding its blunted point into the moss. He drew a knife from his hip with his good hand and slashed it across his exposed neck under his helmet. The Thyremoin collapsed to his knees. A low gasp escaped his lips, his mouth contorted in pain, and then stilled.

I stood there for half a breath, almost in complete disbelief. He'd thrown himself into death. He'd been too injured to go on by his judgment, and his strategy was to give in. His helmet, like Damovanor's, had been designed leaving the throat exposed; where a bevor or gorget would be, there had once been a strip of leather. The years of cutting through the same material, however, had frayed the leather to little better than strips dangling from his collar. In a land of Young Gods, it was a fine strategy if you had nothing to protect, but with me, he had laid out our victory on a silver platter. Now, he would be trapped in Morthia's realm for the next few days, and we could finish this skirmish amongst ourselves in peace.

I spotted the Silver Tongue under the yew tree. Minthisha had been set down at the roots and was digging into a little hollow beneath the tree. The Flayed chewed a section of skin; her other hand staunched the blood flowing from her leg. One of Theodoulos' remaining knights had drawn a secondary sword and was encroaching on her. Just as I was about to intercept the knight, I heard the first groan of metal.

Something *popped* as if it had been hammered into place, and the dead Thyremoin *shivered*. It was far too soon for his resurrection, yet it was happening. I threw myself forward on my bad leg. Theodoulos tried to charge at me, but Geocelin cut him off. The Thyremoin gasped and shook against the ground, but even that tantrum lasted a fraction of a second. I had not made it three yards before Luthor was up, on his feet, sword in hand.

There was no delay, no momentary confusion. The man behind his visor recognized me and retrieved his weapon. Whatever advantage I hoped to have slipped between my fingers. I could not see his eyes behind his visor, but his mouth, bloodied and crusted, was not curled in satisfaction nor flexed with anger. If Luthor was aware, this was nothing more than duty to him.

He parted his bloodied mouth to taste the air, and suddenly, his visor turned to the yew tree. With less than a glance, our fight was forgotten.

Luthor passed Theodoulos' companions and ours, never breaking from the sure path to the tree. Minthisha was there at its roots, elbows slick with mud, hands working in the earth. The Silver Tongue stood before her with a battleaxe at the ready.

Before Luthor could meet him, I stepped back into his line of sight. To my surprise, he stopped, considering me once more. There was a stillness to him that unnerved me as he decided if I was enough of a threat. The only suggestion of emotion I caught was a tilt of his chin as he adjusted his focus. He wrapped two hands around his blade and crouched into a fighting stance.

A calm understanding settled between us. *Thee or me, Morthia shall feast.* This would not be a frantic flurry of blows but a match, cold and decisive. One counter. That's all I promised myself.

Alanus' vassals had attacked me with incredible speed. I knew his stance and the form he would use. I'd seen it a hundred times before. I could counter one blow before he had me, but that would be my contribution, and Minthisha would have a fraction longer to tear open the sealed door. The Thyremoin shifted his back foot.

He hit like a crash of lightning. My knees buckled, my ankle slipped, but there was just enough give to his strike to allow me to push myself under him and slip through his swing. I reset, standing just behind him with my sword still in my hands. I could hardly believe it, and then I saw him take a stiff step. A new arrow shaft had appeared underneath his right shoulder, pinned into the tabard, stuck under the plate armor. He did not stop to remove it, but it caused enough pain to alter his posture. He favored his left side as he circled me. I caught a flash of the Flayed behind him, knocking another arrow with shaking hands from the ground. She'd yet to stand, but she braced her back against the corpse of the soldier of the Green as she aimed again.

A skirmish had broken out between Theodoulos' men and Geocelin. I heard metal and the pop of flame.

A glitter of vibrant light caught my eye, and I refocused. When the sunlight dipped into the shadow of Luthor's visor, a radiant light flickered where eyes should have been. This was not just the hand of Morthia. There was something else, something slipping from between the cracks of the armor.

One more bout, I told myself. *Just one.*

The vassals had given me some warning on their sudden bursts of speed when they drew from the wind; with the Thyremoin, it was a mere hitch of breath that forewarned his attack. I braced myself for the second strike when Luthor suddenly leapt away from me, dodging the wild swing of a battleaxe. The Silver Tongue had thrown himself into the fray. The Thyremoin struck back at the Silver Tongue, leaving me a brief opening.

It was not a sudden turn of the tide. Two foxes fighting a bear stood a better chance, but we didn't need to win. We had to divide Luthor's efforts and keep away when he tried to overwhelm us with speed or force. The reckless maneuvers he'd used when we first entered had been abandoned for a more cautious style. If I struck out at him, he countered or dodged instead of taking the blow as before. If he had to choose between taking one of our strikes, he slipped away from me every time. Despite how effortless it all seemed, he was being cautious with me. He knew I was a Deathless as well.

But our luck didn't hold forever. We'd fallen into a rhythm, grown accustomed to each other's steps, and a single break in the pattern led to deadly consequences. Where the Thyremoin would have defended against me, he showed me his back. I stabbed into the flesh of his hip beneath his armor and hit bone. In exchange, the Thyremoin had driven his sword into the Silver Tongue's throat. The Silver Tongue was dead before he hit the ground. We sprang away from each other, backing into a wider circle as we readjusted our grips and footing.

How much longer would I have to hold out?

"Minthisha!" I called over my shoulder, hoping the presence inside of her would respond to her old name. I chanced a glance behind me, but my eye caught on a pale blue tunic first. Theodoulos was limping along the courtyard's edge, toward the yew tree. I saw him slip past Luthor, eyes wild as a hare's. No one followed him. Where was the Flayed? Geocelin?

The Thyremoin's ribbon, muddied and bloodstained, scraped the ground. It flicked just before he lunged. My time was up.

The injury slowed Luthor to something I could offset with quick, conserved steps and good timing. Though I was nimble with a sword, any swing I was forced to meet threatened to throw me off balance. There were limits to my endurance. I would have to retreat or break within a few short phrases. But I miscalculated as well. Sooner than I expected, I saw myself in a position to meet a sword strike I could not oppose.

Then, suddenly, the head of a war hammer had smashed into the Thyremoin's pauldron. The blow was clumsy and unpracticed, but it was hard enough to force Luthor back. Geocelin staggered, holding the weapon's shaft in an awkward two-handed grip like he'd never so much as swung an axe before in his life. I had to pull him out of the way before Luthor's next swing decapitated us both.

As I did, I saw that flash of blue again. Theodoulos was behind us, beneath the tree. Had he found Minthisha already? He would be upon her in moments.

"Goss! The witch!" I shouted.

The canary turned and cursed, catching sight of Theodoulos.

In a second, the Thyremoin was upon me. My leg caught in the wrong way, and I was forced to abandon my first instinct. Instead of lunging for the gaps in armor at his legs or trying to slip past his swing, I threw myself into the path of his swing and swiped at his exposed chin. And the decision caught him off guard as well. He threw himself back, breaking his own momentum to evade my wild swipe. He tried to recover and rush in again, but his sword was ill-positioned, and a strike that should have impaled my chest glanced off my shoulder.

I felt the heavy metal on my collar and then, suddenly, a hand on my shoulder. The Thyremoin locked me in place, shifting his hold on the hilt to angle the sword up to my neck. Cool metal touched the delicate skin beneath my jaw. I dropped my sword. My hands clamped down on the flat of the blade, trapping me in a losing contest of strength. Luthor pressed in close, mouth stretched open as if he were bellowing, but only a breathy whimper escaped. I pushed. Luthor pushed back.

Then, suddenly, the tension snapped. The blade slipped too far up, nicking my neck, and the Thyremoin's hold broke as he collapsed to my side. Geocelin swung down the war hammer again, trying to follow what must have been a lucky strike to his leg. I did not have time to interfere as Luthor whipped around and thrust his blade into his attacker. I heard the little punch of breath escape Geocelin as the sword sank into his chest. The Thyremoin pressed in closer. Sharp, gauntleted hands wrapped around the boy's neck and squeezed.

I made so many glorious promises in my mind as I watched Luthor twist his sword in Geocelin: I would throw myself into the fray; I would rescue him from the Thyremoin with a sudden surge of swordsmanship and skill that would crack mountains and beat this creature into submission; I would feed Geocelin his communion and help him limp back to his little fortress; and they were all the bitter fantasies that I knew I would abandon. The Thyremoin's attention was occupied, and behind me, Theodoulos was closing the gap between himself and Minthisha.

My run was sluggish, but my path was clear. Theodoulos was stumbling over the yew tree's roots, knife in hand. He fell more than once, a trail of blood dragging behind him from some vile injury to his chest. Minthisha must have heard him, but she went on, engrossed in her incantation, mouth moving soundlessly as the wind churned.

Then he had her. Theodoulos grabbed Minthisha by the hair, and she did not resist. She pulled her hand from the mud and reached up, touching the boy's chest, and something was said between them that made him hesitate. I closed the gap between us then and yanked Theodoulos back by the collar. I had to kill him quickly, but I had no weapon. My sword lay abandoned by Geocelin's corpse, and I could already hear the Thyremoin behind me.

I reached to pry the knife from Theodoulos' hands. He released Minthisha and squirmed against me, desperately keeping his hold on the knife. Minthisha did not run. She did not chant or dig. Even if she was moved to flee, there was nowhere to go. I had to get her away. I had to draw the Thyremoin somewhere else. But I was not going to be fast enough. If I dropped Theodoulos, he would take his knife and cut Minthisha's throat. If I kept struggling for his knife, the Thyremoin would cut through both of us.

My heart raced. A shadow passed over us as the glittering white knight arrived on a crumpled leg. His swing arched forward with such grace that it was almost hypnotic to watch, and I knew it would cut clean through my neck.

Suddenly, there was a hand on my shoulder, and I was guided two steps back. There was a shift in the air as something popped. The sword froze, suspended mid-thrust. Minthisha was leaning back, her foot pressing one glinting jewel into the dirt just before her. A feather's width from her chest hovered the point of the Thyremoin's blade, wet and red, captured in her pocket of suspended time.

"There you all are," Minthisha said, looking into the visor of the Thyremoin. "What are you still doing here? Aren't you tired?"

Luthor's body jerked behind her like a wolf trying to free itself from a trap, but the arm would not move as he frantically pulled until I heard something pop and give. He was stuck.

I had moments—seconds—and I pulled the dagger from Theodoulos' grip. The boy screamed, clawed against my leg, bit. I ignored him, driving the blade up and through the writhing Deathless' mouth.

His breath of life sighed into me; that final soft gasp fluttered from my chest to my fingertips. And something once suspended came crashing down on us.

The End

Luthor and Minthisha collapsed as if they'd been cut from strings. I stumbled to the Yew Mother, as if I could revive her, as if I had not released whatever power there was locked away in the Thyremoin. She was dead before I touched her. Her body lay curled at the base of the tree, nestled in its roots.

I sat back, heaving, and I heard the boy. Theodoulos. He was still there on the ground. His moans grew more furious, more broken, until he was screaming.

He cursed me. He called me a monster. The snot-ragged boy's eyes were red with rage—fear.

"What did you do? What did you do?" he shouted again and again.

I didn't need to answer. We both could feel it. It was in the *air*. There was a change, something in that radiance, a crack, a split, a shift in the ground, and we could feel it. It was building, like a wave pulling back from the shore to build and build and build. Soon it would crash and sweep us all away.

From how Minthisha had described the Blight, I'd expected it to be slower. I almost felt cheated. I would not be festering under the stars for a week. No. This was happening now.

"Why? You bastard! You damned evil bastard!" Theodoulos cried.

He crawled to me and punched my gambeson. He curled his hands around my neck and squeezed. And squeezed. I fell back against the tree roots, letting my shoulders rest. He would strangle me, and I'd let him.

"Why couldn't you leave it alone? What did I do? What did I do wrong?"

Mica had been the man of inspiration, of comfort. I'd been a distant father, a brutal comrade, a sullen partner. This, however, needed no words. I watched a rage so like mine seethe through him and felt such shame to ever recognize it. But Theodoulos' grip relented, his fingers softened, and he fell back.

"Fight back!" he shouted.

"Theo—"

"Close it! Stop it! It's not time! It's not my time!"

He damned the gods and begged for their mercy.

Then it was spent. He crumpled and began to weep. Tentatively, I sat up and reached for his shoulder. My hand did not so much as brush his arm before he collapsed into me. He clutched me and screamed into my chest, and I just held him, feeling so very small.

"I'm sorry, boy."

We felt the weight, the pull, the flood as the sun burned red and the sky faded black. All around us, the walls of stone shifted, and a terrible, great power, like the heartbeat of a beast older and grander than the giants, thrummed through us. Whatever had been built around us was falling.

I could feel Morthia's touch and the beckoning promise of his domain.

Dunes of ash as far as the horizon were blown about by harsh winds, snapping the trees and toppling those final towers. But there, in that cold, hard place, there was a bud. A sprig of green had spread its roots and dug deep in the waste. The storm could tear it apart, or it would weather and endure. I would not see the fate of that little plant, but I had seen its start, and that was enough.

Theodoulos drew back and swallowed.

"What's it like?" he asked.

"It's quiet. It's soft and frightening, but then there's bliss, and shapes, and light, and breath. Then there's nothing."

"Don't leave me alone."

"I'll walk with you there. Every step."

I could taste ash on my tongue.

Morthia was waiting. He'd always been waiting.

He stood in the shadows of the yew tree, watching me as I considered where we were going, that hidden place—nameless, unknown, forgotten. I wondered if he'd ask if I wanted to escape it, though he'd never spoken to me before. Of course, he said nothing. Gods ask nothing of mortals. They command. They declare. They cannot see the weight of men's lives the way a man can. We'd clawed this bargain out of him, and he was no more disappointed to see it go than for the sun to turn over the sky to the moon.

He turned away in his thick black cloak and walked on into a place I'd never followed. I knew it was where my sons had gone. My brother. My friends. My rivals. My pains. My loves. We'd all see what was on the other side, but we all had to walk there alone.

But I stayed here for a while longer, feeling the boy shake against me. For a long time, I could hear only his staggered breaths. Dark eyes flashed red as he watched the dappled sunlight fall through the trees. And I thought of a lone plant sprouting in the new sun.

With one inhale, the blackness rolled in. With one exhale, we were gone.

The Young Gods and Their Servants

The Nameless Unblinking Eye

An observer of all things that have been and will be, intuitive and unclouded. The most widespread of its brothers, but found in excess among scholars and the downcast. Patron of devoted Acolytes.

Rivialt the Cretinous Flayed

A spirit too volatile for their container, assertive and sensational. Their connection to the body once lauded, now lamented, no longer adored by healers but adopted by the ambitious. Patron of their Flayed children.

Koroe the Flaming Heart

A bridge of connection, impassioned and vigorous. A favored goddess of soldiers and birth mothers. Patron to the devoted Heartless.

Malmon the Liar

A conduit of pleasure and self forever punished, contrite and indulgent. A known goddess of traitors, self-proclaimed or sentenced. Patron of repentant Silver Tongues.

The Seven Hands

A mock body, deft and amiable. Once the obligatory god of servants and lesser men. Patron to bound Fingermen.

Toothless Deiviknot

A being of the earth chipped from bone, enduring and stagnant. Oldest of his brothers, known to all, unremarkable to most. Patron to the weary Toothless.

The Old Gods and Their Domains

Amivia, Lady of the Flaming Heart

Not a beginning. A cycle eternal, unbroken as winter to summer.

Sibdeot the Twelve Hands of Ambition

Many hands striking many deals and forging many paths in a world that does not satisfy.

Lotinus the Wonder

The lies behind secrets as infinite and graspable as the stars.

Fuemog the Six Feats of Virtue

All that steadies. All that endures. All that devotes.

Wroungemout the Worm

All things foul in decay consumed. All things tender and small seeded.

Bellium the Weeping and Raging

The rebellion of the spirit brought too close to itself.

Morthia, King of the Flies

The end of all things.

ACKNOWLEDGEMENTS

A big thank you to any member of my online audience. This is a melodramatic present for you at the end of the day. Sharing my love of dark books that vaguely relate to a FromSoft series is truly a wonderful community experience. You are the reason this book has any of the visibility or production it does have. Thank you for watching and listening and just being around. Because of you, I was able to hire professionals. Which, of course, means I can thank Nathan J. Anderson for providing absolutely stunning covers for this piece way back when. And thank you to Sam Willow from Scrollwork Edits for enduring this piece for its copy edits.

If you are one of the many members that donated your time or money to a charitable cause in exchange for this book, thank you doubly. It was an honor and a pleasure to read about what you did for your community.

This was a piece I finished and put on the shelf for a long while. I can't help but thank Brandon, Christian, Jake, and Meagan for being stunning critique partners during this book's conception when it was a totally different beast. Thank you to Ray, who came in clutch and helped me tear this manuscript apart. And thank you to the blue jay that helped me keep it all in tune.

ABOUT THE AUTHOR

Frances B. Corvo is the silly pen name for this author who goes by the name of Frankie. She likes to write books that are a bit dark and has been having way too much fun comparing books to games in other places.

Before this, she published a book about a teenage monster hunter who just wanted to give his girlfriend some flowers: A Delivery of Flowers

You can find her stuff around at Fashionable Crow

BlueSky:@fashionablecrow.bsky.social

Tiktok: @fashionablecrow

Youtube:@FashionableCrow

Instagram: @fashionable_crow

This book wouldn't be possible without your support, guys.

www.ingramcontent.com/pod-product-compliance
Lightning Source LLC
Chambersburg PA
CBHW071342300726
48976CB00006B/1739